# Snaked

Everyone is Connected—Watch Your Back

P G Robertson

# Contents

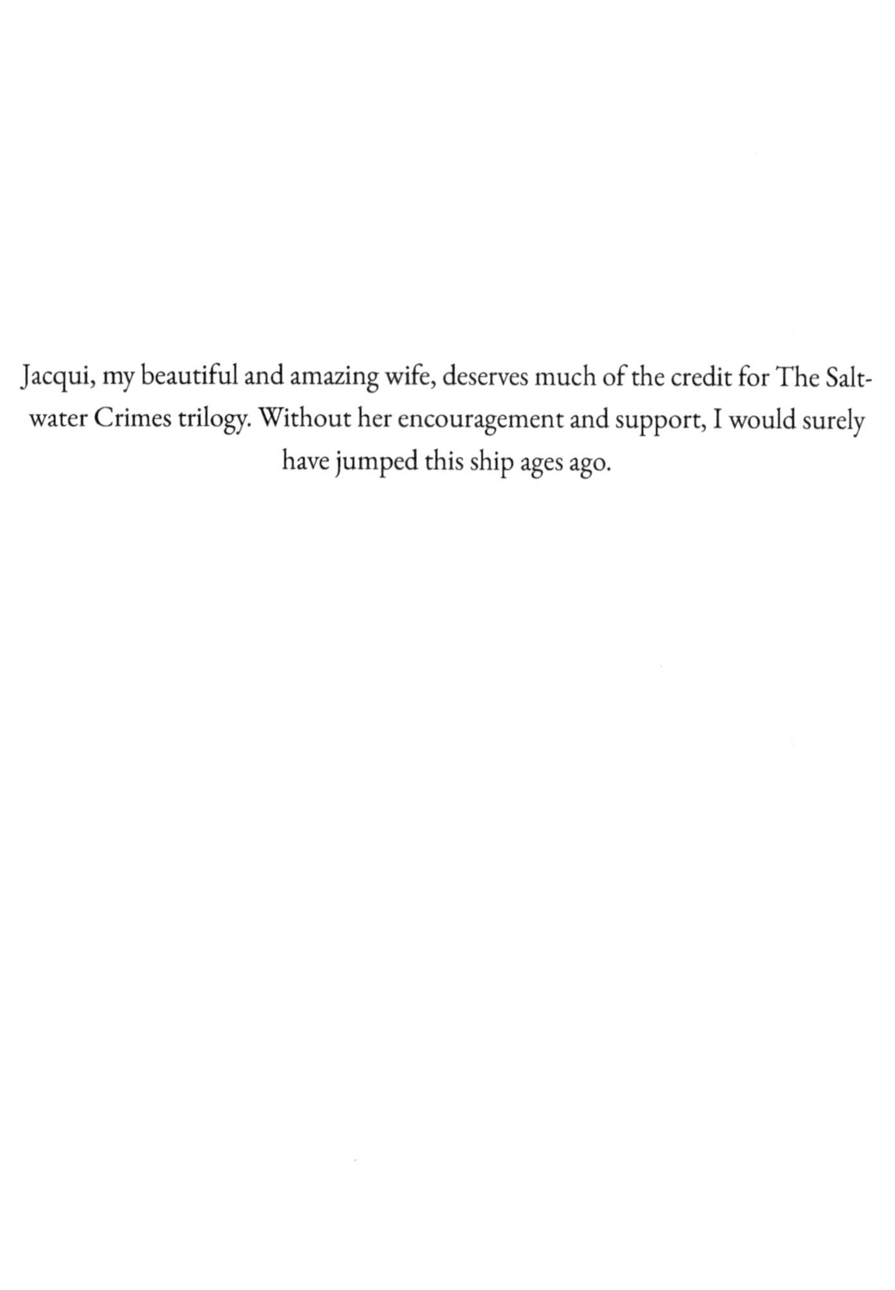

Jacqui, my beautiful and amazing wife, deserves much of the credit for The Saltwater Crimes trilogy. Without her encouragement and support, I would surely have jumped this ship ages ago.

# Prologue

As far as assignments went, this was one of the easiest ever—also one of the most pleasurable. Previous jobs had caused some difficult moments, but he had no option but to take those calls and complete his tasks, no matter how distasteful. Today was an exception. What could be better than a trip to Bondi Beach, enjoying the sights of a sparkling Sunday morning?

Between transit cards and phone pings, it had been childishly easy to follow the woman. For those that had the means and knew where to look, privacy was a delusion of yesteryear. He spied her walking from the surf and zoomed in for a better look. The woman paused briefly to wrap a bright yellow leg rope around the tail of her board before exiting the water. The way she moved displayed a certain confidence, unflappability even, definitely someone comfortable with herself. Even from this distance, she cut an impressive figure, the type of figure that came with care and constant activity. He watched voyeuristically as she struggled to change, using a large multicoloured beach towel as cover, a tough move, as Australian as a day at the beach itself.

The watcher tore his eyes away from the woman to check on his beautiful iridescent riviera-blue BMW coupe, blatantly parked in a loading zone. He was unsure which of the two was more beautiful. His boss, or bosses—he was never entirely sure of that point—would probably not be happy about his expensive glistening phallic symbol. He was supposed to blend in and stay under the radar, although he would take care to indulge himself only on weekends. However, this was the perfect situation to explain away his extravagance. Such machines as his were a dime a dozen in the rarefied sea air of Sydney's Eastern Suburbs. If called to task, he would argue that he *was* blending in—at least today.

He noticed a parking inspector a hundred metres away and walking purposefully towards his illegally parked car. The man was not worried, and he amused himself for a few minutes as the inspector punched his number plate into her handheld revenue earner. She looked up sharply and frowned before she moved on empty-handed, as he had known she would. The man had made sure of that. The casual observer would assume that the car was owned by some VIP with the council in his pocket. After the recent series of highly publicised exposés into council corruption, each shamelessly leaked by the state's anti-corruption watchdog, no other conclusion made sense.

The man looked back towards the object of this Sunday excursion, now collecting her things and making her leisurely way off the beach and up onto the grassy foreshore. It was time for him to go as well. He had what he'd come for. Glancing from the corner of his eye to see if anyone was watching, he popped the engine of his beauty into action. The crackle and rasp of the sports exhaust made his neck tingle. A few heads snapped around for an instant, mostly men, unfortunately, before they turned back to sipping their lattes.

Back in his apartment, the man put on some latex gloves and printed out the series of photographs he had taken. He soon picked out a favourite, a closeup of impressive clarity. She was one fine-looking woman, that was for sure, the type of woman he had imagined sitting in the passenger seat of his BMW as they wove through the hills on their way to his weekend getaway, the one with impressive views over vineyards and golf courses. His groin stirred impulsively as he thought about what they might do each evening, winding down after their days of indulgence.

In his heart of hearts, he knew that these fantasies would never happen. Tomorrow, after his task was complete, he would stash his flash new car and crawl back under his cover, dissolving back into an otherwise bland and unremarkable existence. It was a genuine pity, but mostly for the woman. In his experience, once his boss, or bosses, had someone in their sights, they rarely turned away.

## Chapter 1

# The Hidden Side

Detective Ange Watson was lost in a blissful dreamy state, the type that comes after a relaxing holiday, the body refreshed and the mind cleansed, both back working as their maker had intended. While one part of her brain was occupied with navigating her VW Tiguan along the busy highway, the other part flipped and flopped, this way and that, thinking through the permutations and combinations of the past few months. What a mess the Gold Coast operation had turned into. Certain that she had it all figured out, she was made to look like a bumbling novice who was out of her depth. The weeklong surfing vacation had been just perfect, a welcome segue between that dismal Gold Coast episode and the promise of moving to Sydney.

She looked across at her impressive passenger, dozing peacefully despite a bumpy stretch of road. Brett Tompkins was certainly one fine specimen of a man—tall and rugged, handsome but not pretty, confident but not arrogant, keen but not gushy, thoughtful but no pushover, just about right in most respects. On the negative, the fact that Brett was also a detective and a colleague of sorts was not ideal, something which had already caused some difficult moments. Brett had also suffered PTSD after a traumatic undercover operation that had gone sour. It had turned his life upside down and destroyed his marriage. He was slowly rebuilding himself, but the damage ran deep.

Not that she was perfect herself, her long history of relationship disasters an impediment to truly letting herself go. 'Male fails' was the term that she had coined to describe her track record with men. It had been frustrating, being able to reveal a murderer but unable to find a decent man. Ange was sufficiently self-aware to realise the pivotal role she had played in her past failures. Brett

Tompkins was not in that category, although it was still early days. She hoped she wouldn't trip herself up this time around.

An incoming phone call jangled loudly through the VW's speakers, making Ange jump from her thoughts and rudely pulling Brett from his slumber. It was her mother. Ange's heart missed a beat. Her mother never called unless something serious was afoot.

Perhaps it was the fact that she had gone off to boarding school at a young age, or perhaps it was just how things were between them, but Ange and her parents rarely engaged in small talk. Some of her girlfriends spoke to their parents and siblings every other day. At one point, Ange had worried that she was a terrible daughter and started ringing twice, even three times per week. After just two weeks, her mother had set the record straight. 'Angela. Your father and I are quite worried about you. You've been calling us a lot lately. Is something wrong? Are you sick?' Ange stopped this aggravation soon after and fell back into their former relationship, where most phone conversations were on a need-to-know basis.

'Hi, Mum,' answered Ange. 'What's up? Is Dad OK?'

'Your father's fine. He's off in Dubbo at the races with his mate Ernie Paton. They have high hopes for that filly they purchased together at the yearling sales a while back. I think I've heard this all before,' replied Jane Watson, ending the sentence with a resigned sigh, one tinged with obvious affection for her horse-trading husband.

Ange knew how much her father loved his horses, a passion that was centred around enjoying time with his mates rather than any deep love of actual horse racing. Living on a farm can be a lonely existence, and her father's expensive obsession seemed a reasonable bargain for the comradery he enjoyed.

'Oh good. I sometimes worry about him, all alone working the back paddocks.'

'I think he enjoys the back paddocks more than the home paddock sometimes. Anyhow, it's your brother Joel. I'm worried about him.'

'What's he done this time?' asked Ange. That her younger brother may have gotten himself into trouble did not surprise Ange one bit. Joel had a solid record of chasing the latest fad without looking under the surface of the pond into which he was jumping. In fact, he had badly broken his leg once, when they were kids, jumping from a large river gum into the creek and landing on a submerged log. It was lucky that Ange had been there. Joel had been threatening to dive in headfirst before she had talked him out of such stupidity. Even now, after all those years,

Ange shuddered at that memory and what might have happened had she not been there.

'He's gone and invested all his money in cryptocurrency. I don't even know what that is, quite frankly. He has a young family to support now, and he can't just keep jumping at these get-rich schemes. Your father and I can't afford to keep bailing him out.'

'Has he lost all his money again?' asked Ange, feeling that some pressure was soon to be exerted on her own meagre savings.

'No, nothing like that. He tells me that his money has quadrupled since he invested.'

'So, what's the problem, then?' replied Ange, annoyed with herself over the smidgen of jealousy that she was feeling.

'Well, him and Sarah have gone and contracted to buy a flash new house in Rouse Hill. It's way out of their league. Your father and I told him to cash out his cryptocurrency and shore up his position, but Joel won't hear of it. He keeps insisting that it will double again before he needs to settle. I think he's even factored this into his budget. You know how your brother is.'

'That sounds like Joel. So where do I come into this picture?' asked Ange, curious how this would become her problem. However, this wouldn't be the first time. Becoming a police officer had been an invitation for even her most distant relatives to lean on Ange to make their speeding ticket go away. When she told them that this was not something she could fix, they would often turn against her, as if her reluctance to play a corrupt police officer was a personal slight.

'Could you look into the company he invested with? It would make your father and I sleep more easily if we knew his investment was legitimate.'

Ange knew she had no option but to agree, notwithstanding that she knew almost nothing about investing in cryptocurrency. 'OK, Mum. I know someone who might know something about crypto. What's the name of the company?'

'See Factor Futures. Spelt C-F-A-C-T-O-R. Apparently, it's a fund run by some famous tech genius. Thanks, darling.'

'Give Dad my love. I hope his horse racing weekend is as successful as Joel's cryptocurrency investment.'

'I wish,' said Jane Watson before she hung up from the call.

'Family,' said Ange as she turned and smiled at Brett. 'Sorry to wake you with that sort of nonsense.'

'It's interesting. Australian regulations don't currently allow punters to bet with cryptocurrency, but there are plenty of overseas outfits that do. It's only a matter of time. I reckon that stuff is as dodgy as all hell,' commented Brett.

With that provocative comment, Brett curled up in his seat and promptly drifted back to sleep, leaving Ange alone with her thoughts and daydreams. She sorely wished that she could fall asleep like Brett just had. Her inability to calm an overactive mind would never let her drift off once an idea got in the way. She was certain Brett could sleep on a barbed wire fence if the situation demanded.

The advice of fellow boarding school inmates on how to navigate life had offered grand statements like 'follow your dreams', or 'you can do anything', or another favourite, 'you've got this', a catch-all when other platitudes failed. Even then, filled with a healthy dose of privileged enthusiasm, Ange remained a pragmatist, her country roots welding a deep work ethic into an overactive imagination. Constantly following one's dreams seemed like a precarious addiction. Her mind had always been filled with dreams, born of both day and night. However, Ange believed that constantly moving forward was the key, exploring the full extent of one's boundaries, probing your limits, momentum taking you to places unthought of.

Her mother and father had met at a school dance during their second-to-last year of school. Her father had been boarding at the Armidale School for boys, TAS for short, and her mother at the New England Girls' School, or NEGS. It had been a fait accompli that Ange and her two brothers would follow in the footsteps of their parents and board at their alma maters. Notwithstanding those first few awkward and lonely months, Ange had loved her time boarding at NEGS, an establishment that offered extracurricular activities such as dressage and show jumping. That Ange had excelled at rifle shooting over equestrian pursuits should have offered her teachers some insights into the woman that she might become. Unfortunately, the magnetism of a big city had eventually drawn all three children to Sydney, and it seemed likely that any family tradition built around TAS or NEGS was in serious trouble. It was even worse in Ange's case. She felt the prospects of having her own family slip away with each passing year.

Certainly, a career as a detective had never been an entry in her 'what I want to be when I grow up' notebook. Who would have thought that this pathway lay ahead? Farm girl becomes a gritty detective, pursuing hardened criminals around the country. Her current nemesis, a sophisticated narcotics syndicate, had certainly pushed her boundaries and tested her limits. During what had started as a vanilla-style missing persons case, Ange had stumbled on a clever importation operation, one that had delivered multiple murders amidst a path of destruction. The case had been frustrating and Ange had seemed constantly one step behind.

Ange and her colleagues referred to their quarry as simply the syndicate, which was code for *we have absolutely no idea what we're dealing with here*. Her new boss, Senior Detective Sally Anders at Major Crimes in Sydney, was convinced that the syndicate had tendrils in the department. Ange agreed.

The latest instalment on the Gold Coast had ended badly. Whilst she might have collapsed the syndicate's latest import and distribution operation, they had thwarted Ange at the last minute—a somewhat embarrassing ending to her chase. All momentum of their investigation had been lost.

It hadn't been all bad, though. Her reunion with Brett Tompkins had gone well. They had fallen into an uncomplicated relationship—the type survived by busy people with busy jobs and independent lives. It thrilled Ange to have a steady relationship with someone she genuinely liked and respected, not to mention the physical side of their relationship and how madly attracted she was to Brett.

Their week-long surfing holiday at Agnes Waters on the mid-coast of Queensland had given Ange time to regroup. Whilst she tried to see the best in people, her job hoisted a fair share of lowlifes her way and she feared the hard edge they honed. It was easy to blame the job, but she was sufficiently self-aware to realise that this edge had always been part of her makeup, recalling her competitive streak that would flare up during school sport. She also acknowledged that this trait had cracked a few relationships, leaving some good guys broken and wondering where they had gone wrong.

Her failures to make any deep progress with the syndicate had hardened this edge, and she was smarting about her own underestimation of Lomax and Smith, the two thugs responsible for the deaths at Namba Heads. They had resurfaced on the Gold Coast with disastrous consequences, theatrically disposing of Eddie Falconi, someone who Ange had figured as the syndicate's kingpin. She couldn't believe how wrong she had been about Lomax and Smith—and Falconi, for that matter. They had been one step ahead at every turn and had played Major Crimes for fools.

There was simply no way Ange was going to let them get away with it.

When Brett had woken up from his second catnap of the drive, the pair had switched seats and Brett had taken over the driving duties. He wasted no time in tackling the elephant in the room.

'So, I guess you're going after the syndicate as soon as we get back?' he asked casually, looking straight ahead, as if he was commenting on the weather.

Ange looked at Brett sideways. They had both made promises to put aside the ins and outs of their work during their surfing holiday. Evidently, the holiday was over. 'Of course. I feel like an idiot. I was so certain that Falconi was the boss and that Lomax and Smith were dumb muscle that I considered no other possibilities.'

'We were all fooled by Falconi. That he liked to portray himself as a big fish didn't help. However, it just doesn't seem plausible that Lomax and Smith would be the kingpins,' commented Brett.

'I agree. My guess is that they were simply dancing to the tune of another puppeteer, one higher up the chain. Whoever it is must be super-arrogant to have played us so overtly. It was almost as if they were taunting us and boasting about how much smarter they are. We must have been close, as it doesn't seem plausible that there would be room for too many more egos as large as Eddie Falconi's.'

'What's your plan?' enquired Brett, taking his attention off the road for an instant and looking her squarely in the eyes.

'I've been thinking about that.'

'Really, I would never have noticed,' replied Brett teasingly, his broad smile showing a level of awareness that Ange found gratifying. It was nice to think that he was attuned to the way her mind worked.

She smiled back comfortably, joining in the repartee. 'And don't tell me you aren't pissed off with that mob.' Brett's failure to respond confirmed this allegation.

'I figure I need to circle back to where it all started. On my way back to Sydney, I plan to pay Joe Kramer a visit. I feel somewhat responsible for what happened to Ted Kramer, so I think it's also the decent thing to do.'

Brett looked up sharply. 'Visiting Joe Kramer is a bold move, seeing as Ted was his son.'

Ange had ensnared Ted Kramer after cracking open the case in Namba Heads, and Major Crimes had then sequestered him away in the boondocks, keeping him off-grid as a potential witness against the syndicate's activities. Ange was almost certain that Lomax and Smith had killed Ted Kramer, but the local police were well out of their depth. Worse still was that Major Crimes had been ordered to abandon pursuit of the syndicate and Ange was moving to Sydney to work at head office.

Paying Joe Kramer a visit would be confronting. Not only was Ange feeling partially responsible for the demise of his son, but Joe Kramer remained a painful thorn in Ange's side. A prominent environmental activist from the New South Wales north coast region, he was the reason Ange had been ignominiously dragged in front of SACC, the Standing Anti-Corruption Commission, and portrayed as a dodgy cop by the media. While Joe Kramer seemed to have gotten away with his little scam extorting property developers, his son, Ted, had not been so lucky.

'You are not to blame for what happened to Ted Kramer. He made his own choices in life. When you lie down with dogs, you catch fleas,' said Brett kindly, breaking the silence of Ange's self-recriminations.

Ange knew this to be true, but Ted had also been no master criminal—more likely just a lost soul who had veered onto the wrong side of the tracks. Without Ange getting involved, Ted would probably still be meandering aimlessly through life, perhaps a minor player in the recreational drug scene, but he hadn't deserved his ultimate fate.

'Anyway, I want to mend a few bridges back in Byron. I'm not cut out to play the role of a dodgy cop, even less so to go undercover. I don't know how you do that,' she said, looking towards Brett, his eyes now firmly back on the road.

This was one thing that niggled Ange. She simply could not fathom how anyone could operate undercover and take on a completely different persona. The other night, after their lovemaking, she had lain awake for hours pondering this thought. Was the Brett she was sleeping with the real one, or was he playing a part, one where she was a ship in the night? Even after such a wonderful holiday together, she remained uncertain about the obvious complexity locked away inside Brett's personality. She needed to be sure about the person who she was lying in bed with at night.

At times, he would withdraw from her and disappear into some dark place or another. Ange had seen this before with one of her school friends, someone who had ultimately taken her own life. It really troubled Ange that she didn't know quite what to do when her Brett vanished. Then suddenly, as if someone had flicked a switch, he would be back, the warm and confident guy Ange was so attracted to. She worried he might not return one day.

After a moment's silence, she brushed these dark thoughts aside and turned back to the topic at hand. 'I can't believe that there isn't something we missed. I figure Joe Kramer is as good a place as any to start.'

'What do you want me to do?' asked Brett. He had only ever been on the fringes of this investigation into the syndicate. Ange felt grateful that he was supportive of her plan.

'Falconi must have left some clues through his gambling outfit. Have you come clean with your colleagues at BeaBet?'

BeaBet was a start-up online gambling outfit. Brett had gone undercover to play the part of a Gold Coast property developer/entrepreneur, a supposed investor in BeaBet, looking for evidence against organised crime. They hadn't specifically targeted his work towards the syndicate, but Major Crimes knew that organised crime preyed on problem gamblers who might suit their needs. Now, BeaBet was ostensibly being purchased by eZee Bet, another online gambling house that Eddie Falconi had been behind. That the two worlds had collided had come as a shock. In hindsight, it shouldn't have been any shock at all.

'Yes, I came clean after Falconi's demise. The boss and I workshopped this at length. In the end, I felt somewhat obligated to let my colleagues know what they were involved in. It also wouldn't hurt to maintain some friends in the business, so to speak. Even though eZee Bet is no more, organised crime and gambling are perennial buddies.'

'Keep digging around Falconi. He was a larger-than-life character who wasn't short on ego. He would surely have been reckless at some point, either with a former mistress or perhaps the way he lived his life and flashed his money around.'

'OK. It'll take me several weeks to finish up on the Gold Coast, so I'll do my best. I gather that this needs to stay under the radar?' queried Brett.

The mention of their mutual boss, Senior Detective Sally Anders, reminded Ange of their conversation a week or more back. 'Absolutely. Sally and I are almost certain that we have a rat in the house.'

Ange failed to mention the minor fact that Lomax and Smith had left a conspicuous target on her back, even more reason to remain discreet. A less determined person would have let sleeping dogs lie. Lomax and Smith had made it quite clear that Ange was in their sights when they'd left a note showing her picture and the GPS coordinates for Ted Kramer's resting place.

This overt warning was a little piece of information that she saw no reason to disclose to Brett—for the time being, at least. Her mum had once told her never to believe the glossy magazine version of life. Keeping some mystery was the real secret to a healthy relationship. Ange didn't always agree with her mum, but this advice suited just nicely for the moment.

Their Sunday breakfast at a quaint coffee shop in Childers broke this somewhat dark train of thought. Ange and Brett put aside their crime-fighting personas, blending into the crowd like any other tourists on a surfing holiday.

The casual observer would never have guessed their deadly concerns.

# Chapter 2

# Parting Blues

Ange had left her car at Brett's place during their surfing holiday to Agnes Waters. They had abandoned any pretext of secrecy some weeks ago, as it had seemed pointless to continue that charade. It had been a long drive back and Ange planned to leave the following day to make her slow way south to Sydney. Cooking dinner was out of the question.

When the option was available, Ange always chose Japanese. They settled on a small teppanyaki bar Ange had discovered in her first few days at the Gold Coast. The chef even recognised her and made a special effort, seeing as she seemed to be on a date. All her previous visits had been solo, and she suspected the chef fancied her. Japanese culture intrigued Ange; the cute and almost childish side that foreigners saw concealed a ruthless streak, one with an edge as hard and sharp as a Katana sword.

That night, their lovemaking took on an urgency that was both exciting and disturbing. As she drifted off to sleep, exhausted and spent, she wondered why they had felt that way. Were they subconsciously aware of the difficulties their relationship would likely face? Was this a potential 'last time' moment that they didn't recognise?

While Ange felt she was entering an exciting new phase in her life as she moved to Sydney, she knew that Brett would be returning to familiar ground and soon come face-to-face with his ex-wife and children, as well as the reality of everything that had led to their messy divorce. Conversely, Ange hadn't lived in Sydney since her university and police academy days. The prospect energised her. Sydney was one of the world's most exhilarating cities, after all. Perhaps a desire to get on with life was the source of her urgency. At any rate, her dreams that night were not at all the dreams of someone who had just enjoyed a wonderful surfing holiday.

The morning light had cast a disconcerting shadow over the pair as they made their awkward goodbyes. The peck on the cheek seemed incongruous with the desperate lovemaking of the previous evening. Her surfboards and clothes tucked in the back of her southbound VW SUV, Ange plunged deep into thought, probing the implications of her past ten days.

Once she hit the Pacific Highway, Ange pulled herself from those disturbing thoughts and called her colleague Billy. She hadn't spoken to him for a couple of weeks.

'Hi, Billy, what have you been up to lately?'

'Clearly not as much as you have, although I caught Covid while you were on holidays. That Gold Coast operation came crashing down with an almighty dull thud,' he replied.

Ange ducked that leading question. 'How was Covid? I've been lucky enough to avoid it. Hopefully, I'm one of those medical marvels and some pharmaceutical company will pay royalties to access my DNA.'

'It wasn't all that bad. I was sick for a few days and then exhausted for a few days after that. My mate Nelson was far sicker than I was. I'm pretty sure that I caught it from him. Well, that's what I'm telling him, anyway. I'm sure you'll get it sometime or another, Ange. You're good, but I wouldn't say that your blood is worth bottling. Anyhow, how was the holiday?'

Ange smiled at the image of him beavering away in his tech supercentre at Major Crimes in Sydney. Billy's enthusiasm for his job was contagious. 'It was brilliant, Billy. I even tried my hand at fishing for flathead. Without luck, I'm afraid. You know how much I love eating that fish. Anyhow, how are things at head office?'

'It's been pretty tense around here. The boss has been like a bear with a sore tooth after what happened on the Gold Coast. I can't believe that the entire operation has been shut down like that. Lucky for me that cybercrime is a growth industry. I seem to be getting busier and busier each day. On the bright side, I hear that you're moving down to Sydney. It will be good to have your smiling face around.'

'Thanks, Billy. I know how the boss feels. It's ridiculous in the extreme to abandon pursuit of the syndicate like that, just because we ruffled a few high-profile feathers.'

'Well, boss, I think the death of Eddie Falconi counts for more than ruffling a few feathers.'

'Whose side are you on?' admonished Ange, the laughter in her voice showing that she was enjoying the repartee. 'I wondered if I could ask a favour, Billy?'

'Sure thing, although your *favours* sometimes stretch the friendship. What do you want?'

'My brother Joel has put all his money into cryptocurrency. My mother and father are worried that he has gone out on a limb. Do you know anything about cryptocurrency?'

'A fair bit. My course of cybercrime delved into cryptocurrency. It sure opened my eyes to how it might be useful for criminals. I have invested in crypto myself. It's been going gangbusters lately. What currencies does he have?'

'I understand he has invested in a fund of some sort. Something called cFactor Futures.' She was about to spell out the name of the fund in full when Billy interrupted.

'I know cFactor. It's a fund that invests in a basket of cryptocurrencies to help spread the risk. It's the first of its kind in Australia and has gotten heaps of attention in the crypto community. Started by a tech entrepreneur called Ethan Tedesco. As I understand it, the fund is targeted at mum and dad investors who don't really know about crypto but want to jump on the bus. That guy sure has his finger on the pulse. I'm pretty certain that your brother is in good hands, but let me look into it and ask around my mates.'

'Thanks, Billy. I appreciate it. You'll have to give me a lesson in cryptocurrency sometime.'

'Sure thing. Anytime, boss. Drive safely.'

Before long, Ange saw the turn-off to Mullumbimby, the home of Joe Kramer. She figured that he could wait for a day or so. There were a few things that she needed to set straight in Byron Bay before she tackled Joe Kramer. She kept heading south and took the turn towards Byron.

The drive into the iconic coastal town took Ange past the Byron Bay industrial estate and offered the perfect opportunity to cross one name off her list. Bell surfboards were her not-so-secret addiction, an expensive addiction at that. Not that any of her former boyfriends had ever attempted hijacking her heart with diamonds anyway, but she might remain hostage to a Bell surfboard—well, for a few weeks at least.

It was 10 a.m., and the shop-cum-factory would have been open for hours. Their relaxed coffee hangout was a magnet for local surfers needing to secure their first coffee of the day, forced to work in the nearby factories and businesses when they would rather be in the water. Ange was pleased to find a parking spot outside, a lucky break which had become increasingly rare during her four-and-a-half-year stint in Byron. The guy at the front counter recognised Ange immediately and commented that they hadn't seen her around for a while. Ange ordered a flat white and brushed off his implied query with a bland 'work stuff' reply.

'Is the boss in?' she asked.

'Yep. He's upstairs. You know where his office is, don't you?'

While her coffee was being made, Ange wandered around admiring the latest surfboards, impressively displayed like expensive pieces of artwork, which was what they really were—individual creations handcrafted in-house. Ange was sorely tempted by a baby-blue longboard on display, the practicalities of squeezing yet another surfboard into the VW the only thing stopping her short of making a snap purchase.

'Hi, Ange. I wasn't sure that I would see you again,' came the breezy greeting from the mezzanine level. Gus Bell moved easily and confidently as he made his way down the staircase. Ange noted that Gus had become no less handsome in the past few months.

'Hi, Gus. Do you have time for a chat?'

'Sure. I see you're having coffee. How about I join you?'

The pair made their way outside and sat at the end of a large trestle table. Ange took a sip of her coffee before tackling the object of her visit.

'Gus, I know it all seemed weird when I left Byron. I took a promotion. Part of that promotion had me posing as a cop of uncertain character on the Gold Coast. We took advantage of the SACC catastrophe,' explained Ange.

'What, you were working undercover?' replied Gus, intrigue lighting his eyes.

'Not exactly, but sort of. I had to keep it tight, even with my friends. Sorry about that. Anyhow, playing the role of a dodgy cop didn't sit well with me and I'm certainly not cut out to go deep undercover.'

The conversation took a pregnant pause as the guy behind the counter brought out Gus's coffee. He shot his boss a knowing smile. Gus waited until his employee was out of earshot before speaking.

'That was all so strange. I had wondered if I had offended you. Anyway, I never for a moment thought that you were dodgy. Are you still based on the Gold Coast?'

'No, that job is done. I'm heading back to Sydney, where my new department is based. How is business?' she asked, quickly changing the topic. Ange had no desire to get into the specifics of her job. People watched too many crime dramas these days, and revelations about Ange's job often forced her to turn disappointingly vague.

'Business is booming. We can't keep up with demand. We've sold all our display stock five times over and we have a six-month waiting list. The world seems to have discovered surfing as an antidote to their Covid straitjackets. And that's on top of the crazy number of people who had moved into the region in the past twelve months. I sometimes wonder if Byron will be loved to death and we all might lose our idyllic lifestyle.'

Ange wasn't sure whether to be sad or relieved that she couldn't whisk that baby-blue longboard into the back of her VW. 'I hear you. My friend Kerrie—you know her—she's said the same thing to me.'

Gus looked resigned to this inevitability. 'I suppose change is inevitable and we will adapt. We call it progress, but I sometimes question that it really is.' His face brightened at the thought of their mutual friend. 'And as for your mate Kerrie, her blog posts aren't helping with the backlog. We always get a spike in enquiries after she borrows one of our boards for a photo shoot. It's a good problem to have. I owe her big time. How long are you in town? Do you have time to have dinner?'

'A couple of days. As a disgraced detective, my social calendar seems remarkably free at present. I would love to have dinner. I know that it's short notice, but how does tonight suit you?'

'Perfect. Let's meet at the pub for a drink at 7 p.m. and work out where we want to eat from there.' Gus glanced at his watch. 'I must go. Another shop in Brisbane wants to stock our products. I need to humour them, as I don't have any stock available right now. However, things can change, and it makes no sense to burn bridges. See you this evening, Ange.'

With that, Gus picked up his empty coffee cup and took it back to the counter. Ange liked how Gus did that, not expecting his staff to clean up after him. She sat in the courtyard finishing her coffee amidst thoughts of having dinner with Gus Bell. Notwithstanding the comfortable rapport that existed between them,

Ange was keen to learn about the JayTee Foundation that Gus and his father had established to help talented young regional surfers like Jake Thompson. In some ways, Ange's efforts in investigating Jake's untimely death were obliquely responsible for the foundation.

Ange followed Gus's lead and took her own cup back to the counter, which led her to a last lap of the surfboard gallery. She reluctantly dragged herself away from the baby-blue perfection and moved towards her car, wracked by non-buyer's remorse and envy that a stranger would soon enjoy that beauty.

Her phone rang suddenly, thankfully upsetting the train of thought that was inexorably heading towards placing an expensive purchase order that she could ill afford. It was her boss, Sally Anders.

'Hi, Ange. I have some information for you. Where are you right now?'

'I've just driven into Byron Bay. Why do you ask?'

'A burner phone was recovered from Ted Kramer's duplex, where he was living out west. It had only registered one call. His duplex had been ransacked, but Ted had hidden the phone in a packet of muesli,' explained Anders.

'I presume he had another phone?'

'Yes, he had been given another phone, but that was being monitored. I think it's safe to say that he wanted to have an off-the-record conversation. That he made that single call before his death is suspicious. We traced the number, and it's registered to a Tyler Ball. It looks as if he's based in Mullumbimby, going by his call data. Can you poke around while you're in the area? Keep it low-key if you can. We aren't supposed to be looking any further into this mess, as you well know.'

'Understood. I'll look around and see what I can learn. Actually, I was planning to visit the station and catch up with my old boss. I can trust him. Are you OK with that?' enquired Ange.

'Yes, of course. Jim Grady and I go way back. Take your time. I've approved some additional leave for you. You're ostensibly attending to personal matters that you didn't resolve before we transferred you to the Gold Coast. Hopefully, you can find something for us to go on.'

'OK. I'll get back to you if I learn anything.'

The drive into town took Ange past the Byron Bay Police Station. There was never a time like the present, so Ange swung into the car park and crossed this off her to-do list. Sally Anders was one cool customer. Her unexpected connection with Ange's old boss, Sergeant Jim Grady, surprised Ange, but it explained in part why she had been plucked from Byron Bay and promoted to Major Crimes. Ange had secretly called him Bosley during those first few years in Byron Bay, an affectionate nickname from her time as a young girl back on the farm in Tamworth, playing Charlie's Angels with her girlfriends.

She saw her old Toyota Camry parked in the car park. They still hadn't fixed the ding she had made in the bumper, backing into a signpost rushing to a crisis. It was funny how the subconscious anchored itself to places and objects, visual or auditory memories, how the smell of a former lover could evoke powerful memories in an instant. The Toyota Camry carried some confronting memories for her, and one of the worst came rushing back.

Ange had been called to a tragedy involving the death of a young mother and her two small children. According to neighbours, the woman's abusive former partner had turned up unexpectedly at the house, yelling obscenities. The man had a record of methamphetamine abuse and appeared to have been having a major drug-induced psychotic episode. In a moment of unimaginable horror, he had doused the family in petrol and set them all alight, killing everyone, himself included.

Ange had held herself together for most of the day but had ultimately lost it when she'd finally finished with her duties and was alone in her car. Collapsing her head on the Camry's steering wheel, she had sobbed uncontrollably for ages. It was no surprise that she held a deep loathing for those who profited from addiction.

Counselling had helped rationalise the horror of that tragedy, but nowhere near as effectively as the events of a few weeks later. Ange had located and helped rescue a small boy abducted by his estranged mother. The look of relief in the eyes of the boy's father and the obvious love between the two had helped more than any counselling ever could. That was her job—confronting the constant ebb and flow of the human condition, the yin and yang, replayed countless times across the community she served.

She suddenly shook herself, unsure of how long she had been sitting in the VW, staring blankly ahead. Hers was a tough job, simply brutal at times. Luckily, the station had been a place of great comradeship and support, so she quickly turned her back on past nightmares and walked through the front door. There was a new female constable at the counter whom Ange didn't recognise.

'Is the boss in?' asked Ange casually.

'I think so. Who's asking?' replied the young constable, somewhat warily.

Ange smiled at the young woman, genuinely looking forward to seeing her old boss again. 'Just tell him it's Ange. He'll know who you mean.'

# Chapter 3

# Byron

Ange couldn't suppress the smile that blossomed when Sergeant Jim Grady, aka Bosley, her former boss, walked through the door.

'Look what the cat dragged in. Where have you been hiding?' asked Grady, keeping his smile to the wry variety. He knew full well where Ange had been hiding, having been integral to her promotion to Major Crimes.

'You know. Here and there,' answered Ange, a tinge of irony sitting alongside her breezy and nonchalant tone.

Grady led Ange through the swing doors and into the bowels of the station. A few eyes widened at her impromptu appearance. She had left the station some months back in apparent disgrace following a torrid affair at the hands of SACC, the state's anti-corruption watchdog.

Grady confronted the stickybeaks head-on. 'Look who came to pay us a visit. We all need to congratulate Detective Watson here for pulling down a major drug importation and distribution operation while operating undercover on the Gold Coast.'

The eyes and ears of the station opened even wider at that news. Everyone knew just how tough it was to operate undercover.

Grady was enjoying himself. 'What? Did you guys actually believe that our very own Ange was dodgy? I can't believe you fell for that charade. Talk about gullible!'

Some eyes smiled, some stayed wide, and some looked sheepishly downcast. It was easy to deduce who had been sticking the knife in whilst Ange had been up north. 'Good to know,' thought Ange to herself.

With that bit of fun under his belt, Grady ushered Ange into his office for a chat, closing the door behind him to keep out prying eyes and ears.

'So, tell me, how did it go? I had a call from Sally Anders the other day. Did I tell you we go way back?' asked Grady.

'No, you forgot to mention the fact that you and Sally Anders were besties. It explains a lot,' replied Ange, trying vainly to look miffed. She found it impossible to get truly upset with Bosley. 'The operation was brutal, actually. We completely underestimated who we were dealing with and they made us look like fools.'

'Hang on a minute,' replied Grady. 'You shut down a highly sophisticated narcotics operation. Don't underestimate what you achieved.'

Ange knew this to be true, in part at least, but she was not about to cut herself any slack, despite the encouragement of her former boss. 'Perhaps, but the syndicate will pop up somewhere else soon enough. What really grates on me is that I let Lomax and Smith get away. They were the same two goons who we believe murdered the trawlerman from Namba Heads, Dave Fletcher. How will I face his wife and tell her I let them slip through my fingers?'

'How do you think that happened? You must have had them under surveillance,' observed Grady shrewdly.

'Well, we thought we did. Sally and I are both convinced that we have a mole in our midst, probably moles plural. That can be the only explanation for how they knew what we were up to. They played us right to the end. For goodness' sake, we'd even tagged their car with a GPS tracker—which they clearly knew about. What's even worse is that they had the arrogance to throw all this back in our faces and expose just how stupid we were.'

'How so?'

'We were about to close in on Eddie Falconi when they murdered him. I was convinced that Falconi was the kingpin of the entire operation, but even he was expendable. The syndicate had already shut up shop by the time we moved in. Did Sally tell you that Lomax and Smith led us to Falconi's house before they left town? They even left a warning note for me personally.'

'What sort of note?'

Ange grimaced. Evidently, Anders hadn't told Grady everything. 'A picture of me with a set of coordinates showing where Ted Kramer's body had been buried in the scrub out west. That's how we found him. We thought Kramer had simply absconded, not that he had been brutally murdered.'

A pregnant pause developed as Ange studied the floor, the sullen mood finally broken by Grady. 'What are you going to do next?'

'Sally Anders has been ordered to abandon the joint task force and focus on stuff in her own backyard. She's being pressured from all angles for straying out of her lane. Perhaps our Queensland colleagues have their noses out of joint after the Gold Coast disaster? Who knows? She's also concerned that the syndicate might have some lofty connections.'

This news clearly annoyed Grady. 'Surely you're not planning to leave this rest? I know you. You won't want to give up this chase so easily. Anyway, it seems ridiculous to think that the mob you're chasing would be constrained by any state border lines. If they're operating in Queensland, then they'll be operating in New South Wales for certain.'

Ange looked up from the floor and fixed her former boss with a determined stare. 'Well, that's why I'm here. I need your help.'

'Sure, tell me what you need.'

'It seems as if Ted Kramer purchased a burner phone. He made one call before he was murdered. We can't be sure of the dates and who was responsible, but my bet is that Lomax and Smith paid him a visit because of that call.'

'Who did he call?' questioned Grady, asking the obvious.

'A guy called Tyler Ball. He was in Mullumbimby when he took the call. My guess is that he was a bit player in the syndicate, which then put Lomax and Smith on the job. I can't go anywhere near Tyler Ball until the dust settles a little. We need to assume that any obvious moves I make against the syndicate will circle back and slam into Sally Anders. Sally and I are not backing down, but we need to stay under the radar if that's possible.'

'I presume you want me to look into the well-being of Tyler Ball?'

'Correct. Maybe see if you can track him down and bring him in for questioning. I can help guide you on that front, but I would need to stay behind the scenes. Ball can't have been thrilled that Ted Kramer called his personal phone. My bet is that he has gotten rid of that and has a new phone by now.'

'What angle should we run to track him down?' asked Grady, now fully invested in the chase.

'I would go vanilla and stick with supply. If he was in direct contact with Ted Kramer, it's plausible that he was part of Kramer's small-time street network. I'm going to pay Joe Kramer a visit, ostensibly to bury the hatchet, so to speak. If I'm honest, I feel partly responsible for Ted Kramer's death.'

Ange saw the look in Grady's eyes and cut him off before he could speak. 'Yeah,

I know. He made his own bed, slept with dogs, got fleas, all that stuff. Anyhow, the real reason for my visit is to see if Joe Kramer has any information to offer, perhaps something we missed.'

'OK. How long will you be in town?'

'A few days, at least. Probably until the end of the week. Sally Anders has me on extended leave for *personal reasons*, or something lame like that.'

'Great. How about you come over for dinner? Barb would love to see you, and perhaps we can talk about something other than work.'

Ange's diary was filling up fast. 'Love to. How about Wednesday night?'

'Perfect. I'll keep you posted about Tyler Ball. Do you know anything about him?'

'Nothing. Although, given that he was the first and only person who Ted Kramer called from his new burner phone, we need to assume that they were good mates or close associates.'

'OK, see you Wednesday, then. You know the address. Let's say 7 p.m. Don't bother bringing anything. Oh, and make sure you pass out a few of your patented death stares at a couple of your former colleagues as you leave, the ones who were quite prepared to throw you to the dogs. I would start with Walton and Lynch. Man, those guys can sure talk shit, and they covered you in plenty of it. It took every bit of my self-control to let it slide and keep our charade alive.'

'With pleasure,' concluded Ange as she stood up and made for the door, readying herself to unleash some displeasure. It was cold comfort, but the generous smiles from some of her more trusting colleagues proved adequate compensation.

## Chapter 4

# I'm Back

As Ange walked back out through the reception-cum-waiting area, she saw that the large government-issue clock on the wall was approaching midday. Rather than decide to brave the inevitability of a frustrating lap around town searching for a car park, Ange opted to leave her car at the station and walk into town.

She stopped to speak to the young constable at the counter. 'Hi. I'm going into town, so I'll leave my car outside if that's OK. It's the white VW SUV.'

'Sure, Detective. I'll make sure you don't get a ticket,' said the young woman with a wide and generous smile.

'I'm Angela Watson, by the way. Most people call me Ange. How long have you been here?'

'I know who you are. I'm Breanna White, but everyone calls me Bree. I've been in Byron for just on two months now. This is my first real posting and I'm finding it much more challenging than I expected. Well done on the Gold Coast. I can't imagine how difficult it would be to go undercover.'

Clearly, tongues had been wagging while she had been speaking with Bosley. 'Byron is a plum gig. I loved my time here. The sarge is a great person to work for, so my advice is to stick close and lap up everything he says and does. Nice to meet you. I guess I'll be an hour or so. Catch you then.'

With that, Ange walked out into the midday sun. The glare caught her off guard, so she picked up her sunglasses from the VW before wandering into town. At five minutes past midday, she called her friend Kerrie. Being a successful lifestyle influencer meant you had to look the part, so Ange knew Kerrie would never miss her Monday Pilates class. Kerrie maintained a perpetual aura of energy and vitality around her, something that Ange loved to soak up. More than once, Kerrie had lifted her out of a dark place caused by her work. Ange wondered how anyone could remain so upbeat all the time.

She rang Kerrie's number as she crossed over the railway tracks. The phone rang many more times than was usual for Kerrie. Lifestyle influencers stayed very close to their phones. Ange wondered if she had lost touch and Kerrie was into some new craze, the next Zumba perhaps.

Kerrie answered. 'Hey, girl. What have you been up to lately?'

'Oh, this and that. I presume you have just finished Pilates. Is the gorgeous Charlie still running the class?'

'No, unfortunately. He hooked up with one of the other instructors and they started their own outfit. I've stayed with the old class. You know me, loyal to the hilt. I'm just sitting down for lunch and my usual salad. Gosh, I'm getting predictable. Enough about me. Tell me about you.'

Ange knew exactly where Kerrie was sitting, as they had shared lunch there on innumerable occasions. It was just around the corner.

'Well, I just finished my case up on the Gold Coast. Back from a week's surfing holiday up north.'

Kerrie's timing was impeccable. Just as Ange was walking through the door of the small cafe, she asked, 'When are you coming to visit us?'

'How about now? I just walked in the door.'

Kerrie shrieked with delight. She could be over the top sometimes, but Ange couldn't ask for a more loyal and generous friend. She gave Ange the biggest of hugs, filling Ange with a wonderful warm feeling, a feel-good, best-friends buzz that almost brought forth tears.

'How long are you in town? You must stay with us. Mike finally moved his office out of the downstairs bedroom. You can stay as long as you wish.'

'Fantastic. Thank you. A few days at least. I need to mend a few bridges here before I head back down to Sydney. I have a dinner date this evening with Gus Bell. You know him, don't you?'

'Oh yes. The delectable Gus Bell. How did you go on the Gold Coast man-wise, while we're on the subject?'

'Well, I sort of hooked up again with that guy I had a fling with at Namba Heads?' Ange had given Kerrie the full download of her frustration and disappointment after Brett had suddenly skipped town and left her high and dry.

'Turns out we work for the same outfit.'

'A man of considerable mystery. I like it. How very James Bond.'

In between fits of laughter, the two girls caught up on the latest news in their lives. There was always lots of laughter when they got together. Kerrie knew absolutely everyone in town and always had the latest gossip about who was doing what, also who was doing who—her specialty, in fact. Not that she was a terrible gossip herself, other than with Ange. Somehow, Kerrie seemed a magnet for the juiciest and most salacious news in Byron.

Once they had finished lunch, Kerrie suggested they meet back at the house so that Ange could get settled. 'I've got a photo shoot this afternoon, so I need to get changed and all glammed up. Have you checked out the surf? The guys at Pilates were telling me that there was some solid swell about and The Pass was on fire this morning. You should take advantage and grab an afternoon surf.'

Kerrie insisted on paying the bill, so Ange started walking back to the car. Along the way, she came across the young constable she had met at the station earlier.

'Hi, Constable,' said Ange as they passed. 'It's Bree, isn't it?'

'Yes, Detective. I'm impressed. Most people forget the "girl at the front counter",' replied Bree, making air quotes over the last phrase. 'It's lucky I ran into you. I have a confession to make.'

Ange was still smiling at her observation. 'Go on. It can't be too much of a confession. We only met this morning.'

'I left a note on your car. I hoped that you would have time to give me some advice. It would be good to get your perspective on how to get ahead. Also, how to deal with some guys around the station. They treat me like their housemaid.'

'Sure, happy to do what I can. It can be tough coming into a new station. Byron Bay can also be cliquey and a hard place to make new friends. How about we catch up for a drink? Tell you what, I'm meeting someone at the pub tonight at 7 p.m. Why don't we meet there at 6 p.m. and we can chat then over a glass of wine?'

Bree readily agreed to that plan and the two traded numbers in case something came up in the meantime. As Ange walked back to her car, she remembered back to when she'd first turned up at Byron and considered what advice she would give to the younger version of herself. She had never thought of herself as a mentor, more of a perpetual mentee. Despite suddenly feeling disturbingly old, Ange was secretly chuffed at being asked to help guide Bree.

She pulled Bree's note off the windscreen and tucked it in her pocket before jumping in the VW to drive across to Kerrie's house and unpack. In less than an hour, a wetsuited Ange was clutching her midsize board and wading into white water at The Pass, keenly observing where the best waves were forming. There were some nice ones swinging around the headland. A tingle of anticipation and excitement surged up through her neck muscles, making her hair follicles stand on end, the DTs of a lifelong addiction that would never wane.

Even though it was officially spring, the water was crisp and cool as it slowly seeped into her wetsuit, enlivening her with a sudden burst of energy. The break comprised three sections. The outer section featured the largest waves, but these were messy and disjointed. The inside section offered the smallest and cleanest waves, but size progressively bled away as they swept around the headland and turned towards the light breeze. Ange chose the middle section for her session as it seemed to strike just the right balance.

Even though the surf seemed crowded for a Monday, it was nothing like the throng of eager beavers that the weekend would have held. Ange was thankful for that and immediately latched onto a nice shoulder-height wave. Turning quickly down the wave face, she was soon racing across the crystal-clear swell, the afternoon sun warming her face and turning the water ahead into a sparkled canvas of sequined light. As she pulled out of her exhilarating ride, she marvelled at her situation, a reminder of how fortunate she was to live in a country that afforded her such a miraculous lifestyle, something that she was determined to protect.

In what seemed like an instant, the sun was low on the horizon, casting disconcerting shadows in the water. Ange was no warrior for surfing into the evening, stories of late-afternoon tragedies all too vivid. As she was towelling off at her car, she heard a somewhat familiar voice call out her name. It was a guy she'd dated a few times, a genuine, full-blooded 'male fail'. He had completely duped Ange into believing he was single, only for her to find later that he had a wife and two children. It had been Kerrie who'd joined the dots and warned Ange away, which was a rather poor effort for a detective. The nerve of that guy, smiling her way and acting as if nothing untoward had happened. Perhaps he fancied his chances? She tasered him with a death stare that successfully wiped the smile off his face.

In any event, Ange needed to hop to it if she was going to make her 6 p.m. drinks appointment with Bree.

# Chapter 5

# Not Fungible

Ange walked into the Byron Bay pub bang on 6 p.m. She never ceased to marvel at the iconic watering hole, perched on the stunning foreshore overlooking the bay, a nexus between the town and the beach. The place was absurdly popular.

Ange saw Bree sitting patiently at one of the tall tables, off to the side and in a quiet section of the bar. She saw glimmers of recognition from several faces as she weaved her way through the end-of-day crowd. The Byron Bay of today was an eclectic mixture of tourists, long-term locals, new seachangers, people reinventing themselves, and those breezing through on their way to some place or another. Not so long ago, the crowd would have been truly international, but Covid had proved a formidable change agent. An avalanche of Australians from all over the country had tumbled into Byron, transitioning this once-sleepy hippie village into yet another iteration of cool.

Bree saw her coming and stood up, immediately asking Ange what she would like to drink. While Bree headed to the bar to grab Ange a glass of Riesling, Ange took advantage of her strategic vantage point to make a thorough reconnoitre of the crowd. The number of unfamiliar faces surprised her. It suddenly dawned on her that Byron was already no longer her town. It had taken years to be considered a true local, but only months to become just another tourist again.

Drinks in hand, Bree thanked Ange for agreeing to meet with her, explaining that she was still finding her feet. Being the only woman at the station hadn't helped.

'How did you get into the job?' asked Ange.

'I went to school in Lithgow and sort of fell into it, more by accident than as a conscious career move. I play hockey and hoped that the police service would be sympathetic to my training needs. It hasn't quite worked out that way.'

'Sounds serious. How good are you?'

'I haven't made the national side yet, but I feel that I'm close. There are a few retirements in the wings, so I hope to get a shot at making the team in the next couple of years. The trouble is that there's no money in a sport like hockey, so I need to support myself. When I'm training and competing, it's like holding down two jobs.'

'I'm impressed. Does the sarge know about your sport?' asked Ange.

'No, I haven't been game to broach the subject as yet.'

'Have a word with him about it. If that doesn't help, let me know. He owes me. Anyhow, what did you want to speak with me about?'

Bree looked apprehensive, taking a sip of her drink before replying. 'How should I handle the men in the station? I'm no shrinking violet, but I don't want to make life difficult just to prove a point. Should I headbutt them or stay all sweet and bubbly? Two of them have asked me out already.'

Ange knew how difficult it could be to join a new station. 'That's a hard one. It was easier for me, as I arrived at the station as a detective and had some seniority. I think headbutt them when the time is right. They won't respect you otherwise. They'll still talk behind your back, but at least you'll have some breathing room around the station. And let me guess who asked you out. Walton and Lynch?'

'Correct. You should hear what they say about you. Your turning up today was a bit of a shock.'

Ange's ears pricked up. 'Tell me what they've been saying.'

'My favourite is that you were having an affair with the sarge. The next best is that you were cradle-snatching Billy, the guy I replaced.'

'I love them both dearly, but that would be like having an affair with my father or my brother. Actually, next time you're in Sydney, I need to introduce you to Billy. He's an accomplished tennis player and competes in tournaments all over the place. I think you two would get along. So, what else?'

'That you were taking money under the table from some activist and the only reason you've gotten away with it is because you're a woman.'

That last one hurt. Ange could cope with childish dating gossip, but her blood quickly boiled at those suggestions. Walton and Lynch were marked men.

Bree saw the annoyance on Ange's face. 'It was good of the sarge to let them know what had really been going on and that you were undercover, but now they reckon the sarge is protecting you because of the affair. Those guys will not stop. Talk about small minds.'

Ange finally laughed at that, realising that those imbeciles were simply putting their own ignorance in plain sight. She moved on. 'So, how is the hockey going? Do you have any other hobbies to keep you busy?'

'The hockey is taking a bit of a breather at the moment. I think I'll have to play on the Gold Coast, as the local competition isn't up to scratch. I'm also a bit of a collector in my spare time. I like to flip things I pick up at flea markets and second-hand stores. I do quite well at that. My mum and I have been doing this since I was a little girl. It helped pay for my hockey trips. There are loads of great stuff around. Not in Byron. Everything is too expensive here. The real action is in the small towns.'

This level of gumption and ingenuity impressed Ange—it was the type of enterprise that country kids like herself had engaged in. Her most profitable venture had been collecting dried cow manure and selling it in town. Bree's hustle sounded much more appealing.

'I've also been dabbling in cryptocurrency lately, that and trading NFTs. Those things are crazy, but I've done really well. So much so that I might stop the flea market gig,' continued Bree.

'What are NFTs anyway?' asked Ange, interested in speaking with someone who could explain this new term being thrown around in the media.

'Non-fungible tokens. Mostly digital artwork, but they can be anything. They're a variant of the blockchain technology used in cryptocurrency. While I sort of understand how they work, I can't say that I fully understand the value proposition. I've cleaned up with some of my NFTs and lost all my money on others. Overall, I'm way up.'

'How much money are we talking about?'

Bree's face was full of energy, evidently animated by the conversation. 'Well, my best was a CoolCat playing tennis that I purchased for just over two thousand dollars. It's now worth well over fifty thousand. I think the success of Ash Barty has had something to do with that.'

'Holy moly,' Ange exclaimed. 'How does that make sense?'

'Well, it's like any collecting. Scarcity and appeal, mostly. But I agree, most of it makes little sense. One similar, that I paid two thousand for, dropped to zero in days. One big downside is that all the transactions are in Ethereum, a cryptocurrency, and there are brokerage fees when buying and selling crypto, not to mention the transaction fees associated with the NFT itself. Lots of people are doing very well out of it. Anyhow, I can't complain. Well, today at least. Tomorrow could deliver another *I should have sold yesterday* moment. The whole crypto space can be intense.'

Ange could have stayed and spoken to Bree for ages about cryptocurrency and NFTs, but she saw Gus Bell coming their way. She stood up to introduce them. 'Hi, Gus, this is Bree, a newly minted constable at the station. Bree, this is Gus, the maker of the coolest surfboards on the planet. That's something you should get into while you're here. I took a surfing class soon after I arrived in Byron and have been hooked ever since. It also helped me make some new friends, which was a bonus.' Ange paused and gave Gus a look of someone resigned to their fate. 'My surfing addiction has been much to Gus's benefit, as I'm always lusting after at least one of his new surfboards.'

Bree could obviously take a hint, so stood up and readied herself to leave. 'Thanks for catching up, Ange. If you ever want any info on NFTs or want to invest yourself, please let me know. Also, I'll remember your advice and wear my head protection around the office in case an opportunity comes along to break some eggs.' Ange laughed at that.

Gus gave Ange a peck on the cheek. 'That's interesting. I've just spent the day with the team discussing how we approach cryptocurrency at Bell Surfboards. We need to accept that more and more transactions are going this way. There seem to be loads of people around here who've made a lot of money in crypto recently. We also spoke about NFTs and whether we could link an NFT with our JayTee original artist surfboards, a type of certificate of authenticity. As best I can determine, each time a board sells, the JayTee Foundation would get a clip of the ticket.'

This was a new concept that Ange hadn't considered, although she was clueless as to how that might work. 'How is the foundation going anyway?' she asked.

'It's going well. The Foundation now has four promising young regional surfers under our wings. I really think we can use NFTs to our advantage and perhaps get a global reach.'

The rest of the evening focussed on surfing and what each of them had been doing these past few months. Ange was naturally circumspect about her own recent experiences and Gus seemed to understand and respect this reticence. Some of the awkwardness between them remained as Gus struggled with the boundaries of her work and the circumstances of Ange's abrupt exit from Byron some months ago in apparent disgrace.

At least she could speak about surf spots like South Straddie and SuperBank and the swarms of surfers that now plagued these places. Gus mentioned he had recently experienced a man-made surf park and thought that perhaps these might provide some relief. Ange was yet to try or even see one of these facilities, but she found it hard to imagine it would be as stimulating as the natural version. It was yet another case of technology and innovation changing the way things were done and shifting paradigms, just like cryptocurrency and NFTs.

This sort of thing often happened to Ange, where the universe would speak to her in this way. Most others let opportunities constantly pass them by without ever noticing, incapable of taking advantage. Ange wasn't one of those people; she just didn't yet realise how loudly the universe was screaming at her that night.

## Chapter 6

# Coded Secrets

Ange woke early Tuesday morning, eager for another surf. The swell was holding up, but cloud cover made the water more imposing and less comforting. She surfed for almost two hours and caught a bunch of waves, which proved a decent workout. Coffee and some avocado toast at her favourite cafe caught her reading some articles on her phone and reflecting on her discussion with Bree. Tales of illegal deals on the Dark Web, all facilitated by crypto, confirmed her feeling that this new frontier would be a magnet for anyone up to no good. Understanding cryptocurrency and NFTs needed to be a priority.

She drove back to Kerrie's house and found the place deserted, which came as no surprise. Kerrie and Mike were busy and active people. The concept of an early retirement in Byron Bay was a fantasy reserved for Kerrie's lifestyle blog. After a shower and change, Ange rang Billy, her font of all knowledge when it came to technology. She could hear him tapping away on his computer as he answered the call, multitasking as always. 'Billy, do you have some time to give me a lesson on cryptocurrency?' she asked in her sweetest voice. She heard the click-click-click of his keyboard come to an abrupt stop.

Billy was immediately at his enthusiastic best. 'This space is so hot right now and we always seem to be one step behind. Crypto is the favoured currency for those into something dodgy. It's such a super cool idea. What do you want to know?'

'Let's start with the basics. What actually is cryptocurrency, and how does it work?' asked Ange, pen poised over her trusty notebook.

'So, OK, to understand cryptocurrency, you need to know about blockchain. I'm sure you've heard of blockchain. It's called that because it's blocks of data, and they form a chain. Each cryptocurrency coin is its own blockchain, and every transaction associated with the coin gets bundled up and added to the blockchain. Think of a giant ledger, with an infinite number of pages, where every transaction is recorded and balanced.'

'Who manages the ledger, a bank of some sort?'

'That's the clever part. The ledger is maintained by no one and everyone at the same time. With Bitcoin and other cryptocurrencies, for example, a cloud-based public ledger records every transaction and adds it to the blockchain. Let's say you start with a single whole Bitcoin—it's the original and the one most people have heard about. A single Bitcoin can be subdivided down to eight decimal points. Each time you spend a fraction of your Bitcoin, the transaction is recorded on the blockchain and your Bitcoin is balanced to reflect your spend, which is then broadcast around the globe via the internet. I sometimes think of it as an endlessly growing conga line of people dancing around the globe.'

'Billy, you know I'll never get that image out of my head. I can see it now, a gigantic conga line of partygoers, all in Hawaiian shirts, probably dancing to that song by Gloria Estefan of the same name. So, how do I get a Bitcoin or one of the other cryptocurrencies?'

'You can buy them through a cryptocurrency broker, exchanging any of the major hard currencies. You can then trade your crypto for goods and services from vendors who accept your cryptocurrency. The two biggies are Bitcoin and Ethereum.'

'If we stick with Bitcoin for the sake of the discussion, who makes a Bitcoin in the first place?'

'That's the totally brilliant bit. The inventor of blockchain and Bitcoin is a mythical person who goes by the name of Satoshi Nakamoto, but his real identity is unknown. Some say he's an Australian or Canadian and that the Japanese-sounding name is a ruse, but nobody really knows. Anyhow, he created a system whereby Bitcoin miners can create new Bitcoin, a sort of reward for doing all the work of bundling Bitcoin transactions into blocks and adding them to the blockchain. To achieve this, they need to solve some highly complex cryptographic calculations, which use a lot of computer power. All those computers chugging away use vast amounts of electricity. Globally, this has been estimated to be about the same electricity as a medium-sized country uses at present, and it's continually ramping upwards. I also read a prediction somewhere, where Bitcoin mining in

Texas will account for some twenty-five percent of the capacity of their electricity grid by 2026.'

As fanciful as it all sounded, this conversation had Ange fully engaged. 'You're kidding me, aren't you? You're having me on, Billy.'

'I'm not kidding. There have been cases of national electricity grids being compromised by Bitcoin miners in some countries. The problem is that Bitcoin is getting harder and harder to mine. Every four years, the set of calculations ratchets up, so Bitcoin mining is likely to become an energy problem of some significance. Cryptocurrency is a super cool idea, as no one person, company or government controls the currency. Bitcoin is the original and certainly commands the most value.'

'I sort of get it, but I still don't understand where the value is,' Ange said, flipping her phone to the other ear at the thought of all those computers chugging away, no doubt generating significant amounts of heat.

'Well, with Bitcoin, there will only ever be a limited number mined, so it comes with inbuilt scarcity. The value of any one cryptocurrency is essentially determined by its popularity. The more popular, the more desirable, and hence the more valuable. But the biggest appeal of cryptocurrencies is that you have a global and somewhat democratic currency that isn't controlled or manipulated by any company or government. As a result, early adopters were either IT geeks, disaffected types who wanted to stick it to the system, or those up to no good who wanted to stay incognito. Crypto fuels the Dark Web for sure. It's totally brilliant, isn't it? The combination of scarcity and the escalating cost of mining new coins embeds inflation. However, the real reason for the recent crazy growth in value is more about speculation and using cryptocurrency as a high-risk hedge against an economic or geopolitical collapse.'

Ange's phone buzzed in her ear, signalling an incoming call and interrupting her chain of thought. She pulled the phone away from her ear so she could see who was calling.

'Sorry, Billy, that was my mother calling. I'll need to ring her back. How did you go with the fund I asked about?'

'Oh, that. Sorry I didn't get back to you. cFactor looks totally legit to me. The guy behind the fund, Ethan Tedesco, is a home-grown tech luminary. He's the real deal, even sits on the prime minister's industry round table for technology. I had a look at how that fund is going. If your brother had brought in as little as twelve months ago, his investment would have tripled as a minimum. I think I might invest some money in cFactor. It makes sense having a spread of currencies to mitigate any concentration risk. I reckon this bull run on crypto assets has only just begun.'

'Thanks, Billy. My head is already spinning about cryptocurrency. How about we continue my education at a later date?'

'Sure, boss. I'm not going anywhere. Speak soon,' said Billy, ending Ange's first lesson in Crypto 101.

As soon as she had hung up from her call with Billy, she rang her mother to pass on the good news. 'Mum, it still seems too good to be true, but my colleague checked out the fund that Joel invested in. It seems like the real deal, although something that goes up that fast must come with some risk. Mum, you must let Joel grow up eventually. He's a big boy who should be able to look after himself by now.'

'OK, darling. Thanks. You're probably right, but it doesn't stop a mother from worrying.'

'How did Dad's horse go in Dubbo?'

'Ran fifth. Boxed in on the rails, apparently. I would love a dollar for every time that I've heard that excuse. He still had a smile on his face when he came home, so I guess he had a good time, despite how the horse performed.'

Ange's dad was forever convinced that his current horse, or the next, or the one after that, would win him a start in the Caulfield Cup. On reflection, Ange was almost certain her dad knew he was being used. However, being recognised as a successful racehorse owner was a badge of some honour amongst bushies and almost everyone had a racehorse or two. The phone calls from mates wanting to know how her dad's horse was looking for Saturday kept them connected, their shared love often a pathway to other conversations. Ange had learned the absolute worst tips came from racehorse owners. She was sure her dad and his mates knew this as well, and the charade that they played was more about friendship than hopes of valuable insider information.

When back home on the property during school or university holidays, Ange could remember sitting around the dinner table discussing the latest trainer's report. His dad would get recordings texted to him and the family would listen intently, as if they were privy to the most secret of insights. Then, following the inevitable disappointment of another middling run, the trainer would ring back with a series of rote excuses. 'We got boxed in on the turn'; 'should have let him run wide on the straight'; 'tough run today but the jockey really likes the horse'; 'I think we'll set her up for a bigger race in the city'; 'it wasn't worth showing everyone how good she is today'—stuff that kept the dream alive and ensured that her dad kept paying the training and agistment fees.

Each horse always won at least one race and her father's office proudly displayed the many winning photos of far too many horses. This seemed part of the game and in tacit agreement that every owner deserved one win. Considering all the mouths that needed feeding, the racing industry desperately needed enthusiastic owners like her dad. It was all harmless fun and something neither Ange nor her dad regretted. He was a smart man, and Ange was certain he knew what was going on. Living on a farm can be a lonely existence, and her father's expensive obsession seemed a reasonable bargain for the comradery he enjoyed.

If nothing else, she loved driving with her family to picnic race meetings in the region, occasionally even a trip to Newcastle or Sydney to watch her dad's pride and joy gallop around the track. These experiences had imbued a certain fondness for the horse racing industry and the people she had met along the way, and she signed off from the call with her mum with a smile of affection for her dad and his folly.

When Billy had hung up from the call with his boss, he sat back in his chair and reflected on their relationship. She had been his lucky break. Not only was she someone who Billy enjoyed working with, she had recognised his IT skills and pushed him forward at every opportunity. He was super grateful that Ange had convinced Senior Detective Sally Anders to recruit him from the Byron Bay Police Station.

The fact was that Billy was having an absolute ball in his new job as an IT maestro within Major Crimes. It was every bit as exciting and stimulating as he had imagined back at university in Armidale. The pay might not hit the lofty heights that he had dreamt back then, but he was grateful nonetheless. Given the meagre sum noted on his weekly pay advice, that Ferrari, the one ready to prance out of the poster pinned to his bedroom door, could wait. It would have to. His time would come, he was certain of that.

Lurking in the dark realms of cyberspace, Billy was learning every day. It was another world, one where people somehow seemed to behave worse than normal. He was certain that perceived anonymity was the key to this tendency. Scamming or stealing from an arbitrary email address was much easier than robbing actual stuff from actual people, someone who could look you in the eye.

Cybercrime was highly lucrative too, certainly much more so than robbing someone's house or car. It was also easier once you knew your way around. Billy figured that he could make a brilliant cybercriminal in a few years, knowing all the right tricks to evade the authorities. Perhaps Spectre might reach out one day. Billy had just seen the latest James Bond movie, and everything led to Spectre and 007. Deep down, Billy secretly wished he was Q. The parallels were obvious in Billy's eyes, even if not in those of his mates.

During the events of the Gold Coast, he had become obsessed with the online gambling industry. Policing this seemed incredibly hard, seeing as it was online. There were scads of illegal outfits based overseas, often with Aussie-sounding names, luring in the punter with beguiling introductory offers. Legitimate outfits operated on a voluntary code of conduct, requiring them to report suspicious gambling activity, problem gamblers, and anything that resembled money laundering. Not so the online outfits, where money was the only rule to play by. Punters also came from overseas, another complication that made regulation a mere annoyance for anyone who wanted to work around the system.

During the Gold Coast project, Billy had reconnected with Nelson, a mate from university who now worked at the tax office. It had surprised Billy when Nelson had confessed that he enjoyed gambling online with his mates. Billy had to admit that it was fun, particularly if one had a good head for numbers and didn't mind doing the hard yards to understand what lay behind the odds. Even though he would still lose money in the end, Billy factored in the entertainment value and felt he came out in front.

Nelson was a real find, not only good fun but also a great connection. Having a close contact in the tax office was a bonus, a privilege that Billy took seriously. He certainly didn't want to abuse Nelson's trust. Wherever money flowed, the tax office would be interested, and they should surely be able to help each other out in the future. They already had, in fact. Nelson had pointed Billy in the right direction during that breathtaking fraud case, one where the CFO of a major construction company had fleeced over eight million dollars to support his gambling habit. The scale of that, from just one company, made Billy realise cybercrime offered enormous opportunities for his career.

## Chapter 7

# Connecting Dots

Ange mulled over her conversation with Billy during a walk on the foreshore before grabbing some pho at her favourite Vietnamese hole-in-the-wall. She wanted to continue diving down this rabbit hole whilst it held her attention. She rang the station and recognised Bree's voice.

'Hi, Bree, it's Angela Watson here. I hope your day is going OK.'

'Have there always been so many demanding citizens in Byron Bay?' asked Bree straight up.

'Yes, and no. It's getting worse, that problem, that's for sure. Hey, I was wondering if you were free this evening. I need to pick your brains on something. I'd also like to introduce you to a friend of mine. If there's one person you need to know in Byron, it's my friend Kerrie. Once you know her, you know everyone who's anyone.' Ange had only to think about Kerrie to elicit a smile.

'What could you possibly need my advice about?' asked Bree incredulously.

'Well, our conversation yesterday evening has got me thinking, and I need a lesson in the NFT marketplace. I figured you might be a good place to start.'

'OK, I'm definitely no expert, but few people are. I would love to. I get off work at 5:30 p.m. I could meet you by 6:30, perhaps?'

'Perfect. Let's try somewhere else other than the pub this time. I know a nice wine bar. I'll text you the address.'

'See you then. Someone with an angry scowl on their face just walked in. I'd better go.'

Ange immediately texted Kerrie.

*Are you and Mike up for a drink at the Loft tonight? There's someone*

*I'd like you to meet. You might also learn something useful*

Kerri just texted back a thumbs-up emoji.

*Great. I'll see you and Mike at home and we can head downtown together. Catch you later. A xxx*

Ange then texted Bree.

*Confirmed. 6:30 p.m. at the Loft in Jonson Street. My friends are called Kerrie and Mike. C U then*

She didn't receive a reply immediately. Bree's angry visitor evidently had her attention. It was some forty minutes later before Ange's phone pinged with another thumbs-up emoji. She spent the rest of the afternoon back at the house, catching up on emails, doing some washing, the sort of stuff that you could put aside for a while, but not forever. By the time 6 p.m. came around, she felt on top of her chores and was ready for a drink. Kerrie texted to say that she and Mike were running late and would meet her at the bar, so Ange caught an Uber into town. It arrived late as well, so by the time she arrived at the bar, Bree was sitting on her own, looking decidedly lost. Her face brightened when she saw Ange walk through the door.

'Sorry about that. You know how it is. You think you have plenty of time and then suddenly you're running late. My friends should be here any minute. I'm staying at their house, in fact, but they were also running late and decided to come straight here from whatever they were doing. To fill you in, Mike invented some parking app and sold it for millions. He now invests in start-up ventures. Kerrie is a super-successful lifestyle blogger, leveraging her own Byron Bay lifestyle. When you meet her, you will realise why she's so successful. Kerrie knows anyone worth knowing, so she's a good contact to have in town,' explained Ange. She glanced towards the entrance to see Mike and Kerrie arriving. 'Speak of the devil. Here they both are. Kerrie and Mike, meet Bree. Bree is a new constable over at the station. She sort of replaced Billy. Kerrie, I'm sure you've met Billy.'

'Oh yeah, Billy. He's cute,' commented Kerrie with a wicked smile. Mike just rolled his eyes with a resigned look. Evidently, Billy was not the only guy that Kerrie found cute.

Ange also rolled her eyes. 'You're incorrigible, Kerrie. Anyway, I wanted to pick Bree's brains about NFTs and I thought you guys might find it interesting. Bree, tell Kerrie and Mike about your side hustle.'

Mike piped up. 'Oh, NFTs. Those things are crazy. Everyone's talking about them and trying to work out how they can make money off this technology. It's a super-interesting space right now.'

Bree seemed a touch nervous, being put on the spot like that. 'I'm no expert in NFTs, but I have been trading in them for over a year now.'

'Tell them how you got into the space, Bree. From the beginning. It's impressive,' prompted Ange, trying to give Bree some encouragement and confidence.

'Well, I started collecting stuff with my mum when I was a young girl. We used to trawl through second-hand stores and flea markets. When I wasn't playing hockey, Saturdays became a lap of the local garage sales. Turns out that I have a bit of an eye and started flipping whatever I picked up via online marketplaces like eBay and Facebook.'

Ange interrupted. 'Oh, I forgot to mention that Bree is hoping to make the national hockey side in the next few years. Who knows, she might even become our very own Olympian that we can cheer for.'

'Wow. Impressive,' said Kerrie. Ange could almost see her brain ticking over with ideas on whether she could use Bree in some gig or another.

Bree blushed and continued, slightly embarrassed by the attention that Ange had foisted on her. 'About a year ago, one of my mates put me into the world of NFTs. I can't say I understand the technology, but I've done really well. As I explained to Ange, for every NFT that goes up, there are two or three that go down. I'm a momentum buyer and keep an eye out for the online chatter and popularity stakes. I made more money last year on NFTs than the past five selling the physical stuff. Also, now that I have a full-time police job, collecting, storing, and selling hard collectibles is impossible. I can buy and sell NFTs on my phone. Here, I'll show what's in my wallet.'

With that, Bree opened an app on her phone and twisted it around so the others could see. She flipped through a series of small digital icons. None of them looked valuable or impressive.

'Show us the one that's worth fifty thousand dollars, Bree.'

Kerrie and Mike didn't seem at all fazed by that revelation. Bree scrolled through to find a rather sketchy catlike figure brandishing a tennis racquet. 'I just got lucky with this one. I put it down to the Ash Barty effect.'

'So, tell us how these things become valuable?' asked Ange.

'My theory is that it's simply a popularity contest. Also, like any collecting, a key factor rests in who else owns one. If a celebrity buys an NFT you're collecting, then the series will often go through the roof. Sometimes, there's something else that goes with the NFT, like being part of an exclusive community. Probably the most famous NFT is the Bored Apes Yacht Club. Has anyone heard of those?'

Kerrie piped up. 'Yes. I understand they go for millions of dollars and owning a Bored Ape is a must-have amongst A-listers. Rumour has it that a couple of Yacht Club members frequent Byron Bay.'

'Correct. But there is no proper guide to what will be successful and what will be a flop. The successes are wildly successful, and the flops are usually a total wipeout. And then there are the scams. A while back, someone listed a bunch of bored-looking apes that weren't the real thing. They looked just as good, if you're into that type of art, but these apes were all looking to their right. All the real Bored Apes look to their left. The real ones are worth millions and the fake ones are worth nothing.'

Mike asked the obvious question on everyone's mind. 'When are you going to sell your CoolCat NFT?'

Bree looked reflectively at Mike. 'I'm not sure. I think that I'll keep her. Perhaps she can be my mascot for when I make the Olympic team. Sport and NFTs go well together. I think that's where I'll focus from now on, NFTs with a link to something tangible like a sportsperson or a team, perhaps a music star even. An NFT doesn't need to be a piece of digital art. It can be a video or a song. Some NFTs are even one-off interviews with sports stars. The digital art space is crowded and messed up now, so it's getting harder to pick winners.'

'So, how do you buy an NFT?' asked Kerrie. Ange looked her way, knowing her entrepreneurial side would figure out the angles that might work for her business.

'First, you need a digital wallet containing some Ethereum cryptocurrency. I use a platform called OpenSea to buy my NFTs. It's essentially a giant marketplace where buyers and sellers meet. Anyone can mint an NFT and connect it to their wallet, which is why the marketplace has become so crowded so quickly. I think now, in the main, you need to have a real brand behind you to get noticed. Think of some of the big sports teams, the Indian Premier League cricket, companies like Adidas and Nike. When an organisation like that mints a series of NFTs, they have instant credibility. The issuer can also build in scarcity, which helps underpin value.'

Bree then looked a little sheepish, as if she was on uncomfortable ground. 'If I'm honest, I would love to mint my own series of NFTs when I make the national or Olympic teams. It could help fund me through what's otherwise an amateur sport. If I could pull that off, then I wouldn't also need to hold down a demanding job.' Bree paused and glanced at Ange. 'Like a police officer, for example.'

Ange laughed. 'Tell me about it. However, I think my second career as a professional surfer is unlikely, particularly given how badly I surfed this morning! At least you have some credentials, Bree.'

The evening wandered through a series of conversations, enjoyed over some share plates. Bree was fascinated with Kerrie's job and how she had created her own brand. Kerrie was her brand, and the authenticity of her personality showed through in the online version of herself. Ange always felt that this was Kerrie's secret weapon, the ability to harness the force of her personality in almost any situation.

Mike, on the other hand, was like a secret agent, not able to spill the beans on his next big investment. Given the speed with which these ventures came to market, he seemed to be constantly worried that another smarter and better-funded version might swamp his latest project. Bree tried her best to elicit some gems from Mike, but the best he could offer was caution on how difficult tech investing was.

Ange insisted on picking up the tab, seeing as she was a house guest of Kerrie and Mike's. Bree had easily paid for her dinner and she was becoming more and more impressive in Ange's eyes. It didn't surprise her that the nebulous world of crypto and NFTs was a magnet for scammers and those up to no good. This train of thought reminded her of another recent scam.

'By the way, Kerrie, did you ever receive those cosmetics you ordered from GlitterStrip?' Ange asked, still smarting about being outwitted. GlitterStrip had been used as a front to distribute narcotics to the Gold Coast streets, courtesy of its mail order business and the unwitting help of Australia Post. Lomax and Smith had cleaned out any evidence before Major Crimes raided GlitterStrip.

'Yes, they arrived. They're not bad. I'm hoping to get some work off them at some point.'

Ange quickly weighed up how open she should be with Kerrie; however, she was one of her closest friends, after all. 'You should be careful with GlitterStrip. I'm not supposed to tell you, but they were a front for distributing narcotics.'

Kerrie seemed completely unfazed by this revelation. 'Well, I assumed they were involved in something untoward. Why else would you have been so interested? Anyhow, I understand that one of the large pharmacy chains has taken the business over.'

That Kerrie was so comfortable caught Ange by surprise. It shouldn't have. Kerrie's business operated online, where scams were nothing personal. Ange swam in a different pond, one with sharks that could take a chunk out.

# Chapter 8

# Epic

Ange awoke early with a start. Something was different about the morning's aura. Even the cackling kookaburras seemed more compelling, optimistic even, somehow crisper, calling Ange to get out of bed and seize the day. Following the advice of those feathered larrikins, she rubbed her sleepy eyes and looked out the window. No leaf ruffled. The pressure of the moderate south-easterly breeze had disappeared overnight, leaving a sparkling morning in its place. These were the mornings that a surfer lived for, where still conditions and residual south-easterly swell merged to create epic days.

She wasted no time getting changed—hastily pulling a tracksuit atop bathers, throwing her wetsuit and towel into the back of the VW on top of her surfboards, and quickly driving off to check out the action. Opting to chance her arm at the beach breaks, she made a beeline for one of her favourite spots, a kilometre south, yet still under the watchful eye of the Cape Byron Lighthouse. She arrived to find the small parking area already jammed full of cars. A surfer appeared from his van, frantically getting himself ready and jogging away down the sandy track. As soon as Ange got out of her car, she could hear the crack of waves breaking, a series of lightning strikes, the type of crack that was reserved for large clean peaks.

She didn't waste any time checking the conditions; she knew that the surf was on. After desperately struggling on her wetsuit, she selected her six-foot thruster, the one with plenty of rocker and a tapered tail. If the gunshots going off on the other side of the sand dune were anything to go by, steep take-offs and tight lines would be the order of the day. A quick wax of her board, followed by a furtive glance around to check that nobody was watching as she hid her car keys, and Ange was soon hotfooting it down the boarded track.

As she crested the dune, she took in the scene laid out before her. The sea resembled mottled deep blue glass, moulded over thick swell lines, rhythmically marching toward the wide sandy beach and their inevitable demise. A series of obvious peaks stretched up and down the beach. Ange stood for a moment surveying the situation, before hastening one hundred metres south, where she could see a strong rip that had formed between two sandbanks. Whilst a rip was a swimmer's nightmare, it could also be a surfer's delight, welcome relief from a tiring and difficult paddle through the impact zone. Sometimes weaker rips moved around as the tide or conditions changed, messing up the wave face as the escaping water met the incoming waves. Ange's chosen rip was deep blue, suggestive of a substantial channel between the sandbanks, something that would be unlikely to move around. Of course, this perfect setup was ephemeral and everything would change once the next big south-easterly blow had its way.

Ange dropped her towel on the soft sand, and excitement got the better of her. She was soon bunny-hopping over the crashing shore break and into clear water, then sliding onto her board and paddling frantically. The rip soon gathered her up and whisked her out to sea. About halfway, she admonished herself for forgetting to complete her usual deep stretch of sleepy muscles on the beach, such was her excitement. She would need to ease into the session as the waves looked intense.

Now abreast of the breaking waves, she was taken aback by their size and power. Their perfect form had created a deceptive impression from the beach, where they'd looked manageable and cruisy. These A-frame monsters were anything but cruisy. Ange looked around at the handful of surfers in the line-up. As was often the case, she was the only woman, a familiar scenario and of no bother. One guy latched onto a huge peak, taking off at the apex and quickly slotting into the almond eye of a perfectly formed tube. Like all talented sportspeople, he made it all look so easy. Ange knew it was anything but.

She picked up the shoulder of a mid-sized wave to warm up, gauging the wave's characteristics but safe from the bulk of the power. Some tentative turns and a poor attempt at a cutback, and she shot into the channel and the racing rip. A couple of paddles later, and she was back in the line-up. It was a dream setup, the type of session that one experienced once or twice a year at most.

Sufficiently warm, she paddled further into the take-off zone, where the apex, or peak, would break first before it quickly peeled across the sandbank. The surfer's challenge was to make the drop and get set for a race across the face, making a beeline for the shoulder and the safety of the channel. A decent-sized peak rolled across the glassy sea. Ange was in the perfect spot and had the right of way. She could go left or right—she chose right, her forehand.

Not one to chicken out, she took a deep breath and stroked into the wave. After a quick jump up, she sped up rapidly as she took the long descent down the wave face, almost losing her balance backward as the power took her by surprise. Collecting herself to complete the drop, she carved into a long deep bottom turn, striving to maintain the precious speed she had garnered on the way down. Looking ahead, she could see the wave folding over. Ange tucked up close to the face and crouched, making innumerable tiny adjustments to keep a tight line.

The trick with navigating a tube ride was to avoid drifting low and being caught flat-footed, a position that inevitably led to a painful crushing as the wave overtook the rider. Equally calamitous was edging too high on the wave face, a fatal error that would see the rider carried over by the lip toward a dramatic explosion of body and board. Ange's micro-adjustments happened in an instant as the mad rush of adrenaline fired off muscles autonomously, trained by countless repetitions and drawing from experience.

Safely through to the shoulder, she pulled over the back of the wave face and collapsed onto her board, safe in the channel and ready to paddle back out. One of the other surfers paddling alongside turned to her. 'Nice tube. You were in deep. You handled that brilliantly. I didn't think you were going to make it.'

'Thanks,' replied Ange. 'That was a rush. The wave was so fast that I wasn't certain what had happened.'

'A tube ride is such a sensory overload. I usually need to pick it apart frame by frame to get a proper picture of what happens once that lip folds over. Believe me, you were in deep.'

'How amazing is this?' asked Ange, still buzzing from her ride.

'Yes, it's one of those rare moments when the surfing gods clap their hands. A northerly is due in late morning, so we've lucked out with the transition of weather patterns. Make the most of it,' said the surfer as he paddled back into the line-up, quickly pivoting to make a late take-off into a large peak that had reared up in front.

Ange followed this sage advice on her paddle back out to the line-up and painstakingly replayed her memory, examining each snapshot in minute detail and reliving the splendour of that fleeting moment of perfection. She really made the most of the session, surfing well past the point of fatigue. She caught so many waves that she lost count. One ride merged into another, making it hard for her to remember them all. It wasn't all chocolates and roses, as she also collected plenty of dustings along the way.

Some days, a bad wipeout could spoil the day and destroy Ange's confidence. The worst such wipeouts were failures at take-off, when the wave face was at its highest, its own intimidating Niagara Falls. Such a failure resulted in a painful melee of body, board and churning sandy white water. While this was a terrifying experience, it was the embarrassment that hurt most. Every surfer made take-off errors, but there was nothing worse than failing before you had begun—the equivalent of a golfer's air swing on the first tee, right in front of the clubhouse, or a cricket batman's golden duck, bowled on the first ball and sent packing. Today, success when achieved was so intoxicating that the worst wipeouts were mere trifles, just another hurdle on the way to perfection.

Ange saw the predicted north-easterly breeze before she felt it, an incongruous ripple off to the left and out to sea, out of place atop the mirrored water. As it gathered pace, so did the surfers, frantically securing their last rides before the onshore breeze spoiled the party. A mere thirty minutes later and the waves were a mushy mess, tumbling and rolling incoherently, difficult to ride and signalling it was time to pull up stumps.

As she stood on the beach, wetsuit draped over her board and wrapped in her towel, she relived the special moments of her morning. The great turns, one re-entry move that she had been especially proud of, and the tube rides, of course. Some surfers insisted that a tube ride was better than sex. Tube rides were decidedly rarer, even with Ange's spasmodic sex life. Perhaps this would be the fate of surf parks, where perfect man-made tubes might spoil such rare thrills. She could not imagine ever tiring from regular sex with someone special, whereas if she scored tube rides at will, it would likely trend towards boring.

Having successfully faced the morning's waterborne challenges, she decided that now was a good day to face another.

## Chapter 9

# Return to Mullumbimby

As she resolved to take the picturesque drive to Mullumbimby, she reflected on the last time she had visited the stately country town. The dawn raid on the home of Joe Kramer had resulted in the apprehension of his son, Ted, a chain of events that ultimately led to his murder, presumably at the hands of Lomax and Smith. Ted's death was the reason that Ange wanted to visit Mullumbimby; however, that was just one source of tension between her and the Kramer family.

Joe Kramer's side hustle, leaning on property developers to support the Byron Bay Coastal Protection Society, had riled Ange. Worse still, it had ended with her being called before the state's anti-corruption watchdog, SACC, and made out by the media as a dodgy cop. Even though Ange and Sally Anders had used this unfortunate turn of events to their advantage, that Joe Kramer had bested her in that exchange still rankled.

Not wanting to make the drive and miss Kramer, Ange had called the society over her sushi lunch in Byron. A young woman had answered her call.

'Hi, Byron Bay Coastal Protection Society. How can I help?' came the breezy voice.

'Hello. A relative who passed away left me some money and I'm looking at donating to a suitable charity. A friend suggested I speak to Mr Kramer, who I understand founded the Byron Bay Coastal Protection Society. I'm up in Byron on holidays and I wondered if Mr Kramer might be free to see me. Would he be available either this afternoon or tomorrow morning?'

'Oh, great. I'm sure it would please Mr Kramer to see you. He is in the office now, so how about I check his availability? Would 2 p.m. suit you if that works for Mr Kramer? May I ask who's calling?'

Ange knew full well that Joe Kramer would make time for a potential donor. 'Two o'clock works for me. My name is Gloria White.' Ange's time incognito had honed her ability to spin a yarn, calling on her alter ego from the Gold Coast operation.

The young woman put Ange briefly on hold but was back in an instant. 'You're in luck. Mr Kramer is free at 2 p.m. as well. Our address is 57 Stuart Street, Mullumbimby.'

'That's perfect. Let me write that down—57 Stuart Street. Got it,' she lied. Ange knew exactly where Joe Kramer lived.

As soon as she had hung up from that call, she rang Billy in Sydney.

'Hello, Billy.'

Ange knew full well that her sickly sweet voice would instantly raise warning bells. 'Yes, boss,' was his tentative reply, sensing that a curly request was coming over his bow.

'Remember when we raided the Kramers' house in Mullumbimby? Do you have access to the evidence log? Given that Major Crimes bundled us out of the investigation on the very next day, we never got a good look at whatever was taken as evidence. Seeing that we *are* Major Crimes now, I wondered if you could have a look at this for me?'

Billy was cautious. 'Where exactly are you at the moment?' he enquired warily, correctly deducing that Ange was up to her usual tricks.

'I'm still in Byron, but I'm about to drive over for my two o'clock appointment with Joe Kramer. Well, the appointment that Gloria While has with Joe Kramer.'

'You know we've been told to lie low on pursuing the syndicate,' warned Billy.

'Just passing on my condolences to Mr Kramer,' commented Ange offhandedly, as if sugar wouldn't melt in her mouth.

'OK, boss. I'll poke around where I can. You're going to get me into big trouble one day.'

'Who, me? Never,' she said, hanging up the call amidst Billy's sigh of resignation. Ange knew he would be smiling.

So, there she was, driving down the main street, admiring how the avenue of palm trees framed the impressive historic buildings, the overall effect heralding how important the town had been in the local area. Byron Bay had well and truly taken over, but Mullumbimby would have once been a prestigious place in which to live and do business. This changing of the baton had seen Mullumbimby fall into disrepair before hippies and the alternative set had rolled into town. The stratospheric prices of Byron Bay real estate had certainly heralded a new era of prosperity for Mullumbimby, as greenchangers and seachangers on a budget had discovered this beguiling and cheaper alternative.

Ange swung her VW into Stuart Street and parked outside No. 57, taking advantage of the centre aisle and a large shady tree. A sharp bark from a large dog was an immediate echo to the clunk of her closing car door. Ted Kramer had a blue cattle dog, Bluey, if her memory was correct. She had grown up around dogs back on the farm, and her own much-loved pet had been a red cattle dog. She had named him Buddy, and that he was. When Ange came home from boarding school, she would arrive to find Buddy already waiting expectantly at the front gate. How Buddy knew she was coming home was a mystery to everyone. Some dogs had a connection with their masters that science could never explain.

Ange walked over to the front gate just as Bluey came racing around to greet her. Ange knew to take care of blue cattle dogs; their reputation for a short fuse was well deserved. Bluey had a worried and questioning expression on his face. Ange carefully opened the gate and gave Bluey a roughhouse pat, bending down to give his neck a good massage. Bluey stared straight into her eyes, imploring her to answer his question. She heard a voice from the veranda and looked up to see Joe Kramer standing there, hands in his pockets, watching how Ange dealt with Bluey.

'He's been like that with anyone he associates with Ted. It's freaky how he knows who to ask for information in his own way, and who to distrust. He must like you. He bit one of Ted's mates. If Bluey hadn't, I probably would have. A genuine piece of work that guy is. I doubt he'll be back, and good riddance.'

Ange looked up at her nemesis. 'Cool dog. I had one myself. Buddy, a red dog. It's amazing how they know. A genuine sixth sense. His name is Bluey, isn't it?'

'Yes, but Ted didn't call him that much anymore. He preferred Blue Dog once that children's cartoon show became all the rage.' Bluey's ears pricked up at the mention of his alias. 'We normally call him that, but he responds to both. A very smart dog is our Blue Dog,' explained Kramer, his affection for Bluey obvious.

Joe Kramer seemed relaxed, not so much of the smug activist that Ange remembered. 'I presume you are Gloria White, here for our two o'clock meeting? I thought that a new donor falling from heaven was too good to be true.'

Ange stood up and faced Kramer. 'I know we haven't been on the same side of things, but I wanted to pass on my condolences about what happened to Ted. Nobody deserves that fate.'

Kramer sized up Ange before replying, assessing whether she was being sincere. 'Thanks. Ted wasn't a bad guy. Perhaps a bit confused and easily led. I must take some responsibility for that, but I tried to protect him from the crowd he had fallen in with. I should have done more, but I guess there comes a point where your children need to take responsibility for their own decisions in life. I miss him. I wouldn't win any awards for best dad, but it was great to have Ted around and back in my life.' Kramer's words hung awkwardly in the air whilst the pair contemplated the reality of what had transpired. A young life wasted in horrific circumstances, precipitated by Ange's investigation at Namba Heads.

'Sorry for the pretence about Gloria White, but I wanted to make sure you were in, and I wasn't certain that you would want to see me.'

Kramer fixed Ange with a long stare. Bluey collapsed onto his belly and watched the conversation between the two, as if he could speak human. His eyes followed every word, as if imploring someone to provide some news about his master.

'I know we don't see eye to eye, Detective, and that you don't agree on my methods, but I get a lot of that. I'm sorry that you copped a beating in the press over the SACC affair. That wasn't fair and certainly not my intention.'

'So, it was you who went to the press?' asked Ange, more a statement than a question. 'That was pretty brazen, especially while SACC had you under the spotlight.'

'The whole thing was a crock. It pissed me off and should never have happened. The reason I was confident that they wouldn't find anything was that there wasn't anything to find. I was worried that SACC would manufacture something to justify themselves, so I went on the offensive. Unfortunately, you were a casualty of that.'

This revelation surprised Ange. She wasn't prepared to let Joe Kramer off so easily. 'So, leaning on developers is OK, then?'

'Someone needs to look after the environment and it all costs money. Who better to pay than the group who profits most from destroying it? And by the way, I don't have any council officers in my pocket, as SACC alleged. The internet makes it super easy to keep track of who's doing what. I can find all the information I could ever want in planning and development portals. Of course, it always helps when I'm working with a green council, and it's my right to have the odd word in the right ear. Anyhow, I figure my role is not only to limit the impact of development but also to educate developers. There's always some way to improve a project's environmental footprint.'

Kramer's pragmaticism shouldn't have surprised Ange. The Byron Bay Coastal Protection Society was like any other venture. It needed money to survive, and Kramer was a survivor, if nothing else. 'Perhaps you could be a little less aggressive about the way you go about it, then. The police service doesn't need the distraction of dealing with complaints from developers about your methods.'

'I get that, but some of them are so bloody arrogant. Boils my blood and I can't help myself. Anyhow, I'm sure concerns about developers aren't the reason for your visit to Mullumbimby. I understand you've gained a promotion. Congratulations.'

Ange carefully measured her response, taking a moment to assess Kramer and whether he was being honest with her or taking the piss. The last thing Sally Anders needed was a complaint precipitated by Kramer, who undoubtably would have friends in high places, perhaps a wealthy patron who knew someone of influence. She made these assessments in an instant, still unsure. Kramer sure was a wily customer. She pressed on. 'Is there anything that you have found about Ted that could help us bring those responsible to justice?'

'Nothing that I can think of. Your lot took most of his stuff away. I gather you've found nothing worthwhile.'

Ange was still uncertain about how to deal with Kramer. She eased forward slowly. 'Ted was really a minor player in the operation, so I'm surprised that they felt the need to murder him. He must have known something that worried them. Do you know a guy called Tyler Ball, by any chance?'

Kramer's expression quickly hardened. 'That lowlife. I'm certain he was the guy who got Ted into trouble in the first place. He was also the person who Bluey bit. As I said, our Blue Dog is an excellent judge of character.'

Ange's pulse quickened. 'What was he doing here?'

'Well, he wasn't paying his respects for sure. Bluey caught him skulking up the rear stairs. He must have come through the neighbour's property and jumped over the back fence. Bluey was making a hell of a racket, and I came out to see Tyler scooting off the same way. I think Bluey got a piece of Tyler as he jumped the fence. I haven't seen him since. Good old Bluey,' said Kramer, turning and motioning for Bluey to come over for a pat. Having heard his name on several occasions, Bluey was alert to this possibility and gratefully moseyed over to Kramer to receive his treat.

Ange thought about this revelation for a moment. 'He's also not answering his phone. I guess he was looking for something. Any idea what that might have been?'

'I've thought about that myself. He would have known that your lot had have been through the place with a fine-tooth comb. You didn't exactly keep a low profile during your morning raid.'

'If you think of anything, can you let me know?' Ange handed over her business card to Kramer just as his mobile rang. Kramer excused himself and took the call, turning his back to Ange.

She crouched down and Bluey came over for a pat. She tousled his head again, much to his delight. Something caught her eye as Bluey's dog tag ran through her fingers. She stopped and rolled it over. One side of Bluey's tag contained his name in large red italic lettering. The other side was a jumble of incoherent words, discreetly engraved into the sliver metal tag. Some words were hard to read. It seemed incongruous, so she quickly whipped out her phone and took a series of closeup pictures, choosing different angles each time.

Kramer hung up from his call. 'Anyhow, Detective, I must go. There's a kerfuffle over in Nimbin that I need to check out. I reckon I might see some of your colleagues. I'll let you know if I hear of anything, or if Tyler or any of his mates come around again.'

'Did you know any of his other mates?'

'No. Tyler was the only one I heard Ted speak of. He was always going on about Tyler.'

'OK. I look forward to hearing from you should you think of anything that might help. Don't speak to anyone else, if you wouldn't mind.'

Kramer looked inquisitively toward her. 'Is this all under the radar, then?'

'Yes, and no. There has been a loss of momentum, but since I started this train wreck back at Namba Heads, I need to see it through,' lied Ange. A loss of momentum was a gross understatement of the facts. She gave Bluey one last tousle as Kramer headed back into his house.

She left Mullumbimby pondering what on earth Tyler Ball might have been searching for.

## Chapter 10

# Secret Stash

Ange rang Billy on the drive back to Byron. 'Hi, Billy, any luck with the stuff about Ted Kramer?'

'Nothing worthwhile. It's weird, but I can't see any phone records. I'm sure we got those as part of the investigation?'

'I'm sure we did. That is strange. I'll speak to Sally Anders about it. What about bank statements?'

She heard Billy's fingers flying across his keyboard. More than once Ange wished she could navigate herself around a computer even half as well as Billy could. 'Yes, I have them. I'll flick them to you, but there's nothing of any real interest. Just bits and pieces and everyday purchases. Looks like he was getting some sort of stipend from the Byron Bay Coastal Protection Society to make ends meet.'

'OK. By the way, Billy, did Ted Kramer have a laptop?'

'Yes, he sure did. A Dell XPS laptop.'

'Do you know how thoroughly we examined it?' asked Ange. She heard Billy's mouse clicking away.

'I wouldn't say that we went though it with a fine-tooth comb. Just the usual emails and documents that might have looked interesting. The report seems to dismiss any information stored on the laptop as low value.'

'Can you see if you can get your hands on it? I think it may be important.'

'What reasons can I use? I can't just waltz into the evidence store and walk out with it, particularly when we aren't supposed to be looking in this cupboard.'

'Yep, you're right, Billy.' Ange went silent for a few moments while she thought through the problem. 'I think I may have an idea. Expect a request from Sally

Anders to come through tomorrow.'

'What am I looking for? Is this another of your needle-in-a-haystack brainwaves?' asked Billy.

'Perhaps. But Tyler Ball was searching for something in Mullumbimby. We've been through his phone, but we know something was missed. Ted's computer seems like a good place to look.'

'Where are you going with this, boss?'

'I don't know, Billy. We know Kramer was being paid for his services, and presumably he was paying for his own narcotics. We found some cash when we raided his house, but we know that this was likely the same cash that had been used to pay off Dave Fletcher, the trawlerman. Presumably Kramer retrieved that after Fletcher's murder.'

'Keep talking, boss,' prompted Billy.

'What if he was using crypto for his activities, and the cash we found was a one-off? If we could establish a pattern, then perhaps it might point us in a different direction.'

'Seems like a long shot to me, boss, but I'll do what I can. I hope that you aren't sending me on a wild goose chase.'

'I would never do that to you, Billy. Thanks. By the way, Bree passed on some office gossip the other night. In the world according to our old colleagues, Walton and Lynch, you're my toy boy.'

'Honestly, those guys are pathetic.'

'I could do a lot worse in my choice of toy boy, Billy,' joked Ange, showing her good humour over the situation.

'Funny, boss,' said Billy with a nervous-sounding chuckle, suggesting that the idea wasn't completely abhorrent to him. 'So, when should I expect to hear from Sally Anders?'

'In the next day or two. Speak then, Billy.'

By the time Ange had arrived back in Byron and attended to her omnipresent inbox, it was time to head over to dinner with her old boss. She picked up a nice bottle of South Australian Riesling on the way. As Ange waved her phone over the EFTPOS terminal to pay for the wine, she recognised the already digital nature of money. She couldn't remember the last time she had used actual cash to pay for anything. Crypto wasn't as big a step as she had thought only a week ago.

Ange had been looking forward to having dinner with Jim and Barbara Grady. It had been an exhilarating day on many fronts and a home-cooked meal was a rare treat. Ange hadn't eaten at her boss's home all that often, but she knew what a terrific cook Barb Grady was, undoubtedly the major contributor to the few extra kilos being lugged around by her husband.

Ange understood full well that she had totally lucked out by scoring Jim Grady as a boss and mentor. He had exerted a positive and supportive influence on her career, keeping a watchful eye on her progress, especially in those early years at the station. Her promotion to detective had come quite early in her career as a police officer and she knew that there were many naysayers who begrudged her success.

The Gradys greeted her warmly. Barb was interested to hear about her sojourn on the Gold Coast, not so much the work side of things but more about what it was like to live in that growing city. Barb explained her interest. 'You know, there was a time when we considered that the Gold Coast would be a great place to retire. We were so lucky that we purchased this house when we did—at least we'll have some options. We wonder how long we can afford this lifestyle. Byron is changing so much and becoming so expensive.'

'The Gold Coast is still an enigma to me. A major city sitting on the edge of the Coral Sea. On one side, I met some lovely young families, everyday people, living and working happily amongst the glitter. On the other side are the scammers, attracted to the Gold Coast's glitz and glamour like a magnet. Major Crimes put me up in this stunning waterfront home that was confiscated as a part of a financial crimes case. Just a few doors up, I met a lovely elderly woman called Ada, and her dog, Franky. She'd lived there most of her life and reminded me of my favourite aunty from Tamworth. A few doors to the other side lived Eddie Falconi, as smooth and sharp as they come. Unfortunately for him, Falconi became a victim of our investigation, evidently killed to clean up any loose ends. I can't think of any other place in the country where all of that could sit on one street.'

Barb Grady's ears pricked up. 'I read that Falconi had committed suicide. Something about financial pressures.'

'A staged suicide, like the trawlerman Dave Fletcher in Namba Heads. I never saw Falconi's murder coming, as you know, boss,' admitted Ange.

Barb took the cue and headed to the kitchen to plate up their meal and let Jim and Ange continue their discussion.

'By the way, we did some work looking for Tyler Ball. He appears to have disappeared without a trace. We found out where he lived, a farmhouse out of town. According to my officers, it looked abandoned.'

This was not good news. 'When was Ball last seen?'

'I rang the letting agent who handles the property. There was a card in the door. Apparently, the agent has been trying to get in for almost a month and install some new fire alarms. A month would be my best guess,' replied Grady.

'What about his rent? Wouldn't he need to pay weekly?'

'Not in this case. The agent said he paid cash, six months in advance. A model tenant, in her words.'

'Cash? Isn't that unusual nowadays?' enquired Ange.

'I had the same response. The agent said that it would surprise us how often cash is used to pay rent in the region. I asked her why and she felt it was probably because some people just wanted to stay off the grid or under the radar, leave as little trace as possible. She also remembered that Tyler Ball asked if he could pay in Bitcoin or Ethereum. Apparently, this is more and more common and something she's looking into for the future. In her experience, most landlords still perceive cryptocurrency as a high-risk form of payment.'

'Can you do me a favour, boss?' asked Ange.

'I'm not your boss anymore, you realise. But, yes, of course,' replied Grady.

'Could you contact Sally Anders with a request that Billy examine the laptop and phone records of Ted Kramer? Ball and Kramer were known associates, and Kramer rang Ball from a burner phone just before his death. It would seem a legitimate fear that you might have concerns about the well-being of Ball and are trying to locate him.'

Grady fixed Ange with a sideways grin. 'I get the distinct impression that you're not really all that concerned about the welfare of Mr Tyler Ball.'

'You know me too well. Not only did Ted Kramer make that fateful call to Ball, but Joe Kramer caught Ball snooping around the house after the death of his son. Their dog, Bluey, bit him, which was apparently quite gratifying. Joe Kramer blames Tyler Ball and his mates for leading his son astray. Ball was looking for something, so I think it's worth trying to understand what that something might be.'

'OK. I'll contact Sally. We'll also keep looking for Ball. I'm not sure we have enough to gain access to his phone records. It might help if someone made an official missing person report. What about Joe Kramer? He could report Ball's disappearance.'

'Yes, but I still don't completely trust Joe Kramer. If you can't find anyone else, let me know and we can consider that option. Ball is definitely a key person in all of this. We really need to find him.'

With that, the loud ring of a bell coursed through the house. 'That's Barb's way of telling us that dinner is served. She loves to find any occasion to use that bell. It reminds her of when the kids were at home. It was her trick to bring everyone to the table before dinner went cold,' explained Grady as the pair stood up and moved towards the dining room.

The rest of the evening ebbed and flowed effortlessly around family and friends. Barb didn't miss the opportunity to probe Ange about her love life, in a kind motherly way that resulted in Ange disclosing more that she might otherwise have done.

She left the Gradys' house well after 10 p.m. Jim Grady's parting words echoed as loudly as their clanging dinner bell. 'You need to be careful, Ange. People associated with your investigation have a habit of going missing.'

## Chapter 11

# Balls Up

Some weeks back, Tyler Ball had been slumped on his kitchen chair in front of his laptop computer, twirling a pen around in his fingers and deep in thought. He was getting nowhere fast with his project and stood up to stretch his legs. As he rose, he felt a twinge in his calf muscle where that bloody dog had nipped him. It was lucky that he had been wearing jeans as the mongrel hadn't broken skin, but the bruise the dog had left was still painful enough. The worst part of the whole exercise was that he had learnt absolutely nothing. The bite mark was all he had to show from that failed excursion.

Tyler had been at it all evening, trying to hack into Ted's digital wallet. He knew that it was a super long shot without Ted's dongle, but he had to try. After all, Tyler reasoned, that money was really his. He was the one who had convinced Ted to get on the cryptocurrency freight train. Ted had often boasted about how much he had invested in crypto, and Tyler knew Ted spent none of his ill-gotten gains, money earned from acting as a petty drug dealer and running errands for Tyler, all paid in Bitcoin or Ethereum. Tyler had done the maths and Ted's crypto stash was significant. Cryptocurrency values were still skyrocketing. One gig, four or five years ago, where he had paid Ted the equivalent of $5K in Bitcoin, was now valued at over $250K. Ted must have millions in his wallet.

It was a pity about Ted, but heck, business was business. That was how Tyler rationalised the situation. The people that he was working for had blamed Tyler for the mess that had become of their Namba Heads operation. It hadn't been his fault, just because Ted had turned witness. If anything, it was their own fault. They were the ones that had botched mopping up those bodies. If they had done a better job, none of this would have come back to bite them. Nonetheless, Tyler had done as requested and rung them the moment that Ted had contacted him. He didn't know what had happened to Ted. He didn't want to know.

It was Ted who had given him the idea to move to Portugal and live off his crypto savings. If he could add Ted's stash to his own, he would have more than enough. He'd done some research, and Portugal was the place to go. Their tax laws hadn't caught up with the new world order of digital currencies, and there were plenty of beautiful places where he could live cheaply and stay off everyone's radar, not to mention all the beautiful Portuguese women.

Tyler was sick and tired of living like a hermit, stuck out in the sticks in the bland brick-veneer house that he'd rented. It had been hard work building his nest egg while maintaining a low profile and keeping his head down. He still had some clients to service to keep some cash trickling in, but he was fast losing interest in being a drug dealer. It all seemed so old-school when compared to trading in crypto and watching it go up every day. Some of his NFTs had gone up as well, but the ones that he'd sold to Ted were a bit of an anomaly. Tyler wouldn't bother stealing those back. He'd almost felt bad about selling them to Ted.

Notwithstanding his own minor fortune, he still wanted Ted's crypto to give him a nice buffer on which to retire gracefully. The stuff was just sitting there, ripe for the taking. Even better was that Tyler was probably the only person who knew about it. He desperately wanted to get his hands on the dongle that unlocked Ted's digital wallet. Tyler knew that Ted had one; he'd seen him use it one time when they were transacting over something or other. Tyler could even picture that dongle in his mind, an innocuous-looking ticket to paradise. He needed to have another go at breaking into Ted's house. If not the dongle, he might uncover Ted's seed phrase, the other way into his digital wallet. Ted had probably hidden it under one of his old martial arts trophies. That would be the sort of hiding place that Tyler would use.

He would need to deal with that bloody dog, but perhaps he could distract him with some meat of some sort. That might work. Come to think of it, he wouldn't mind having a look in that mongrel's kennel. Ted adored that dog. Tyler wasted a few minutes searching up on his laptop for something suitable to feed a dog, something that wouldn't leave any trace. Chicken wings seemed to be the best option, and he resolved to get Bluey addicted when he next visited Mullumbimby.

Feeling that he finally had a way forward, he stood up once more and limped into his kitchen, snapping on his absurdly noisy kettle to make a cup of tea. 'How on earth could any company design such a pathetic product as that kettle?' Tyler thought to himself as he leaned into the fridge to retrieve a bottle of milk.

He neither heard nor saw whoever came up behind and expertly wrenched his neck, severing his spinal cord in an instant. Before it stopped working, Tyler's brain worked out that he wouldn't be moving to Portugal after all.

## Chapter 12

# The Long Drive

Ange spent the morning after her dinner date with the Gradys wandering aimlessly around Byron. The north-easterly had destroyed any chance of a worthwhile surf, so she opted for a long walk that took in the iconic lighthouse, a beacon visible from almost anywhere in town. Seeing as Byron Bay was the most easterly point in Australia, it seemed a logical spot on which to plonk a lighthouse, but she could imagine nowhere more spectacular. The coastline stretched both north and south, with long sandy beaches punctuated by a series of headlands, forming one of the most impressive vistas in the country. It was no surprise that Byron proved such a magnet for those looking to build a new life.

Not one to tread water, Ange decided it was time to head back to Sydney. She rang Kerrie and organised to meet for lunch and explain her plan to leave that afternoon. Kerrie was visibly disappointed but understanding shone in her eyes. Ange was someone who needed to keep moving, not in the literal sense, more a statement of intent on how to tackle life. 'Keep moving forward' would be a reasonable epitaph. This was not unlike Kerrie in many respects; however, the new digital world allowed Kerrie to move forward without moving house, something not so easy for Ange and her career.

Ange had packed and was on the road by 2 p.m. She saw the turn-off for Namba Heads ahead, causing her to consider visiting the sleepy coastal village. In the end, she opted to keep driving. Her failure to apprehend Lomax and Smith would make for a tough conversation should she run into Sharon Fletcher, the wife of the trawlerman that the two thugs had murdered. Of course, if it wasn't for the roaring north-easterly wind, the prospect of a surf at Sliders, one of her favourite breaks, might have overcome those concerns.

Once she had settled into her drive, she rang Sally Anders. 'Hi, boss. Can you talk? Preferably away from prying ears.'

'I'll ring you back, Detective,' replied Anders before abruptly hanging up.

Ange was another twenty minutes down the road before her boss called back.

'Sorry about that. I was busy defending our record with the bigwigs. Frankly, I'm not sure how long I can hold them off. They want blood, and mine seems to be preferred. There's something unsettling about all this pressure that's piling onto us. When are you coming back to Sydney?'

Ange reflected on this pressure and her boss's capacity to stay cool under its weight. It was the first time Ange had ever heard a shiver of defeat creep into her voice. She felt that their relationship had progressed sufficiently to ask about something that had been bothering her for ages. 'Boss—who exactly is piling the pressure on you over this? I gather that it's someone high up in the food chain. I think it's fair that I know who we risk pissing off.'

Sally Anders was silent for a few seconds. Disclosure was not one of her strong suits. 'Point taken. Chief Superintendent Bold, who keeps mentioning the commissioner whenever he unloads on me.'

'Whoa. It's nice to know it's not someone important,' commented Ange, a healthy dose of sarcasm dripping off her voice.

'Bloody Bold is a study on how to climb over your colleagues to get to the top, and the commissioner is more a politician than anything else. Who knows who's pressing their buttons—probably the police minister or one of his political cronies. Anyway, you leave them to me. That's why I get paid the big bucks,' explained Anders, no slouch in the sarcasm department herself.

'OK. Thanks for filling me in, boss. I appreciate it. I'm on the road now. My visit to Byron Bay will probably make life even more interesting. I tried to keep my visit as discreet as possible, but it's going to be difficult to maintain radio silence.'

'On that point, I've already received a request from Jim Grady, asking if Billy could look through Ted Kramer's laptop and phone records. I presume you had something to do with that?'

'Yes, that would be me.'

'What's your angle on this, Ange?'

Ange filled her boss in on the basic details of what she had learned. 'I called in a favour with my old boss to help track down Tyler Ball. It turns out that Ball has also disappeared. However, before he went missing, Joe Kramer caught Ball trying to enter their house up the back steps. In fact, Ted's dog, Bluey, bit him.'

'Any ideas what he might have been looking for?'

'It looks more and more obvious to me that Tyler Ball was Ted Kramer's colleague, and the call made by Kramer from his burner phone ultimately got him killed. There must have been a reason for the syndicate to take that step. Either Kramer knew something he wasn't telling us, or he possessed some information that he didn't realise was significant.'

'He could have simply been looking for the cash you guys recovered when you raided the Kramers' house. If Ball and Kramer were both working in the Namba Heads operation, then Ball would have known about the cash,' deduced Anders.

'I've thought about that. The seizure of the cash was no secret, and the cringeworthy Sergeant Darren Billings was on the syndicate's payroll, so we need to assume that this wasn't about the cash. There had to be something else that Ball was looking for.'

'Any ideas?'

'None that are particularly well formed. That Kramer wasn't forthcoming about his links with Tyler Ball is also interesting. I was off the case by then, but how did Kramer explain his involvement in the operation when you guys interrogated him?'

'Kramer insisted that he never knew who was behind the syndicate's activities and that his instructions all came via his burner phone. Those calls and texts were all dead ends when we traced the numbers, and his personal phone records showed nothing of interest. We also looked through the emails, documents and photos stored on his laptop, which were totally unremarkable. Over all, his story seemed plausible, and we concluded that Kramer was indeed the small fry that he insisted he was.'

'But they must have paid Kramer for his services. How did he explain that?' probed Ange.

'He said that they had paid him in product, which would not be out of the question. This seems like old ground to cover, Detective. I'm not sure it's relevant.'

'Maybe. That Ball has disappeared and Ted Kramer is the only link makes it worth looking into, at least. Anyway, if Ted Kramer was paid in product, he would have needed to convert that to cash and we didn't find any evidence of that. I have a hunch that there's a lot more to their relationship.'

'OK, Detective, I'm happy to humour you. I know that you have some theory or other rolling abound in your head. I presume you'll fill me in one day?' replied Sally Anders, seeming to appreciate that she was being afforded only a fraction of the story.

'If my theory is right, then Ted Kramer's laptop should show us something to link their activities. We should also try to track down Tyler Ball, and we can't leave all that to Jim Grady.'

'OK. I'll get Billy onto the laptop, ostensibly looking for clues as to the whereabouts of Tyler Ball. By the way, I've had all your stuff up picked up from the Gold Coast. I've put it in storage for you. Do you have somewhere to stay?'

'No, I hadn't thought all that through.' The revelation that she had ignored this minor matter came with some embarrassment to Ange. She was essentially a vagabond. Uncertainty over her relationship with Brett rudely surfaced, interrupting her train of thought. She hadn't heard from him for a few days. Was this a sign, or was he too busy? She hadn't thought to ring him either, which was also disquieting. It wasn't like his name hadn't come up. Kerrie had probed every facet of their relationship. Sally Anders snapped her from falling down this mineshaft of doubt.

'We have a serviced apartment you can use until you get settled. I'll send you the address and the instructions on how to get into the apartment. I'll block it out for two weeks while you find somewhere to live.'

'Thanks, boss. My mind was on other things. I should be back in Sydney tomorrow evening. Will that be OK?'

'Yes, that's fine. I'll get Peter Fredericks to make the arrangements and send you the details. I'll have to get your car back, though. You can use one of the work cars when you need one.'

'Sure. I've really enjoyed this car. I'll bring it into the office on Monday and hand over the keys.'

'OK. See you Monday, then. Drive carefully.'

As she drove southward in her soon-to-be-relinquished VW, Ange's mind continued to spin with all the permutations and combinations of what she had learned over the past few days. When she was not tumbling these thoughts over and about, the many doubts and concerns over what to do with Brett and their relationship crashed through. The nondescript Port Macquarie motor inn, with its lumpy bed and ubiquitous tacky bedcover, didn't help matters. After a restless night, at least she scored a pleasant surf, tucked into the corner at Lighthouse Beach, one of the few places protected from the north-easterly. The water was markedly cooler, and the waves were small and weak, but she enjoyed a great view of the coastline through the distinctive and unique lens of the surfer. Sitting out the back on her shortboard under the gaze of the quaint lighthouse, patiently searching for the ride of the day, was cathartic, providing some time to think through her issues and concerns between rides.

She found a nice cafe for a leisurely breakfast. Her phone pinged with a message from Peter Fredericks containing an address for her temporary Sydney accommodation, along with the PIN number for a lockbox containing the key. On the road by 10 a.m., she settled into the four-hour drive through to Sydney. In any other circumstance, she would have taken the time to stop at a few places along the way, Forster or Blueys Beach, perhaps. Truth be known, she was suddenly feeling lonely. Another night playing solo-traveller showed little appeal in her current frame of mind. It would be nice to have a companion along for the ride, even better if that companion was also a surfing buddy. Someone like Brett Tompkins.

Almost as if her mind had been read, her phone buzzed. It was the man himself. 'Hi, Brett. I was just thinking about you.'

'I hope those were nice thoughts.'

She didn't see the need to act cool about her feelings. 'I'm driving back to Sydney and was wishing you were here.'

Brett didn't exactly gush out his own feelings, choosing instead to deflect from giving these away so readily. 'Have you stopped anywhere for a surf? It's rubbish up here on the Goldie.'

'I caught a few small ones this morning in Port Macquarie, tucked up in the pocket at Lighthouse Beach. Nice spot. I'm on my way back to Sydney now. When will you be finished up there?'

'I still have a lot to do. I've found something interesting, which is why I'm calling you.'

It dismayed Ange that work was the only stimulus for Brett to call her. She didn't respond to Brett's teasing revelation, instead waiting patiently for him to continue.

'I guess you heard that the local police have written off Eddie Falconi's death as a suicide.'

'What a crock. They're either lazy, sloppy, or crooked.'

'I know, but it has helped us out in a roundabout manner. I still haven't officially left BeaBet, so I made some enquires with the administrator appointed to liquidate eZee Bet. They're in a holding pattern for the time being, but they plan to sell the company along with any assets that we can't get our arms around. Anyhow, on behalf of BeaBet, I expressed an interest in acquiring some of their assets once they were ready to dispose of them. They sent me a list.'

Ange was back to her old self, intrigued and engaged by this direction of travel. 'OK. Sounds interesting.'

'Remember when we went to that party at Falconi's house on Cronin Island and you were admiring his artwork?'

'Yes, I do. I'm no expert, but anyone could tell that they were expensive pieces.'

'You were spot on. However, they were just his everyday round-the-home pieces of art, not the high-end stuff.'

Ange was all ears. 'What do you mean? That he has more art stored away somewhere?'

'When I probed the administrators about the art, the guy dropped his guard somewhat. He mentioned truly international works, even one by Salvador Dalí. I pushed him on why that was the case. Apparently, they found a trail to Singapore and something called a Freeport. Falconi has several valuable pieces of art stored there. I gathered from the conversation that it won't be easy for them to get their hands on the stuff.'

'What's a Freeport?'

'The way the administrator explained it to me, it's essentially a stateless warehouse. Anything stored there is deemed in transit and out of the reach of governments. It's often all about avoiding the tax man or hiding illicit goods. These facilities allow you to buy and sell your art anonymously and it never leaves the warehouse. I haven't fully got my head around the idea, but it all smells dodgy to me. Anyway, I thought you'd like to know. The administrator wasn't forthcoming about how Falconi got the money out of eZee Bet to purchase these expensive pieces of art. I guess he could have used the same trick as he used to get the money in.'

'What do you mean?'

'Well, he could easily have set up his own offshore betting account and collect on a series of winners. I know we're supposed to stay off-grid, but exactly how Falconi funneled his money offshore would be good to know.'

'Thanks, Brett. That is all super interesting. I'll do some research myself. Let me think through an angle to find out how Falconi was moving money offshore without ringing any alarm bells. Maybe it was through his art? Falconi seemed to have lots of tricks up his sleeve.'

'OK, then, I best get back to it,' said Brett, his voice betraying some discomfort.

'Let me know when you're back in Sydney,' Ange enquired, trying to stay cool and nonchalant. She could sense that Brett needed breathing space.

At the next opportunity to pull off the highway, she searched podcasts on Spotify, typing in search terms like 'Fine Art and Money Laundering', 'Art and Tax Evasion', then adding 'NFTs and Money Laundering'. That last search turned up a plethora of podcasts to keep her busy. Even a cursory glance at the titles suggested NFTs were manna from heaven for someone up to no good.

The rest of the drive to Sydney was a blur of Freeports, despotic government officials, lessons on how to squirrel assets away for a rainy day, and a 101 on using fine art to evade taxes and pay bribes. One fact that blew her mind was the estimated US$100 billion in assets held in a Freeport in Switzerland, all considered in transit and out of reach. One didn't need to be Einstein to deduce that not all these assets were squeaky clean.

## Chapter 13

# Meanwhile—Back in Sydney

After the call from Ange enquiring about cryptocurrency, Billy decided he needed to upskill. Being an investor himself in no way made him an expert on the ins and outs of this rapidly growing sector. His course on cybercrime had only dealt with the basics, and he had merely skated across the glossy surface of the crypto world until this point—just one in an avalanche of twenty-something first-time 'investors' attracted by this shiny new phenomenon. In the eyes of Billy's generation, crypto promised to break the mold of the stodgy investment products contrived in the world of their parents and in partnership with complicit governments. The stories of overnight Bitcoin millionaires exploding across social media channels presented a brilliant opportunity for scammers and unscrupulous marketers. Big profits came with big risk, an investment axiom which seemed lost on 'coiners'.

Billy wasn't the only tech-head in Major Crimes, but nobody else seemed to be an expert in crypto and blockchain. The sector had all the ingredients for fertile ground, and he knew from his course that criminal activity was rife. His career could only go forward if he could position himself as the in-house expert.

In the world of nefarious financial activity, cryptocurrency presented a conundrum. On the one hand, the ability to transact under the radar, around the globe, and beyond regulation was highly appealing. Whatever regulation existed was woefully inadequate and perpetually one or two steps behind. Some local jurisdictions were focusing on the point of conversion to hard currency. This made sense for the moment, while crypto wasn't mainstream, but more and more products and service providers were coming on board and allowing customers to transact with crypto. Billy could see rafts upon rafts of legislation on the horizon as regulators sought to plug this leaky boat.

On the other side of the crypto coin was the blockchain itself. Cryptocurrency gave the impression that it was secret and anonymous, but the opposite was true. Sure, provided you could keep your crypto transactions away from prying eyes, you remained cloaked in secrecy. However, once someone had the thread of a crypto transaction and knew where to look, the entire history could be unlocked. Every person who had played a role had their crypto alter ego recorded in the blockchain—forever. It wasn't as if their name, address, and telephone number were on display, but there were ways and means to work this out. Billy was intent on learning these ways and means.

As soon as Ange hit the outskirts of Sydney, she abruptly crashed into everyday life, distracting her from her education on unscrupulous uses of Freeports.

Brimming with hope and opportunity, the city drew people from all over the globe, and its growth showed no bounds. Despite reeling from its extended Covid lockdown trauma, Sydney was bursting back to life. Ange had largely skipped being incarcerated by the virus, something she attributed to the warmer weather up north and her outdoor lifestyle. Hitting Sydney and its stifling Friday afternoon traffic jams proved a shock. She would never have found her temporary digs without the help of satellite navigation.

As Ange sat in the traffic, she reflected on the complex relationship she held with Sydney. Just on eighteen when she'd first moved to town for university, she had arrived with a teenager's view of the world, excited about her future and the role that the city would play. Now, she was older and wiser, also a battle-scarred veteran from her time working the Western Sydney streets as a junior constable. To say that she was battle-scarred was no understatement, and a disturbing incident from her days on the beat in Western Sydney had come flooding back.

Ange and her partner had been called to a disturbance in Fairfield. Calling the incident 'a disturbance' was a gross understatement. It was a full-blown racially fuelled battleground. As soon as they arrived, both sides of the altercation turned their hatred of each other against the two police officers, joining forces and surrounding the vehicle, rocking it violently and striving to smash the car windows. Ange was terrified and pleased that her partner, who was in the driver's seat, could extract them without casualty. At least their capitulation seemed to quell the battle. Perhaps each side had found some common ground in their mutual hatred for the police. Ange and her partner didn't wait to see if hostilities resumed. They were ill-equipped to tackle such an incident, and it should have been the riot squad who attended to that skirmish. Ange had had nightmares about the incident for months afterwards.

Then there was the last time she had stayed in Sydney, her reputation challenged by SACC, the state's integrity attack dog. These experiences had left her with mixed emotions about moving back. As she approached Darlinghurst and the address of her apartment, she made a vow to smell the roses and take the best of what Sydney could offer, and try to accept the worst as just part of life—or part of her job. Car parking was something that fell into the worst category, and she scrambled around for ages looking for somewhere suitable, finally squeezing into a jam-packed fifteen-minute zone.

By the time she had retrieved the keys to the apartment, worked out how to access that basement car park, and arrived back at her car, she found a council parking inspector taking photos.

'What seems to be the problem, Inspector?' asked Ange in a pleasant enough voice. She was surprised at this attention given that she had taken such care to park legally.

'Are you the owner of this car, madam?' questioned a burly and officious-looking parking inspector.

'No, not really, it's on loan for the moment.' Ange was interested to see where this was going before she came clean with her identity.

'Well, this car is parked illegally. You're over the yellow line. Here, you can clearly see.'

The man paused to show her an image that he had just snapped using his phone. Ange was furious. He had taken the photo at an angle, making it look as if the nose of her car protruded across the yellow line.

Ange walked to the front and took her own series of photos, one perpendicular and another from a position a metre ahead of the car, an angle that made it look as she was parked well behind the yellow line.

She showed the two photos to the parking inspector. 'These are the photos that I'll be showing my boss.'

'That's fine. You can always take the council to court if you have the time and the energy. I'll back my word against yours, any day,' he said with a smirk.

Ange put her phone back in her pocket and pulled out her wallet, flipping it open so that the inspector could clearly see her detective's badge.

'I wouldn't count on it. You know that the public lumps us all together as one and the same. I appreciate that you have KPIs to meet and budgets to make, but this sort of dodgy behaviour gives us all a bad name and makes my job harder.'

A brief battle of wits played out, but the parking inspector was simply no match for Ange's best *I dare you* stare. A full ten seconds elapsed before the inspector knew he had been beaten.

'OK. I'll let you off this time,' he said in a condescending tone, as if he was doing Ange a big favour. 'Just don't do it again,' he added as he abruptly turned and went on his merry way, off to bludgeon some other hapless motorist.

Ange's blood boiled. It took every element of her self-control to keep her anger in check. 'Do what again?' she thought to herself as she hopped in her car and drove away. 'Park legally? Bloody hell. Welcome to Sydney, Ange.'

The next two weeks presented a blur of activity, where everyday life rudely interrupted her train of thought at every turn. Finding a suitable place to live, at least one that she could afford, proved a nightmare. Ange wanted to live in the inner Eastern Suburbs, midway between the beach and the city. Needing to extend her temporary rental of the apartment another week, she finally found a neat little one-bedroom apartment in Edgecliff, a short walk from the station and on the Bondi Junction–Town Hall line. There was no parking, so it was a blessing of sorts not to have a car, as life would be an incessant and frustrating search for a parking spot. There was a laneway out the back of her apartment block she could use when she had a work car overnight, but it wasn't somewhere she would feel comfortable leaving her own car permanently.

Her apartment was small, and Ange was pleased for her meagre possessions. She liked to leave a small footprint, opting for quality rather than quantity. She appreciated the small storage area where she could stick some boxes and stash her surfboards. Her lovely JayTee, with its impressive mural, was proudly displayed in the small living room as her sole piece of artwork.

Her introduction to the Major Crimes head office was taxing—getting sorted with her passes and security clearances, being assigned a desk to work at, learning the ropes of her new job. There were courses and training that she had to complete, and she arrived home each night exhausted. It was good to see Billy again occasionally, even though he worked on another floor of the office building. Peter Fredericks breezed in and out, and Sally Anders was as busy as ever. Everyone else was a stranger.

Notwithstanding her foreign work environment, she was loving being back in Sydney. The dog-eat-dog side of the city surfaced rudely on occasion, but there was always something to do and someplace to go, even without a car. Her daily exercise doubled as an exploration of her suburb and surrounds. Energy and activity pulsed through the city, and it was impossible not to find this intoxicating.

Within days of being in the office, she was assigned a case involving white-collar crime, a fraud case involving another CFO. This one had been extremely clever, siphoning small amounts of money autonomously over a wide range of transactions. The company had discovered the fraud during stress testing of a routine software upgrade.

There seemed to be a lot of this stuff going around where CFOs were involved. While it was nothing like the fraud case on the Gold Coast, which had tallied over $8 million, $300,000 was nothing to sneeze at and was well worth Ange's attention. Her job was to work out who else was involved and what they knew about the scam. It was routine stuff, but interesting enough to keep her mind occupied.

Ange had made contact with her friends from university during her first week in Sydney. They seemed thrilled that she was back in town and organised a lovely Sunday breakfast catch-up at a coffee shop in Bronte, one facing a park. Takeaway coffees in hand, the fathers oversaw the kids as they played. Ange watched in awe as the children gathered around the inanest piece of play equipment, a foil to facilitate learning about themselves and each other.

Once her girlfriends were settled, they wasted no time in addressing an issue of concern. After all, it would not do for their family to mix with the wrong crowd. 'So, tell me, Ange, what was going on with that corruption enquiry that you were involved with?' asked Amy, one of her closest and more adventurous friends from university. Amy had lured Ange into many a sticky situation back in the day.

Ange's suspicions that tongues would wag over that affair were proven correct. She made her best effort to fend off these worries. 'Oh, that. It was all a ruse for an undercover operation I was involved with,' she said nonchalantly, gilding the lily somewhat and ending any deeper exploration of that affair. Questions about work often fell flat when detectives were involved.

At each juncture, the thread of the conversation inexorably veered towards the many trials and tribulations of being a young parent. Occasionally, and not unrelated, were discussions about real estate prices and the next housing move that their growing families would demand.

No matter how hard she tried and how much interest she feigned, Ange remained a foreigner to the countless interlocking moments that made up the lives of these families. The children were just delightful, but there was one major insurmountable problem that she couldn't get past. None of them were hers.

## Chapter 14

# Back on the Trail

Almost six weeks had passed by since she had arrived back in Sydney, and Ange was making solid progress on her embezzlement case. It was proving an excellent distraction, and she had hardly given the affairs of the syndicate another thought. She was sitting in a nearby coffee shop taking a mid-Friday-afternoon break when she received a call from Jim Grady.

'Hi, Ange. How are you settling into things in Sydney?'

'It's great, boss.' She still called him that on reflex, despite that no longer being the case. 'I'm enjoying Sydney but missing the lifestyle of Byron.' Ange failed to mention just how deeply she was missing her friends in Byron Bay.

'It seems like another boatload of immigrants has descended on the place since you left. I don't know where this is all headed, if I'm honest. Anyway, that's not the reason for my call. We've spent the past month or more looking for Tyler Ball. He seems to have disappeared from the face of the earth.'

'Have you found anything interesting?'

'Nothing obvious. We searched his phone records, and they show his phone stopping ringing soon after that call from Ted Kramer. Also, a search of his bank accounts yielded nothing useful. It's obvious to me he was up to no good, as he had no obvious means of support. The only inflows came from sporadic deposits from a company called Swyftx, all smallish amounts and just enough for him to live off. I looked them up and they're a mainstream digital exchange for cryptocurrency. They rate highly and seem totally legitimate. I had our latest recruit on the case and she uses the exchange herself. I think you met her, Breanna White.'

'Oh yes, I did. Bree seems like a gem to me. That is interesting about Tyler Ball.

Cryptocurrency pops up at every turn nowadays.'

'The real estate agent who managed the place where he lived she gave us access. It was completely bare. The agent was upset that she couldn't re-lease it, as Ball had obviously skipped town. Seeing as he paid six-monthly, there wasn't much that she could do.'

'OK. Thanks. It sounds like Ball has either gone to ground or he's buried somewhere in it.'

Grady paused for a moment before wrapping up the call. 'Ange, I don't think that there's much more I can do about Tyler Ball. I'll keep my eyes and ears open, but I can't throw any more resources his way. Have you guys gotten anywhere?'

'No, I've been tied up getting settled in the office,' replied Ange. Grady's question came as a reminder. She needed to check in with Billy and see if he'd gotten anywhere with Ted Kramer's laptop.

'I understand. By the way, I haven't written this up. I figured it best to stay under the radar after hearing that Sally had suspicions about a mole.'

'Yes, good idea. I understand you need to move on, boss. That he's gone missing so comprehensively tells me something. Thanks for your help.'

Ange jumped in the lift and went down to pay Billy a visit.

'Hi, Billy. What's up?' she said in her sweetest voice.

'Oh, hello, boss. I've been busy with my investigation into corrupt councils. Everyone uses WhatsApp these days, which makes it hard to trace communications. Luckily, everybody slips up eventually.' He fixed Ange with a mischievous grin. 'It's good to see that you've dragged yourself off the executive floor to pay the lowly workers a visit. How are you settling in?'

'Very funny, Billy. It's OK, but I prefer the engine room to the executive lounge. You should know that about me. Anyhow, I was wondering, did you ever get around to examining Ted Kramer's laptop?'

'No. Actually, I forgot all about it. They never sent it up from evidence.'

'That's disappointing. I'll chase it up with Sally. I think it's important. When his laptop arrives, can you dive straight into it? Let me know whatever you find in person. No need to waste time writing anything up.'

'OK. I'll get onto it when I can,' replied Billy.

Ange sometimes felt guilty about sucking Billy into her projects. She knew he struggled to resist her many requests, no matter how hard he tried. 'You're a gem, Billy. I don't know where I would be without you.'

Billy seemed unsure whether to beam or grimace at such ingratiation.

She was barely back at her desk for a few minutes when she saw Brett Tompkins' name come up on her phone as an incoming call. Her pulse quickened. Brett was proving to be a conundrum. As much as Ange hated gushy men, she would have expected some rekindling of their personal relationship. Perhaps being so overtly work colleagues, rather than undercover operatives with alter egos, was a problem? Maybe dealing with an ex-wife and their children was challenging him? Whatever was going on, they had only spoken one time since parting ways at the Gold Coast.

'Hi, Ange. Have you settled into Sydney OK?'

'Pretty well. Busy. Finally found a place to live nearby, so I feel as if I'm getting on top of things,' answered Ange. Not prone to gushiness herself, she kept a businesslike tone in her voice, noting that Brett had neglected to ask about where she was living.

'You know that stuff we found out about Eddie Falconi and his artwork stored overseas? Well, I kept digging further. Even though I'm officially out of BeaBet, I convinced my partners to keep me on the books as a consultant. I thought it might come in handy.'

'That sounds like a good idea. Were your partners OK with that?'

'No, not really, but Sally has something over the founder, so they probably didn't have any choice. Anyhow, I kept in contact with the administrator of eZee Bet and made him think we might be interested in acquiring the business.'

'Is BeaBet genuinely interested in acquiring it?'

'I doubt it, although the name is better than ours. BeaBet doesn't need a client list of drug dealers and money launderers on its books. Anyway, I told him we were interested in expanding, particularly into Asia, and we might be interested in acquiring a worthwhile international client base. I was wondering about a possible Singapore connection and the Freeport where Falconi had his artwork stored. Turns out I was off the mark on that. However, the administrator told me that there were only a couple of overseas clients, but that they were big clients.'

'Where were they based?'

'That's the interesting part. All three were in tax havens. Cayman Islands, Bahamas, and the Jersey Islands.'

'How big were these clients?'

'The administrator wouldn't tell me, although he doubted BeaBet would be interested in acquiring those clients. Apparently, eZee Bet was haemorrhaging some big losses from those three. I think the administrator feels that he's in deeper than he wants to be. He shut up shop after spilling that piece of information. I reckon he would be worried about who might pay his bill. Those guys usually rely on asset sales to pay their account. Anyhow, I presume you're still digging around Falconi and his activities. I thought you might be interested.'

As interesting as this was, Ange would have been more interested if Brett had asked her out so they could discuss this over dinner, but that invitation had not been forthcoming. She put that disappointment behind her and reflected on their conversation.

Brett's update supported her theory that Falconi had been using fake bets to launder money out of the country. She had to admit that Falconi's operation had been brilliant, with his drug dealer clients settling their debts through eZee Bet, all disguised as legitimate gambling losses. The international winning gamblers were most likely proxies for Falconi himself, money that he could use to pay off others and buy his expensive art, safe and securely stored in the Freeport. eZee Bet probably showed a modest profit overall, enough to sustain his lavish lifestyle and keep the regulators happy.

As Falconi had showed so comprehensively, gambling drew criminals like bees to honey. When the words *illegal gambling* were mentioned, Old World images of colourful racing identities or shady casino owners sprang to mind. Almost everyone had a favourite movie show or TV series involving dodgy bookies or casino shenanigans, or both. The new world of gambling was moving online, making it harder to track and even harder to regulate. That didn't mean that traditional forms of gambling weren't part of the story; it was just that the real action was elsewhere, at least in Ange's eyes.

Like most everyone, Ange was not above buying a Lotto ticket or having a bet at the races. However, the new world of betting was 24/7 and certainly not confined just to horse races. In the past couple of weeks, she had spent some time hanging out with Billy and his mate Nelson. Surprised to learn that they liked to dabble, Ange took advantage of the opportunity to learn something about the new world of online gambling. She could certainly see how addictive it was, recognising the psychology embedded in the platforms themselves. According to Nelson, online gambling apps harnessed the same five golden rules that applied to addictive video games: immersion, fascination, progression, reward, and mastery, all designed to secure one more bet.

Nelson also had an interesting theory that online spread betting was the perfect way to launder money. All one needed was a maths geek to write an algorithm and unleash a bot that placed lots of small bets and took contrary positions. All you would lose would be the house margin. There would be fluctuations day to day, but the yield over time would be quite predictable. Domestic betting companies were tightly regulated and required to stay alert and report illegal betting or money laundering. It was the overseas black-market outfits that were harder to control. They weren't precious about where their money came from, and a steady flow of losing positions was manna from heaven.

The syndicate had proven to be extremely clever, and Ange felt that whoever was behind the operation would be unlikely to allow the same play twice. Still embroiled in gambling and money laundering investigations, Brett would hopefully be alert to anything which resembled the syndicate's signature. Ange was now convinced that she needed to look in a different direction. She just wasn't entirely sure what direction that was.

## Chapter 15

# Bondi Beach

The somewhat relaxed off-duty version of Ange was mulling over her Friday afternoon calls from Jim Grady and Brett Tompkins as she sat on the train, clutching her public transport surfboard and on her way to the Eastern Suburbs for a surf. She should have been worrying about her embezzlement case, but that seemed ordinary and mundane when compared to the activities of the syndicate.

She had woken up early and hoped that either Bondi or Bronte Beach would deliver what the surf report had suggested—clean shoulder-height waves amidst bright sunshine. She had nicknamed her new-old surfboard Franky, in honour of the endearing Labrador she had met on the Gold Coast. An expert judge of character, Franky the dog also had teeth and could mix it up in the heat of battle, at least according to Ada, his mistress.

Her Franky was decorated with evidence of an active life. He might not be pretty, but he was structurally sound and a solid performer, perfect for crowded surf breaks and even public transport. 'What's another ding between friends?' was Ange's attitude, one that empowered her to muscle through the Sydney throngs, both in and out of the water.

She dared not take her magnificent JayTee swallowtail shortboard on public transport, resplendent with its one-of-a-kind mural. JayTee lived a bubble-wrapped existence in Sydney, precious about when and where he surfed. It seemed natural to Ange, ascribing names and personalities to her surfboards, good friends and companions to her passion as they were. Gus Bell had taught her what to look for in a board, explaining what should suit her surfing style and level of ability. Naming her surfboards, however, was all Ange.

A fortnight after arriving in Sydney, Ange had picked up Franky at the Bondi

Junction Cash Converters for a song, abandoned because of some surface discolouration and a few dings, a victim of a society that demanded the latest and flashiest to feel good about itself. She'd taken Franky out for a few surfs since, and he had turned out to be a rough diamond.

The deserted and uncrowded beaches of her last surf trip to Agnes Waters just before moving back to Sydney were a far cry from what she was experiencing now. Surfing in Sydney was best described as *every man and woman for themselves*. She had learned to take on a Franky persona—the real Franky, that was, the canine version. All friendly and nice until someone stepped over the line. Ange, like Franky, could bite back. It was not her preferred way to surf, but she wouldn't catch a single wave unless she played the game the Sydney way, scrambling over everyone and everything to get on top.

Even despite these waterborne annoyances, Ange loved Sydney. Despite being a country girl at heart, she relished the energy and activity that pulsed beneath one of the world's great cities. It was exhilarating, frustrating, elegant, ugly, breathtaking, and disturbing—all at the same time. However, Covid had left deep scars in Sydneysiders, wounds that had not yet healed.

Public transport was a case in point. What had once been the preferred way to travel in Sydney was now a pill to be taken sparingly. People had retreated into their four-wheeled cocoons, laying claim to their personal patch of infrastructure, clogging roads and fraying tempers. On the plus side, for someone without a car, trains were nowhere near as busy as they had been before the pandemic. Despite enduring the ire of an occasional traveller who felt that surfboards belonged in the water, Ange felt a certain satisfaction sitting there on the Bondi Junction train with her pet board that early summer day.

Ange was enjoying her little one-bedroom apartment in Edgecliff. It was noisy, cramped, and all that one would expect of inner-city accommodation on a budget, but it was smack bang amongst the action. Just a short walk to the train station, she could be sitting in the Major Crimes office, just off Bathurst Street, in less than twenty minutes. There was also still some novelty value to walking along a jam-packed New South Head Road to the Edgecliff train station on the weekend, Franky tucked under her arm and looking like a fish out of water—so to speak.

Arriving at her station, Ange expertly manoeuvred Franky through the barriers, navigated a precipitous escalator, then another, ultimately spilling through some large doors into an expansive indoor bus station. The 333 rolled in, perfectly timed to make easy her decision on where to surf. Ange smiled as she edged into the bus, catching some 'what's a surfboard doing on my bus?' stares. Franky was her special care dog, after all.

In mere minutes, Ange was standing on the Bondi Beach foreshore. It was staggering to think that such a stunning place could sit within one of the world's largest and dynamic cities. She never tired of that view and wished her modest salary could stretch to a beachside apartment. If her job was indeed *following her dreams*, then she was light years away from realising one of those abodes.

Ange made her way down onto the sand and chose a spot just north of the Icebergs Swimming Club. Despite the sunny day, the ocean clung tenaciously to winter, and the water was still cool. She was pleased to pull on her 3mm steamer, as opposed to the stalwart members of the Icebergs, who swam without such luxuries, every day of the year. She walked gingerly into the water as the cold seeped into her wetsuit. Minutes later, she was forced to duck-dive under a crashing wave, and the water stole her breath away, concurrently chilling and exhilarating. Ange quickly forgot any discomfort when she turned and picked up a small wave on the paddle out, the perfect way to ease into her Sunday session.

She was glad to have arisen early. People were streaming onto the beach, in tune with the rising sun and creeping warmth. As her session progressed and the crowd increased, waves became harder and harder to come by. Ange tried every trick in her arsenal to score her fair share of rides. She was 'snaked' on two occasions, where a greedy surfer jumped the queue and cut her off, one of the most hated moves in surfing. Everyone became brutally focussed on catching a wave and all courtesies vanished. Beg, borrow, or steal—whatever it took. Playing the female card was of no use whatsoever. Not only were there more women surfers in Sydney than she had seen elsewhere, but they were good—and tough.

As she eased into the back end of her session, watching the growing number of surfers compete for limited waves, Ange's mind drifted once again towards Brett, a fellow surfer of some skill. Pushing the wrong side of mid-thirties, she dreaded the prospect of needing to similarly compete on the dating scene once more. Sydney demographics would work squarely against her. She'd done the math on her last trip to Sydney and before rekindling her relationship with Brett, a mental conundrum to take her mind off that distressing anti-corruption matter. In raw terms, there were six percent more females than males in the Eastern

Suburbs. When you took out the married men, this imbalance stretched to a full ten percent. No wonder her single girlfriends complained about a dearth of eligible men.

A sudden wipeout on a large set wave shook Ange from her daze. Still sitting, she shifted her weight onto the tail of her board, tilting it almost vertically in the water and quickly pivoting, placing herself in the prime spot to take the wave. Now facing in the right direction, she timed her move perfectly, the action of the board popping up also shooting her forward. Yelling toward another surfer who was looking to drop in on her prize, she took two brisk, confident paddles and she was up and away. It turned into the best wave of her session, taking her almost fully in to the beach. She contemplated paddling back out, but the throng of surfers looked even more imposing from that perspective and she called it quits, reasoning that she had enjoyed the best of the morning waves, getting the jump on lazy Sunday sleep-ins as she had.

By the time she had indelicately squelched off her wetsuit, the cool breeze had chilled her to the core. She ditched her usual freshwater rinse at the communal outdoor showers on the foreshore, settling for a brisk towel-down on the beach itself. After a rather sketchy under-the-cover-of-beach-towel change of clothes, one where sand ended up in all the places it shouldn't, she was soon warm and snug in her tracksuit and hoodie, looking for all the world like any other itinerant surfing day-tripper—perhaps one of the Covid-stranded Bondi-loving backpackers who persisted.

As she stood there watching the action and soaking up the sun, shaking out the remnants of sand that had found its way into her pants, a guy sauntered over. Good looking, in a rangy shaggy dog way; tall, thin, and fashionably dressed, in a beachie, hippie sort of way. She assumed he was also looking to get into her pants.

'Would you like to buy some weed?' he said in a slow, raspy voice, almost offhandedly.

Ange didn't know whether to laugh or cry. On the one hand, that this guy had unwittingly offered drugs to a detective was spectacular. On the other, Ange had brought no identification to the beach with her. All she carried was her transit card and a few banknotes to buy breakfast. It wouldn't do to leave her badge unattended on the beach. It was safe and sound in her apartment, her usual habit during these urban surf outings.

She pointed to a guy she had spotted earlier, standing on the foreshore with a large camera, taking photos of the beach scene, conspicuous with his large DSLR and humongous lens. 'See that guy up there? He's my colleague in the police service. It's your lucky day. I just had a great surf and I'm feeling in a good mood. I suggest you hotfoot it out of here before he points that thing at us and I'm forced to arrest you.'

The guy couldn't have gotten off the beach any faster, disappearing rapidly up a back street. Ange figured he would be unlikely to return, but the whole affair put her in a suddenly dark place. A bit of pot was not something she was particularly worried about. Personal cannabis use was increasingly being decriminalised and hardly the worst thing someone could do. It was those who profited from the misery of others that riled her. Mobs like the syndicate.

'What am I doing?' Ange questioned herself. 'This is my day off and I'm supposed to be enjoying myself.'

With that, Ange and Franky also disappeared into the back streets, grabbing some coffee and a pastry in a relaxed coffee shop that she had recently discovered. Caffeine and delicious carbs quickly restored her good humour.

## Chapter 16

# Hidden Trails

Mondays were moving day as far as Ange was concerned, particularly when she had enjoyed a weekend off. Mostly free weekends had proved an unexpected benefit of moving to head office and working in Major Crimes. When working in Byron Bay, she was never really off duty, permanently on call should something or someone hit one fan or another. Given she had slipped into the Gold Coast investigation directly from Byron, she hadn't contemplated the realities of her new job.

Ange had a long list in her trusty notebook, an eclectic collection of things to follow up, things to leave alone, things to speak with Billy or her boss about, the odd scattered grocery item, who to ring and who to avoid—and, of course, her incessant light bulb ideas. It was those light bulb moments that usually provided the most inspiration and breakthrough, but those same moments got Ange into the most trouble. Most ideas arrived while she was out exercising or surfing—they were usually the good ones. It was those ideas that came in the middle of the night that she had to watch out for. Those tricky suckers were often part inspiration, part hallucination, and usually part crazy-thoughts. Separating the inspiration from the madness proved very tricky.

As soon as Ange arrived in the office, she wandered over to see her boss, discreetly closing the door behind herself.

'Hi, boss. Jim Grady rang me on Friday. Tyler Ball has vanished and they don't have any clues as to his whereabouts. It's quite plausible that he has met a similar fate to Ted Kramer.'

'Yes, I know. Jim rang me as well. Did Billy find anything on Kramer's laptop?' asked Anders.

'Evidence hasn't sent it up. Could you chase them for me?'

'For goodness' sake. Those guys act as if anything in the evidence room is theirs and theirs alone. I'll give them a nudge. Anyhow, what do you hope to glean from his laptop?' asked Anders.

'The fact that Ball was skulking around the Kramers' home suggests that Ted Kramer had something of value which interested Ball and his associates. I've got a hunch Ted Kramer was into crypto and maybe the pair transacted that way. The estate agent who managed that property where Ball lived mentioned that he wanted to pay in cryptocurrency.'

'That seems like a gigantic leap. Isn't cryptocurrency anonymous?'

'I guess, but I'm still learning about how crypto works. I'm sure Kramer and Ball would have left some crumbs for us to follow.'

'OK. Good luck with that. Remember to stay discreet. My life is difficult enough without another *please explain* demand from upstairs.'

'Will do, boss,' said Ange before she left the office and made a beeline for the lift to pay Billy a visit. No time like the present.

Billy was only one floor down and the lift car seemed tediously slow. She would have preferred to use the fire stairs, but security was tight, and she didn't wish to be stranded in the stairwell again. On that last occasion, she had been forced to trek all the way down to the ground floor. Then the security system wouldn't let her back into the building, seeing as she hadn't exited normally.

Stuck waiting for the lift, she reflected on the state of play. The fact was, the trail to the syndicate had hit a stone wall; however, Ange knew that she needed to keep plugging away and searching for an opening. Her plan was simple on the face of it—follow the money. She hoped that Ted Kramer had left a clue on his laptop that they could reveal an avenue that she could explore.

Wherever large-scale narcotics were being distributed, there would be significant revenue that needed to be sanitised and dealt with. The tales of Pablo Escobar and his associates were no myth, and the amounts of cash involved boggled the mind. Like most of her profession, Ange had become engrossed by the Netflix miniseries on Escobar.

Another thing that Ange had become engrossed in was podcasts on financial crimes and money laundering, which often involved cryptocurrency and NFTs. Like Billy, she had reached the conclusion that financial crimes were a huge growth area and developing expertise in this area would be a sound career move.

These weren't crimes that the average Joe could investigate. They were complex concealed scams, usually run by smart people. And there were a lot of them, providing ample opportunity for an equally smart and determined detective.

One thing she had learned during her time on the streets was that the average petty criminal was not particularly smart and usually screwed up with at least one dumb mistake. Her favourite experience was the thief in Byron Bay who had taken off his sunglasses to better see what he was doing, only to leave them sitting on a shelf on his exit. Ange could have gone down the DNA route, but the guy's scratched initials had made her task easy—evidently he'd been worried that his mates might steal his precious sunnies. Honour among thieves was a hugely overblown concept.

It was money itself that usually brought white-collar criminals undone. Flashing around an expensive car or boat when you have a mediocre office job will raise at least one eyebrow. Taking too much from one victim also increased the risk. Some of the best scams stole a small amount each time, nothing that anyone would notice. The textbook examples involved hidden computer algorithms which siphoned off cents, or even a fraction of a cent, over millions of transactions.

Greed was a factor, but ego often played a part, where the criminal felt the need to prove how clever they were, ironically revealing that they weren't particularly clever after all. The tough ones were those who treated stealing money like any other job, all businesslike and not allowing emotions or their own ego to get involved. In fact, some criminals used ego on the parts of their victims to assist their scam. The podcast on Bernie Madoff and the way he'd positioned himself as a darling of the New York City elite had fascinated Ange. Ego and wanting to run with the cool crowd were powerful motivators readily exploited by scammers.

Once she had eventually made it to Billy's floor, she moseyed over to his work area, not so much a desk as a technology multiverse carrying four monitors packed with gobbledegook. 'Hi, Billy. I was wondering how you're going with Ted Kramer's laptop.'

'Oh that, sorry, I haven't even touched it,' replied Billy. He glanced at one corner of his desk, where a silver laptop sat, piled under papers and documents. 'I needed to get some work done on my official corruption investigation. Remember to use WhatsApp when you need to keep your messages secure. I was getting nowhere until a mistress of one politician under investigation spilled the beans.

All hell has broken loose and now his wife is piling on.'

'Beware a woman scorned,' commented Ange.

'Let's have a look at it now.' Billy rolled his chair sidewards and retrieved Kramer's laptop. He plugged in a power adapter and opened it up. A sticker had the numbers '0719' written in marker pen. 'That's the password to fire up the laptop. We must have gotten that from him when he was being interviewed.'

The computer booted itself up. The lock screen displayed a magnificent late-afternoon beach scene, showing a surfboard leaning up against Kramer's van, Bluey chasing some seagulls, and an attractive long-legged woman sitting in a camping chair taking in the sunset. Ange had never actually met her, but she assumed that the woman was Amy Lightfoot, Ted's former girlfriend. Ange remembered Kramer had mentioned their regular camping trips during questioning.

'Quite a scene,' she commented. Pangs of desire to be transported into that scene surfaced unbidden.

Billy typed in the password, revealing the desktop. He then clicked on the icon for Google Chrome and the familiar browser interface popped up. Moving the cursor to the top right, he clicked on the letter T, confirming this was Ted Kramer's laptop. This also revealed his Google email address, a predictable combination of his name and birthdate @gmail.com. Billy then clicked on the nine dots hiding a series of Google Apps, including Kramer's Gmail application. A long list of emails came up, littered with spam and marketing blurbs. The laptop had been dormant for over six months now, so this was to be expected.

Billy gave this list a cursory glance. 'I'll have to go through that later. There are loads of emails here.'

'Can you search for emails from Tyler Ball?'

Billy ran a search for the name Tyler. 'Nothing, boss. Perhaps Ball was using a pseudonym. They are criminals, after all. I guess I should scan through these, looking for suspicious emails that might be from somebody like Ball. They also may have communicated some other way. I'd use WhatsApp or one of the other encrypted messaging services if I was into something dodgy.'

He clicked back to the browser interface and opened Kramer's photo library. Ange could see that Kramer was obsessed with three things. Surfing, Bluey and Amy Lightfoot. She noted that there weren't any photos of his father, Joe Kramer, or indeed his mother. Ted Kramer really had been a lost soul. Billy didn't give these too much attention and quickly skipped back to the main Google browser page.

'That's interesting,' Billy commented, pointing to a small round red icon flying a skull and crossbones flag.

'What's that, Billy?'

'It's an application called RedBrd, a play on the infamous pirate with the long red beard. It shows that Kramer has a digital wallet. *Had* a digital wallet, more correctly.'

'Cool name. Can we access his wallet?' she asked, her pulse quickening. RedBrd seemed appropriate given her developing sense of the crypto trading routes—the perfect symbolism for someone up to no good.

'Almost impossible without his password and his dongle,' Billy replied, clicking on the icon to open the app, displaying a login request and a suggestion that now would be a good time to deploy one's dongle.

'You're talking another language now, Billy. Bree, the young constable in Byron Bay, has a digital wallet to store her NFTs, but I have no idea how they work. Enlighten me.'

'Digital wallets or NFTs? NFTs are way too weird for my liking.'

'Digital wallets, you nong,' chided Ange with a chuckle.

'Remember your first lesson on blockchain? Well, in its raw state, blockchain isn't exactly the most user friendly of inventions. It was, pretty much, an invention to warm the heart of math geeks everywhere.'

'Really Billy? I would never have guessed,' teased Ange.

Billy was in his element and totally ignored her mockery. 'So, your cryptocurrency lives on the blockchain of the original coin that was minted and is controlled through a super long number called a digital key. It also comes with some things called public and private keys. Think of the public key as like your home address, something which is publicly available information, the thing you give to your delivery driver when you purchase something online. To access your mailbox to retrieve the delivery, you need your own private mailbox key. Whereas you are happy to give your home address to the delivery driver, you're not likely to give them your mailbox key. You will want to keep your mailbox key safe, so you wouldn't store it anywhere obvious, like on top of your mailbox, for example,' explained Billy.

Ange shifted uncomfortably, thinking about how lax she was with her apartment key when she went surfing. She probably should get one of those lockboxes installed, but they just seemed like an invitation for a robber to break in. What to do with your keys when you were out surfing was a riddle to be solved another day. 'I understand, Billy. The public key is your address, and the private key is the thing that lets you in. That's a good analogy. What do private and public keys look like?'

'Both are very long series of uppercase and lowercase letters and numbers that are almost impossible to remember. The characters need to be entered perfectly, so you can imagine that needing to remember a billion characters like that, just to make a transaction, is simply impractical. Enter digital wallets—which can store all your public and private keys and allow you to access them simply and easily to make transactions, almost like online banking. If someone needs to send you some crypto, you would give them your public key, the equivalent of your address, and they would essentially send the crypto to your public key. Your digital wallet would then access your private keys and complete the transaction. There's a lot more going on in the background, but that's the gist of it.'

Billy paused to check that his student was following his lesson before continuing. 'There are different types of digital wallets. A cold wallet is one that uses a dongle, whereas a hot wallet is purely a software application, usually cloud-based. There are also paper wallets, which are essentially a printed set of your digital keys. Personally, I would worry too much about losing my piece of paper. I think the cold wallet is the most secure, but nothing is foolproof from misfortune and stupidity. In the old days, before digital wallets came along, crypto was stored on the hard drive of your computer. There are stories about early crypto investors losing tens of millions of dollars' worth of crypto stored on a hard drive, others forgetting or losing their digital keys and never being able to retrieve their currency.'

'I get it, but wouldn't your wallet be a target for hackers and scammers?'

'Absolutely, and there have been instances of wallet platforms being hacked and crypto being stolen. That's why I like a cold wallet that uses a dongle. I need my password, which I have memorised, and my dongle, to access my crypto wallet.'

'Yeah, but what happens if you lose your dongle? Or, in my case, accidentally go surfing with it and drown it in seawater?'

'That's OK. Your wallet generates a thing called a seed phrase. This is another crazy long code, and that's the one thing you do need to write down and store somewhere safe, like under a tennis trophy back at your mum's house. People tend to go the extra mile with hiding their seed phrase. Just in case you were wondering, mine isn't stored there anymore, as Mum has been threatening to give my trophies away if I don't come and collect them. *Dust collectors* is the term she uses.'

'OK. I think I understand how this works. So, the most viable option for us to gain access to Ted Kramer's wallet is to find his dongle and his password,' summarised Ange.

'Or his seed phrase, but he'd be more likely to keep his dongle nearby and handy for quick and easy access to his crypto. Let me go through the evidence logs and see if any dongle was recovered when we raided his room in Mullumbimby.'

'What's a RedBrd dongle look like?' asked Ange.

'There are loads of different dongles which can hold multiple different coin wallets. You can get them from lots of places. Most people buy them online. Some are USB dongles and others use Bluetooth.'

Billy clicked away and pulled up a series of images showing cold wallets from a series of vendors. None seemed particularly impressive or noteworthy, which Ange supposed made sense for something that was the secure key to a small fortune. She wouldn't have wanted to wear a Rolex, had she ever owned one, walking around Blacktown during her time as a Western Sydney constable.

'Finding his dongle is our best way in. Going by what I know of Ted Kramer, I reckon I could work out his password. Most people choose pretty inane passwords based on combinations of their pet's name, car brand, superheroes, sports, that sort of stuff, usually with some numbers or special characters embedded. The inane passwords some people use would amaze you. *Password* and *Qwerty* are my two favourites. However, for cryptocurrency, people up the ante and chose a more complicated password than their usual garden-variety password used for online shopping. Luckily, I have some pretty cool software tools that can help me with that, the same ones that hackers use.'

Ange again shifted with discomfort. She knew her own favourite was quite lame and made a mental note that she needed to review her passwords at some stage. 'OK. Thanks, Billy. Let's pursue that angle first. Let me know how you go.'

'Will do. It shouldn't take long for me to review those evidence logs. If we strike out there, I guess we'll need to search his house again?'

'That won't be easy without a warrant. I can't imagine Joe Kramer readily allowing us access. I'll bet Ted's mate Tyler Ball was searching for the dongle when he tried to break in. Lucky Ted's dog bit him before he got anywhere. Fingers crossed that it turns up in the evidence room. If it's not there, then I guess we'll need to work out a way to convince Joe Kramer to let us search Ted's house again—which is not my preferred option. I'll pop back tomorrow morning and see how you went.'

'OK. I'll do what I can. I need to jump to it and finish my angry mistress report. I reckon the papers will have a field day when all that gets leaked,' replied Billy with the boyish smile of someone who was having fun—certainly more fun than the corrupt politician was about to have.

Billy's smile was infectious. Ange caught the lift upstairs and walked back to her own desk, feeling uplifted from their discussion. She saw her mobile showed a missed call from Brett. Her heart rate quickened and her face contracted. Perhaps she at least might make some progress with her personal life today. She punched on the missed call icon and rang his number.

'Hi, Ange. How are things?' came Brett's reply.

'One step forward and one step back. I'm getting nowhere fast.'

'Aren't you working on another embezzlement case?'

'Oh yeah, that. I've got that under control. The woman involved in the embezzlement was hooked on the pokies. She confessed once we fronted her with the evidence. She seemed relieved in a roundabout manner. I'm slowly preparing all the reports now. I was referring to my lack of progress with the syndicate,' replied Ange.

'Actually, that's what I'm ringing you about. My curiosity got the better of me, so I pulled rank on the eZee Bet administrator and asked him about the artwork that Falconi has sequestered away in his Freeport in Singapore. He sent me the list of paintings Falconi owned, complete with valuations from Christies.'

'So, what are we talking about here?' enquired Ange.

'I'll send it over, but the valuations total over fifty million US dollars. Apparently, if you know what to buy, fine art has had a strong run in the past few years.'

'Holy moly. There must be some expensive pieces in all of that.'

'Falconi sure must have been raking in the cash. I can't believe that he could risk that amount of cash being siphoned off through BeaBet, but there you go. The administrator sounded a lot more chipper when I spoke to him this time. I think he now feels his bill might get paid after all. Now that he's seen those valuations, he'll probably add an extra zero to the end.'

'Who says crime doesn't pay? Thanks for this. How are things going with you, Brett?'

'I'm stuck in the middle of a bureaucratic pile-on. This money laundering case will be high profile and big news. All the wannabes are sticking their nose in. Reminds me of my personal life.'

'What do you mean?' answered Ange, trying her best to keep any testiness from showing in her voice.

'Well, I'm spending as much time as I can with the kids, but Chrissy is similarly sticking her nose in everywhere.'

Ange took that piece of news on alert. She hadn't really considered the ins and outs of a split marriage amidst Brett's return to Sydney. 'Perhaps we can catch up sometime when you get your head above water?' asked Ange, her pangs of uncertainty finally getting the better of her.

'That would be great. I'll organise something when I finally get my shit together. Catch you later.'

Ange was all too aware that guidance on a likely date had not been forthcoming.

## Chapter 17

# Light and Light Bulbs

With both her love life and hacking Kramer's crypto wallet on hold, Ange had left work early to take a long walk and was wandering somewhat aimlessly, a perfect allegory for her current state. Happenstance and a lack of attentiveness to where she was going delivered her an inspiring change of scenery. There, in a quiet park perched on the Elizabeth Bay hillside, she encountered a discreet series of ponds filled with large and colourful koi carp. They seemed to be highly sociable fish and were obviously well fed. As she walked over to the water's edge, they came swarming towards her, eager to see what snacks she might be bearing.

Sydney was like that, surprises hidden everywhere, particularly where the harbour was involved. It was a remarkable landscape, and the CBD had made the most of the opportunities to keep the water in sight. Regrettably, newer and more modern skyscrapers had obscured any view of the water from Ange's office in Bathurst Street. The captivating seaway was a spectacle of which she never tired, so she sat down on a park bench to take in the sunset. Her vigilant fishy friends soon lost interest and swam away to look elsewhere for their sustenance. Typical, just like her other relationships. All fun and games until reality came knocking.

Above all else, Ange loved late afternoons, when the soft afternoon light revealed subtle troughs and ridges, creating a fleeting depth to the landscape. The rolls and folds of the harbourside cliffs created a remarkable canvas, a relief of sorts, the tendrils of the many gullies like arteries, draining the land and keeping the harbour fresh and alive. Popping lights were spreading across the thousands upon thousands of homes that clung to the hillsides, folded into the gullies and crevices, all straining for a glimpse of the iconic waterway, each no doubt jealous of the lucky ones perched waterside.

Activity was constantly transforming the harbourside scene below, a stupendous painting that never sat still, an evolution of light and colour that made Sydney one of the world's most beautiful cities. The daily exodus was well underway, a reverse osmosis to the morning's invasion. In the distance, she could see the Manly Ferry, filled with work-weary commuters on their way home from Circular Quay. That seemed like a nice way to travel to work, at least when the weather was good, leaving your peninsula suburb and being plonked right on the doorstep of the city's financial hub, never having left the water.

The contemplative scene below soon plunged her back into thoughts of the syndicate and the many characters that she was investigating, many of whom were now dead or missing. Covering tracks seemed an impressive skill of the hidden figure, or figures, who sat atop this heap of misery makers.

Brett had sent across the list of artworks that Eddie Falconi had sequestered away in Singapore, and Ange had searched the artists online before she'd left the office. One thing was for sure: Falconi had expensive tastes in art. The podcasts and online research that Ange had undertaken on art and money laundering showed that the world of fine art was a most opaque and secret world—your status in life and who you knew were as important as how much money you possessed. Some of the leading galleries were obsessed with ensuring their artwork found a suitable home. If you were an aspiring art collector, following in the footsteps of prominent galleries and collectors was every bit as important as the art itself.

The most impressive of the paintings that Falconi had possessed was a striking untitled piece by Joan Miró, the colourful subjects folded and twisted to portray Miró's unique perspective. With no sale history, the valuation posed a wide range. Six to ten million US dollars, the valuer had stated some two years prior. Ange had delved further into the works of the Spanish master, finding that prices had risen even further during the pandemic. The valuation of Falconi's painting was probably on the low side, and the valuer had stated that 'the painting would be keenly sought after'. This research caused Ange to become quite a fan of the artist, although she was never likely to own anything more than a cheap print.

She pondered how Falconi could have siphoned all those funds out of the country without raising the eyebrows of any authorities. If Falconi could do it, the financial border must be a sieve, allowing money to flow every which way, inevitably leading her train of thought back to the world of cryptocurrency and NFTs. This surely seemed a far easier way to shift money around the globe, seemingly undetected and out of reach of any one jurisdiction. Ange felt certain that this was where the action lay. She resolved to stay focussed on this direction.

A young woman being towed along by a boisterous border collie stumbled by to interrupt her train of thought. The dog strained against his lead, insistent that he needed to say hello to Ange. As she pandered to the young dog, Ange shared a brief conversation with his owner, learning that 'Shadow' was a Covid puppy. Ange figured that Shadow liked the spotlight and could do with some training, but that was not her problem. She had other more sinister shadows to spotlight.

The first thing she did upon arriving at her office building on Tuesday was to pay Billy a visit.

'Hi, Billy. Any luck with finding Ted Kramer's crypto dongle?'

'Nothing. Frankly, I think we need to search Kramer's house again. The wallet vendor is a major player, but they're based overseas and out of our jurisdiction. It's just not in their interests to assist investigators like us. Gaining a reputation as a turncoat to the authorities would likely be the ruin of them.'

'Seeing as we aren't supposed to be looking, I can't just waltz up and ask for another search warrant. However, I seem to have made some peace with Joe Kramer. I guess I could ask him, but I reckon his permission would come with a sting in the tail somehow. Let me think about that,' said Ange, the dejection of another blind alley obvious in her voice.

'You could also look for Kramer's seed phrase at the same time. That would work just as well.'

'Explain exactly how finding his seed phrase will help us, Billy?'

'Well, the other term for seed phrase is recovery phrase. It's like an emergency fail-safe should you lose your dongle or password, for example. Imagine you went surfing with your dongle and ruined it. Your secret recovery phrase would let you retrieve all of your crypto, even without the dongle.'

'I see. Recovery phrase seems like a better term, although I guess it's way too simplistic for tech-heads like you, Billy.'

'Very funny. OK. Let's stick with recovery phrase from here on, seeing how technically challenged you are. Anyhow, if we could find his *recovery* phrase, we could restore his wallet and then access what's in it,' summarised Billy.

'What are we looking for? Give me an example of a recovery phrase, Billy. I guess that's another unintelligible sequence of letters and numbers.'

'No, it's not, actually—well, not in its English format. A recovery phrase is a series of either twelve or twenty-four words. Like AGENT NUCLEAR CREEK and so on. The system uses cryptology to randomly generate the phrase for you when you first set up your wallet. If someone knows your phrase, they can access your digital wallet. The order of the words is important as well. You can generate your own seed phrase—sorry, *recovery phrase*—but that's a more advanced option, as the last word acts as a checksum that adds another level of validation,' explained Billy. He saw Ange look down at Kramer's laptop. 'Even Kramer wouldn't be stupid enough to record his recovery phrase in a document on his laptop. Anything connected to the internet is too easily hacked.'

A grenade suddenly exploded in Ange's head. She fiddled with her phone as Billy resumed whatever he'd been doing before she had interrupted. He saw an email arrive in his inbox. It was from his boss, the one who was standing right beside him. He turned around and gave her a questioning look.

'Could you open up the pictures that I've just sent you, Billy?' Ange asked as she leant over his shoulder.

Billy clicked on the first image, a silver tag of sorts. He could see some words and letters engraved on the tag, but they were hard to read. He clicked on the next image, one showing the same tag but from a different angle and exposing some more of the words.

'Could that be a recovery phrase?' she asked hopefully.

'Sure could. Where did you get these pictures, boss?'

'They're photos of Bluey's dog tag—I took them when I visited Joe Kramer in Mullumbimby. I would have brought it up earlier if I'd known what a recovery phrase looked like.' Ange paused and gave her colleague a taunting smile. 'See, Billy, I actually do listen to your info dumps.'

'Well, a dog tag seems like as good a place as any to store your recovery phrase. Hopefully, we can assemble the complete set of words from these pictures. Why did you take those pictures, boss?'

'It just seemed out of place. Why would Ted Kramer go to all the trouble of engraving a cryptic string of letters on his dog's tag like that? It made no sense.'

'That was quick thinking. It was also a good idea to take your pictures from different angles so that the light could expose the letters more clearly. He sure squeezed them in there.' Billy paused, mouthing each number as he counted up the words. '"There's twelve words engraved on that tag. I think we're on the money here, boss."

The pair spent the next half hour playing a word puzzle of sorts, eyes straining to piece together the twelve words etched into the metal tag. Finally, Billy had the following written on his notepad.

> *erosion slot sustain december apology home canyon crew royal dragon layer drive.*

They stood back to admire their work for a second. 'I could never trust myself to remember that. It's just a jumble of words with little or no pattern. No wonder you need to record it somewhere,' commented Ange. 'Will we give it a go?'

'Why not?' replied Billy as he fired up the laptop and clicked on the RedBrd icon in Kramer's web browser. 'Here goes.'

## Chapter 18

# Word Games

'I'm not familiar with RedBrd, but let me find the option that allows us to recover the wallet using a recovery phrase,' explained Billy as he explored the RedBrd app, eventually finding the Restore Wallet option in the Settings tab.

'What happens next, Billy?' asked Ange.

'The recovery phrase essentially allows us to restore Kramer's wallet onto his laptop. We could even change wallet vendors if we wished.'

'Should we do that for added security?' asked Ange.

'We could, but we'd need to sign up, pay the fee and all of that. Plus, I'm also not sure what the implications of changing wallets might be. I'd need to think that through. However, if we recover Kramer's wallet onto his laptop using this method, nothing really changes and we will simply gain access to his original wallet.' Billy paused for a moment as he weighed up the options. 'I think we should stick with his RedBrd wallet for the time being. We can always revisit this down the track if we need to.'

'OK. I agree with that logic. Let's push on.'

Billy refocused on the task at hand, typing the twelve seemingly random words into a series of numbered text boxes while Ange peered intently over his shoulder. She needed to correct his spelling several times and expressed amazement over how poor Billy's generation was with spelling, victim to an ever-present spell check, a tool not used in the RedBrd recovery phrase entry boxes.

Once Billy had all the words typed in, the pair paused and read the recovery phrase out loud, checking once more for any errors.

*erosion slot sustain december apology home canyon crew royal dragon layer drive*

'Are we good to go, boss?'

Ange paused, reading the phrase out loud until completely satisfied. 'Hit it, Billy.'

Billy's pressed Enter and his screen immediately showed an ominous skull and crossbones symbol, struck out with a thick red diagonal line. 'That's a big fail. I suppose we'd better check the words again.'

With that disappointment, the pair went back and double-checked their mini crossword puzzle. After a full ten minutes, Ange stood up and stretched stiff muscles. 'The words are all correct. It *must* be his recovery phrase. What else could it be?'

'I agree. Perhaps he mixed up the words somehow. That's certainly what I would do if I had my fortune engraved on a dog tag. Let's try them in reverse order.' He looked at the original phrase that they had written down and typed in their second attempt.

*drive layer dragon royal crew canyon home apology december sustain slot erosion*

Same result. Access denied.

'OK. That was probably too obvious, anyway. You'll need to leave this with me. Having a sense of Ted Kramer, the way that he mixed up the words will be fairly simplistic. I should be able to work it out by making sure the checksum is valid.'

'What's a checksum, Billy? You mentioned this before. Honestly, the jargon you IT geeks use is endless,' explained Ange, tiring of her own ignorance in this world of acronyms and loosely fitting words.

Billy's overtly exasperated manner suggested that Ange's jibe was to be ignored. 'The checksum is the twelfth word. It validates the previous eleven words and the order that they've been entered. It's very clever.' His face brightened with a look of admiration. 'I still can't believe that you took a picture of that dog tag. I should be able to work this out. I'll text you.'

With that, Billy turned his full attention toward his screens, leaving Ange feeling superfluous. It would be impossible to concentrate on finishing her report on the poker machine addict. Coffee was in order. Hopefully, Billy wouldn't take all day.

After trading a series of texts with her friend Kerrie, Ange was twiddling her thumbs and midway through her second cup of coffee when she received Billy's text.

*I think I have it. Will wait for you.*

Ange quickly downed the dregs of her coffee and rushed straight back to her office building and up to Billy's desk. 'That was quick, Billy.'

'I figured that he would go something basic. In the end, it was simple. First word swapped with the seventh, second with eight, and so on.'

'How sure are you about this? It wouldn't do to be locked out of the wallet forever.'

'Almost certain. The checksum word was *home.* Even though the words are taken from a list of over two thousand possible choices, to be valid, the twelfth word has to follow certain rules based on the other eleven words—in short, given any series of eleven words, the twelfth word has to be one out of one hundred and twenty-eight of the words on the list rather than the full two thousand and forty-eight. The chance of another viable checksum existing in those twelve words is almost zero.'

'You know that you are speaking in tongues, Billy. I didn't understand half of that, but I get the gist that you're feeing confident about your logic,' observed Ange.

Billy looked towards one of his screens, where the words had been reordered in the text boxes.

*canyon crew royal dragon layer drive erosion slot sustain december apology home*

Rolling his chair to one side, he motioned to Ange. 'Why don't you do the honours this time? Hopefully, you'll have the Midas touch.'

Ange moved in front of Billy's keyboard and took control of Billy's mouse. Moving the cursor to hover over the *Restore* button, she paused before clicking. Billy added some gravitas to the situation. 'Fingers crossed this works. I'm not sure how many attempts we will be allowed before they lock us out. At least if it fails, I can blame you, boss.'

Ange gave Billy a smouldering look that was tinged with irony. 'Hilarious, Billy.'

She clicked Restore, fearing another dreaded skull and crossbones failure. The spinning wheel of success was the cue for Billy to roll his chair back and shove Ange away from his keyboard. 'We're in. The first thing we need to do is to set up a new password.'

Billy clicked the Profile tab. 'There's his wallet address,' he said, pointing to the screen and the letters *5urfD0g5ex@RedBrd.com*. 'That's the address he would give to someone sending him money.'

'Cute,' said Ange. 'That's an amalgam of his photos that we looked at. Even I can remember that. He's just substituted zero for the letter O, and the number five for S.'

Billy then clicked on the option to setup a new password.

'Any preferences on a password, boss?'

'How about we use a password based on Ted's dog, Bluey? Something we could both remember relatively easily.'

Billy typed in 'B!ued0gAWBB'. He then looked at Ange. 'How about that?'

'That works for me.'

Once the password had been validated with a second entry, Billy navigated back to the main screen and a dashboard of sorts was displayed on Kramer's laptop. Ange had no clue what any of this meant. 'Run me through what we have here, Billy.'

'OK, it seems like he has a heap of Ethereum, some Bitcoin and some of the other minor currencies.'

'How much in normal dollars?' asked Ange, not knowing what value the series of numbers represented.

Billy did some quick maths in his head. 'If he cashed it in, I reckon that's worth well over a million dollars.'

'You're kidding me. How did he amass that sum?'

'It depends on how long he had been an investor. This stuff is highly volatile, but if you got in, say, five years ago with a modest investment, it would have grown significantly.'

Billy clicked on the transaction tab, which showed a long list of transfers in and out. 'OK, that's a lot of transactions. He was quite active. It'll take me a while to sift through all that, but I should be able to trace some of what he's been up to.'

'Hold up. You can trace what he's been up to through his crypto? I thought this stuff was completely anonymous.'

'No way. That's the crazy thing. There is nothing anonymous about crypto. Remember what I told you about the blockchain and how every transaction is recorded forever? If you know where to look and what to look for, you can trace transactions far more accurately than holding cash. People confuse anonymity and being outside of the traditional national and international banking systems. Personally, I can't see governments allowing crypto to take over the banking system, but crypto is still in a sweet spot where governments are two steps behind. It will be interesting to see what happens to the value of cryptocurrency when they catch up and increase regulation.'

'I recognise Bitcoin and Ethereum, but not the other currencies showing on the screen. How many different currencies are in circulation?'

'There's really no limit and new ones are being minted all the time. Most fail or become playthings for a select group. Some are out-and-out scams, and there have been some breathtaking pump-and-dump or rug-pull schemes. My favourite was a group that used the Netflix *Squid Game* series to create a squid cryptocurrency, unbeknown to Netflix themselves. Remember what I told you about how value is created by popularity? Those guys were especially clever in exploiting the sudden and immense popularity of *Squid Game*, a show pitched directly at their target demographic. Once the currency had garnered sufficient value and investment, they promptly pulled the rug and pocketed everyone's money.'

Ange knew that while technology changed rapidly, human nature basically stayed the same. 'Nothing surprises me when there's money involved. There's always a scammer ready to pounce on the unwary. Do you have time to start looking into this?'

'I have a window while everyone digests what to do with my report on those WhatsApp communications and the angry mistress. Leave it with me for a day or so.’

‘Oh, before I forget. Will anyone else be able to get into Kramer’s wallet as well—assuming they find his dongle and work out his password, that is?’ asked Ange.

‘I guess so. I’m not really sure. Maybe there’s a way to cancel your dongle if you lose it, sort of like when you lose your credit card and get your bank to cancel it. I’ll look into that.’

Ange stood up from her crouched position over Kramer’s laptop and stretched her arms above her head. ‘This is exciting, Billy. I feel like we’ve made a major breakthrough.

‘Don’t count your chickens before they hatch. I’ll focus on all this tomorrow. I need to tidy up a few loose ends and then head out to a function. I’ll text you.’

## Chapter 19

# Rogue's Gallery

Billy had only been at his desk for a few short hours on Wednesday when Ange turned up on her way to lunch. He had arrived later than usual with a fuzzy head, having drunk far too much the night before. His latest squeeze, Amber, and her friends sure knew how to party, and Billy had failed to resist getting swept up in the fun.

While Billy knew his way around a computer, he was relatively clueless about how to navigate the dating scene. Usually failing to pick up the signals, he was often completely oblivious to when the opposite sex was showing interest. Billy preferred older women, partly because he found them more interesting, but also because they were more direct and usually knew what they wanted.

Amber was a case in point. She had made a beeline for him one evening when he was at the pub with Nelson and his mates. 'The rumours about Sydney are true,' Billy had thought at the time. 'There really are more women than men.'

A handful of years older than Billy, Amber was hot, even when judged by his super-critical mates. Their relationship had leaped into the bedroom and Amber thrilled Billy with her adventurous sexuality, opening his eyes to what a woman really wanted in bed. While Amber wasn't the marrying type, or someone he planned to invite home for Christmas dinner, she was certainly skilled at holding Billy's attention once they were alone.

Amber worked in fashion retail, augmenting her salary with some part-time modelling through a talent agency. The talent in Amber's agency was a shallow invocation. Being attractive and vivacious was the main game, traits which Amber held in spades. She was often called to form part of a glamorous rent-a-crowd at parties and events. This suited Billy, as it would often tie her up on a Friday or Saturday night, leaving him to spend time with his mates. After work, late at night, she would always pay him a visit to 'wind down'.

Amber and her talent agency workmates had been employed to glam up the VIP-only opening of a groovy new rooftop bar in Sydney's North Shore. Even though it was a Tuesday night after such a busy day, Billy had been pleased to tag along. Amber's workmates were all gorgeous. He felt like a movie star amongst all that glamour.

Super fun, also no fool, Amber's equities investment theme was a case in point. Whenever she was working at a large corporate gig, she would quiz the field about their company, disarmingly gleaning insights from all angles. If she liked what she heard, Amber would invest. Not in the slightest bit interested in the headline numbers or financials, she focused instead on the mood and culture of those who worked in the company. This strategy was proving a boon for her portfolio, better in fact than the advice of most stock market 'experts'. Putting aside her total lack of formal qualifications, Billy figured that Amber's true calling was to become an early-stage venture capitalist.

He was happily tagging along with Amber's investment thesis, a nice and unexpected side benefit to the amazing sex he was having. Who knew what other surprises Amber held in that gorgeous head of hers?

'Any progress, Billy? What's happened to you? You look terrible,' Ange commented.

'I may have overdone it last night,' he replied, eyes slitted and showing the telltale signs of an early-morning headache. 'Anyway, I said that this would take a while. I've only just gotten a handle on the scope of stuff in Kramer's wallet. As well as a basket of cryptocurrencies, I did find his collection of NFTs. He's got some weird stuff in there.'

Billy navigated his way to Kramer's dashboard and pulled up his NFT collection. A series of images popped up on the screen, looking for all the world like children's cartoon characters. There was a concentration of bat cartoons, which seemed totally out of sync with Kramer's character.

'Now I am feeling old, Billy. How could those things be of any value whatsoever? Can you explain how NFTs work?' asked Ange. 'What does that stand for again—non-findable totems or something like that?'

Billy laughed. 'Non-fungible tokens. Essentially, NFTs are a blockchain tag that gets appended to an item. At present, that item is mostly digital art, but there's talk of using NFTs to authenticate traditional art, for example. The big advantage of NFTs is that a thing called a digital contract sits behind the NFT. It defines any entitlements and what the rules of engagement are. The reason artists are so interested is that the contract could include a requirement to pay a commission back to the originating artist on every resale, which would remain in perpetuity. Before long, I think that we'll see lots of things underpinned by NFT technology and digital contracts. Think of a title on a house, for example. The digital contract would set out the rights of the holder and any obligations for taxes and duties that need to be paid.'

This explained her conversation with Gus Bell and his plan for a JayTee surfboard NFT. 'OK, I can see how that might work. Things like music or books would seem sensible. Actually, I recently had a conversation with someone about attaching them to limited edition surfboards. So, tell me about the contract—that seems to add complexity.'

'No one really understands their digital contracts, just like those digital disclaimers that pop up every time you install a new app on your computer. Who reads those things? NFTs have attracted some nifty scammers. I forgot to say that most cryptocurrencies include a digital contract as well, in varying degrees of complexity and obligation. Remember the squid crypto I mentioned the other day? Well, the smart contract had laid out exactly what would happen, so the punter who invested in the currency really didn't have a leg to stand on, so to speak. A classic rug-pull. Hardly anyone knows how to read a digital contract properly. If I was a lawyer, that's what I would become an expert in.'

'So how are NFTs made and traded?' pressed Ange, suggesting that she may be enjoying her private lesson.

'NFTs as an investment are still in the too-weird basket for me, so I'm no expert on that front. However, I understand that anyone can mint an NFT, and that there are exchanges where you can buy or sell them. I know that the only currency accepted in the NFT world is Ethereum. Nelson reckons that the reason some NFTs get traded for such crazy prices is that there are so many crypto millionaires out there who don't know what to do with their stash. It's still seen as Monopoly money, as there are only limited legitimate places to spend your crypto. Sorry, but you need to speak to someone else about how the NFT marketplace works.' Billy pointed to the one image that resembled something from the real world. 'I recognise that one. It's one of a series of tokens released by the Indian Premier

League of their star cricket players. Nelson purchased one of those.'

Ange's face lit up. 'I know someone who might help us out. Remember when I mentioned your replacement at the Byron Bay station was into NFTs? Breanna White, but she goes by Bree. Can you screenshot each of the images and email them to me? I'll send them to Bree, and I'm sure she'll be happy to do some research for us.'

Billy went through the process of progressively running through Kramer's NFT collection and taking a series of screenshots, adding each to an email he had composed to Ange. As he stepped through each image, Ange felt increasingly confused about how these images could hold any value whatsoever. Once Billy had finished emailing the screenshots, he opened another browser window and entered a site called OpenSea. He typed in the search term 'IPL', the abbreviation for the Indian Premier League, and looked up some similar images to Kramer's own cricket star. 'Actually, these haven't gone that well. They came on at twenty-five US dollars each, and they really haven't moved at all. The IPL dumped fifty-five thousand of those NFTs onto the market and they sold out in nine minutes. That was far too many to create any scarcity. Nelson probably won't lose any money, but he won't get rich.'

Billy pulled up the statistics page showing the current top-ranking NFTs. They were all cartoon-style images. He could see by the look on his boss's face that she still wasn't getting it.

'Sorry, boss, you'll have to leave me with this. You should have the email. I'll start looking into Kramer's crypto transactions this afternoon. I'll text you when I have anything worthwhile.'

'Thanks, Billy. I just don't get how those cartoons could be worth anything more than a few cents.'

'Get with it, boss. Crypto and blockchain, in one form or another, are going to be big time.'

'Thanks for making me feel old, Billy,' Ange replied with a wry smile, laughing at her misfortune of being old. Her smile soon disappeared under the shadow of a serious thought. 'Before I go, you said that Kramer had over a million dollars in cryptocurrency. How much did he have in Ethereum, then?'

Billy went back to Kramer's dashboard, pausing briefly to do some mental arithmetic. 'A touch over half of that.'

'So, if he had over five hundred thousand dollars in Ethereum, and that's the currency that gets used to trade NFTs, then I reckon we need to get a handle on his NFT collection. Leave that with me. I'll get Bree onto it. You focus on the cryptocurrency transactions,' said Ange. 'And don't worry, I won't bother you until you text me. I hope your hangover improves, Billy.'

With Billy's last jibe, Ange caught the lift to her floor and sat down in front of her computer. She opened up Billy's email, marvelling once more at this craziness. Unlocking her phone, she pulled up the number that she had stored for Bree. It rang three times before being answered.

'Hello, Detective. How are you settling into Sydney life?' came the cheery voice.

'It's Ange to you, Bree. Sydney is great, but I'm not really in the sweet spot just yet. I'm still finding my way around a new office environment. I love living here, except for the surfing. It's way too crowded and aggressive after what I enjoyed in Byron. How's the training going?'

'Quite well. I spoke to the sarge as you suggested and he was most understanding, particularly when I mentioned my Olympic goals. He went in to bat for me and secured some special leave. What a great guy. I can see why you like him so much.'

'Yes, you totally lucked out getting placed in his station.'

'I'm coming to Sydney in a few weeks for the national titles. Despite my poor training regime these past couple of months, I made the state team. I think my past performances got me through. Perhaps we can catch up?'

'Fantastic, and well done. We will definitely catch up. If you get stuck for somewhere to stay, I have a foldout couch you can use.'

'I should be fine. I normally get billeted out with another hockey family, but thanks for the offer. Being billeted out can be hit-and-miss, so let's see how that all pans out.'

'Sure. It's there if your need it. Anyway, the reason for my call is to ask a favour.'

Bree's reply came immediately and unfiltered. 'Anything. Tell me.'

'I wondered if you could look into a series of NFTs that I have come across? Perhaps see if you can make any sense of them for me.'

'Sounds like fun. Where did you find them?'

'It's probably best that I don't tell you at this point. I would prefer you to keep an open mind. You also don't need to get involved in my messy problems. What's your email address?'

'Now you have me totally intrigued,' said Bree. She read out her lengthy email address. 'One word, all in lowercase.'

'Great, I'll send you the email now. Let me know if you find anything interesting.'

'No problems. Catch you later, Detective.'

The habits of her training, where rank and seniority counted heavily, were proving hard to crack for the young constable. 'Remember, my name is Ange. Thanks, Bree. Speak soon.'

She hung up and imagined Bree sitting in the Byron Bay station. Ange could easily conjure up the incessant noise and chatter that came with a busy police station. Her new office at Major Crimes, where her colleagues worked on big and long-term cases, was all quiet and serious. Ange felt some small pangs of regret for what she had left behind. After teetering on the edge for a moment, she pulled herself away from that precipice. She had made her bed, and it was up to her to make the best of it.

Before she got back to her more mundane tasks, Ange updated and reviewed the notes that she had assembled during her crypto journey.

Crypto & NFTs

- *Crypto based on blockchain technology*
- *Blockchain is a giant public digital ledger—kept by everyone*
- *Lots of currencies—Bitcoin and Ethereum most popular*
- *Crypto exchanges flip hard currency and crypto*
- *Crypto uses public and private keys to identify and access. Think of home address as public key and actual mailbox key as private key*
- *Crypto keys stored in a digital wallet. Used to make transactions—almost like online banking*

- *Wallets are hot (web/online), cold (dongle), or paper*
- *Cold wallets use dongle plus password to access. Kramer used a RedBrd cold wallet. Dongle missing.*
- *Wallet can be restored using recovery phrase—comprised of 12 seemingly random words*
- *12th word is a checksum and key to unlocking recovery phrase.*
- *Kramer's wallet holds over $1M in crypto, plus NFTs*
- *NFT stands for Non-Fungible Tokens. Mostly digital art but can be anything. Also, can be 'minted' by anyone. NFTs based on blockchain technology*
- *Bree looking into NFTs. Need to speak to Anders about what to do with cryptocurrency*
- *Crypto transactions are public and traceable, but no international boundaries and little or no regulation*
- *Crypto and NFTs underpinned by digital contract that nobody understands*
- *Scams, steals, rug-pulls, criminals.*

Ange was not planning to invest any of her own hard-earned cash at this point.

# Chapter 20

# Slow Progress

Bored was a state of mind that Ange rarely entertained, but the rest of the week dragged on interminably. Her embezzlement case had fizzled out completely. It was a simple case of a woman addicted to gambling and finding solace in poker machines. There was no master criminal syndicate behind this tragedy. It was more a case of government-sponsored pain and heartache. It had shocked Ange to discover that, across the nation, governments reaped a breath-taking five-plus billion dollars annually from the industry. However, an even more tragic discovery was that the woman had subsequently been diagnosed with early-onset Parkinson's disease. During her investigation, Ange learned that some people undergoing treatment for Parkinson's were prone to gamble irresponsibly. Without someone looking out for them, this risky tendency could easily spiral out of control.

Billy was conspicuously absent in reporting back on the trading activity of Ted Kramer. She was mindful that the continued pursuit of the syndicate was off the books as far as Major Crimes was concerned, so she didn't want to push the envelope and pressure Billy any further. Despite listening to a couple of podcasts on NFTs during her daily walks, she remained perplexed about how these things could ever be considered an investment. How anyone could value a Bored Ape Yacht Club image at over a million dollars escaped her. Perhaps that might be a business venture she could explore. A Bored Detective Surf Club series of NFTs had a nice ring to it. An inveterate doodler, she soon caught herself sketching bored detective stick figures in her notebook.

She filled her boss in on progress over Friday evening drinks.

'Boss, I'm beginning to appreciate the new type of wealth proposed by cryptocurrency. With authorities wanting to tax cryptocurrency profits at the point of exchange for another currency, the concept of paying tax is simply a bridge too far for many crypto investors, especially those whose wealth has been earned illegitimately. As a result, investors hold vast sums of crypto wealth with limited opportunities to spend it. In part, this is driving these seemingly crazy prices for cryptocurrency and stuff like NFTs.'

'Yes, I see how this could create quite a bubble,' observed Sally Anders. 'Have you discovered anything specific that might help us?'

'Well, two things seem obscure. The first is the fact that Ted Kramer had over a million dollars in cryptocurrency. We know he wasn't exactly the most industrious of individuals, so this wealth seems highly suspicious.'

'Wow, that is quite a sum for someone who is essentially a drifter. What's the second?' asked Anders.

'That would be the matter of Eddie Falconi's fine art collection, covertly stored in a Freeport based in Singapore and essentially out of reach. I don't know about you, but a secret art collection worth over fifty million US dollars is extraordinary and also suspicious. Particularly given what he was up to with eZee Bet and GlitterStrip.'

Sally Anders took a sip of her gin and tonic. 'I agree. That all seems questionable. However, neither of those discoveries provides us with any new or concrete links to the upper echelons of the syndicate.'

Ange's expression was consistent with this conclusion. 'Point taken. It's hard to make any steady progress when we're doing all of this off-grid. Billy is my main man, and he seems to get busier and busier.'

'I know. Cybercrime and all its permutations are certainly where crime is going, particularly at our level within Major Crimes. Billy's skills are hot property right now and we need more of him. Unfortunately, my bosses are old-school and very much behind the times. They just don't see it that way.'

'Given how adaptable and agile the syndicate has proven to be, I fear we'll lose the scent completely if we don't run this to the ground soon,' commented Ange in a dejected voice.

'Let me speak to Peter Fredericks and see if he can take some load off Billy for the next month. I'm afraid that if we can't get this sorted by then, then we really must drop this case for good.'

'What should I do about Kramer's crypto fortune? Do I need to report it as proceeds of crime?'

Anders paused for a moment as she thought through the implications of Ange's loaded question. 'Well, we don't really know for sure that his fortune was amassed through criminal activity. We're still considering that point, aren't we?' she postulated, a sly grin creeping across her face. 'Let's keep it to ourselves for a month until we know more.'

This was just the stimulus Ange needed. Whilst she had never exactly been a crammer, a deadline had always provided a powerful incentive. Whether this was rooted in her need to complete her task or perhaps something as pathetic as a basic need to please, she became suddenly re-energised.

That weekend, she took Franky over to the coast for a surf at Bronte Beach. The waves looked like rubbish from the sand, but Ange suited up and paddled out anyway, needing an outlet for her renewed vitality. In her experience, when the surf looked poorly, getting the wetsuit on was the hardest step to take. Once she had braved the initial shock of the cool water and paddled out the back, beyond the break, gently bobbing around on Franky in the clean, clear water, her outlook on life always brightened. She loved looking back toward the coastline that she had just departed, taking in the panoramic view of the craggy headlands and yellow sandy beaches, a special perspective that only a surfer could fully appreciate. Despite the small conditions, Ange surprised herself with a couple of passable rides, certainly enough to make the trip worthwhile. Franky had desperately needed some exercise.

She was hovering over Billy's shoulder first thing Monday morning.

'Billy,' Ange stated in her most businesslike voice, 'Sally is going to ask Peter Fredericks to take on some of your workload so you can focus on tracing Ted Kramer's crypto trades. We only have a month to make some genuine progress—otherwise, we might have to drop the case altogether for good.'

'Peter has beaten you to it. He rang me over the weekend and asked me to send him anything that he could take over. He seemed a bit disappointed with the stuff

I offloaded. I suppose that I did give him a collection of rats and mice, which may have been a bit mean in hindsight.'

'Billy, the boss is really concerned about keeping it low-key. Don't speak to anyone about exactly what you are up to, not even Peter,' replied Ange. 'Now, where are we headed with Ted Kramer's crypto trades?'

'OK. I wasn't completely running dead on the issue. On the weekend, I spent some time with my mate Nelson. The tax office is quite a way ahead of us. It makes sense, I suppose, as they can look at this on a cost and return basis. They realise that lots of profits are being hidden and not crystallising into tax revenue. Given the growth in the sector, Nelson and his team had no trouble securing the right resourcing levels—unlike us.'

Ange knew that resourcing of policing activities was a perennial problem. Building a business case that linked funding and outcomes was difficult, particularly when not all investigations came with a financial payback. 'What did Nelson have to say?'

'Now that crypto has the attention of governments and agencies like the tax office, software tools are popping up. You can imagine that a market created and fuelled by secrecy wasn't initially interested in creating software tools to help with tracing. Nelson put me onto a new app that can link the daisy chains recorded on the blockchains and build a complete picture of a series of transactions. There are also registers of crypto accounts that are now available, which are cross-referenced through the likes of social media and its linkages. These can help identify some actual names of those involved.'

'I'm confused, Billy. How does it achieve that?'

'Sites like Facebook and LinkedIn employ the science of social networking. I'm connected to you and you're connected to Sally, therefore perhaps I might like to connect with Sally. Once I connect with Sally, I get access to all her connections. You can see how quickly this might grow. Well, the blockchain has similar characteristics in some ways. By unpacking a blockchain, then the links to each entry in the blockchain, and so on, we can build a profile of all the connections.'

'Sounds complicated, Billy. How long does all this take?'

'It depends on how deeply you want to go and how widely traded the pool of users might be.'

The continued confusion still showed on Ange's expression. 'Explain, Billy.'

'OK, imagine you wanted to trace a series of transactions from, say, a ring of drug dealers. Once we got our hands on the blockchain of one of those transactions, by tracing the series of blockchains connected to that, and then the blockchains connected to those, then we should be able to identify the common users and any ringleaders.'

'OK. I sort of get it. Surely it can't be that easy—otherwise, we could track anything and anyone.'

'One trick is getting access to the blockchain of a suspicious transaction in the first place. However, it might turn out that the linkages are essentially random when evaluated statistically. Think of the concept of six degrees of separation. Everyone is connected at some level, so there's a point at which the connections are of no value to people like us. Also, if someone was using their crypto to just, say, buy their groceries, then their connections would probably be random and essentially meaningless.'

'I get it. Seeing that we now have access to some suspicious transactions, how long will all this take, Billy?'

'I've downloaded the software, but now I need to work out how to use it. Come back at the end of today and I'll fill you in on where I'm up to. Nelson offered to act as my help desk. I reckon he'll be sick of me by then.'

'Thanks, Billy. Human ingenuity never ceases to amaze me. It certainly seems easier than needing to secure warrants for every customer of every bank involved. I still can't get my head around the paradox of an unregulated currency being so open book.'

After Ange left Billy, she paid a visit to her boss's office on the way to her own.

'Hi, Ange,' said Sally Anders as soon as Ange appeared at her door. 'Peter Fredericks came to see me. I think he suspects that we're up to something and he wants in. I can't have everyone getting involved. There's still our other work to do. We need to keep this tight from now on. I told Peter that you and Billy were helping Brett exit our position in BeaBet.'

'Got it. Hopefully, we'll have made some progress by the end of the week and I'll get back to you.'

Ange contemplated calling Billy to fill him in but opted to brave the lift again and visit him in person. While she was waiting for the lift, she reflected on her boss's excuse. The fact was that she knew very little about what Brett was up to. It stung, being kept at arm's length like that. She arrived at Billy's desk.

'Billy, the boss told Peter that we're helping Brett to wrap up BeaBet. Can you stick to that story? She seems to be worried about being pinged from above on this case and wants to keep it tight between us.'

Billy looked up from whatever trickery he was involved with. 'Will do,' he said, immediately turning his attention back to his sorcery and leaving Ange bemused by the way his focus could shift so instantly and completely. Whereas she would daydream her way to oblivion, Billy's mind leaped from topic to topic, each getting his full attention until he switched to the next. Despite knowing how Billy's mind worked, Ange felt disappointed by this lack of engagement. She had been secretly hoping that he would already have the blockchain nut cracked open.

As Ange made her way back to her floor, she could feel a sense of impatience building. It promised to be a long day ahead.

## Chapter 21

# The Bored Detective Surfing Club

Ange spent the morning shuffling papers on her desk. Even though Mondays were Ange's moving day, she was getting nowhere fast on this particular Monday. She didn't even make it to midday before deciding it was time for lunch, heading downstairs to find something nice to eat before the lunchtime throngs descended like locusts. She was about to exit the building when her phone rang. It was Bree, a bright spot to lighten an otherwise dull morning.

'Hi, Bree. How are beautiful people in Byron Bay travelling?'

'Well, thanks, Detective—I mean Ange. I'll get used to calling you that, eventually. Anyway, I have a bone to pick with you.'

Ange could sense the good nature of this jibe and respond accordingly. 'What have I done now?'

'Ever since you put me on the case of these NFTs, all my other work seems incredibly boring. It's made me realise I want to be an investigator like you.'

Ange was alert to the power of strong role models in forging a career. Jim Grady and Sally Anders were cases in point. 'Well, detectives also often suffer from boredom, but I can help you with your career, Bree. We should talk about this when you come to Sydney. Perhaps I should introduce you to some colleagues and you can get a broader perspective on becoming a detective and what steps you need to take.'

'That would be awesome! That's one thing I wanted to speak with you about. Can I cash in your offer of a couch for this weekend? I know that it's short notice, and no hassles if it doesn't work, but the place where they offered to billet me is way out in the Western Suburbs. If I'm coming to Sydney, I really wanted to be near the harbour and the centre of the action.'

'Sure, that's no problem. When will you be coming down?'

'I need to be in Sydney on Friday, so I'm taking the day off. My flight arrives late-morning. I can catch the train into the office and meet you there, probably around midday.'

'Done. I've already put this in my diary. Any luck with the images that I sent you?'

'That's the main reason I rang you. It's been super interesting but also super difficult. I tracked down a few of the images you sent me. I'd say that the collector of those NFTs is a novice investor.'

Ange walked back into the foyer with the phone glued to her ear. She found a place to sit, one that was out of earshot. 'Why do you say that?'

'They made a couple of rookie errors, like buying fake copies of popular NFTs. It's a trap for young players. I fell for it myself early on.'

'That there can even be such a thing as a fake copy of a digital cartoon image, one that never physically exists, makes my head spin.'

'People just jump in without doing their research. The world of cryptocurrency and NFTs is overweight with scammers and con artists. Anyhow, the six NFTs based on bats were a challenge. I couldn't find them anywhere. They aren't for sale on OpenSea, and Google Lens didn't show any clues, so I wondered if they were real NFTs at all. I guess the concept of a real NFT is also challenging for your mature mindset,' commented Bree, a playful tone creeping into her voice at the last sentence.

Ange loved that the young constable was feeling comfortable enough to throw off at her own mid-thirties view of the world. 'Well, at least I haven't fallen victim to an NFT scammer. Not yet, at least.'

Bree laughed, naturally and without guile. 'Point taken. Anyhow, I eventually found a trace of them in a chat room on the Dark Web.'

'You definitely need to meet my colleague, Billy, the fellow you replaced at the Byron Bay station. You two will get on like a house on fire. I don't even know how to find a chat room on the Dark Web, let alone find any useful information. What did you learn?'

'The NFTs come from a collection called BuzzyBats, and they're super weird. According to the chatter, they're very tightly traded and come in different denominations according to the number of copies released. The top price that I could find was the Ethereum equivalent of around twenty-five thousand dollars, which is also weird. There is no secondary market, and I just can't see how that sort of value can be justified.'

'Can you explain that to me? How is any value determined in the world of NFTs?' asked Ange.

'Well, it's no different from art or other collectibles. First, there's the artistic value, then scarcity, and then desirability. Things like who else is collecting the same range of NFTs—celebrities or well-known collectors, for example. This faddish trait also facilitates some classic rorts. Imagine you're a celebrity influencer, and you let drop that you just purchased an NFT from a certain collection. If you're truly influential, the prices will immediately skyrocket. Meanwhile, you could also have purchased another bunch of the same collection under a crypto alias. As the prices rise, you can progressively sell out the collection owned by your alias, all the while extolling the virtues of the one held by your public persona. It's just another version of the classic pump-and-dump scheme that the stock market has used forever.'

'You know you aren't exactly proving to be a great ambassador for this class of investments, Bree? I'm even less likely to invest now than before—if that were possible. So, tell me more about bats.'

'As I mentioned, they weren't available for purchase through normal channels. However, I kept digging and found a reference to a digital studio by the name of StudioBuzz, which was curious given the use of the word "buzz" in both names. I had a look on the website for StudioBuzz and they're a serious outfit, doing lots of stuff in the digital imagery space.'

'What sort of things?'

'Digital advertising, animations, infomercials, training videos. I really couldn't explore all the things that they do or verify that they had in fact minted those NFTs,' replied Bree.

'I think I understand. My colleague Billy used the term minting to describe the process of producing a new cryptocurrency coin,' commented Ange.

'It's sort of the same. Minting an NFT converts your digital image into an NFT with its embedded blockchain. It can then be traded or sold. I'm pretty sure that StudioBuzz minted these BuzzyBat NFTs, but some parts of their website were password-protected and I couldn't access those pages. That's as far as I got.'

'Thanks, Bree. I'm impressed. We'll use the resources of Major Crimes to track down StudioBuzz. By the way, can you trace the trading history of an NFT in the same way that you can trace cryptocurrency transactions using the blockchain?'

'Absolutely. It's the same technology. In fact, once I have a lead, I can see what other people have in their NFT collections. It's all part of the marketing engine. Sort of like LinkedIn, when you get those notifications to connect with someone and it tells you all the connections that you have in common.'

'OK. Thanks, Bree. I'll get Billy to show you his latest software trickery. I'm hoping that it will allow us to trace connections easily. Let's touch base next week and confirm the arrangements for your trip.'

Ange had completely forgotten about lunch. Her rumbling stomach rudely reminded her it was already on alert that food would be forthcoming. She wandered through the streets in a daze, autopilot taking her to a favourite Korean hole-in-the-wall lunch spot. She ordered kimchi rice to satisfy her belly and sat down. The smells wafting from the kitchen were doing nothing to quell the rumbling. She scratched off a quick email to Billy using her phone.

> *Billy, can you ask Nelson what he can find out about a company called StudioBuzz? I'll fill you in when we speak this afternoon. I think it's important.*

Her phone pinged with Billy's instantaneous reply. She marvelled at the ability of twenty-something people like Billy to deal with emails on the fly, no apparent interruption to whatever else they were doing. Between shovelling forkfuls of rice into her mouth she and Billy traded texts.

> **Billy:** *What does StudioBuzz do?*
> **Ange:** *They're a digital studio that produces, amongst other things, a range of NFTs.*
> **Billy:** *Cool. Making good progress. Pop around after 4 p.m.*

Ange, if nothing else, was no longer bored, and her stomach was no longer grumbling.

## Chapter 22

# Chain Gangs

After her call with Bree, and with the prospect of circling back to Billy later that afternoon, there was absolutely no chance that Ange could concentrate on administrative work. None of it seemed remotely interesting. She whittled away the rest of the afternoon on the internet.

StudioBuzz seemed totally legitimate. Their website even had testimonials from happy clients. She didn't recognise any of their clients, but they seemed like online businesses, vendors, educators, or the like. She was reminded of GlitterStrip, which had seemed like a genuine online cosmetics store until one looked under the hood. GlitterStrip, the mail-order supplier of sunscreen and lip balm, was a cover for a darker side, the mail-order supplier of narcotics, so she knew not to be duped by any facade of legitimacy. Nothing seemed out of place and there was little that she could discern from the public online front door for StudioBuzz. There was no reference anywhere to an actual front door, one with a buzzer or a door handle.

She then spent some time watching instructional videos on how to trace cryptocurrency transactions, of which there were several on YouTube. The jargon and lingo still presented a barrier, but she could form a view of how it might be possible. She reflected on her previous investigations involving bank accounts. Government regulation was making it increasingly difficult to operate a traditional bank account without suitable identification. Crypto had no such regulations, a powerful incentive for anyone wishing to stay incognito.

By the time 4 p.m. came around, Ange was a dangerous and volatile cocktail of ignorance, understanding, and toxic confusion—in the world of crypto, at least. Fortunately, she had Billy on her side. He was so deeply engrossed in his screens that he didn't notice her standing behind him. She watched for a moment as he flicked from screen to screen, each a small window into his thought processes.

Anticipation of what he might have discovered finally got the better of her. 'Hi, Billy. What have you got for me?'

Billy reluctantly pulled himself from this trancelike state to glance back over his shoulder at his boss. 'This is amazing stuff, boss. I knew the basics, but I didn't appreciate the power of these tools to trace movements of crypto.'

'Show me,' said Ange, pulling up a chair from an adjoining desk and sitting down beside her colleague.

'Nelson put me onto several software tools that they use to trace this stuff. Some are in the public domain and surprisingly good for a free service. He recommended a product called BCExplore. It's a paid subscription platform, so I used some of the budget left over from my new computer setup. I could only spring for the entry-level subscription, but it's still very impressive.'

Ange pointed to one of his screens, which showed a series of colour-coded bubbles of varying sizes connected by a spider's web of lines. 'What's this screen showing us?'

'OK. How this works is that the software traces the source and destination of transactions on the blockchain, and then the source and destination of those transactions, and so on. I can go forward and back as far as I want. Each bubble represents a wallet, or user, and the size of the bubbles can depict either the number of transactions passing through that user or the aggregate value of the transactions. I can toggle the system to display either.' Billy clicked repeatedly on a tab, each click changing the image slightly. He pointed to one specific bubble as he did this. 'You can see that some bubbles have high value and low numbers of transactions, and others show the reverse.' He looked towards his boss to check that she was following his demonstration. 'Understand?'

'Yes, Billy. I get it.'

'Right. So, we can also filter out how far we want to go with this, either by numbers of steps from the original blockchain address, or by date range, or by consequence of value, or transaction volume.' He clicked on a tab in BCExplore, which resulted in the bewildering chart of bubbles and lines being displayed. 'This is what I started with,' he explained. Billy then clicked sequentially through a series of screen images, each time rendering a clearer and more concentrated chart. 'And this is where I've gotten to. You really don't need to know the ins and outs of it.'

'OK, I can see that this is a simpler chart, but tell me what I'm looking at,' asked Ange.

'I figured that we're focussed on the big fish in this pond, so I filtered out all the noise. I might have missed a few things, but I'm confident they aren't significant. That being said, I've only been playing with the data for a few hours, so don't hold me to any conclusions.'

'That's good thinking, Billy. We don't have time to waste on smaller players. They can wait for another day.'

'So, I believe this chart depicts the main protagonists in this series of transactions.' He pointed to one bubble in the lower right of the chart. 'This is Ted Kramer.' He then pointed to another larger bubble. 'And I reckon that this is the other guy, the one that's gone missing. What's his name again?'

'Tyler Ball. He's the one Ted Kramer fatefully called from his new burner phone. The call that got Ted killed.'

With this established, Billy moved on. 'This bubble here is Swyftx, a site that exchanges crypto for hard currency. You can see that both Kramer and Ball use the same exchange.' He pointed to another bubble, which also had some common lineages. 'This is OpenSea, the NFT platform. There's not as many transactions as I would have expected for guys with an NFT collection. The software is clever enough to identify major crypto identities like Swyftx or OpenSea.'

Ange pointed to the largest and most significant bubble in the top left of the screen. 'And who's this?'

'That I cannot tell you. Based on the number of transactions and value, it looks like a vendor or trader, or some other type of business. Whoever or whatever this is, they're clever and have gone to some trouble to mask their identity. I can't find anything about them. The more expensive version of the software, the one with an AI engine that sweeps social media to piece together information, does a better job at identifying players. I probably need to upgrade if I can find the budget.'

Ange sat back and thought about what Billy had just described. 'So, we know that Kramer and Ball did business together. I guess that the two-way arrows between them indicate that crypto was flowing in both directions?'

'Correct. Similarly, there are two-way transaction flows between the mystery bubble and Ball, but no transactions between them and Kramer. It's my conclusion that Ball was one step up from Kramer and that Kramer really was a lower-order player in all of this. But anyway, that's not the interesting bit.'

Billy pulled up another window on a different screen. It was the same software but showed a different chart. 'This is the same analysis of Kramer's NFT collection. You can see that he bought NFTs from Ball and some from OpenSea. You can also see that Ball purchased the bulk of his NFTs from the mystery bubble to the left, as well as a few from OpenSea. He bought nothing from Kramer.'

This conversation had Ange's full attention, and her brain strained to take in the avalanche of information that Billy was throwing at her. The mystery bubble on the top left was like a Covid-19 virus, a ball showing lots of spikes, one of which was connected to Tyler Ball. Ange pointed to it. 'What's going on here, Billy?'

'You can see that these charts bear some similarities. The configuration of that mystery bubble you pointed to suggests a vendor of sorts. It turns out that this bubble is associated with StudioBuzz, the company you emailed me about. I had to ring Nelson to find that out. He has the full version of the software. The tax office has way more data and resources than us.'

Ange's mind was racing ahead. 'So, can we deduce that these trades between StudioBuzz, Ball and Kramer are the BuzzyBat NFTs that we found in Kramer's digital wallet?'

'Correct, but that's not the intriguing part.'

Ange waited patiently for Billy to continue. He stayed silent, as if building suspense. She eventually caved to this stalemate. 'Are you going to tell me or not?' she said, smiling at Billy's rare display of one-upmanship.

He pointed to the Covid-style bubble, the one with many spikes. 'Once the NFTs are purchased from StudioBuzz, they practically never get traded again. The only few that have been traded are between Ball and Kramer.'

'What does that mean, Billy?'

'I don't know, but it's super weird. Nelson reckons that NFTs are like baseball cards. They're traded like crazy. That these almost never get traded is bizarre. Some BuzzyBat NFTs should have shown up on OpenSea at some point. Nothing. Nada. Zip.'

'And Kramer has been murdered and Ball has gone missing,' surmised Ange. 'These BuzzyBats seem like dangerous pets to own.' She pointed to the mystery bubble on the original chart of crypto transactions. 'Can we determine if StudioBuzz is involved in this?'

'Probably. I'll need to compare the timing of the transactions and make some conclusions from that. I could ask Nelson, but I'm concerned about stretching the relationship. Hopefully, I can triangulate the value that those NFTs were being traded for. It'll be a lot of work, as I don't think the software is that powerful. Is it important?'

'I think so, but only dig until you're sure of your conclusions. No need to do a complete analysis of all the transactions. We just don't have time. The value of the NFTs will give us some idea about the sums of money involved, which will be interesting.'

Billy turned back to his computer. 'OK. I'll get onto it.'

Ange swivelled Billy's chair around to face her, pulling him away from his precious keyboard. 'Billy, that was fantastic work. I can't believe we've learned all this so quickly. Do you think the criminals know what you can do?'

'Not yet, but I'm sure they'll catch up,' said Billy with a satisfied smirk.

## Chapter 23

# Train Wrecks

Ange knew to leave Billy alone to do his stuff. She could tell how engaged he was in their covert investigation. He would also have other work to do. It wasn't until late Tuesday that Ange received a call from him.

'Nelson got back to me about StudioBuzz. He became more interested once he knew about their involvement in NFTs. This will blow you away. Guess who's behind StudioBuzz?' Billy said in an excited voice, as if he possessed the coordinates to the Holy Grail.

'I guess from your question that I should be able to make a decent guess or two. Unfortunately, I have no idea,' said Ange.

'Ethan Tedesco,' he explained, blurting out a name that he felt Ange would surely know.

Her silence told him otherwise. 'You know, Ethan Tedesco. ET. We spoke about him several weeks back. He runs the crypto fund which your brother has invested in. ET is everywhere and into everything. I reckon Nelson has a crush on him. We all do, actually. He burst onto the scene when I was at the academy and his overnight success almost caused me to quit and build a start-up of my own. He's constantly on the young rich lists and hailed as one of the bright lights of Australia's tech and innovation industry. Until he came along, everyone thought we had to move to Silicon Valley. ET proved that we could do it from here.'

'It's surprising that someone with his profile is connected to all of this.'

'I can't believe he would be involved. ET would have lots of staff and partners of companies that he's acquired over the years. It would be impossible for him to know everything that was going on.'

Billy was clearly an ardent believer, so Ange resolved to rely on her own research. 'That's interesting. Any other progress?'

Billy exaggerated his reply. 'I'll call you, not the other way around.'

In between the mundanities of work and life, Ange read all that she could about Ethan Tedesco. His nickname, ET, seemed a touch obvious and trite. Even though the classic movie by Steven Spielberg had been released back in 1982, before Ange and Tedesco were born, the nickname given to the main character had become the acronym for all extra-terrestrial beings.

As Billy had suggested, Tedesco was indeed everywhere. He seemed to have his hand in so many pies that Billy's hypothesis that he might not be aware of every detail within his conglomerate was reasonable. Tedesco's name was associated with several start-up technology businesses. Billy could probably explain what the companies did, but most of the names meant little to her. His reputed wealth had skyrocketed from ground level to stratospheric in just a few short years. This, it seemed, was not out of the ordinary for tech entrepreneurs.

He was also a regular A-lister in the Sydney social scene and a big supporter of charity events. Ange felt he was neither attractive nor unattractive; in fact, he seemed rather normal for such a superstar. She saw he enjoyed the company of beautiful women, but few faces were repeated. Billy and Nelson would have to wait their turn. Digging a touch deeper, Ange discovered he was the son and heir to the Tedesco fortune, one built on worldly and banal enterprises like waste management and infrastructure construction. Eric Tedesco, the patriarch, had endured his fair share of controversy. Claims of bribes being paid to secure contracts, intimidation, and links to shady characters abounded. A genuine old-school tough guy, it seemed, one who was also a favoured political donor when election funds were required. Ange guessed he had plenty of favours waiting to be called in, not to mention plenty of dirt, all carefully curated for another day and the right occasion.

No such dirt was stuck on Ethan Tedesco's image, and he was an all-around darling of the new world order, one where tech and innovation were the catchphrases on everyone's lips. ET also sat on the federal government's technology and innovation round table, so he would have his own political contacts and conduits, not needing to rely on those of his father. The only dark stain on his character was a reputation for a volatile temper. ET did not entertain fools or failures, particularly when their follies cost him money. This disdain was indiscriminate, and his public brawl outside a cafe on Bronte Beach had embroiled an equally well-known fund manager. Apparently, the fund manager had offloaded a bunch of stock and the resulting drop in stock price had angered Tedesco. The matter was nothing more than a social media moment, both combatants blaming the incident on a late night and laughing away their 'disagreement'.

At the end of her research project, Ange was uncertain and undecided about what to think. She needed to take care and not jump to any rash assumptions, just because Tedesco was successful in a world that was totally foreign to her. She would certainly not be referring to him as ET. He would be plain old Tedesco in her lexicon.

By Wednesday lunchtime, her curiosity finally prevailed, and Ange paid Billy and his tech hypercentre a visit. She arrived to find Billy with a tight and concerned look on his face.

'What's up, Billy? You look worried.'

'Haven't you seen the news? The crypto markets are in meltdown. I'll have to put my early retirement on hold for a while more,' Billy replied with an ironic but drawn smile.

Ange sensed that this attempt at humour was forced. 'How much has it fallen?'

'Some currencies have basically fallen to zero. Even some of the major ones have fallen by over fifty percent overnight.'

Ange was now worried that Billy might be in too deep. 'I hope you didn't lose too much money, Billy. Are you OK?'

'I'm OK, boss. I'm probably sitting about square,' Billy said sheepishly, as if gilding the lily about his actual position. 'The market will correct itself. Luckily, I got in years ago. There are some horror stories out there, people who took out loans to invest in crypto and lost the lot. Cryptocurrency has many layers of risk and return. The promise of supercharged profits with, say, initial coin offerings, comes with stratospheric risk. With the consistent price growth of the past few years, it's easy to become complacent and assume that the only way is up. We all just found out that the way down is more like a cliff than a stairway. People will lose their houses over this crash.'

Billy's face darkened with a flash of anxiety. 'Sorry I haven't gotten back to you, boss. I've been preoccupied.'

'OK, Billy, that's fine,' replied Ange, noting that he had a dashboard in the top corner of one of his screens showing the current prices of Bitcoin, Ethereum and a bunch of other currencies. The mention of houses jogged her memory. 'What's happened to the crypto fund that my brother invested in? cFactor, wasn't it?'

Billy quickly pulled up a chart of the fund's performance. It was the perfect example of falling off a cliff. 'Not good,' said Billy, stating the obvious.

'Oh dear. My brother will not be happy. By the way, Billy. You remember Bree, the new constable from Byron Bay that I told you about?'

'Yes, the one who invests in NFTs. I wonder how she's going. I don't have any NFTs yet, thank goodness.'

'Well, Bree is coming to stay at my place over the weekend. She'll be in Sydney for the national hockey titles, playing for New South Wales. She's coming by the office sometime on Friday, so I'll introduce you. We'll probably go for an early drink after work. I'm sure Bree needs to get to bed early before her competition starts on Saturday.'

'Sounds good. I'm solo this weekend. Amber has a job in the Hunter Valley and she won't be back in Sydney until Monday.'

'Who is Amber, Billy? You haven't mentioned her before,' probed Ange, interested as to why Billy had never mentioned Amber.

Billy looked embarrassed, almost as if he had been caught cheating. 'Oh yeah. I've been seeing Amber for a few months now. It's not serious or anything,' he replied casually. He failed to mention that Amber spent most nights sleeping over at his place. 'Anyhow, I'm making progress with those transactions. I should have something from you later this afternoon.'

Ange left Billy to his crypto dashboards with a bemused smile on her face.

Billy proved true to his word and sent Ange a text just after 4:30 p.m. asking her to come around to his desk.

'Hi, boss. I think we have enough to be confident that the StudioBuzz in the NFT chart is the same as the large bubble we looked at on the cryptocurrency chart.' He pulled up a spreadsheet and pointed to a chart that was simply a mess of lines in Ange's eyes. 'The black bars are the NFT purchase transactions and the red bars are the crypto transactions. You can easily see the correlation.'

'I'll believe you, Billy. This is great stuff. Thanks for your help.'

'Is there anything else you need me to do right now? Peter Fredericks came around asking if there was anything else he could help me with, so I hit him up for a subscription to the pro version of BCExplore. I gave him a quick tour, and he seemed impressed. He's going to put my case to Sally Anders for the extra funding,' explained Billy. 'Don't worry, I pretended it had to do with another case,' he elaborated after he saw a look of concern come over Ange's face.'

'I would have done that for you, Billy. After all, it was me who got you your new computer setup.'

Billy looked anxious that he might have offended Ange. 'I wasn't trying to go over the top of you, boss. It's just that Peter was here. He's also been with Major Crimes longer than both of us, so he probably knows better how to secure funding for this type of stuff.'

Ange smiled. 'Don't panic, Billy, I was only teasing. Let me digest what we've found out so far and I'll come back to you. Catch up on some of your other work so that you have a clean plate when I next come knocking on your door.'

'Thanks, boss,' replied Billy before his eyes flicked back towards his cryptocurrency dashboard.

Ange made a mental note to check up on Billy's funding request with Sally Anders. It wasn't implausible that Peter would be jealous and alert to the potential for Billy to overtake him in the promotion race. Some officers were always glancing back over their shoulder to see who they needed to block from going past. Billy was still young and green, someone easily outmanoeuvred by a more experienced player.

She called by her boss's desk, but Sally was nowhere to be seen. That was a job for tomorrow.

# Chapter 24

# A Bridge Too Far

Ange had arranged a lunchtime meeting with Sally Anders. The pair dodged and weaved through the packed lunchtime crowd towards Chinatown, settling on a nondescript dumpling restaurant. Slipping into a discreet corner table, Ange felt like a spy, meeting to hand over the plans of a nuclear submarine or the like. If nothing else, the Chinese weren't ones to waste time or table space, so they had soon placed their order and were sipping green tea.

'Where are you up to, Ange? Any progress?'

'Yes, more than I expected. By the way, before I forget, did Peter Fredericks speak to you about getting extra funding to purchase some software upgrades for Billy?'

'Yes, he did, in fact. This morning. I wanted to speak to you about that. Is it important? Upstairs has my budget squeezed into a straitjacket.'

That Peter had done what he had promised pleased Ange. 'Yes, I think it's worth the spend. Billy is on a steep curve, learning about tracing suspicious cryptocurrency transactions. I'm convinced that criminal activity in this murky arena is only going to increase exponentially. He's already found out some interesting stuff, and he needs the right tools. Otherwise, we'll always be one step behind, or in this case, two steps behind.'

'OK. You've convinced me. I'll get it sorted. Fill me in on where you are.'

Ange gave her the abridged version of what Billy had found. It was hard without the bubbles and lines of his crypto tracing charts, but she ultimately got her point across.

Sally Anders was a tough taskmaster. 'So, you don't really have anything concrete to go on?'

Ange tried vainly to hide her disappointment at this response. 'I've only been on this track for a couple of weeks. I thought that we'd made some good progress.'

'Sorry, I didn't mean it to come out that way. I just don't see how this is getting us anywhere.'

Ange realised that in her desire to fill her boss in, without the benefit of Billy's charts and flow diagrams, the logic of her argument wasn't clear. She recapped. 'We now know that Kramer and Ball were trading in cryptocurrency and NFTs. They both had NFTs called BuzzyBats in their respective collections. Whereas Kramer brought all of his BuzzyBats from Ball, Ball brought all his BuzzyBat NFTs from a company called StudioBuzz. BuzzyBat NFTs are extremely tightly held. The only time that they've been traded on the secondary market was between Ball and Kramer, and Kramer has been murdered and Ball has vanished.'

'OK, but that only tells us what we already know, that Kramer and Ball were both into something dodgy. So, tell me about StudioBuzz. What do you know about them?'

Ange knew she was now getting to the edge of plausibility. 'StudioBuzz is a tech company controlled by Ethan Tedesco, the tech entrepreneur. You may have heard him called by his nickname—ET.'

'I know who he is. I once got dragged into a case involving his father, Eric Tedesco. We were completely screwed. Evidently, Tedesco the Elder has friends in high places. We were forced to drop the entire investigation before it really got started. Anyway, that Ethan Tedesco, the tech maestro, controls this company, tells you nothing. I'll bet they're big in the cryptocurrency and ETF space.'

Even though she knew what her boss meant, Ange couldn't help but correct her. 'NFTs, not ETFs.'

'Whatever,' said Anders dismissively. 'What does NFT stand for, anyway?'

Ange tried hard not to sound like a know-it-all, something she most definitely was not. 'Non-fungible tokens. They use blockchain technology to protect ownership of things like digital art.' She saw the look on her boss's face. 'Don't worry, I don't get the concept either, but some of them sell for huge money.'

'How huge?' asked Anders.

'Millions and millions of dollars; well, the crypto equivalent. I know what you're thinking. I'm the same. But they do. You know my motto—follow the money.'

'OK. So, we have some crypto trades between Ball, Kramer and the company associated with Tedesco. So what?'

'What if this is just a more sophisticated version of eZee Bet? Buying a BuzzyBat NFT from StudioBuzz is the way to pay for goods received. In this case, those goods are narcotics. Tedesco would easily handle the receipts. He even has an interest in a cryptocurrency exchange business, for goodness' sake. As I understand it, the value of any NFT is essentially whatever a vendor and purchaser agree on, so it would be a case of hiding these payments within all this NFT noise and madness. We only have a bead on this through Ted Kramer and some good luck. Without that, we would never have made these connections.'

'That's a clever theory, but what about the supply side? Any clues on that?' probed Anders. 'Without working out the supply side, all we have is a series of trades that could be easily explained away as normal NFT craziness. You've basically said as much yourself.'

'I've got nothing on the supply side. We've only just started to piece this together, boss,' pleaded Ange, disappointment showing as she confronted this cold, hard reality. After a moment's reflection, her face took on a more determined hue. 'My bet is that they have another version of GlitterStrip running. That was really clever. They could pull that scam off in hundreds of different product categories and we'd be none the wiser. It was only luck that we worked out that GlitterStrip cosmetics doubled as a conduit for narcotics distribution. Now that we have a loose thread in this network of crypto trades, I'm hoping that something will fall apart if we keep pulling.'

Anders looked somewhat mollified, albeit tempered with a distinct air of scepticism. She mulled over what Ange had told her before replying. 'I think you overplay your own hand in the so-called *luck* with GlitterStrip. I suppose that there's no other way but forward,' she said, thus ending the briefing.

After that, they chatted about the shows that they were watching on TV and other inane stuff. Once their Chinese hosts had ushered them along, the pair walked briskly back to their office. On the way, Ange noted that Sally Anders' phone hadn't rung once, a rare respite indeed. Ange wondered if she had turned it off. That would be a first in Ange's experience.

Despite the lunch proving delicious, Ange felt flat and dissatisfied, questioning whether she had made any progress at all. Unable to face the rest of the day, she checked out early and went for a long walk. She had brought her walking gear into work, as she had already planned to walk home. With some extra time on her hands, she took the scenic route.

Alighting from her office block, she headed west along Bathurst Street towards Darling Harbour and then followed the waterfront through Barangaroo. Finding her mark, she then turned right at Argyle Street and ducked under the Harbour Bridge and past the busy nexus that was Circular Quay. Even though it was mid-afternoon, early commuters were streaming onto the many ferries that waited patiently for their customers. That pinch point navigated, she fell to the temptation of walking around the Sydney Opera House, an extra four or five hundred metres. This slight detour was always good value, affording her a fabulous view back towards the Harbour Bridge.

Ange paused for a few minutes to take in the spectacle. The harbour was alive with boats and ferries, making waves that crashed against the revetment wall surrounding the Opera House. Cars and trains were racing over the bridge, not to mention the swarms hidden in the tunnels beneath, all streaming to their homes in the northern suburbs. Tourists were taking selfies of the splendorous scene. It was easy to take this for granted when one lived nearby.

She finally dragged herself away from the view, her track home then skirting the Botanical Garden, before winding its way through Elizabeth and Rushcutters Bay, finally ending when she arrived at her little flat. Almost two hours had elapsed since she had left the office. It was surely one of the great urban walks in the world and lifted her spirits to no end.

After a long shower, she heated a packet of ready-made ravioli, to which she added some bottled pesto sauce, all complimented with a packet salad and a glass of merlot. A recent season of *Bosch* beckoned, one that she hadn't gotten around to watching. She let the trials and tribulations of Hieronymus Bosch take her mind off pursuing the syndicate. There was something comforting about Bosch and his troubles.

## Chapter 25

# Double Vision

Ange arrived to work early, dressed casually. Many traditions had been lost during the Covid work-from-home revolution, but dress-down Friday persisted. In fact, Covid seemed to have stripped a lot of formality from how people dressed in the city. Like all fashion, formality would likely come back at some point. How fashion recycled itself was a mystery to Ange. Instead, she relied on her friend Kerrie to ensure her image was appropriate. Before they had met, Ange had purchased some truly tragic outfits and was relieved to have this burden taken from her. The simple instruction given to her stylist friend was always 'sharp, but comfortable'.

She had been on the train when Billy had texted, asking her to come by his desk when she arrived at the office. Apparently, he had something interesting to show her. Bree was turning up sometime around midday, so Ange texted her the address of the office again, eleventh floor, just to make sure. Bree texted back a thumbs-up emoji, then a brief text of actual words to say that things were running to schedule.

She went straight to Billy's floor and strode around to his desk. 'You had something to show me, Billy?'

'Oh yes, boss. You won't believe this. Nelson and I were talking last night about the collapse in the crypto markets. I mentioned we were the lucky ones, having only lost thousands. I dropped Ethan Tedesco's name into the conversation, imagining the millions that he must have lost.'

Ange interrupted Billy's story. 'Why would Ethan Tedesco have lost millions?'

'Well, that investment fund that he set up, cFactor Futures, for one. As I showed you yesterday, its price has been slaughtered. Plus, with this collapse, there are loads of investors who need to cash in their chips, which is creating a run on the crypto exchanges. ET has a stake in one of those as well. Nelson thinks it's only a matter of time before some of the exchanges blow up with liquidity issues. With all the stuff that ET is involved with, I'll bet he has exposure all over the pl ace.'

'I see. Sorry, I interrupted your story. Go on,' prompted Ange. Billy's story reminded her to check on how her brother Joel was faring.

'Well, Amber overheard our conversation. After I'd finished my call with Nelson, she told me she'd met Ethan Tedesco. A couple of weeks back, Amber was working at a function held in Tedesco's apartment on Point Piper. She said his was the swishest apartment she'd ever seen, one with views over Clark Island to the Opera House and the Harbour Bridge. Apparently, it took up the entire top two levels of the apartment block. She took some pictures. I asked her to send them to me. Here, have a look.'

Billy pulled up a WhatsApp message on his computer email, showing a series of images, which he scrolled through. Ange had to agree that Tedesco's apartment was astonishing. Billy paused at a photo of Tedesco with his arm around an attractive woman, the plunging neckline showing off her assets to perfection.

Billy pointed to the woman. 'That's Amber with Tedesco. She said he was cool, but more ordinary-looking than she had imagined. Amber said that there were lots of celebrities at the party. Tedesco told her not to take any more photos once the party was underway.'

Seemingly not upset that Tedesco had his arm around his girlfriend, Billy casually clicked to the next photo, one taken from the balcony and showing the Opera House framed perfectly by the Harbour Bridge. A bell of sorts clanged loudly in Ange's head. 'Billy, can you go back to the last photo?'

There was something familiar about that photo, but Ange couldn't put a finger on it. 'Billy, can you email that photo to me, please?' She saw the look of hesitation in his eyes. 'Don't worry, I won't post it on Facebook. It's just that there's something familiar about it. It might be just Tedesco himself. I have been doing some research on him.'

'You really do need to get onto WhatsApp, boss.' With that admonishment, Billy went through the tedious process of sharing each image in individual emails to Ange.

'That is interesting, Billy. Thanks for that. Pillow talk often yields surprising information. I promise that I'll look into WhatsApp sometime.'

Billy blushed at the reference to the bedroom, so Ange knew that she had been spot on. While she could see the obvious attraction, she had made a snap judgement that Billy could do better, which was harsh given that she had only met Amber in that photo. Was her harsh appraisal borne of jealousy or intuition? Which reminded her of something.

'By the way, Bree from Byron Bay should be here around lunchtime. Perhaps you can show her the chart of NFTs that you've compiled? I'm sure she'll be interested.'

'I'll be here,' said Billy, his red face trending back towards normal.

'Oh, that reminds me,' said Ange, remembering her sobering discussion with Sally Anders. 'How hard would it be to work out who's behind all those other bubbles—sorry, wallets, the ones trading with StudioBuzz? Maybe one of them could give us a clearer picture of what's underpinning all this activity.'

'Well, since the BuzzyBat NFTs never get traded on any secondary marketplace, I'd need to focus on the crypto side and cross-reference transfers with the timing for original BuzzyBat NFTs transactions, then hopefully find something somewhere that could identify someone. It's plausible, but it would take a team of people and a month of Sundays, and certainly not within the time that the boss has allocated us. We've been lucky so far with finding Ted Kramer's link and gaining access to his wallet.'

'OK, Billy. Let's not waste any of our limited time with the unknowns and keep probing what we have. I'll pop round later today and introduce Bree. See you then.'

Ange went back to her desk to find that Billy's email had beaten her there. She stared at that photo of Amber and Tedesco for ages. There was something important in that photo, but she just couldn't put her finger on it. Needing some inspiration, she went back downstairs to find some coffee. She walked across to the Queen Victoria Building, one of Sydney's most historic and iconic shopping centres, home to luxury labels and designer outlets. The nineteenth-century building oozed elegance, both inside and out. Paying a visit to the QVB, as it was commonly known, always made Ange feel special about working in the city.

One of her favourite coffee shops was on the lower level, part of the rail labyrinth of Town Hall, one of the major train station hubs servicing the CBD. Itself a hub of style and design, the QVB was more like an art gallery than a shopping mall. She sat down in the centre of the basement mall to enjoy her coffee and gaze up at the emporium. Rather than the dark Victorian place its name conjured up, the building felt light and airy, courtesy of a domed glass-panelled roof, bookended with dazzling stained-glass windows. The overall effect was impressive and uplifting, a sensory experience that shifted her mindfulness and allowed her subconscious to take over.

She was only part way through her flat white when the light bulb exploded. Needing to test her inspiration, she gulped down the last of her coffee and raced back to the office. Pulling up the photo again, she looked past the people and stared at the painting. That was the object which had triggered her subconscious memory. She minimised the picture and dragged it to one side of her screen, after which she opened the email that Brett had sent her containing the valuations from Christies.

She opened them in sequence, coming to one simply entitled 'Emily'. She clicked on the attachment and an explosion of colour jumped from the screen, the signature of one of Australia's top-selling Indigenous artists, Emily Kngwarreye. The same painting was hanging on the wall of Ethan Tedesco's apartment in Point Piper. How could that be? Someone was taking the piss. At least it gave Ange an excuse to ring Brett Tompkins. The phone almost rang out before being answered.

'Hi, Brett, how are things with you?' Ange said after Brett had answered.

'OK, I suppose. How are you?'

'I'm good, Brett,' replied Ange, picking up on the strained hesitation in Brett's voice. Now was not the time or the forum to get into anything personal, so she jumped right into the object of her call.

'Remember those paintings that Falconi had stored in Singapore? Can you check with the administrator that they haven't sold them already?'

'OK. Why do you ask?'

'I just came across one of those paintings in an apartment in Point Piper. It was there recently, before you sent me the valuations. Something isn't right.'

Now Brett was interested. 'Which painting? Not the Miró?'

'No, not the Miró. One by an Indigenous Australian artist called Emily Kngwarreye. I'm never totally sure how to say her name properly.'

'I remember that one—a mess of colourful bright lines, one that looked like nothing and something at the same time.'

'That's it. Can you check with the administrator and get back to me?'

'Will do. I'll ring you back as soon as I can.'

Ange sat back in her chair and stared at the two images. There were several explanations for how the painting was being proudly displayed in Tedesco's apartment. Perhaps the Freeport had made an administrative error, or they had some scam going and the administrator hadn't checked their facts. Maybe the administrator was even in on the arrangement.

It was just approaching midday before Brett got back to her.

'The administrator wanted to know why I was asking. I didn't tell him, but he seemed quite alarmed now that he knows I'm with Major Crimes. He contacted the CEO of the Freeport, who was quite indignant that he would suggest something untoward. She emailed him a picture of the actual painting that they held in storage, complete with today's copy of the *Straits Times*. I'll send it over.'

'Thanks, Brett. This is most unusual. I'll let you know when I find out what is going on,' she said, pausing for a moment. 'Perhaps we should catch up for dinner sometime?'

Brett was silent for way too long, not a good sign in Ange's eyes. 'Oh yeah, that's something I wanted to speak with you about. I've moved back in with Chrissie and the kids. I wanted to tell you in person, but I've been avoiding it. I'm sorry, but I'm doing it for the kids,' Brett pleaded.

Ange was furious. She took in a deep breath, trying to cool her heels before replying. This was where the harsh realities of having an affair with a colleague came home to roost. 'I get it. You need to look after your family. It's not as if we'd made any commitments to each other.'

Brett seemed relieved that the conversation hadn't descended into a series of angry recriminations. 'The kids are loving having me back home. It's tense at times, but I'm loving being around them full-time. Perhaps we can go surfing sometime?'

'Sure, just let me know,' replied Ange as calmly and offhandedly as she could. She knew that this had been a glib offer to ease his way out of the conversation, so she hung up to let him off the hook. Chrissie was unlikely to be happy about Brett going surfing with his former squeeze.

Ange sat back in her chair once more and clasped her hands atop her head as swirling emotions surfaced. If she was being honest with herself, she had known something was amiss in her relationship with Brett, or whatever it was they'd been doing. Despite these suspicions, she was furious that Brett had not been man enough to tell her in person and had taken the coward's way out. It was normally Ange that did the dumping, and it was an unpleasant feeling to be on the receiving end. At least he had done the deed via a phone call and not a text message—she would have exploded if that had happened. Ange guessed that Brett had officially joined her growing collection of 'male fails'.

'Two nuclear bombs dropped, and it's not even lunchtime. I thought this was going to be another vanilla-style dress-down Friday. How wrong I was,' she thought.

## Chapter 26

# Bree Breezes By

Ange mulled over the disheartening news that Brett Tompkins had thrown at her. There was no point in creating a confrontation over their insipid breakup. She still had to work with him, a problem of an office romance. The job persisted even when the relationship had fizzled.

In her defence, she hadn't known that they were colleagues when they had first met back in Namba Heads. She had been impressed with his surfing ability, none the wiser that Major Crimes had drafted him to work undercover. Their relationship—romance, fling, whatever one wanted to call it—had developed naturally amongst the sunshine and the waves.

Ange reasoned that if anyone was at fault, it was Brett. He had known she was a detective and he should have known the risks. Upon finding out about this dalliance, their mutual boss, Sally Anders, had been less than impressed. Ange had hoped that they could navigate their way through the workplace landmines, but she hadn't factored in Brett's former wife and the love for his children. If nothing else, Brett and Chrissie must have loved each other before he'd gone off the rails. Perhaps these embers were being reignited?

Never having been a 'woe is me' type, Ange dived back into the case of double vision she had stumbled upon. She needed to understand more about the ins and outs of fine art, so she resolved to seek some advice from the best and brightest. She started by ringing the Art Gallery of New South Wales. Met with one of those annoying automated answering services, she clicked her way through a long list of options before being put on hold. Finally, after a good ten minutes of advertorials, a hollow male voice answered. 'How can I help you?'

'Good afternoon. I would like to speak with the gallery director, please,' Ange said in her most important-sounding voice, the one she reserved for gatekeepers and officialdom.

'I'm sorry, the director doesn't work on Fridays,' replied the monotone voice.

'OK. Well, can I make an appointment to come and see the director on Monday?' she asked, ratcheting up her voice until it was approaching her 'let me speak to the manager' incantation. She did not appreciate being stonewalled.

'I can check with his assistant. May I ask who's calling?'

Ange hit him with the big guns. 'My name is Detective Angela Watson from Major Crimes here in Sydney. It's extremely important that I see the director as soon as possible. What's his or her name?'

'Mr Brendan Carmichael. Hold on while I speak to his assistant,' replied the receptionist in a distinctively more agreeable tone before placing Ange on hold again. In less than sixty seconds, a sharp-sounding woman came onto the line.

'Hello, Detective. Mr Carmichael can slot you in at 10 a.m. Monday. Does this work for you?'

'Perfect. Where do I come?'

'Come to the main gallery entrance and tell the desk that you have an appointment with Mr Carmichael. Someone will come down to get you and sign you in. Perhaps arrive ten minutes early to make sure all these formalities are complete by 10 a.m. May I ask what this is about?'

'I'd rather not say. It's a highly confidential matter, and it's best that I speak to Mr Carmichael in person. Thanks for your help.' Ange figured that this approach would ensure that Brendan Carmichael would be ready and waiting for her visit.

Ange then spun her wheels, attending to emails and some administration. She didn't feel like starting something new and remembered about checking in on how her brother Joel was faring with the collapse of the cryptocurrency markets. She rang her mother.

'Hi, Mum. How's Dad's latest horse going? Any wins lately?'

'Terribly. She was a bleeder. They had to retire her. They've already purchased another one. Honestly, for such a smart man, your father can be so stupid. The useless thing is lazing around eating grass that should be reserved for sheep.'

Being a bleeder meant the filly bled from the lungs under racing conditions. Such a horse was usually an expensive liability and routinely put down in the racing industry, but her father was a softie at heart and his retired racehorses usually roamed around the farm in idle luxury for the rest of their days. Not every racehorse owner had access to a lovely home paddock.

'How has Joel gone with his investment and the collapse of the cryptocurrency markets?' asked Ange, getting to the purpose of her call.

'Not too bad. He came asking for a loan to tide him over last week, and your father forced him to sell half his investment. That was like pulling teeth, getting Joel to agree to that. He's lost the rest but made money overall. That boy sure is blessed with a lucky star. He won't have factored in the tax he'll need to pay, but I guess that will be a problem for him and his accountant at tax time.'

'Oh good. I was worried about him. Speak soon. Say hello to Dad for me.'

As Ange hung up from the call, she smiled at the thought of her father, a shrewd man, despite his weakness for racehorses. Her brother, on the other hand, had inherited none of that shrewdness but somehow survived his many misadventures—always had done. It had driven Ange crazy when they were growing up. She would plod along steadily, doing the right thing, whereas Joel would stumble from one hare-brained scheme to another, yet somehow find his feet in the end. She dared not mentioned that she knew someone in the tax office, as Joel's tax problems would likely become hers.

She looked up from these thoughts of the farm to see Bree stepping from the elevator, dragging a large and unwieldy duffle bag on wheels. Major Crimes didn't have any reception desk per se, so Ange went out to greet her junior colleague. 'Hi, Bree. Good flight?'

'It was fine, thanks. The only hard part was lugging this humongous bag around the city.'

'Leave your bag against the wall. There are some people that I'd like you to meet.' Ange first took Bree to meet her boss. 'Hi, boss, can I interrupt you for a moment? I'd like you to meet Breanna White, Billy's replacement at the Byron Bay station. Bree's an expert on NFTs. She also helped look for Tyler Ball.'

Anders stood up and warmly greeted the young constable, giving her a firm handshake and a genuine smile. 'It's nice to meet you. Thanks for helping us try to locate Tyler Ball. Perhaps you can give me a lesson in NFTs as well,' laughed Anders, as if this might be a bridge too far.

Bree looked Anders confidently in the eye as she shook the hand of her superior. 'Sorry I couldn't help more with Tyler Ball. He seems to have completely disappeared or gone to the ground. Don't worry about your lack of knowledge of NFTs. I suspect even the so-called experts know less than they make out. It's such a new and emerging field. A great place to launder money, if you ask me.'

'What brings you to Sydney and our neck of the woods?' asked Anders.

'I'm playing in the national hockey titles this weekend. Detective Watson kindly offered me her couch.'

Ange inserted herself into the conversation. 'It's Ange, how many times do I need to tell you?' She looked at Sally Anders. 'Bree hopes to be an Olympian in the next few years. She's going to mint her own range of NFTs to fund her campaign.'

Anders appeared suitably impressed. 'Well, thanks for dropping by and good luck for the weekend.'

After the pair left Anders' office, Bree commented on how impressive Sally Anders seemed. Ange agreed. Her appreciation of her boss's ability had not been dulled by time and proximity.

The next stop, and the real reason that Ange had put Bree through the pain of dragging her duffle bag around town, was down a level to Billy's desk.

'Billy, I'd like you to meet Bree. She's the one who's been helping me with the NFTs.'

Billy stood up from his desk, showing how tall and fit he was. 'Hi, Bree, great to meet you. How have you fared during this crypto crash?'

Bree grimaced. 'I've been smashed. The market's going berko. Luckily, I'm a cautious investor and never put too much money down on the table.'

'Me too. What's happened to the NFT market?' replied Billy.

'Well, the junk has been completely wiped out. When a correction like this happens, everybody tries to offload their junk first. The problem is that there aren't any buyers. You can imagine what this means for the price of something like an NFT, which is already volatile at the best of times. It's still not great, but the good stuff has held up better.' She looked across at Billy. 'Do you have any NFTs, Billy?'

'No, I haven't made the plunge yet. I'm into a basket of cryptocurrencies, and the same thing has happened. The junk has been hosed out and the major currencies have held up better. Perhaps you can be my NFT advisor?' said Billy with a smile, his boyish charm shining through.

Bree smiled in a non-committal way, avoiding any direct answer to Billy's hypothetical question. 'The other issue is the level of liquidity in the market. That's the problem right now. People are panicking, and liquidity has dried up. It might take a while, but the desirable stuff will come back. I'm thinking of buying rather than selling at the moment.'

Ange was mildly amused at this exchange, an insight into twenty-something investment strategies. She refocussed the conversation. 'Billy, why don't you show Bree your chart of the NFT trades?'

Billy turned back to his computer keyboard and pulled up the chart he had compiled earlier in the week. He pointed to the bubble on the lower right. 'This bubble represents the NFT trades for Ted Kramer.'

Ange could see Bree's blank look and stepped in to explain. 'Ted Kramer is where all this started. It was his NFT collection that I sent you. Someone murdered him earlier this year.'

Billy continued, pointing to the adjacent bubble to the left. 'This bubble connected to Kramer is that of Tyler Ball, a known associate of Kramer's.'

'He's the guy I went looking for. That guy has totally vanished without a trace,' piped up Bree.

Billy seemed interested in that fact. 'I didn't realise that was you. This bubble on the far left, the one that looks like a Covid virus, is a company called StudioBuzz.'

'Yes, that makes sense. I'm pleased my research gave you a lead on that,' commented Bree.

'Oh, I forgot to mention that Bree was the one who uncovered StudioBuzz. On some chat rooms on the Dark Web, apparently,' explained Ange.

Intrigue showed in Billy's eyes. 'Bree, what would a nice girl like you be doing lurking on the Dark Web?'

'I buy nothing until I've done some research on the Dark Web. Criminals love to brag, so if something is untoward, it normally shows up there. I presume that the spikes emanating from the StudioBuzz bubble are other people who have purchased NFTs from them.'

Billy took back control of the conversation, pointing to his screen. 'These two bubbles that are common to Kramer and Ball are Swyftx and OpenSea. There's another thing that's strange about this chart. StudioBuzz doesn't trade with OpenSea. I'm not sure how they did that.'

'Yes, that is strange,' observed Bree. 'There are alternative NFT exchange sites to OpenSea, but presumably they should have shown up on your chart. Perhaps StudioBuzz has somehow created its own exchange?'

'That makes sense,' Billy remarked. 'I don't fully understand how this marketplace works. Anyhow, not a single BuzzyBat NFT has been traded through OpenSea. The only two that have ever changed hands were direct transfers from Ball to Kramer.'

Ange noted the gory details. 'And those two characters are missing or dead.'

There was a pause in the conversation before Bree asked a killer question. 'What has happened since the crash on Wednesday?'

'Good question. I haven't looked. Let me refresh the chart.' Billy clicked away on his keyboard, making the image flicker briefly. There didn't appear to be much change, although two Covid spike bubbles had grown. 'That's weird. I would have thought that at least a few collectors would have offloaded some BuzzyBats.' Billy clicked on the bubble that had grown the most. A series of trades came up in a small pop-up window.

Bree was right onto it. 'No way,' she exclaimed loudly. 'Whoever that is has actually purchased more BuzzyBats since the crash—and for big money.'

Billy clicked on some of the other bubbles. 'And what's even weirder is that not a single BuzzyBat appears to have been sold.'

'This is not normal trading behaviour. Something very weird is going on here, Detectives,' concluded Bree.

Billy looked a touch embarrassed. 'Actually, she's the only detective here. I'm still a lowly constable.'

Bree laughed out loud. 'So, you're just like me—only smarter.'

This was the perfect form of flattery in Billy's eyes, making him blush discernibly. 'I don't think so,' he said sheepishly, unable to recover his cleverness for any sort of decent riposte.

Ange put an end to this impromptu gathering of the mutual admiration society. 'We're heading home on the train and then walking over to have drinks and some pub food at the Four in Hand in Paddington. Meet you there in an hour and a quarter, Billy?'

Billy did not hesitate to join in. The last hour had provided Ange some deep insights. She liked the manner in which Bree had handled herself around the office, and the way Billy and Bree had bounced off each other was telling. Their generation approached technology with a different mindset, one Ange needed to foster and harness.

After a disconcerting start, the day had ended on a high note, and Ange sensed the trio had made some solid progress.

## Chapter 27

# Letter Bomb

After wrestling Bree's large duffle bag up the stairway into Ange's flat, the pair took quick showers and dressed casually for drinks. Ange couldn't help but smile to herself when Bree asked for an opinion on how she looked. She looked great in Ange's eyes, brimming full of health and vitality, the most attractive feature of all. If only Ange could bottle that sauce, she would be well on her way to that oceanfront apartment on the eastern beaches.

It was only a ten-minute walk from Ange's apartment to the pub. By the time they had arrived, the pub was busy—not pre-Covid heaving busy, but busy enough to create a pleasant atmosphere. Ange had somehow avoided catching Covid, whereas Bree had not been so lucky, or perhaps she had been the lucky one. That was still a mystery. Bree had succumbed immediately after the last Byron Blues Festival, where she had been on duty. Luckily, she hadn't fallen seriously ill, unlike one of her friends, who had been sick for weeks and was now suffering long Covid. Ange expressed scepticism that this was a real thing, but Bree argued the case well, finally convincing Ange of its validity.

Billy waltzed in while they were standing at the bar and waiting to be served. Ange picked up the first round of drinks and they found a comfortable place to sit. The conversation weaved its way around surfing, hockey, and tennis, then onto the latest news about Byron Bay, the source of their common connection. Ange hardly got a word in edgeways, although she was pleased to hear that Bree was planning to sign up for surfing classes once she had a break from hockey training. The world of cryptocurrency and NFTs barely rated a mention.

At about 9 p.m., Bree confessed she needed to get to bed early. She was scheduled to play three games the next day. Hopefully, they would win their pool and make it through to the finals on Sunday. She made a point of inviting Ange and Billy to come along on Sunday, assuming her team made it through. Ange was a definite starter and Billy seemed keen, just the right sort of keen—not too little and not too much. Bree was similarly circumspect on the walk home. 'Billy seems nice,' she commented casually, looking straight ahead and giving nothing away, as any elite sportsperson should.

Bree was awake early the next morning. Ange had remained carless, or else she would have offered to drive. The state hockey centre was at Sydney Olympic Park, which was a bit of a trek from Edgecliff. Ange suggested Bree catch a train to Strathfield and then get a taxi to the hockey centre.

The surf forecast was terrible and, since Ange was already up, she amused herself by taking her coffee and breakfast at a cafe before dealing with some shopping chores. She arrived back at her flat after midday, planning a quick shower before heading back out for some exercise. As she approached the door to the foyer of her apartment, she noticed some envelopes sticking out from her mailbox. Resting her grocery bags on the ground, she retrieved a jangling set of keys from her pocket and unlocked her mailbox. She recalled Billy's explanation of private and public digital keys as she extracted a larger-than-expected pile of haphazardly stacked mail. Equating such a complex concept to something as mundane as collecting one's mail was a clever analogy.

When Ange was a young girl back on the farm near Tamworth, one of her daily jobs was to collect the mail after being dropped off by the local primary school bus. Her dog, Buddy, was always waiting patiently for the bus to arrive. He loved to accompany her on the longish walk to the homestead. Buddy would even bark if she forgot to check the mailbox. Such was this ritual.

In between throwing sticks for Buddy to retrieve and keeping an eye out for black or brown snakes, she would finger through the mail on her rambling walk home, making up stories about what each letter contained. Fortunately, besides being her mate, Buddy was an excellent snake dog. Her city cousins had no such protections, needing instead to navigate snakes of traffic. At that stage of her life, Ange would take the slithering variety any day. It was amazing how familiarity helped one cope with life's diverse challenges.

Email had not yet been a thing and the physical version, the real thing, played a crucial role in connecting rural folk with the world. The letters to watch out for, as she had learned from the look on her dad's face, were the ones sent by the bank. Those missives, unmistakable with their big red logo, invariably resulted in a deep scowl. Her father usually flung them onto the sideboard unopened, building upon a pile of their similarly tattooed cousins.

Old habits died hard, so Ange stood in the foyer and thumbed through the sheaf of envelopes, putting aside junk mail to be binned, separating the odd letter worthy of consideration, until she came to a blank envelope—no address and not even sealed. She extracted the solitary item inside. A photo, it seemed.

Turning the photo over, she couldn't suppress an involuntary gasp when she saw it was an image of herself. She immediately recognised the location as the south end of Bondi Beach, just near the rock shelf that formed the Icebergs' swimming pool. Unmistakable. The photo appeared to have been taken from a vantage point on the foreshore, north of where her towel lay. It captured a wetsuited Ange wading from the shallows, clutching Franky under her arm, her bright yellow leg rope already unfastened off her ankle and snaked over her shoulder. The surf looked crowded, and she remembered that day. The memory came in a rush and she realised who must have taken the photo. It was the guy who she had used as a ruse to scare off the cannabis dealer. That was ironic. She maintained sufficient composure to carefully place the photo back in its envelope, preserving any fingerprints that might remain.

Ange's head spun wildly with this revelation. She whipped around in reflex, then raced back to the street, peering into cars parked nearby, then staring up at the buildings opposite, hoping to see who might be watching. Finding nothing obvious, she walked back to retrieve Franky and move to the relative safety of her foyer. Ange noticed her hands were shaking, annoyingly so. She fumbled to find the correct key, fumbled again trying to open the foyer door, each bumbling attempt adding to a sense of exposure that was bordering on frantic. She barely remembered making it into her apartment. It wasn't the first time that the syndicate had sent her a message like this, but this was far more personal. She felt violated.

Dumping her shopping bags on the floor, she put the jug on for a cup of tea, just like her father would do upon opening those letters from the bank. Cup of tea in hand, Ange collapsed on her couch, the one that was currently also Bree's bed. This ritual of taking tea slowly retrieved Ange's composure. She realised it wasn't concern over her own safety that bothered her; she was furious, positively incandescent at this invasion of her privacy. It was her job to peer into the secret lives of others, not the other way around.

Someone had clearly sent the photo as a warning, cleverly executed, and easily dismissed as that of a friend or admirer. She knew it would yield no fingerprints, such was the lack of any other distinguishment.

Her initial shock slowly wore away, to be replaced by a sense of excitement. She was on the right track and someone was worried. She was suddenly hungry and not just for food.

## Chapter 28

# Executing

Ange put aside her unwanted fan mail for the moment. She would speak to Sally Anders about it on Monday before jumping to any conclusions. Bree arrived back from her day's exertions around 7 p.m., exhausted and spent. Excitedly, her team had made it through to the finals. Her semi-final was to be played at 10 a.m. the next day, with the final scheduled for 3 p.m.

Ange ordered some takeaway Indian food from a nearby restaurant, adding in an extra serving of rice to replenish Bree's energy reserves in readiness for her strenuous next day. She wandered over to pick up the food while Bree took a long, hot shower. As soon as they settled down to dinner, Bree asked Ange if anything was wrong. This was perceptive. Ange had felt that she was acting completely normally.

'No, nothing really, just a surprising development in a case I'm working on,' replied Ange. She didn't want Bree to feel like an imposition, adding, 'It's great having you here, Bree. I'm enjoying the company. How about we watch a show that I've been meaning to watch, the one about the collapse of WeWork?'

They had barely finished dinner and were less than one-third of the way through the movie when Ange saw Bree was having trouble staying awake. As they were sitting on Bree's impromptu bed, Ange called stumps, piling the dishes into the sink until morning. After getting herself ready for bed, Ange popped her head around the corner to say goodnight, only to find that Bree was already fast asleep, obviously not nervous about her big games the next day.

Ange, on the other hand, did not sleep anywhere near as deeply or peacefully. The movie hadn't helped matters and she endured one of those terrible nights, where her frenetic mind raced to make sense of the *letter bomb* which she had received. Ange awoke twice during the night feeling flustered and sweaty.

Ange was up early on Sunday morning and traded texts with Billy.

> **Billy:** *Did Bree make the semi-finals?*
> **Ange:** *Sure did. I'm planning to accompany Bree out to Olympic Park. Do you want to tag along?*

Billy replied with a thumbs-up emoji and, as this was getting all too hard by text, Ange rang him. 'Hi, Billy, the first game is at 10 a.m. We're heading downstairs shortly to find some breakfast and then make the journey out to the venue. I'm planning to catch the 8:02 train from Town Hall to Strathfield. Why don't you meet us there?'

'Easy. I should be able to find you. I'll see you at the game if I'm running late,' replied Billy before hanging up.

Ange gave Bree a spare set of keys in case they went their separate ways during the day, and they headed to a local cafe that was on the way to the train station. With such a strenuous day ahead, Bree tucked into a solid breakfast, whereas Ange limited her calorific intake to some avocado toast and coffee. Billy was already waiting on the platform when they arrived for their 8:02 train to Strathfield. He waved when he saw the two women coming down the escalator.

'Oh, Bree, I forgot to tell you that Billy wanted to join us. I hope you don't mind,' said Ange casually.

'Cool,' was the full extent of Bree's opinion on the matter.

The games proved far more exciting than Ange had imagined: fast-paced, highly physical jousting matches, certainly not affairs for the fainthearted. Even though Ange didn't understand the subtleties of the sport, she could see how Bree played in a calm and measured way, always in the thick of things, or thereabouts, conserving her energy wisely for when it counted. It was thrilling being part of a tribe and barracking for your team. Both Ange and Billy yelled loud support for Bree whenever she made a dash down the field on attack.

Bree's team won their semi-final easily, but the final proved a torrid battle against the Victorian state team, their archrivals. Bree's team got off to a flying start, scoring twice in the first twenty minutes. Like all champion teams, Victoria rallied and fought back, scoring their first goal early in the second half. From there, it was a nail-biting finish, with Bree's team just holding off their rivals to win 2–1. After the presentations, Bree came over to see Ange and Billy. They both congratulated her with big hugs.

'Thanks for coming, guys. We nearly blew that game. We relaxed once we scored our second goal in the first half and then became tight once Victoria came back at us. I'm glad we got the job done in the end, but we were lucky in those last ten minutes. The momentum was with Victoria, and I wouldn't have liked to go to extra time had they levelled the scores. The team is heading to a pub nearby to celebrate. Do you guys want to join us?'

'Thanks for the offer, Bree. I've got a big day tomorrow. I'm sure Billy will join you,' replied Ange, making sure that Billy didn't miss any opportunity. 'How about I take your gear back to the apartment and you guys have fun? You have a set of keys. What time are you flying out tomorrow?'

'I don't leave until the evening. I wanted to do some shopping and have a walk around the city. I hope that's OK?'

'Of course. I might be gone by the time you get up. Make yourself at home. We can touch base during the day.'

Ange looked at Billy. 'I'm sure Billy will see you safely home.' He was like a deer in the headlights with absolutely nowhere to go.

The pair left to join the team, and Ange threw Bree's duffle bag over her shoulder. She ordered an Uber on her phone and was home in less than thirty minutes. She settled in to watch another episode of *Bosch* to calm herself down, eventually heading to bed around 9 p.m. Thankfully, she must have slept deeply, as she didn't hear Bree come in.

The next morning, Ange tiptoed around and quietly exited the apartment around 7:30 a.m., choosing to grab breakfast in town so as not to disturb her houseguest. She tucked the nefarious letter in her handbag, a heavy weight borne of both concern and anticipation. Upon arriving at the office, she swung by her boss's office to discuss the letter. Sally was nowhere to be seen, nor at 9:15 a.m. when she left to make her appointment at the art gallery. She spied Peter Fredericks and asked him where Sally was, only to learn that she was in Canberra for a national symposium on organised crime. She wouldn't be back in the office until Wednesday.

That was a pity. Discussion about the letter would have to wait.

# Chapter 29

# Finery

The Art Gallery of New South Wales was in The Domain, only a twenty-minute walk from Ange's office. In no hurry, she crossed into Hyde Park, the country's oldest public domain, taking time to enjoy the magnificent central spine, a cathedral of massive centuries-old fig trees. Pausing briefly to take in the Archibald Fountain, she then crossed over into The Domain, arriving at the imposing front door of the gallery some fifteen minutes early, appropriately inspired by her pleasant jaunt.

Ange approached the front counter and informed the middle-aged woman that she had an appointment with the director. Ange could see the woman's mind working. 'No, you don't,' it said.

'May I see some ID?' said the woman in a stern and offhanded manner, most likely expecting to be offered a driver's licence.

Ange used her official credentials sparingly; however, now seemed an appropriate use of force, so to speak. The badge brought on a marked change of attitude in the woman.

'Thank you, Detective. I'll get someone to come down and get you.' She handed over a visitor's book and asked Ange to sign in. 'Don't worry about the details, just your name. I'll fill the rest in for you,' she said, now all smiles and cuddles.

Ange needed only to wait a few minutes before a smartly dressed thirty-something woman walked over. 'Hello, Detective. I'm Annabelle Fraser, Mr Carmichael's PA. Let me take you upstairs. Do you come here often, Detective?'

'No, not nearly often enough. Occasionally I come to the special exhibitions, but my visit today has reminded me to make better use of the gallery. I just live nearby, so it's crazy that I don't come here more often. Thanks for organising this appointment at such short notice,' said Ange. This seemed to please Ms Fraser no end. That was a secret tactic of Ange—always stay on the good side of the gatekeeper.

She was ushered into the director's spacious office, where a well-dressed forty-something man and a similarly well-dressed middle-aged woman stood up to greet Ange.

'Hello, Detective. I'm Brendan Carmichael, the gallery director.' Carmichael gestured towards the woman. 'May I introduce Janis Jones, the chair of our audit and risk committee? We've just finished a meeting and I thought it was worth her staying.'

After shaking hands with Carmichael, Ange shook hands with Jones and introduced herself. Whereas Carmichael's handshake was decidedly insipid, Jones's handshake was firm and confident, an important insight for a one-time country girl.

'So, how can I help you, Detective?'

'Thanks for agreeing to see me at such short notice. I wanted to ask how a notable painting could be in two different places at the same time.'

'Well, that would be impossible. Perhaps you are referring to a study, or maybe one painting resembles the other, perhaps a different size. Artists often do variations on a theme, leading the uneducated eye to believe that they have seen the painting before,' replied Carmichael, clearly having gauged Ange as someone who might possess this delinquency.

Janis Jones entered the fray, to the obvious annoyance of Carmichael. 'Or one of them could be a forgery.'

'Despite what you read in the papers, forgery, at least one that would confuse a gallery or a serious art dealer, is quite rare. What type of painting are we talking about?' said Carmichael, trying to regain control after Jones's interruption.

'It's a major Indigenous Australian artist,' replied Ange. She turned up some heat. 'I'm sure that you will have this artist well represented in your gallery.'

A concerned frown had passed over Carmichael's forehead, quickly replaced by a knowing smile. 'Yes, well, Indigenous Australian art would be one of the easiest kinds to copy.'

'Why is that?'

'Well, for one, they're all relatively modern. Older artworks, something from, say, the nineteenth century, would need to show appropriate levels of ageing. Second, the materials that would have been used are quite common and still easily obtained. Third, Indigenous art is often simplistic and bold, which makes it easier to emulate. What stratum of artist are we talking about?'

Ange didn't wish to let on the name of the artist. There was always a chance that someone knew someone who knew Ethan Tedesco. He was a well-known supporter of charity, which might extend to the gallery itself. She chose her words carefully. 'Paintings by this artist sell for hundreds of thousands of dollars, even millions.'

'Oh well, that is quite a rarefied air in the world of Indigenous Australian art. I suppose if someone had access to the original, they could create a decent facsimile. They are quite unsophisticated paintings in the main. Many of these artworks were created within state-sponsored studios. That this same art can now command hundreds of thousands of dollars, even millions, is testament to the success of that project.'

Ange surprised herself with a rush of proprietorial anger on behalf of Indigenous artists. 'Haven't art galleries and collectors profited most from Indigenous Australian artwork? I'll bet the original artists were paid a pittance for their hard work, a mere fraction of the millions being charged in the flash galleries.' Ange had taken a distinct dislike to the pompous Brendan Carmichael. She couldn't help but notice the faintest of smiles sneak into the expression of Jones.

'Perhaps, but the art of curation is every bit as difficult and important as the art of creation,' said the self-important Brendan Carmichael.

Ange didn't believe that for a moment, but she wasn't here to cross swords with the gallery director. 'I understand. Moving on, if one had two copies of the same painting, how would one prove which was the original?'

'Provenance is the most important part. Identifying whose hands the work has passed through and establishing a verified trail is critical. This is often a problem with some Indigenous art—not the stuff produced in the studios but works produced outside of those. They have sometimes passed through countless hands. When the artist becomes successful, the full extent of their works shows up everywhere. Until they become valuable, establishing provenance had been of no importance.'

Carmichael paused, looking up and to the right, as if consulting a privileged encyclopedia on artist attribution, one that he alone possessed. 'A forensic comparison would analyse the paint and canvas composition, as well as things like brushstrokes and how the paint was applied. There are some specialist firms that one can hire to verify a piece of art, but their services don't come cheaply. Of course, if you could find an old valuation, then the valuer will have completed the background work, particularly for a work as expensive as you purport.'

Ange handed over her card. 'Would you mind sending me the details for those firms used to verify originality, please?'

Carmichael looked down at Ange's card. Major Crimes maintained a certain cachet that could be useful. He looked up and fixed Ange directly in the eye. 'Sure. We have little use for firms like that. Like I said, forged artwork is not as common as the media has led you to believe.'

Ange knew that this was as far as she could go for today. Indigenous art was evidently not Carmichael's preferred, but Ange had learned a great deal. It would seem that if one wanted to forge a piece of art in this country, then important Indigenous Australian art would be a good place to start.

Ange stood to take her leave. 'Thank you, Mr Carmichael. This has been most helpful.'

Carmichael then asked the question that had been playing on his mind. 'I hope that none of our paintings are involved?'

'No, you don't need to worry.' She saw Carmichael visibly relax. 'Not yet, at least,' she added. Ange could be cruel, particularly when it involved the sport of bursting a bubble of self-importance.

Janis Jones stood as well. 'I'm about to go as well. I'll walk you out, Detective.'

Once they were in the hallway and out of earshot, Jones turned to Ange. 'Don't believe a word he said about forgery being unusual. Between us, it's a massive problem globally. The thing is, it's not in anyone's interest to look too closely. Don't discount forgery in your case, despite what Brendan may have said. If you find anything interesting, particularly if it might affect our gallery, I'd appreciate a heads-up—if you can, of course. I report to the auditor general, so the existence of widespread or systematic forgery would be dynamite and something I need to know about.'

Jones handed over her business card to Ange, who mused that this was, of course, what a good chair of the audit committee should be worried about.

'Also, the world of art gallery directors is a study of upward mobility, each looking for the next job in a more prestigious gallery. It wouldn't help their cause to rock the boat. Don't waste your time trying to get someone to break rank—it just won't happen. Believe me. I've tried,' said Jones with a telling smile.

Ange was left with the distinct impression that the relationship between Jones and Carmichael would be testy at best.

## Chapter 30

# Meet ET

Ange wandered back towards the office deep in thought. The matter of this double vision was an important riddle that needed solving. Sure, the Freeport and the administrator of Falconi's affairs might be involved in some sort of cover-up, but that seemed highly risky behaviour with their respective reputations on the line and under the scrutiny of police. Also, the logistics of moving a painting in and out of a Freeport and dealing with customs sounded like a lot of trouble, but she would need to check the dates of Amber's photo and match them with the Singaporean newspaper. Her visit to the art gallery had reinforced her suspicion that one painting was a forgery, but it was impossible to tell which one from her computer screen.

It was almost 11:30 a.m., so she ducked into a Vietnamese restaurant for an early lunch. She had recently discovered this hidden gem by accident, tucked away in an alleyway beside a watch repairer that Ange had sought. Pho was one of those meals that Ange could eat for breakfast, lunch, and dinner. The mere act of eating a bowl of pho was calming. Unless a change of clothes was close at hand, the boiling hot potion of noodles and broth wasn't something to be gulped down in a hurry.

By the time that Ange had slurped down the last tasty noodle and drained her broth, she had determined a plan of attack and she strode back to the office full of purpose. First step was to identify what type of car Ethan Tedesco drove. A search of vehicle registrations shows that he, in fact, owned three cars. A black Mercedes G Wagon, the fast and furious version; a white Tesla Model S, for when his appearance obviously required a green hue; and a green Lamborghini Huracán, brash and noisy like its owner. Ange mused that she owned three surfboards, so they at least had something in common.

Given that she knew where Tedesco lived, Ange proposed to pay him a visit. No search warrant would be required. It was just a friendly visit to give him a heads-up that his painting might be a forgery. He should be interested in hearing that news. Ange wandered across to Billy's desk, but he was nowhere to be found. She saw Peter Fredericks in the distance, but he was racing out the door with a pile of documents tucked under his arm. Ange didn't want to bring anyone else in on this, so she went up a floor to her office and sent a text to her young colleague.

*Billy, can you come by my office when you get back to work, please?*

Ange's text went unanswered, but Billy eventually waltzed in around 2 p.m., accompanied by her houseguest. If Ange didn't know better, she could have sworn Billy was standing two inches taller. Bree was carrying several shopping bags. The pair walked over to Ange's office.

'Hi, boss. Bree and I caught up for lunch. She's about to head back to Byron Bay,' explained Billy, unable to wipe the huge grin off his face.

Bree held up her shopping bags. 'As you can see, I celebrated our win yesterday with some retail therapy.'

'I thought you two might get along. It's always nice to celebrate with some credit card carnage,' said Ange. They all laughed at this truism.

'I'll head off now and pick up my stuff from your apartment before catching the train to the airport. What do you want me to do with your keys?'

'Just leave them on the kitchen table and slam the door behind you. You'll still be able to exit the foyer,' explained Ange.

'Perfect. Thanks for having me, Ange. It's been a great weekend. Winners make grinners. I hope to see you again soon. Maybe I'll make the national team and you can come to an international game. India is touring next year. They're always a tough team to beat, even at home.'

Ange said her goodbyes and left Billy to escort Bree to the lift. Ange was waiting at his desk when he returned from these farewells. 'Billy, would you mind checking the exact dates when Amber took those photos with Ethan Tedesco?'

'Sure. I'll text her now,' said Billy. Within seconds, his phone buzzed with a reply. He looked up at his boss. 'Are you set up on WhatsApp yet?'

'Not yet, Billy. Give me time.'

'Here, give me your phone and I'll set you up now for you.'

Ange handed over her phone. In no time, Billy handed it back to her and it pinged with her first WhatsApp message—from Billy, of course. She looked at the date on the original message and realised that it was just under two weeks before the date on the *Straits Times*. It did not rule out a rushed transfer from Singapore to Sydney, but that seemed of low probability. She was heavily persuaded by her forgery theory. 'Billy, how would you like to meet Ethan Tedesco?'

'Yes, definitely. Nelson would be so, so jealous. How are you planning to arrange that, boss?'

'We know roughly where he lives, and I know what cars he drives, so I figure we can wait for him this afternoon and knock on his door. I'm sure that he'll want to speak to us.'

'Truly, boss. Are you really so last century? Why don't I log in to the traffic cams in the area and we can see when he drives by?'

'You can do that?'

'Yes, sure. Peter Fredericks showed me how to do this a while back. We have permanent access to that sort of stuff. Send me the number plates and I'll organise an alert.'

'OK, great. We should be ready to jump as soon as an alert comes through. I'll organise a car from downstairs.'

Around 4 p.m., Billy swung by. 'Boss, you didn't tell me that one of these cars was a Lamborghini. Those cars are beasts. Lamborghini green is ridiculously easy to spot.'

Ange immediately dropped whatever she was doing, and the pair were soon driving across town to meet Tedesco. Even though peak hour was some time away, the traffic was intense, reinforcing Ange's decision not to own a car in Sydney. It took them a good forty minutes to make it across town and onto the rarefied real estate of Point Piper.

There was only one plausible block of apartments to fit Amber's description and support the aspect of her photos. The two officers parked their car on the street and walked up toward the locked foyer. A large intercom panel was mounted in a small alcove next to the main door. They knew from Amber's visit that Tedesco occupied the top two levels, so Ange started at the top button. It didn't even ring. She tried the next button down. It rang out. Continuing with her trial-and-error approach, Ange pressed the next button down. This time, a gruff male voice answered.

'Hello.'

'Hi. Are you Mr Ethan Tedesco?' asked Ange.

'No, Ethan's on the next level up. The next two levels, actually.'

'OK. Thanks. I tried his buzzer but there wasn't any answer.'

'Keep trying. He has an enormous apartment. He might have been on the top floor. I know that Ethan's home, as I heard him drive in. It's hard to miss that car of his.'

'Thanks, that's helpful. I'll keep trying.'

She rang the next buzzer up again. It rang out with no answer. Heeding the advice of her previous discussion, she pressed the buzzer again.

Another unfamiliar male voice came over the intercom. 'Can I help you?'

Ange glanced at Billy with hopeful eyes. 'Am I speaking to Mr Ethan Tedesco?' she replied.

'Yes. Who's asking?'

Ange held her badge up in front of the camera atop the intercom panel. 'I'm Detective Angela Watson. I wondered if I could speak to you about something.'

'It's not convenient. Please make an appointment at my office and we can speak then.'

Ange was not so easily dismissed. 'It would be better if we did this now, Mr Tedesco. It concerns your apartment, in fact. I think you'll want to hear what we have to say.'

There was a long pause, as if Tedesco was weighing up his options. 'OK. I'll open the front door and send a lift. Just get in and the lift will take you directly to my apartment.'

The foyer door buzzed and Billy pushed through, holding the door for Ange to enter. No sooner were they in the lobby than the far lift pinged and a light flashed. The pair exchanged glances and walked into the lift. It deposited them directly to a waiting Ethan Tedesco. Amber hadn't been exaggerating. It was quite an apartment.

# Chapter 31

# Mates' Rates

As the lift door closed, Ange noted it was a brilliant mosaic of silver, emerald and gold lines, clearly an advantage of owning the entire floor—even the lift was a feature. She introduced herself and Billy, shaking hands with the casually dressed Tedesco. He pointed to a spacious sitting room nearby. 'Make yourself comfortable,' said Tedesco, following behind and fiddling with his phone as he walked.

'Ah yes. I thought you looked familiar. I read about you a few months back during that SACC investigation,' said Tedesco casually, as if he was commenting on the weather.

'Damned Google. That bloody SACC affair will haunt me to my grave,' thought Ange to herself. Keeping her cool, she summoned a casual air in responding to her obsequious host. 'You should know not to believe everything that you read in the papers, Mr Tedesco.'

'Call me Ethan, please,' said Tedesco, turning on his not-inconsiderable charm. 'So, what is this about, Detective?'

A tall and elegant Vietnamese woman silently appeared, interrupting the conversation. 'Do you want anything to drink?' asked Tedesco.

'Just some water, please,' replied Ange. Billy nodded.

'I'll have the same. Thank you, Tham,' said Tedesco, politely dismissing the woman before turning his attention back to Ange. 'You were saying?'

'We have concerns that one of your paintings may be the object of forgery,' said Ange.

'Which one?' asked Tedesco alarmingly.

Ange scrambled with her phone to open the photo taken in Singapore that

Brett had sent her. 'It's a large paining by Emily Kngwarreye. I believe you have one the same?'

A brief look of annoyance flickered across Tedesco's face before he quickly regained his composure. 'I do. It's in the other room.'

'Can we see it, please?' asked Ange.

Tedesco stood and took them into an even more spacious sitting room, one that showed the full panorama of Sydney Harbour. It was breathtaking. Tedesco motioned to the painting on the wall. 'There it is.'

It was hard to decide which was the most impressive sight. The Opera House and the Sydney Harbour Bridge, or the explosion of light and colour that was the hallmark of Emily Kngwarreye's work. Ange held up her phone. It was indeed the same piece of artwork. They stood looking at the stunning painting for a minute before Tedesco led them back into the smaller sitting room. It was hard to leave that magnificent room. Their drinks awaited.

'You said that this was a forgery case? Presumably there is another copy. Mine is patently the original, as you can see. I have a proper valuation as well.'

'The other copy was discovered in a warehouse overseas. How did you acquire yours?' asked Ange.

'I purchased it some eighteen months ago from a business associate.'

'And it's been here all that time?'

'Yes, I think it sits nicely against the view, don't you?' observed Tedesco conceitedly, relishing his trophies of success.

'I agree. It is most impressive,' said Ange. It was impossible to argue with the truth. 'Would that business associate be Mr Eddie Falconi, by any chance?'

Tedesco didn't look as surprised by this revelation as Ange felt he should have. Either that, or he was a formidable poker player. 'Yes, it was, in fact. That was very sad about Eddie taking his own life. I knew he had some money worries, but it wasn't worth killing himself over.'

'How did you know Mr Falconi?' asked Ange.

'Well, we mixed in the same circles socially from time to time. I was sitting with him at the cricket one day when I mentioned I was redecorating the apartment and on the lookout for a signature painting, something with lots of colour and high impact. One thing led to another, and I purchased the painting some six months later, or thereabouts.'

'Would you mind telling us how much you paid?' asked Ange. Billy was just sitting there, all starstruck. He looked like he was in love.

'I'm not prepared to disclose that information, Detective. As I mentioned, my painting came with a valuation, one from a top-tier firm.'

'That would be Christies, I presume?' suggested Ange.

If any of that rattled Tedesco, he was doing a terrific job of hiding his discomfort. 'There are several quality firms that I'm happy to rely upon, Christies being one of them.'

'Fair enough. Did you agree to pay Mr Falconi the valuation price?'

Ethan Tedesco delivered Ange his best multimillion-dollar smile, one brimming with confidence. 'I'm sure you know how trading works, Detective. A fair price is what a buyer and seller agree to shake hands on. Mr Falconi seemed quite eager to offload the painting, so let's just say that I was more than happy with the price we settled upon.' As quickly as his smile had blossomed, it hardened in an instant. 'I'm quite certain the other painting, the one on your phone, is a fake. I suggest you check that out more fully.'

Tedesco stood up from the sofa. 'Look, I need to be at a fundraiser this evening. Let me call the lift for you.'

Tedesco's expression signalled that his patience for this conversation was at an end. He made for the lift and pressed the down button. Billy was still of no use, but Ange had what she had come for, so she was happy to leave Tedesco to his supposed fundraiser. Within seconds, the lift pinged and the brilliantine doors opened. After taking their leave, the two police officers were soon being whisked down to the lobby.

Billy finally found his tongue. 'That went well, considering. Very cool.'

Ange looked at him sideways. She wasn't sure if he was serious or joking. 'I thought you might propose to him, Billy.'

Billy looked surprised by that joking accusation until understanding flushed his expression. 'No, not that. Hilarious. I meant considering the pressure he must be under business-wise.'

'How so?' asked Ange.

'The crash in crypto markets has followed a rout in tech stocks. The entire sector is being murdered in the markets. I imagine ET has a lot of worried investors on his back right now.'

The tech rout was news to Ange. 'And now we come knocking on his door, essentially telling him that his million-dollar painting is worthless. If he was associated with Falconi and narcotics, he knows that we've made the connection. Narcotics is one of the few recession-proof businesses going around, so I wonder how much cross-pollination exists in his investor base. That could be interesting. I doubt that was our last encounter with Ethan Tedesco.'

The drive back to the office plunged Ange deep into thought. She had proven the link between Falconi and Tedesco, but she needed to rattle Tedesco's cage more strenuously. She would need to speak with Brett to probe the Singapore connection and hopefully prove that Tedesco's painting was the fake. Ange could then circle back on Tedesco to further probe his relationship with Falconi. And then there was the angst of speaking to Brett following his recent admission.

Billy was speaking during Ange's mental gymnastics. 'I think that's an angle on how we might crack the NFT matter.' She seemed distracted. He waited for a moment before speaking again. 'Were you listening to my idea, boss?'

Ange, in fact, wasn't really listening, caught in her own whirlpool. 'Go for it, Billy. I trust your judgement.'

As things turned out, she should have been listening more closely.

# Chapter 32

# Reputation Matters

It was approaching 6 p.m. by the time Ange and Billy were back at their desks. Not wanting to kick the can down the road, Ange concluded that now was as good a time as any to ring Brett.

'Hi, Ange. How are you?'

Ange could hear plenty of noise in the background, people yelling and having fun. 'Fine, thanks, Brett. Is it OK to talk?'

'Sorry, I'm picking up the kids from soccer practice. Let me walk around the clubhouse to get away from the racket. Hang on for a moment.'

Once the noise abated sufficiently, Brett spoke. 'That should be better. What can I do for you, Ange?'

'Remember that painting that we've been looking into? Well, I saw its doppelganger today, hanging on the wall of Ethan Tedesco's luxury apartment in Point Piper.'

Brett whistled before commenting. 'Wow, Point Piper is expensive territory. How did the painting look?'

'Impressive. There's no way that I could tell whether it was a fake. It might be. I don't know.'

'What are you thinking?' asked Brett.

'Could you turn up the heat on that mob in Singapore where Eddie Falconi had his artwork stored? I guess it wouldn't be good for business for the market to hear that they played a part in Falconi's two-card trick, which is my strong suspicion.'

'Sure thing. The kids finish at 6 p.m., so I should be home by 6:30 p.m. Singapore is a few hours behind us, so I might catch someone still at work. By memory, there were some contact details on the signature block of the email sent by the administrator.'

'Great, Brett. Thanks.' Ange looked at her own watch and saw that it wasn't yet 6 p.m. 'So how are things otherwise?'

'OK, I guess. The move back to Sydney has been a bit of a culture shock. I'd gotten used to being my own man and marching to my own tune. I'd also forgotten how busy it is, juggling work and family.' Brett's voice trailed off, perhaps signalling this admission had been a step too far.

'That's good, Brett. Speak to you later on, then. I'm not doing anything this evening, so ring me as soon as you have news from Singapore,' said Ange in a somewhat clipped tone. Brett had opened the can of worms and exposed a gaping hole in her life, one progressively slipping out of reach. She would love to be in Brett's shoes right now—with kids, that is—guiding them through a busy life and being part of their noisy journey. With that depressing thought, Ange closed her computer and gathered her things. She called down to Billy's floor to say goodbye, but he was on the phone and engrossed in his computer screens. Ange waved a distant goodbye from the foyer. Before the lift doors closed, Ange glanced aroun d the office floor. There were still several people hard at work.

'Is this the extent of my life?' she thought in a moment of self-pity. Her call to Brett had left her feeling that life might slip through her fingers, consumed by a thankless job. She picked up a ready-made meal-for-one at the supermarket on the way to her apartment. At least the ever-reliable Harry Bosch was on standby.

Brett rang back before she even had time to heat her meal. 'Hi, Ange. I spoke to a guy at the Singapore Freeport facility. He gave his title as director of operations. Looking past the fact that they help people hide things and avoid taxes, they're an impressive operation. They were one step ahead. After my previous enquiries, they had commissioned an authenticity analysis themselves. He's going to send it to me. I'll forward it to you once it arrives.'

'But couldn't that just be a self-serving report to keep their reputation intact?' asked Ange.

'I asked the same thing. The director told me they simply cannot afford to gain a reputation for dealing in forgeries and counterfeit goods. As soon as I had raised my initial concerns, they sent the painting to their sister facility in Switzerland. Apparently, they use a cutting-edge firm to do their work. On top of the usual colour, paint and canvas analyses, the firm uses sophisticated artificial intelligence to analyse brushstrokes and painting techniques. The director said that they were ninety-nine percent sure of its authenticity. That such a firm even exists shows that forgery is a big problem in the world of fine art.'

'So where is the painting now?' asked Ange, with a sudden sinking feeling that she would lose this part of the trail.

'On its way back to Singapore. I know what you're thinking, but I think it's safe. Getting it out of the Freeport means dealing with customs and border controls. It would be hard to do that without proper authority.'

Ange relaxed somewhat at that news. She took in a sharp, deep breath before continuing. 'OK. Thanks. I hope that the new authenticity report will be enough to secure a court order to access Tedesco's apartment and retrieve his copy.'

'Where are you going with this, Ange? How does knowing that Tedesco owns a fake piece of art help us?' asked Brett.

'I know that it's not illegal to be duped by your mate Eddie Falconi. However, it will give us a licence to dig into that transaction and probe the flow of money. If Tedesco is involved in the syndicate, then this will surely rattle him, maybe even shake him off his rarefied perch. Who knows what will happen? He might do something stupid,' replied Ange. She heard a woman yelling in the background.

'OK. I see where you're going. Ring me tomorrow if you need anything else. I've got to go. Dinner. Catch you later,' he said, hanging up.

Ange looked at her stone-cold meal and thought, 'Nice for some, having a home-cooked meal prepared for you, shared around the dinner table with family.' Despite the good news about the painting, her conversation with Brett had left a slightly bitter taste in her mouth, one that even a nice glass of wine could not wash away.

There were so many unanswered questions running around in her head. Falconi appeared to have been siphoning off huge sums of money offshore. Were these funds for his own benefit or for the syndicate's benefit? Why Falconi would go to so much trouble to scam his mate Ethan Tedesco was another mystery. Perhaps the rumours of his financial stress had been true, and he'd needed some actual cash to tide him over and maintain his lavish lifestyle? Then again, maybe it was a simple case of one-upmanship, a demonstration of who was the smartest and more cunning A-lister? In her experience, the motives of criminals to do what they did could usually be distilled down to ego, greed or necessity—sometimes a little of all three.

Fortunately, Harry Bosch and his desperate troubles carried Ange away from her own, temporarily at least. Collapsing solo in a cold bed brought them rushing back again, rudely disrupting her hopes for a restful sleep. It was another long night.

# Chapter 33

# Closing Ranks

The authentication report, when it arrived mid-morning, was a solid piece of work. Ange felt sure that they could secure a suitable court order once she had her hands on the Christies valuation. She reasoned that Tedesco's version of the valuation would be a facsimile, just like his painting. The Swiss authentication report made for interesting reading, and she was in no doubt that they had analysed the real thing.

Ange went for a walk to think all this through. The only theory that made sense to her was that Falconi had commissioned the forgery, sold the fake to Tedesco, and then kept the original for himself. This didn't implicate Tedesco in any illegal activity. Based on their interview, Tedesco patently believed his painting was the original. If Tedesco and Falconi had been doing any illegal business together, then selling a fake to Tedesco would be a breathtaking move by Falconi. If it wasn't so serious, it would be funny.

And then there was the fact that Tedesco controlled StudioBuzz. If the world of fine art was mysterious and opaque, the world of cryptocurrency and NFTs seemed like a black hole. Somehow, attacking through this door seemed much more difficult and uncertain. By the time Ange had returned to her desk, double-shot flat white in hand, she had resolved to spend the day following the only concrete lead she had—the forged artwork.

An application to secure a court order to seize the painting from Tedesco's palatial home would need to be signed off on by Sally Anders. Ange rang her phone on the off chance. It went straight through to her voicemail. Ange didn't bother leaving a message, instead walking over to speak with Peter Fredericks.

'Hi, Peter. Do you know when the boss is due back? I just tried her phone. It went straight to voicemail.'

Peter looked up from his desk. 'Tomorrow. I assume first thing. You won't get her today. She's with the bigwigs and politicians. What's up? Anything I can help with?'

'I need her signature on a court order. I'll get it ready today and ask her to sign it first thing tomorrow.'

'What's it about?'

Ange surmised that any need for secrecy was over. Seeking a court order would end all that. Nonetheless, she moved closer to Fredericks and lowered her voice. 'I want to seize a painting from the home of Ethan Tedesco. I'm certain it's a forgery. What's even more interesting is that he purchased it from Eddie Falconi.'

'Wow,' said Fredericks, now fully engaged in the conversation. 'How do you know he purchased the painting from Falconi?'

'He told me himself when Billy and I visited him yesterday at his apartment at Point Piper.'

'What led you to Ethan Tedesco? How did you know he had the painting in the first place?'

'Blind luck, really. The administrator uncovered the painting as part of Falconi's estate. Then I noticed the same painting in a photo that Billy's girlfriend had taken. She was working at Tedesco's place as part of some event,' said Ange to explain this good fortune.

'Boy, that really was a stroke of luck,' commented Fredericks wistfully. 'ET's a big wheel around town. You'll need to be careful that he doesn't run you over. Make sure you dot your i's and cross your t's on the court order, Ange.'

'I hear you,' said Ange before she walked back to her office.

Once she had completed drafting the court order, Ange spent several hours learning all that she could about forging art. She concluded that Falconi's scam would be relatively easy to execute if you had the original in your possession. There were plenty of talented yet struggling artists who would be happy to create such a forgery, one that would be almost indistinguishable from the original.

This, in itself, was not necessarily illegal. There could be valid reasons for the owner to commission a copy to display while keeping the original safe. The art of commissioning duplicate copies of expensive jewellery, which the owner might wear to avoid the risk of loss or damage, was its own industry. Making a copy of the valuation and placing it alongside the forged artwork was child's play. It seemed like an easy trick to pull off.

Falconi's was an exceptionally devious and clever scam, but his motives were not clear. The most plausible explanation was that Falconi really was under financial pressure and needed the money, but had been unwilling to part with a beloved painting. Ange had once read an interview with a high-profile business identity who had gone bust in dramatic fashion. That fallen star had lamented that losing his artwork was the most painful part of his collapse. Whatever the reason, it would be spectacular if Ange could prove that the victim of this sting, Ethan Tedesco, was also his partner in crime. She also reasoned that Eddie Falconi was unlikely to have restricted his treachery solely to the realm of expensive fine art, and it seemed quite plausible that Falconi was killed because he was a double-crosser or skimmer, not simply because the police were on his tail.

Ange walked to work on Wednesday and threw a change of clothes in a backpack. The direct route might have been quicker, but she had heard or read somewhere that taking a fresh path was great stimulation for the mind, something that was always welcome. Her winding trail passed through the somewhat gentrified Kings Cross, once the epicentre for organised crime in Sydney through the 1960s and '70s. She imagined what it must have been like to be a detective during that lawless period in history, when police and organised crime had gone into business together.

After she had found her way through the labyrinth that was Woolloomooloo, she crossed Hyde Park and strode down Bathurst Street to her office building. It was hard to imagine that another word existed with more o's than Woolloomooloo, and Ange was still rolling that wonderfully symmetrical name around her tongue, making inappropriate rhymes and ditties in her head, when she arrived at her office floor.

She saw that Sally Anders was already ensconced in her office and decided to strike immediately. She retrieved the court order from her own office and went over to get her boss's signature. Sally looked stressed.

'I didn't realise that dress-down Friday had moved to Wednesday,' said Anders, looking Ange up and down.

'Nothing you haven't seen before, boss,' said Ange lightly. Anders looked as tight as a drum. Ange pushed on with the object of her visit. 'I wanted your signature on a court order to retrieve a painting from the home of Ethan Tedesco.'

Anders looked up sharply and stopped whatever she had been doing. 'Fill me in, Detective.'

Ange gave her the full rundown on how she had arrived at her conclusions, ending her chronology with, 'And that's why I want this court order, boss.'

Anders had listened impassively to the story before speaking. 'And all of this has happened while I was in Canberra?'

'We caught a lucky break with Billy's girlfriend, for sure,' observed Ange.

'OK. Let me read this over and I'll see what I can do. I hope you haven't mentioned the syndicate?'

'I referred to Eddie Falconi as a *person of interest, now deceased*. You may get quizzed on that and need to disclose Falconi's name, but I can't see how that's relevant given the value of the painting and the evidence that I've put together,' answered Ange.

'Nothing would surprise me with that investigation,' said Anders before elaborating on the source of her tension. 'What really riles me is that I copped a total grilling in Canberra about our record of dealing with organised crime. It was all that I could do to hold myself and keep my temper in check. This thing with Falconi, and now Tedesco, is a perfect example of how things work in this town.'

Ange smiled at the thought of an incandescent Sally Anders in full flight. 'I would have enjoyed seeing you spit the dummy at those guys. Have the usual suspects already warned you off Tedesco?'

'Not yet, but I can sense that pressure is about to come raining down on us from up high. You watch,' said Sally Anders with a grim and fixed look in her eye. Ange could almost feel the raindrops falling.

That sobering reminder on the way the world worked triggered Ange to broach the other warning shot fired across her bow. 'Boss, can you wait for a moment? I need to get something from my office. Do you mind if I grab Billy? I think he needs to hear this as well.'

She hastened to her office and retrieved the mystery envelope, now carefully stored in a clear plastic ziplock bag, before popping down to Billy's floor. She almost needed to forcibly drag him away from whatever he was doing on his computer, such was his level of focus. The pair filed into Anders' office.

'I found this letter in my mailbox on Saturday.' She handed it over to her boss.

Anders looked at the front and back before stating the obvious. 'No postage stamp, writing or identifying marks. What's inside?'

'A single photo of me, taken at Bondi Beach a few weeks back. I remember exactly when it was taken and who took it. Well, not exactly their name and address, but enough to know that he wasn't a photographer for *Surfing Life* magazine.' Ange then told the story of that day and described what she knew and what she thought. 'This is clearly a warning message that tells us three things. One, that they're watching, and two, they know where I live, and three, that they were brazen enough to slip the envelope into my mailbox without mailing it.'

Billy entered the fray. 'It could be an admirer...'

'That's very kind, Billy, but I'm inclined to go with a warning. But your point is relevant. The way that this was done could always be passed off as a compliment, rather than a threat.'

'I agree with Ange. This is concerning. It would be a brazen move to lean so overtly on a detective at Major Crimes. Then again, who knows what might happen once we turn up the heat? You need to be careful, Ange. You live alone, right?'

Anders waited for Ange to nod her answer before continuing, 'I don't think you should remain in your flat, at least for a while. We can put you up in a serviced apartment we keep nearby. Billy, can you accompany Ange back to her place right now and pick up enough stuff for at least a week? Take a car from downstairs. I'll get the apartment organised. Things might get messy if we turn up the heat on Tedesco and he's in bed with the wrong people. If he's innocent and it fizzles, then all we've lost is a few days' rental. Send the photo to forensics and get it checked for fingerprints, but I seriously doubt we'll find anything.'

Ange and Billy looked hesitant. Anders waved them away. 'Go on. Off you go. This is not a negotiation. You can collect your court order when you return.'

The pair walked out of the office and made for the lift. 'Boy, that conference in Canberra sure put the willies up the boss,' murmured Billy. Ange was about to agree with him when her phone rang. Glancing down, she saw the caller was Gus Bell.

'Hi, Gus. What's up?' answered Ange.

'Hi, Ange. I'm coming to Sydney for a few days and wanted to see if you were free to catch up for dinner on the weekend sometime. I'm down attending a sporting goods conference and I'm looking for some pleasant diversions.'

'I would love to, Gus. Let me just see what I have on,' replied Ange, genuinely excited about the prospect of putting her work aside for an evening. She checked the diary on her phone before confirming. 'I'm sure Saturday night will be OK, but please don't take it personally if I need to cancel. Things are crazy here right now.'

'Great,' said Gus. 'I understand with work. I'll book something and text you the details. Is 7:30 p.m. fine for you?'

'Perfect. See you Saturday night,' replied Ange before hanging up. This was a pleasant surprise indeed.

## Chapter 34

# Deciding What's Important

Billy double-parked and waited in the car outside, amusing himself on his phone while Ange hastily assembled a selection of clothes and personal items into a wheeled suitcase and duffle bag. She looked wistfully at her surfboards stuck in the corner. Her resplendent JayTee shortboard might forget how to swim. Who would walk Franky?

She was back at the car inside twenty minutes and loaded her luggage into the boot of the car. About to jump in the passenger seat, she paused and then spoke to Billy. 'Sorry, I forgot something. I'll be back in a second.' She rushed up the stairs and soon returned with Franky under one arm and her wetsuit draped over her shoulder. What followed was an interesting exercise in transport logistics, Franky occupying the entire passenger side of the car and Ange sitting in the rear seat directly behind Billy. They caught some strange looks from other motorists during the drive back to the office.

While Ange manoeuvred Franky this way and that, Billy helped carry her bags up the lift and followed her across the office floor with a distinctly bemused look on his face. Peter Fredericks saw this procession and followed them into Sally Anders' office.

'Are you guys going on a surfing holiday?' asked Fredericks with a wide grin.

'Ange needs to move house for a while,' explained Billy.

'Why?' asked Fredericks.

Anders answered that question. 'A rat infestation. They need to be exterminated before Ange can move back.' She looked at Ange before continuing. 'All our usual places are full. I'm working on some other options. I'll come and get you when I find something suitable.'

'Oh, I forgot to mention, boss. When you were busy in Canberra, I filled Peter in on the basics of the forgery matter. I figured we were past acting coy. The proverbial will hit the fan once we cut this court order loose,' explained Ange.

As Ange and Billy gathered the luggage and made for the door, Anders turned her attention to Fredericks, handing him the signed application for a court order. 'Peter, could you find a magistrate to sign this, please?'

Fredericks scanned the application before speaking. 'Interesting. I'll see what I can do.' He wandered slowly back to his own office, reading the application as he went, in no obvious hurry.

The rest of the day was a waiting game. Ange had a sense that pressure was building, like when a cyclone was coming down the coast, gathering force in the warm waters of the Coral Sea. The wind was whipping up some heavy air, fuelling a hell that was about to break loose.

Despite these feelings of impending chaos, the day ended in a fizzle. Peter still hadn't returned with any signatures on her court order. Anders had found an apartment two blocks away, so Ange eventually drifted out of the office and settled into her temporary digs. The apartment was pleasant enough, perhaps a touch clinical, but it boasted slivered views through the adjoining high-rise buildings and was more spacious that her own low-rise flat.

She was suddenly at a loss and feeling like an itinerant traveller, dislocated and directionless. The bland impersonal decor certainly wasn't helping. At least she could log in to her streaming services on the television. Once she had found some food in the streets downstairs, the ever-dependable Harry Bosch helped restore some sense of familiarity to her existence.

Billy arrived home to find Amber stuffing her stay-over clothes and toiletries into a duffle bag.

'What's going on, Amber?' Billy asked, surprised to find her there.

'I'm so angry with you, Billy. This relationship is done.' Amber's expression of loathing said more than her words had described.

Billy's first thought was that Amber had somehow learned of his weekend spent with Bree, although he failed to see how that would be the case. He felt suddenly guilty, made worse by the knowledge that he had called Bree every day this week, multiple times in fact. 'What do you mean?'

Amber fixed him with a stare so frigid that it caused Billy to shiver within. 'I had a call from my boss at the talent agency. He sacked me on the spot. *Indiscretion* was the word he used. I trusted you with those photos. You promised not to spread them around and now I've lost my job at the talent agency. I really enjoyed that job.'

Billy was both sorry and indignant at the same time. 'I'm sorry that happened. I really am. Only my boss has seen the photos. It was important. How did they blame you for that?'

'Ethan Tedesco complained to the owner of the agency. Apparently, they know each other. Tedesco insisted that I be sacked. My boss made me feel so small and pathetic, like a gold-digger or a celebrity chaser.'

'How did he know it was you?' asked Billy. A sinking feeling was creeping into his voice.

'Two detectives coming around asking questions about some painting. I guess one of those detectives was you, Billy?' said Amber in a deeply sarcastic and accusatory tone.

'I'm not a detective,' was all Billy could say. His mind was racing through the implications of this development. He would need to disclose all this to Ange.

Amber's sarcastic tone showed no sign of letting up. 'Whatever, Billy. Clearly, your job is more important than your relationships.' She went to the bathroom to retrieve a cosmetics bag.

'I still don't understand. How did that come back on you?' asked Billy.

'All the girls knew I was dating a detective. It wasn't hard to work out, was it? I was proud of dating you, Billy, but I can see now that we run in very different circles. It's time for me to move on. Next time, maybe you'll think twice before throwing someone under the bus so recklessly.'

Billy had nothing to add to that assessment. If he was honest, his weekend with Bree had raised questions about his relationship with Amber. Sure, she was beautiful and sexy, but they had little in common—other than a love of sex and socialising. He would miss the sex for sure, but he didn't feel as gutted as he should.

He stood silently until Amber had finished packing. When she was done, she hoisted the duffle bag over her shoulder and turned to give him a peck on the cheek. Stepping back, she dangled her set of keys in front of him before dropping them theatrically into the palm of his hand.

'Catch up later, Billy.'

All Billy could muster was, 'I'm sorry, Amber. Take care.'

And that, as they say, was that.

# Chapter 35

# Poor Timing

Ange paced around the office, waiting for Peter Fredericks to return with the court order. She had rung his phone a bunch of times, but her calls had gone straight through to voicemail. He finally rocked in just after lunchtime, waving the court order as he approached Ange's office.

'I had a devil of a time finding a magistrate who was prepared to sign this. It's not exactly a life-or-death situation. As soon as they read whose house we were targeting, they started asking some tough questions. Anyhow, I finally got it done. Good luck with it,' said Fredericks, dramatically flopping down the document on Ange's desk, as if to underscore his efforts.

Ange scanned the document and checked that everything was in order. 'Thanks, Peter. You're a champion.'

She strode to Billy's desk. 'Hi, Billy, we need to pay your boyfriend another visit. Can you set up an alert for his fleet of cars again? We need to catch him at home. I'll organise something suitable for transporting a large painting. I'm not sure what we'll do with it, but I want to get it in our possession as soon as possible.'

'Sure thing. By the way, Amber broke up with me last night. Apparently, Ethan Tedesco complained about her indiscretion with that photo. Her boss at the talent agency sacked her on the spot. She was very upset with me.'

'That's disappointing, but it also shows that Tedesco is rattled. Are you OK?'

'Yeah, sure. It was never a long-term thing with Amber, but she was fun and I'll miss her company,' replied Billy flippantly, the look on his face suggesting he would miss more than just her company. 'I'll send you a text when ET turns up at his home.'

Ange checked in with Sally Anders before putting this train in motion. 'Hi, boss. Peter has finally gotten the court order signed by a magistrate. Any last words before we pull the trigger?'

Anders was as cool as a cucumber. 'No, Ange. Go for it. Do everything by the book with Tedesco. Take Peter if he's free, otherwise get Billy to accompany you.'

Ange waited around the office, aimlessly shuffling papers and dealing with emails. It was after 6 p.m. when Billy's text came through. Peter Fredericks was nowhere to be seen, so Ange pulled Billy into action and the pair went downstairs to collect the white van that she had organised and drive across town to Point Piper.

'He came home today driving his black AMG Mercedes G Wagon. I don't quite get those cars,' commented Billy. 'ET doesn't strike me as an off-road type of guy, one who likes to rough it in the bush. Those things are fast and imposing. I guess it comes in handy when he needs to project a tough-guy image. I'd take the Lamborghini any day.'

Arriving at Tedesco's apartment block, Ange knew which button to push on the intercom this time around. Tedesco answered in an instant. 'Hello, Detectives. Let me buzz you up. You know the drill.'

Tedesco was waiting in front of the lift when the two officers arrived at his apartment. He looked relaxed and confident, which was not the reaction Ange had been hoping for. She had wanted to find him angry, frustrated and rattled by their intrusion.

Tedesco even reached forward to shake the hands of both officers, not the actions of a guilty or troubled man. Something wasn't right.

'How can I help you?' asked Tedesco, with just the barest hint of a smile veiled behind his question.

Ange held up the court order and handed it over to Tedesco. He showed no intention of reading it, keeping his eyes firmly fixed on hers. 'Tell me what we have here, Detective?'

'We have reason to suspect that your untitled painting by Emily Kngwarreye is a forgery, and the court order permits us to take it for analysis.'

Tedesco turned and walked into the larger sitting room, the one with a view to die for. The painting by Emily was now gone, replaced by an equally bright and impressive Ken Done original of the Sydney Harbour itself. 'I'm sorry, you're just too late. After your visit, I felt the need to get it checked out myself. The painting is on its way to Switzerland for analysis as we speak. I'm sure they will confirm that mine is the original.'

'How is it being shipped?' asked Ange, hoping that they might intercept it.

'My corporate jet was taking some executives for investor briefings in Zurich, so I threw it on board. It's going into storage at a Freeport facility, and they're doing the analysis for me. Do you know what a Freeport is, Detective?'

Ange had no intention of pleasing her smart alec host by expressing any overt signs of disappointment. 'I do. It's where people hide their wealth from the authorities.'

'That's a touch mean. There are lots of legitimate reasons people like me would use professionals to safely store their expensive artwork.'

'I trust you will send me a copy of the report when it arrives?' asked Ange.

Tedesco suddenly seemed intensely interested in the court order that Ange had proffered, reading it carefully whilst the two police officers stood patiently by, becoming more antsy as the minutes ticked over. After Tedesco had painstakingly read it and reread it dramatically, he handed the paper back to Ange. 'I see nothing in this document that would require me to provide you with that documentation. This only refers to collecting the said painting from my address,' he said with a smile, the sincerity of which was confined to his teeth. The message in his eyes, on the other hand, bordered on malevolence, warning Ange that she might regret meddling in his affairs. 'Come visit again if you're lucky enough to secure a second court order, one more appropriately worded.'

There was nowhere for the two police officers to go with that. Ange had no intention of degrading herself by agreeing with Tedesco and reacting to his taunt. She collected the document and turned toward the lift.

'This has been fun,' said Tedesco as they walked away. 'Let's do it again. *Not!*'

As soon as the lift doors closed, it was Billy who vented their frustration first. 'What a tosser. That guy is a total FIGJAM.'

Ange glanced his way. 'What, pray tell, is a FIGJAM, Billy?'

His eyes flashed with distaste. 'It's an acronym for Fuck I'm Good Just Ask Me.'

Despite the gravity of the situation, Ange could not help but smile. 'Sounds like someone has fallen out of love.'

'I wanted so badly to wipe that smug smile off his face,' admitted Billy, his tone of voice confirming that he was no longer an ardent fan of the man.

Ange silently stewed over this depressing development on the drive back to the office. She knew that the painting would arrive at the Freeport facility well before she could mobilise Swiss authorities, even if they were remotely interested. The provenance of an Indigenous Australian painting would hardly be a consequential matter. The tiny landlocked country had forged its economic strength on the reputation as a discreet fortress to keep safe the wealth of others, the source of which seemed less important than the quantum. Sure, international pressures were creating cracks in Switzerland's fortress-like border, but that was a slow-burning battlefront that wouldn't help Ange's cause.

However, the most galling feature of their visit was Ange's sense that Tedesco seemed better informed than he should be. Once more, she felt one step behind, a perpetual condition which had plagued her chase from the outset, going right back to the Namba Heads investigation. Tedesco had known full well about Ange's strategy, and he had comprehensively blown her out of the water.

As soon as Ange and Billy had dropped off the empty van in the car park, they made their way up to the office, shoulders slumped and sullen looks telltale signs of how their visit had gone. Ange was immediately summoned into her boss's office.

'Ange, I told you to do this by the book,' said a stern and grim-faced Sally Anders.

'I did, boss. Every i dotted and t crossed.'

'I just copped fifteen minutes of abuse from the police commissioner. Apparently, she's had a call from the PM's office accusing her of allowing rogue officers to harass prominent business identities. Eddie Falconi's name also came up, and the suggestion was that our harassment caused him to commit suicide.'

Ange couldn't help herself. 'What a crock. Surely you've pushed back on such nonsense?'

That question remained unanswered for the moment. 'I hate being outmanoeuvred, but I hate politics getting in the way even more.'

'Boss, during this entire case, going right back to Namba Heads, I feel that we've always been one step behind. Nothing stacks up. I'm open to the possibility of coincidence, but there are far too many for my liking. What do you want me to do?'

'You've got until the end of next week. If we don't have something concrete to go on, we really need to drop this pursuit. I can dodge and weave until then, but don't step out of your lane. Based on my last conversation, you will get run over and squashed if you stray offline.'

With that depressingly vivid image, Ange walked by Billy's desk to say goodbye before catching the train home. Billy was hard at work. He looked up, his face showing a fixed and determined glare. Like any accomplished tennis player, Billy would hate being bested like that.

'Look at this, boss.' Billy ran through a series of video clips that showed the comings and goings of Tedesco's cars.

'Tedesco comes home in the Lamborghini, driving way too fast, then drives back out in the Mercedes some forty-five minutes later. You can't see through his tinted windows, but I'll bet the painting was in the back of his car. He returns four hours later, ahead of our visit. He knew we were coming for sure.'

'I agree, Billy. He was waiting for us with his script already written.'

'What are we going to do? I don't like being played as a fool. More so when I idolised Tedesco and the entrepreneurial spirit that he stands for.'

'I'm not sure, Billy. Let me sleep on it. Whatever we decide, we only have a few days to execute. The heavens have just opened on the boss, and there's only so much she can do before the dam bursts,' replied Ange, failing to mention that she was standing directly below the dam wall.

## Chapter 36

# All Hell Breaks Loose

Even though her temporary digs were just around the corner from the office, Ange stuck with routine. She packed some clothes in a backpack and walked the super long way into work on Friday: through the city, past the art gallery, then circumnavigating the Botanical Garden, past the Opera House, under the Harbour Bridge to Barangaroo, then sticking to the harbourside through to Darling Harbour, before following Bathurst Street to the office. By the time she had arrived, a dark realisation was forming in her mind about why she was running second in every episode of this case.

Billy texted before she had time to shower and change. It sounded urgent, if such a thing was possible in a text.

*Boss, you need to come and see what's happening!*

Ange visited him and his computer screens straight away.

'What's going on, Billy? You look like someone who's just won the lottery.'

'Look at what's happening to those NFTs.' He pulled up the screen showing the BuzzyBat NFT ownership graphic. He pointed to the Covid-like spike. 'Look what happens to StudioBuzz. This chart was yesterday afternoon.'

He overlaid another screen. 'This was 10 p.m. last night. Look what's happened.'

Ange could see that the Covid spike of StudioBuzz looked like it had eroded slightly, as if it was falling apart.

Billy clicked on another image. 'Now look at the same graph at 7 a.m., when I came in this morning.' Ange could see that StudioBuzz had lost the bulk of its spikey connections.

'Let's update the chart to now.' He clicked on some buttons, instigating a rolling wheel to show that the chart was updating. Once displayed, there were only three spikes coming off StudioBuzz, one of which was Tyler Ball.

'What's going on here, Billy?'

'We've got them on the run. They're pulling back all the NFTs. Our plan worked,' said Billy, as excited as Ange had ever seen him.

'What do you mean by pulling back? Anyway, what plan, Billy?' she said hesitantly.

'The one I told you about the other day. See that new bubble over here, the one coming off Ted Kramer?' replied Billy. He pointed to a small bubble that was connected to Ted Kramer, now deceased. 'That's Bree,' he proclaimed proudly.

'What do you mean, that's Bree? How could that have happened?' she said, a sense of dread growing within.

'I sold one of Ted Kramer's BuzzyBat NFTs to Bree through OpenSea. I wanted to find out what might happen, and it worked. They're spooked. They're trying to pull the BuzzyBat NFTs out of circulation.'

Ange was incandescent. 'Billy, you should have told me about this. Not only might they go to ground, but you might also have put Bree in danger. What made you do this on your own?'

'I didn't do this on my own. I told you about it when we were coming back from Tedesco's apartment. You told me to go for it. If I recall correctly, your exact words were, *I trust you, Billy*.'

Billy's strident defence triggered a vague recollection, and she knew Billy was telling the truth. If anyone was to blame, it was herself for not listening to her colleague.

Billy turned away from his computer and looked quizzically at his boss. 'What do you mean, Bree might be in danger?'

'Use your brains, Billy. Whoever is behind StudioBuzz must be astounded to see Ted Kramer trading NFTs. If my hunch is correct, they also know that Ted Kramer is dead, and that Tyler Ball has probably joined him in the afterlife. They wouldn't have been worried about either of these guys posing a threat. Now, they find that a dead person has traded an NFT to a new entrant. How easy would it be for them to find out she was a police officer? Alternatively, they might think that she was an accomplice of Kramer or Ball and might have information that could hurt them.' Ange paused for a moment, thinking through the implications of this startling development. 'Could they track her from this purchase?'

A grave look spread across Billy's face as he considered Ange's question. 'Yes, I guess they could. Collectors rarely hide away their NFTs like they do with crypto. Part of the fun and attraction is bragging about your collection. Any digital company that trades in NFTs like StudioBuzz would surely have access to software at least as powerful as what I'm using. All Bree would need to do was post one of her NFTs on social media, and it would lead straight to her.'

Ange thought back to one of her earliest conversations with Bree. 'Billy, can you do a scan on social media posts for a CoolCat playing tennis?'

Billy did as Ange requested, and Google did its magic. Bree was on the first page, but under a different name. Constable Breanna White was even more savvy than Ange and Billy had figured, employing an online alias. 'Lily', as in lily white. 'Snow' might have been another more obvious pseudonym, but Lily seemed appropriate. Ange guessed Lily might even be Bree's hockey nickname, yelled out on the field to confound the opposition. Rather than an actual photo, Lily was an avatar of Bree, large glistening eyes staring intently from a lily-white face, framed by dark hair fashioned in a short bob. Bree, aka Lily, looked for the world like a strangely familiar character from a Japanese anime.

Ange immediately pulled out her phone and dialled a number from her favourites list, her old boss in Byron Bay, Sergeant Jim Grady. 'Hi, boss, we've got a problem. I need your help.' Ange then gave Grady the entire story.

'Boss, can you keep an eye on her? Bree's smart, but she's still green. I'm concerned that she might be in danger. She's clever enough to use an online alias, but we just don't know how sophisticated Tedesco and his cronies might be,' concluded Ange.

'She can move in with Barb and me. Barb will enjoy the company. We're rattling around in that house now that the kids have left home. Don't worry, Ange, she'll be fine. I'll tell everyone in the office that she has Covid and needs to isolate. That damned virus must be of some use.'

'Thanks, boss. Appreciate it. Can you jump on it? I have a feeling that this whole affair is about to blow up.'

After she had hung up the call with Grady, Ange turned to her now-worried colleague. 'Billy, come with me. We need to speak with the boss.' Ange turned and strode towards her office with Billy trailing sheepishly behind.

As they approached her office, Sally Anders tried to wave them away. Ange was not so easily dismissed and opened the door, interrupting the call that her boss was on. Interjecting herself like that was not Ange's style, and Anders quickly realised that something was up, dispatching her caller with a sharp, 'Sorry, I need to call you back.'

She turned to Ange. 'What's up?'

Ange gave a more fulsome account of the events that had led to this intrusion, also detailing her last call to Jim Grady.

'OK, Ange, no actual harm done. Billy, that was reckless of you. What were you thinking?'

Billy looked embarrassed. 'Bree and I had been talking about this for a few days, more as a theoretical exercise. When Tedesco roached us like that, I saw red and put the ball in motion. Sorry, I won't do it again.'

Ange pulled him off the hook. 'It's my fault, boss. Billy told me he had a plan, but I wasn't listening properly. I basically gave him a blanket approval.'

Sally Anders sized up both officers before speaking. 'OK. Shit happens. What really matters now is what we're going to do about it.'

'Follow the money, boss,' Ange said without hesitation. 'I'll bet Tedesco is hedging his bets on how far we might have gotten, and any cryptocurrency associated with StudioBuzz is being hived off somewhere safe.'

Ange turned to Billy. 'Billy, your mate Nelson at the tax office. How high up is he?'

'Nelson's in the tech division. He's quite high up for someone my age. He speaks highly of his boss, who's all of thirty-two years old. It's a very young division.'

'Can you see if Nelson can set up a meeting with his boss? Give him a basic heads-up of what it entails.'

'Will do,' replied Billy. 'Is there anything else you want me to do?'

'Do as much research as you can on NFT trades and how easy it might be to trace someone like Bree. We need to know if she really is in danger or if we're overreacting. Let me know when you have the meeting set up with your friend at the tax office,' said Sally Anders.

As Ange and Billy turned to leave her office, Anders had one last directive. 'Can we keep these latest developments between us three for the moment? I'm probably jumping at shadows, but I'm sick and tired of being second-guessed.'

Back at her desk, Ange pondered this latest development. As it stood, she hadn't assembled any hard evidence against Tedesco. In a rare moment of self-doubt, she wondered briefly if she was already too old for this new world order. Hopefully, criminals remained basically the same, no matter how they plied their trade.

# Chapter 37

# New Addresses

Ange took a wander down along the harbourside before heading back to her apartment. Billy had organised a meeting with Nelson and his boss at 9 a.m. on Monday. The walk home helped Ange think more constructively about the day. Wracked by guilt that she might have inadvertently placed Bree in peril with her own lack of attention, she resolved to stay on the offensive with Tedesco.

Her phone buzzed with an incoming call.

'Hi, Bree. Is everything OK?'

'I'm fine, Ange. It feels weird staying with my boss. Barbara is so nice, also a much better cook than I am. Anyhow, something strange has just happened.'

'How strange? Tell me.'

'Billy rang me to make sure I purged my social media profiles. He wanted me to double-check for any obvious clues that link me to my usual OpenSea profile. Something strange happened when I logged into my account,' replied Bree.

'How strange?'

'Well, I received an offer to purchase an NFT, one showing a bumblebee dressed in drag. It was weird. It might be nothing, but that was the first time that someone had ever marketed to me like that on OpenSea. I didn't recognise the vendor, but it looked legitimate. It's probably nothing, but I thought it worth letting you know.'

'Thanks. I really can't see any significance, but I'll discuss it with Billy. Keep your head down for a few days, at least until we get a sense of where this is going.'

Still walking, she rang Billy. When he picked up the call, she could hear from the background noise that he was still in the office.

'Hi, Billy. I hear you contacted Bree and told her to check her social media accounts. That was good thinking. Did she tell you about the strange offer she received on OpenSea?'

'No. What offer?' Billy replied.

'The offer to buy a bumblebee NFT.'

'She didn't click on the image, did she?' asked Billy, with a sudden sharp edge to his voice.

'I don't know. Let's ask her. Why do you ask?'

'I've been reading about the finer points of NFT security protocols. I found out that there's a vulnerability that can be exploited on OpenSea. Exploited in lots of places, actually. Someone who knows what they're doing can create a phishing NFT that swipes a user's IP address.'

'Hold up, Billy, what does that mean and why would this be a problem for Bree?'

'If you know an IP address, it's pretty easy to identify a location,' replied Billy.

'What do you mean? If someone skimmed her IP address, then they would know where she is?'

'Well, not precisely. More like her general location. Only the internet service provider can identify her exact address, but the person would have to hack the ISP to get it, which as you can imagine would be difficult to do.'

'So, let's assume that her IP address has been skimmed. That means whoever posted that bumblebee NFT now knows that Bree is in Byron, but not exactly where she's staying. Correct?'

'That's right. She should be OK, particularly after cleansing her profile and social media posts of any information that might easily identify her. We still should tell her, though.'

'Let me join her on this call.'

Ange stopped and sat down on a rock wall on the water's edge and added Bree to the call. It rang for a disconcertingly long time before Bree finally answered. Given that she was sort of in hiding on account of being watched, she looked around to check that nobody could overhear her conversation.

'Hi, Ange. I was just speaking to the boss. He's keeping me busy. What's up?'

'Hi, Bree. I have Billy on the line. That NFT that was messaged to you—did you click on the image?'

'Yes, I did. It was OK, but not especially clever or something that I was interested in. Why do you ask?'

Billy answered Bree's question. 'It could have been a phishing NFT to skim your IP address. There's a vulnerability on OpenSea that I found out about. It's too coincidental that you received that offer directly after transacting the BuzzyBat. We should assume that they know your general location.'

A thought had formed in Ange's mind while Billy was speaking. She verbalised her theory. 'If it is what we think it is, then it probably means that they haven't identified you, so that would be a positive. Bree, you should be extra careful until we work out what to do next.'

'But surely we can use this to our advantage, perhaps lay a trap?' suggested Bree.

'Let's not get ahead of ourselves, Bree. We need to think this through for a bit. I'll get back to you,' said Ange. 'Keep your wits about you, Bree. Billy, can you stay on the call?

Ange and Billy waited until Bree had left the call. 'I like her style,' said Billy, clearly impressed with Bree's chutzpah. 'I need to work through how we might leverage this development. I'll do some more research. Leave it with me over the weekend.'

The intense melee of the week had put her date with Gus Bell in the background of her frenetic thoughts. Bree was safely in the care of Jim Grady, and there was nothing she could do about Tedesco until Monday. Ange suddenly found herself quite excited by the evening's prospects. Gus texted mid-morning to say that he had made a reservation at a Turkish restaurant in Surry Hills. She searched the restaurant on her phone and saw that it looked casual and relaxed.

Since taking on her new job with its higher pay packet, Ange had noticed her bank account was growing faster than usual. At this rate, she might need to consider seeking some investment advice. She recalled Ada from the Gold Coast and her disdain for an investment scammer with the clever nickname of the Pyramid Man. Instead, she opted to invest in a new outfit. Pulling on a cap and sunglasses, she headed downstairs to wander through the city stores, credit card in hand. It took a while to conjure up her shopping mojo, but she eventually became the proud owner of a new dress and sandals, perfect for the summer ahead.

By the time she made it to the restaurant that evening, Gus was already seated in the corner. He stood up as she entered the room. 'Hi, Ange. You look fantastic,' he greeted her with a wide smile, genuine appreciation shining in his eyes.

'Thanks, Gus. I took in some retail therapy today. You look very urbane yourself.'

'I try to get to Sydney as often as I can, so I have a few pieces that don't require board shorts to complete the ensemble,' replied Gus, his smile growing. 'Actually, my dad sent me to boarding school down here, so I have lots of friends from that time.'

They sat down, and he poured her a glass of wine from an already opened bottle. Ange noticed he had chosen a quality Riesling from Clare Valley in South Australia. She wondered if that was coincidence or if he had remembered her preference in white wine from their last rendezvous.

'Me and my brothers went to boarding school in Armidale, which wasn't all that far afield from Tamworth. I boarded at NEGS. My parents also boarded in Armidale. They met at an interschool dance, in fact. Why Sydney? Wouldn't Brisbane have been closer and more affordable?' asked Ange.

'Probably, but like you, my father had gone to the same school, and his father before that. Dad insisted he squandered his education to become a bum surfer, and he wanted me to have an equal chance at squandering mine.'

'I would hardly call becoming a global sporting icon a squandered opportunity,' replied Ange. 'Anyhow, you seem to have taken the business to another level.'

'I suppose some things stuck. The business degree gave me a decent grounding in the basics. Anyhow, it's looking as if the old-school tradition may come to a grinding halt with me.'

'Tell me about that. I'm surprised you haven't married. Before you start, I'm certainly not one to judge. My relationships represent a series of almighty train wrecks.' It was a bit freaky that Gus was having similar thoughts over lost family traditions.

'I'll take that as a compliment, but it's a situation entirely of my making.'

'There are way too many options to interpret that response, Gus. You'll need to explain that further.'

'Well, being the son of a surfing legend, in Byron Bay of all places, was quite beguiling for an impressionable young guy. This resulted in a carousel of beautiful girls and shallow relationships. By the time I realised I was the town playboy, I was mid-thirties and strangely lonely. It made me reconsider what I was looking for.

I've been much more cautious and discerning since I woke up. I shouldn't be too hard on myself; most men don't grow up before they reach thirty. It just took me longer than usual.'

'I can't believe that there wasn't somebody riding the carousel who ticked the right boxes.'

'There was one girl who had it all, but I was stupid and taking my role as the local playboy too seriously. She eventually saw through me. Evie married a lawyer in Melbourne, where they have three children. Anyhow, enough about my disasters—what about the gorgeous Angela Watson? I'm sure your dance card remains full to the brim.'

'Funny. I haven't heard that expression since I left Tamworth. I somehow seem to always pick the wrong guys,' replied Ange with a wry smile.

'What about that surfer you were seeing from the north coast?'

'That was a pity. His children and former wife came back into play. I'm not bitter about that. He probably made the right choice in his family. It was lovely being able to share my passion for surfing, but I've definitely moved on,' lied Ange, neglecting to mention her occasional early-morning and late-night yearnings.

After those mutual disclosures, the evening blended into a series of stimulating conversations. Before they knew it, they were the last pair left seated in the restaurant. Ange had always found Gus extremely attractive but had always considered him off limits. As they hugged goodbye beside Ange's Uber, they promised to do this again as soon as time and circumstance would allow.

As she had drifted off to sleep after her lovely and stimulating evening with Gus, Ange had resolved to take a rare Sunday sleep-in. Unfortunately, the glaring Australian summer sun could inflict insomnia on even the most accomplished sleepyhead, so she was up early. She instinctually checked the surf forecast. Although the outlook for decent waves was bleak, the weather was warm and sunny. The beach beckoned.

Following her disconcerting photo shoot at Bondi Beach, she needed to stay well clear of the Eastern Suburbs. She studied a map of Sydney and decided that Manly looked nice. Stuffing a wetsuit and some beach gear into a backpack, she grabbed Franky and headed downstairs, making a beeline for Circular Quay and the ferry terminal. Cap pulled down over sunglasses and trying to stay under the radar, she felt self-conscious walking through the CBD, so she jumped onboard a light rail train heading in the right direction. It was still early, and she hid herself in a corner of an almost empty carriage, using Franky as a shield from any prying eyes.

Once at Circular Quay, she found a seat to enjoy some coffee and wait for the Manly Ferry. She was not the only crazy person, as a couple of other surfers turned up, lucky ones with a partner to keep them company. What a fantastic ferry trip it was, around the Sydney Opera House and out to the Manly peninsula. Sydney Harbour was at its splendiferous best, a genuine jewel in Sydney's crown. As Ange came abreast the Bradley's Head lighthouse and the ferry made its slow turn towards the northeast, she glanced south and scanned the Point Piper skyline. Her gaze settled on what she felt to be Ethan Tedesco's apartment block, and she imagined him sitting way up in the sky, enjoying the view from his lavish penthouse, a smug smile slapped on his face, perhaps sipping a cappuccino made by his maid, or mistress, or whatever Pham was. Even the picturesque journey across the North Harbour failed to extinguish her fiery thoughts of Tedesco.

Alighting at the Manly Ferry terminal, Ange followed her fellow surfing commuters and traipsed the five-hundred-odd metres eastward toward the surfing beach. The surf report had been spot on. Whatever waves rolled in were bunched up close together, patchy and insipid courtesy of the north-easterly wind of the past few days. The water looked nice, so Ange took advantage of the splendid day and wandered north along the sandy beach. It was some beach, a gently curving bay defined by a line of majestic Norfolk Pines. She loved those pines, an enduring symbol of the beach and holidays with her family. She was standing admiring the view when a passing couple paused their Sunday stroll to tell Ange that the Norfolk pines of Manly Beach were the oldest specimens on the Australian mainland. There was no rush to hit the surf, so Ange chatted with the couple for a few minutes, taking advantage of the opportunity to seek a locals' view of where to find the best fish and chips. Lunch plans settled, Ange left the couple to their walk and kept wandering north until she came to something that resembled a passable break.

Despite the sunny warm day, the water stubbornly held on to winter's chill. Ange's wetsuit was bittersweet, the black neoprene doing a superb job of keeping her comfortable when in the water, but also soaking up the sun's rays when she was sitting on her board waiting patiently for a rare wave. To avoid overheating, Ange was frequently forced overboard for a swim.

The swell interval, that measurement of time between peaks, was a paltry seven seconds. An interval of fourteen or fifteen seconds would have been more to her liking, when deep troughs separated larger peaks and swells carried larger volumes of water. At seven seconds, the waves were stacked up against each other, sometimes even doubling up. All too often, she paddled around chasing a prospective swell that was heading her way, only to find it diminishing in a poorly formed double-up. What rideable waves she caught were mostly weak and from the north. Nonetheless, it was still lovely being out in the water, admiring the view of the headlands north and south and their undoubtedly expensive real estate, then looking back towards the beach and its ring of majestic Norfolk pines.

As Ange was towelling off on the beach, she recalled one wave that had made the trip worthwhile. She had spotted the swell coming when it was some two hundred metres away, peaking above all others. After a series of false alarms, double-ups that had amounted to nothing, she had almost not bothered paddling into position. Once she had a clear line of sight, she could see that the wave was angled slightly from the north, pinching it up against the sandbank she was surfing on. Her first instinct, on account of the swell angle, was to paddle into position for the left-hander, but she was itching for a forehand after her succession of weak, lifeless lefts. Only chest height, the wave reared up as it hit the sandbank, almost catching her off guard. She jumped to her feet and quickly turned Franky to the right, staying high on the wave face to avoid any possibility of being caught flat-footed and stalling. By all reasoning, the wave should have closed out. However, the combination of swell angle and a tapering shoulder meant the ride became an exhilarating drag race. Ange's heart sung as she sped across the wave face, narrowly avoiding being crunched onto the shallow sandbank.

It had been a cracking ride, and as she pulled out, she looked around to see if anyone had seen her performance, perhaps one of the best waves on the entire stretch of beach. Nobody had. Nobody had been even remotely interested in her ten seconds of glory. Surfing was mostly like that, a solitary sport, selfish even, but it was always fun to share your experiences with someone else. Not today. As she stood soaking up the sun, she thought of Higgsy and her surfing buddies on the Gold Coast, then Brett Tompkins and the terrific waves that they had shared.

Perhaps Gus Bell might develop into the surfing buddy she craved. It would be much more fun to be standing there with some friends, sharing tales of their rides of the day.

In fact, in between waves, Ange had thought a great deal about Gus Bell that day. She couldn't fathom why he'd always been considered off limits while she was living in Byron Bay. He seemed so urbane and together; she had just assumed he had a stunning wife and a loving family around him. Gus was definitely food for thought.

Before heading back to the city, she sought the recommended fish and chip shop and enjoyed some lunch under a large Norfolk pine. In her mind, enjoying the outdoors and the majesty of the sea was reward enough, but the ocean sparkled more brilliantly when you mastered your craft and put together some good rides, even if only one. It was amazing how much fun a girl could have with a transit card and her faithful beaten-up old surfboard.

Despite a lingering sense of loneliness, Ange arrived back at her apartment mid-afternoon, tired and satisfied with her day. If nothing else, the day trip had restored her energy levels ahead of what promised to be a busy week.

# Chapter 38

# The Tax Office

Sally Anders rolled into the office on at 8:30 a.m. and collected Billy and Ange for their Monday morning meeting at the tax office. As the three waited for their lift to arrive, she looked around the office and appraised her colleagues, wondering if any of these might feed information to Tedesco and his cronies. This was something she needed to deal with; otherwise, they would perpetually run second in any race concerning their quarry. She rolled various strategies around in her mind during their journey across to the tax office. Billy and Ange knew to leave her alone when she was in such a preoccupied state.

As in many modern buildings, no receptionist greeted their arrival, only a barren foyer bereft of all personality, perhaps appropriate for a tax office. Billy offered to text his mate Nelson, who soon appeared from somewhere in the bowels of the office. After initial hellos and introductions, Nelson led them into a large meeting room, where three people were grouped around a large oblong table.

Nelson made the introductions. 'Let me introduce Sam Cooper, my boss. Sam, this is my friend Billy Bassett, Detective Angela Watson, and Senior Detective Sally Anders from Major Crimes.'

Sam Cooper shook their hands and then turned towards the other two people in the room. 'Since we're talking crypto and international matters, I took the liberty of inviting Detective Cam Paulson and Detective Caroline Russo from the federal police. Our investigations seem to cut across each other more and more frequently.'

Everyone shook hands and seated themselves around the large boardroom table. Sam Cooper opened the discussion. 'Nelson hasn't provided us with any details, so can you fill us in?'

Sally Anders replied. 'We're trying to understand how we might track a large sum of money held in cryptocurrency that was earned illicitly. We have strong suspicions that it will soon be moved offshore—if not already.'

'With crypto, there really is no such thing as offshore,' Sam Cooper responded. 'Provided it stays in crypto, there's little that we can do. The only chance we have is when it's exchanged for another currency. Legislation to report activity covers the major exchanges, and we can ask for any taxes due then. Before that, it's expensive and almost impractical to track.'

'But what about if they exchange it offshore? Wouldn't that get around the issue?' asked Ange.

Caroline Russo jumped in to answer those questions. 'Not really. The problem isn't confined to Australia, and most jurisdictions have brought in similar protections. Australia has tax treaties or agreements with most major countries, but there are still plenty of loopholes to exploit.'

'So, where would you go to exchange your crypto fortune for cash?' asked Ange.

'Definitely Portugal,' replied Russo without hesitation, then adding, 'Perhaps North Africa, if I was desperate.'

'Why Portugal?' asked Sally Anders.

'It's not as if Portugal is acting as a tax haven or anything—it's just that they've been slow to pass legislation. They have plans to bring in laws to close this loophole, but until then, it would be my pick. Portugal is a major country with a strong financial reputation. Money passed through Portugal isn't viewed with the same level of suspicion as, say, Morocco or one of the tax havens,' explained Russo.

'So basically, anyone suitably organised can cash in their chips and hide them away, and there's little or nothing that we can do about it?' concluded Anders, not hiding her obvious frustration.

'That's basically it. Unless, of course, we can first ping them for illegal activity in Australia,' replied Russo. She appraised the three detectives from Major Crimes before asking, 'So, I guess the fact that Major Crimes is involved suggests sizeable sums of money? Who exactly are we worried about here?'

Nelson jumped in before anyone could answer. 'I didn't think it was my place to disclose who you were looking into.'

A flicker of respect showed in Sally Anders before she answered. 'We have concerns that a fellow called Ethan Tedesco has been front and centre of a major and sophisticated narcotics importation and distribution syndicate. You might have heard of him—goes by the somewhat trite nickname of ET.'

The two federal detectives glanced at each other, something that wasn't lost on Sally Anders. 'What was that look about? Are you guys also investigating Tedesco?'

The two federal detectives looked at each other again, holding gaze for an extended period, before Cam Paulson answered. 'Not specifically. His father, Eric Tedesco, has been on our radar for a while.'

'Doesn't surprise me. You do know that he was in my sights some years ago, before he called in some favours from his mates and slithered away?' commented Anders, her loss of face in that incident obvious.

'No, I wasn't aware of that. What was that about?' asked Paulson.

'It was a pretty basic case of intimidation over some building contracts. Our case progressively withered away once Tedesco and his business mates started leaning on our witnesses, not to mention the political pressure that our investigation suffered. If you are looking into Eric Tedesco, don't underestimate the clout he carries in the big end of town,' explained Anders with furrowed brow and pinched mouth. 'Tell me. Exactly why has that snake been on your radar? I would dearly love you to straighten out his forked tongue.'

'He fits a certain profile that we've been interested in,' replied Paulson evasively.

Sally Anders was having none of that. 'What sort of profile? The venomous type?' she asked, opting to stick with her reptilian references.

'Having a Calabrian surname is one factor.'

'Really? How so?' pressed Ange.

'You might have heard about the Ndrangheta mafia families?' explained Paulson.

'How do you spell that?' asked Ange.

'N-d-r-a-n-g-h-e-t-a. The word is a mouthful unless you speak Italian. It's even harder to spell,' replied Paulson.

'Oh, them. Weren't they in the news recently?' observed Billy.

'Correct. We have a task force focussed on the Ndrangheta. They've infiltrated almost every level of Australian society. What makes them especially difficult is their discipline at staying under the radar. They rarely make the mistake of drawing any attention to their wealth.'

Caroline Russo had been fiddling with her phone during Paulson's brief explanation. She looked up to speak to the others. 'Eric Tedesco ticks all the boxes, but his son, Ethan, doesn't really seem to fit the profile for Ndrangheta. He seems far too high-profile to me. By the way, in case you're wondering, Russo is also a Calabrian surname.'

Billy's observation made everyone stop and think for a moment. 'Perhaps in the world of tech entrepreneurs, where brashness and being high profile is part of the game, then Ethan Tedesco fits the profile perfectly. It's just a different perspective, I suppose. In fact, he's one of the more discreet tech wunderkinds.'

'So, how do you track them down?' asked Ange.

'Once we have our sights on someone, we use websites like Ancestry to trace genealogical lines. Extremely strong familial links are a key characteristic of the Ndrangheta, hence why I'm involved. They're exceptionally ruthless but also incredibly secretive, never hesitating to sever any weak links. One is either in or out of the Ndrangheta family, and when I say out, I really mean dead. You need to be careful if you cross swords with them,' explained Russo, the seriousness of her warning clearly displayed in her facial expression.

'What about the surname Falconi? Is that Calabrian as well?' ask Ange.

'I presume you're referring to the guy who committed suicide on the Gold Coast a few months back. I remember having the same thought myself. Falconi is not one of the big and common names, but it originates from southern Italy. So, yes, I would say it's plausibly a Calabrian surname. But that guy also had a high profile, so I didn't think too deeply about him being Ndrangheta,' replied Russo, showing herself as someone who had her finger on the pulse.

'Presumably, going by how you describe the Ndrangheta ethos, they would eliminate anyone caught skimming or double-crossing.'

'Correct,' replied Russo succinctly. 'Going by your question, I gather Falconi was playing those games.'

'You bet he was. So, if Tedesco is part of the Ndrangheta, then I suppose he wouldn't need to be in Portugal himself. A family member could make the trades if they had access to the cryptocurrency, couldn't they?' asked Anders.

'That's correct, but once the money is with the family in Calabria, Ethan Tedesco won't ever get his hands on it again. Going by the look of his lifestyle, my guess is that he would have some funds tucked into a sock drawer somewhere.

The family doesn't normally take kindly to that type of behaviour, which is why I doubt he's part of the Ndrangheta.'

'OK. Point taken. Or perhaps, as Billy suggests, Ethan Tedesco's higher-than-usual profile is appropriate for the new world of cryptocurrency,' replied Anders. She turned to the two tax officers. 'Nelson, is there anything you guys can do to help?'

Nelson and Cooper looked at each other before Cooper spoke. 'Yes, we can monitor movements of any cryptocurrency that you put us on the trail of. Also, we can alert you should we see any patterns of redemption to hard currency.'

'That would be helpful. Billy, could you send Nelson the details of any crypto transactions that we've uncovered so far? Hopefully, this might lead you to others,' replied Anders. She handed over her business card to the two federal detectives. 'Can you keep me posted if you see any red flags flying? I guess that we should have considered the possibility that this is bigger than the usual garden-variety criminal ring. It explains a lot, actually.'

Before they parted company, Caroline Russo amped up the stakes. 'The Ndrangheta have infiltrated all stratas of our society, including government and certainly the police. If this is the Ndrangheta at work, then you need to be alert and careful who may be watching.'

Ange felt a sudden twinge, a reflexive response to the target branded on her back.

# Chapter 39

# An Unexpected Visitor

After walking back to their building in silence, the trio regrouped in Sally Anders' office to debrief their meeting with the tax office and the federal police. They quickly got into a lively discussion about whether Ethan Tedesco was Ndrangheta. The debate had barely taken off when Ange's phone rang with an unexpected caller. It was Joe Kramer.

Ange walked out of the office to take the call, leaving Billy and Anders to keep probing the pros and cons on Tedesco. 'Hello, Mr Kramer. What can I do for you?'

'Hello, Detective. I had an interesting visitor early this morning. I thought you might like to know.'

'Tell me more,' replied Ange.

'A certain Sergeant Darren Billings popped over.'

This was not what she had been expecting. Perhaps one of Ted Kramer's old friends, even Tyler Ball himself, but certainly not Darren Billings. She was instantly on high alert. 'What on earth did he want?'

'He said that he was looking for a friend of Ted's. Someone called Lily. I honestly cannot recall Ted ever mentioning someone called Lily, so my reply was completely candid. Bluey was going crazy. He's been antsy ever since Tyler Ball jumped the back fence.'

'Did Billings say or ask anything else?'

'No, he seemed to accept my response. He was constantly peering over my shoulder, as if she might lurk behind a bookshelf. You've seen the office. There's nothing particularly interesting and certainly nowhere to hide. He did request that I contact him if I see or hear from any Lily, but he took himself off smartly after that. Are you making any progress with Ted's murder?'

'Yes, and no. We're certainly edging closer. I can say that Ted was in way too deep and mixed up with a seriously dangerous crowd. You need to stay vigilant yourself. Even better, keep Bluey close by. Thanks for contacting me. I think it might be very important,' said Ange before she hung up from the call.

She briefed the others, and they were discussing the potential implications of this when her phone rang again. This time it was Jim Grady, ringing from Byron Bay. 'Hi, boss. What's up?' answered Ange by reflex, forgetting once again that her actual boss was sitting opposite.

'Hi, Ange. I just had a visit from an admirer of yours.'

Ange put her phone on speaker so the others could hear. 'Let me guess, that would be Darren Billings.'

'How did you know that?'

'He's been doing the rounds, looking for someone called Lily. What excuse did he give you?' asked Ange.

'That someone called Lily had been staying at the Namba Heads caravan park and left without paying her bill or collecting her stuff. He told me that someone at the pub had suggested that the Lily in question was heading to Byron Bay.'

'Well, that Lily is the digital incarnation of the woman staying at your house. That is most interesting, boss. Let me workshop all this with my crew and I'll get back to you with a plan,' said Ange, abruptly hanging up and turning towards her colleagues.

Sally Anders became suddenly energised. 'Right, I know how we might use this to our advantage. Billy, can you pull up Bree's online profile picture? It's called an avatar, isn't it?'

Billy went to his phone and promptly waved around the digital version of Bree.

'Can you hold your phone up beside Ange, please, Billy?' directed Anders. Everyone instantly knew where this was heading. 'What do you reckon? A plausible likeness?'

'Absolutely. I reckon a short dark bob will suit you, Ange. A change of image might improve your social life as well,' said Billy with a huge grin. Ange shot Billy a look of playful disdain in response.

Anders looked directly at Ange, her voice taking on a serious tone. 'Are you up for this, Ange?'

'Of course. I'll feel better about being on hand for Bree. What about Tedesco?'

'Billy and I will look after Tedesco. It's not as if things are racing ahead on that front at present. You'll need to take someone with you. After our meeting of this morning, I'm not inclined to trust anyone. The trouble is, I've got three officers on sick leave with Covid. This third wave is killing our productivity right now.'

Ange had an idea that she knew would raise eyebrows. 'We also can't really use anyone from the Byron Bay station. That would be way too obvious. What about Brett Tompkins? He hasn't been heavily involved in our activities since we moved back to Sydney, and it makes little sense that he could be a mole. I also don't think we blew his cover as a property developer, so his visit would look legitimate.'

Anders fixed Ange with a direct but silent stare. Ange beat her to the punch. 'Brett and I are no longer dating. He's back together with his ex-wife and kids, marking another spectacular relationship failure in the life and times of Angela Watson.'

'OK. You could either wear a wig or get your hair cut, I suppose. Your call. It probably wouldn't hurt to darken the colour of your hair at the same time.'

'A wig would be impossible to manage in Byron Bay for longer than a day or two. I think it's easier to get a haircut and some hair-colour than mess around with a wig.'

'OK. Haircut it is. Go get that done while I brief Brett. I trust that you'll keep your relationship on a business footing this time, Detective. By the way, don't come back to the office once you complete your new look. Text me when you're done, and I'll meet you at the apartment in town.'

Ange had nothing to say to all that and headed straight downstairs to find a hairdresser who might be available.

A new haircut, particularly one that marked a major change of pace, could be confronting. However, Sally Anders didn't have to laugh out loud. Ange told her as much, struggling to adjust to her new image. 'It looks perfect,' observed Anders, still finding mirth in the transformation. 'The hairdresser did a cracking job. Stick on a cap and some sunglasses, and nobody will recognise you. Did you raise any eyebrows with wanting to look like a cartoon character?'

'The hairdresser hardly blinked an eye. She said mine was a common request.

It's a whole new world out there, boss,' observed Ange, finally finding a smile in her self-consciousness. 'It was also a lot more expensive than I expected. I will be submitting an expense claim. I guess that you have a column titled "disfigurement".'

Sally Anders ignored this news and got down to business. 'I have you booked on the first flight to Coolangatta tomorrow morning. I realise that it's further from Byron, but it's a bigger airport and you're less likely to run into anyone you know. There's a hire car booked in the name of Gloria White.'

Anders asked Ange to stand against the wall and took a headshot of the new-look Ange on her phone. She emailed it off to Billy. 'Billy will drop a new driver's licence around later. Use the credit card you already have in the same name. That was a stroke of luck. Lily White could easily be an avatar for Gloria White.'

'OK. How should I play this, boss?'

'Do what you do best, Ange. Hang out, watch and observe, perhaps make yourself conspicuous around town, but stay vigilant. We need to drag whoever is after Bree out into the open somehow. I'm sure you'll work it out. Brett is flying into Ballina and should be there before you. When Billy comes around later this evening, he will configure a tracking app for your phone so that you and Brett can keep abreast of each other's whereabouts. I've also briefed Jim Grady, but stay clear of him and the station. The less contact, the better.'

Anders paused and grasped Ange by both shoulders in a rare sign of something bordering on affection. 'Are you good, Ange?'

'I'm good, boss. Looking forward to it,' replied Ange with more confidence than truthfulness.

'OK, then,' was Sally Anders' last word on the matter, back to business in a heartbeat.

Billy dropped around later that day to hand over the new driver's licence and provide the details of Ange's car rental. 'I didn't want to go through any of the major brands with their newer cars. There was a discount mob with older cars. I figured it would draw less attention. I hope it's OK. By the way, I like your new look. It makes you look younger.'

Ange wasn't sure what to make of that last comment, so she left it alone. 'Makes sense, Billy. I'm sure it will be fine.'

After Billy had left her alone in her standby apartment, Ange went to the bathroom and studied herself in the mirror. Who was the person staring back at her? She had vowed and declared that she was not cut out for undercover work. Yet there she was, taking on someone else's identity and heading back into the fray. She stood there for ages, floundering in a dreamlike state, dislocated and disoriented, unhinged from reality, wondering who she really was and what she might become. Knowing that the identity that she was assuming was a virtual one did not help matters.

In the end, it was a sense of duty that pulled her from these unsettling and unhelpful thoughts. She felt a burning obligation to bring Lomax and Smith to justice and prevent them from spreading further misery. Joy Thomson and Sharon Fletcher were relying on her, even Joe Kramer for that matter. More pressing, however, was her sense of responsibility towards Bree, someone who looked up to her, placed into danger because of Ange's single-minded pursuit of the syndicate.

Mortally wounding that den of thieves would make a whole lot of things right—even her sketchy makeover. There was no way out of this mess but through.

# Chapter 40

# Northern Light

Ange's flight arrived in Coolangatta just before noon the next day. There was a brief delay, while the passengers patiently waited for a set of stairs to be wheeled over. Once they could finally disembark, the harsh Queensland sunlight assailed the travellers. If the number of Hawaiian shirts was anything to go by, Ange assessed them as mostly holidaymakers, and no one seemed obviously misplaced. Such was the glare radiating off the tarmac, she quickly whisked a pair of oversized aviator sunglasses from her tote bag to ease the journey across to the terminal.

She had packed lightly, focussing on every piece of clothing that might help her look younger. Most notably, her suitcase contained a set of denim overalls which had proven a dreadful waste of money, and those jumbo sunnies, both purchased in a moment of youthful exuberance. Exuberance for youth was perhaps a more accurate turn of phrase, as later, in the harsh light of reality, she had concluded that this snappy ensemble invoked images of a 1980s Cyndi Lauper and was not in keeping with the edgy detective look that she had been cultivating. Neither item had appeared in public before. Kerrie would surely have disowned Ange had she been present.

As she waited for her luggage to arrive, she rang the number for the car rental agency that Billy had organised. NextWeek Car Rentals was off-airport and someone would be around to collect her in ten minutes. 'Minimum one week's hire, paid weekly in advance. Keep the car as long as you want. Your credit card will be charged automatically,' said the balding clerk. 'Sign here, here and here, give me your credit card and driver's licence, and you can be on your way in no time.'

Ange almost made an error filling out the paperwork, needing to turn the first letter A for Angela into a G for Gloria. The clerk accompanied Ange into the blinding sun once more to inspect her new wheels, a plain white Kia hatchback. Before she took possession, Ange walked around and scrutinised the vehicle. She found that one tyre was most definitely illegal. Old habits die hard.

'Sorry, this car isn't roadworthy. The left rear tyre is almost bald,' said Ange.

'It's fine, love. It's one of our best cars.'

If there was one thing that Ange hated above all else, it was being patronised by middle-aged men. Anyhow, love was a feeling, not her name. She dearly wished that she could disclose her real identity.

'I don't think so,' she replied. Ange looked across the road and saw a patrol car parked outside a takeaway joint. 'How about I ask those police officers over the road and we can let them decide?'

The man reluctantly went back inside his demountable office to retrieve a fresh set of keys, those belonging to a similarly nondescript silver Hyundai. Ange observed the car was definitely no upgrade. Its tyres might have been legal, but she pointed out a dent on the passenger door and some scratches on the bumpers. 'We don't worry about that sort of stuff, Love,' said the clerk.

'Sure. That's until I bring it back and you bill me,' thought Ange to herself. She made a mental note that Love might ask the office of fair trade to pay NextWeek Car Rentals a visit. Hiring cars shod with bald tyres put people's lives at risk. Calling her *Love* was worse.

Whilst her little silver Hyundai was a significant downgrade from the VW SUV, it felt good to be driving again. There was a certain freedom afforded by being on the road with a full tank of fuel, even if it was for work. The drive to Byron Bay took barely an hour, and she was soon standing on the foreshore, checking out the surf. There is nothing more depressing for a surfer than to watch cracking waves, out of reach because of work, injury, or lack of equipment. Fortunately, this was not one of those moments. Other than the lack of worthwhile swell, Byron Bay was at its sparkling best. She breathed in the fresh sea air and looked to the horizon, relishing the ocean in all its magnificence. She suddenly felt the urge for some sushi and picked up some fresh salmon and avocado rolls, devoured sitting on a park bench overlooking her beloved Coral Sea.

The next chore was to find somewhere to stay. She had pondered the options on the drive down, concluding that a backpackers' hostel would be the best bet. She knew the options well, having visited each of them in a *professional* capacity in her former life. Ange figured these lodgings would be the most appropriate for her alter ego and drove across town to one of the newest and most upmarket hostels. She pulled her cap down over her sunglasses and approached the front counter. 'Hi, I'm looking for a bed. Do you have any single rooms? I plan to be here for about a week,' Ange asked the young guy at reception. Tanned, longish blond-streaked hair, broad shoulders, absurdly attractive. He looked like a surfer, for sure.

'Sure, you're lucky it's before schoolies week. Once that comes around, you need to book almost a year in advance. I have a single room available, with a shared bathroom. You'll need to be gone within ten days. We're fully booked after that. It's ninety-two dollars per night.'

'Perfect,' replied Ange as she handed over her credit card. 'My name is Gloria White, although I prefer to be called Lily. Gloria is my great-grandmother's name,' she said with a smile.

'Ha. Lily White. Cool. I suppose the other option would be Great, but don't mention the name Great White around here.' He stopped and looked up at Ange with a suddenly sombre expression on his face. 'Another diver got taken at Julian Rocks the other day.'

Julian Rocks was a large volcanic outcrop close inshore and popular with divers. It wasn't the first time such a tragedy had occurred, so this sad news came as no special surprise. 'Are you a surfer?' she asked. Securing a nod, she sought important news. 'How's the surf report looking?'

'Terrible. We seem to be stuck in light north-easterlies. The swell's not predicted to pick up for the next week or more. You might get some beachies at Tallows if you're desperate and get up early.'

Ironically, this normally depressing news made Ange feel better, seeing as she had no surfboard. She could hardly call on Gus Bell to help her out. However, had the surf been pumping, this would have been a massive temptation. She would be able to swim at least, a definite benefit of opting to sidestep the wig idea. As Ange retrieved her key, she felt sure the guy would remember that a young woman who went by the name of Lily White was a guest. She had little to unpack, and her tiny dorm room was nowhere to linger, so she walked back into town to spread the word, starting with a juice bar she remembered.

'One health blast with ginger. Name of Lily. Can you call my name out loud? My hearing isn't so good. Surfing accident,' she asked, her volume on high to make the point.

'How did you do that?' asked the guy standing beside. 'I'm a doctor, up here on vacation.'

'Truly,' thought Ange. 'Just my luck.' Fortunately, she knew enough to make a plausible stab at answering his question.

'I was on a trip through the Mentawai Islands. Burst an eardrum and got an infection,' Ange replied.

'Where were you surfing? I've been there a few times. Amazing place.'

'Rifles. I was flying to make a section and face-planted,' answered Ange, wondering when these awkward coincidences might end.

'Oh yeah. Rifles. That wave can be a handful. How big was it?'

'Only four feet. I made a complete mess of things. Lucky for me, we were heading home. Otherwise, it could have been much worse.'

'Four feet at Rifles is plenty big enough. Which was your favourite break?'

Ange looked over at the girl making her juice, willing her to hurry. 'Well, not Rifles after my crash and burn. Probably Lance's Lefts. I really liked that break, even if it was backhand,' she replied. She was fast running out of names for Mentawai surf breaks, gleaned from surfing magazines and conversations with Brett. Thankfully, she heard a loud 'Juice for Lily' to extricate her from the hole she had dug with this friendly off-duty doctor.

Ange spent the rest of the afternoon spreading the word that Deaf Lily was in town. One more juice and three flat whites, all to go. In between toilet stops brought on by all this fluid, Ange wandered around Byron in a caffeine-and-fructose-induced buzz, checking out the shops and treading the strange line between being discreet and conspicuous. She was pleased that her new image seemed to work, as she saw a few familiar faces who blithely walked by.

That evening, she braved town again, using her ploy to buy some takeaway fish and chips that she enjoyed on the foreshore, seated on the grass under the Norfolk pines. She was feeling mildly confident that this plan might work after a day or so.

## Chapter 41

# Where It All Began

After three days of executing her plan, Ange was nothing more than a caffeine-crazed, juiced-up vitamin bomb, with no leads and quickly becoming bored. Brett hadn't been able to identify anyone remotely suspicious. Fortunately, she had dodged running into her friend Kerrie and Gus Bell on two occasions, so her cover was fully intact.

Her overstimulated imagination pondered whether she shouldn't change identities for good, perhaps start a new diet fad. The 'Lily White Juice and Coffee Blast' was the name she had conjured up. If she could get Kerrie on board to do the marketing, it would surely be an enormous success. On Friday, she hatched an alternate scheme to bring the bad guys out of cover, one that she would discuss with Sally Anders on Sunday—assuming nothing dropped before then.

Once Saturday arrived, she tried a different strategy and hired a surfboard, paddling out into the biggest crowd she could find and introducing herself. 'Hi, I'm Lily. You'll have to speak up. I'm a little hard of hearing.' She tried this for a whole weekend. Other than catching a surprising number of waves, she was nowhere closer to her goal. Despite this failure, Ange was pleasantly surprised how much fun her soft foam hire-board proved to be in the small surf. She vowed to buy herself one back in Sydney, so the weekend hadn't been a complete waste of time. Hopefully, Franky wouldn't be too jealous.

Another surprise on this assignment was how much Ange enjoyed staying in the backpackers' lodge. She had made a point of hanging out in the common areas as much as possible, introducing Deaf Lily and discussing travel stories with her fellow guests. Although international travellers were trickling in, it was a small fraction of what establishments like this had enjoyed pre-Covid. Most of the people Ange met were fellow Australians who were discovering what a diverse and glorious country they lived in. Her favourite encounter was with a couple who had left Melbourne to travel up the centre of Australia, across the top end, and were now heading south and home for Christmas. Their highlight had been Uluru.

'We didn't have high expectations. After all, we'd seen Uluru often enough on TV and in magazines. It blew us away. What an amazing experience to see Uluru rising from the desert plains as we drove west off the Stuart Highway. It was almost surreal to watch the sunset and witness the spectacular colour changes. We now understand what the fuss is all about. The whole desert was like this, one gobsmacking vista and experience after another. The trip is best done in the winter months. Summer in central and northern Australia is brutally hot and potentially dangerous for the unwary or ill-prepared,' explained the travellers.

This and other travel stories made Ange realise how limited her own experiences were. It was something that needed work. She had some holiday leave due and would start planning a trip as soon as this case was done and dusted. Instead of always looking toward the ocean, perhaps she should look west.

After an otherwise uneventful weekend, Ange rang her boss on Sunday evening, adding Brett into the call to explain her alternate plan. 'So, we know they've asked Billings to look for Lily, but whoever secured his services is probably not in town. Why don't I confront Billings and convince him it might be in his own best interests to help draw them out? I'm thinking that I could move down to Namba Heads, and he can legitimately report that he has located me and arrange a meeting. I have a good idea for that, and we can ensure we have appropriately armed officers in place beforehand.'

'It's not without risk, Detective. What do you think, Brett?'

'I think it can work. I can't be seen with Ange-stroke-Lily around Namba Heads after living there for so long, but I could coordinate the action and probably help with surveillance. Two properly armed snipers would do the trick.'

'The trouble is, I don't trust anyone,' replied Anders pensively. It was obvious by her tone that there was a lot behind this observation.

'What about the federal police we met on Monday? If you stress to them how worried you are about leaks, they might jump on board. If experience is anything to go by, we're going to find ourselves in a dust-up at some stage. Isn't it best we bite the bullet and deal with it on our terms? That was a terrible choice of words, by the way,' Ange laughed, relieving the tension that had descended on the call. Despite her bravado, it would be Ange's first such confrontation and the reality of the risks was dawning on her.

Sally Anders broke the pregnant pause that ensued, evidently having reached her decision. 'OK. I'll deal with the feds. Ange, you should really have someone with you in the caravan park. What about Jim Grady? He's a steady hand. It would leave Bree exposed, but surely they would have moved in on her by now. Perhaps I could send Billy up to help? It wouldn't be out of the question that he might come back to Byron and see his old colleagues.'

'I agree with all that,' replied Ange. 'Billy is a familiar face around town. Once you've spoken to Jim, I'll ring him and get cracking on the arrangements. We should be able to move down to Namba Heads on Tuesday, subject to how you go with the feds. Brett, I'll send you an image of the meeting location that I have in mind and how you might circle around and get in position well before any proposed meeting time.'

Ange was all action and tried not to dwell on any dangers. It was like surfing. If you worried too much about the wipeout, you would never catch a wave. 'How are you guys going with Tedesco?'

'We've hit a solid brick wall. A Portuguese citizen has just exchanged a large amount of crypto for euro, but there's nothing we can pin on Tedesco while he stays in Sydney. I admit defeat to these guys being better at this stuff than us. We need more resources. So does everybody,' said Anders, her voice trailing off despondently, lack of resources being a constant bugbear.

Lily White took a lower profile in town come Monday morning. A single Immunity Blast and a mere two flat whites were more than enough stimulation given how energised she felt. She spoke to Jim Grady mid-morning. He would ostensibly take a couple of days off. Barb had insisted on joining him. Ange had some initial misgivings about this but took comfort in having an extra set of eyes. Barb was as sharp as a tack in Ange's experience. Billy arrived at midday. She felt sure Billy hadn't pushed back when asked to exchange his computer screens for the company of Breanna White.

Early that afternoon, Sally Anders called and dropped a bombshell. 'I just received word that Ethan Tedesco died in a car accident this morning.'

Ange's mind reeled. 'How? Where? Surely you don't believe it was an accident?'

'He was driving his SUV on Putty Road, coming back to Sydney from the Hunter Valley. Putty Road is a renowned drivers' road with lots of twists and turns. Apparently, it's a favourite of the weekend motoring set and there would have been a strong police presence on Sunday. Not so in the very early hours of Monday morning. His car failed to take a corner and went over the edge of a steep embankment and exploded in a fireball. The crash started a bushfire that took the fireys ages to bring under control. The traffic investigation unit is looking into it, but I guess that will all take time we don't have. I can't really tell them how to do their job, but I don't believe in this type of coincidence.'

'Me either. They're cleaning up loose ends again, whoever *they* are,' observed Ange.

'Correct. Even worse, on Thursday afternoon I scattered a rumour selectively around the office that we had enough evidence to bring Tedesco in for questioning and secure some search warrants. It now seems certain to me that someone in the office is leaking information.'

'Who do you think it is and what does this mean for our plans?' asked Ange.

'I need to do more work before I'm prepared to make any mole accusations. Regarding our plans, nothing. The turn of events may explain why nobody bit on your Lily White bait. They may have been busy dealing with Tedesco. Keep going with your strategy. I expect to have support from the feds confirmed shortly. They're planning to pull a small crew out of Brisbane, so I see no reason to delay moving in on Billings. I also quizzed them further on whether Tedesco was Ndrangheta and they have established a link. Tedesco's flamboyant and public profile had caught them by surprise and diverted their attention. He was so wildly out of character for the Ndrangheta but, as Billy pointed out, maybe not for a tech wizard and the brains behind their cryptocurrency operations. Perhaps my massive rant when they didn't get back to me about Tedesco helped secure their support for the coming days.'

Anders let all that sink in for a moment before stating the obvious. 'So, we need to assume that we are dealing with the Ndrangheta here. This would explain a lot, like why we never seem to get to the top of the tree. I don't need to tell you how seriously dangerous these guys are. One piece of news that warmed my heart was to learn that the feds also have ratcheted up their interest in Eric Tedesco as a result of our investigation. Who knows, I may finally retrieve the pound of flesh he took from me.'

The first evening edition of the news was abuzz with the 'tragic death' of Ethan Tedesco, hailed as 'a luminary tech entrepreneur'. A special story ran in the *7:30 Report* later that evening, which pointed to the financial stress that Tedesco's companies were under following the tech rout assailing global stock exchanges. The presenter pointed to Tedesco's pioneering role in the now-plummeting crypto markets, theorising on the impact to his empire. The whole thrust was that of a genius grappling with a series of challenges not of his making, implying that distraction or self-destruction might have caused his death.

Ange bought none of these theories.

## Chapter 42

# Rude Awakening

Soon after midday, Ange started the familiar drive down the coast to Namba Heads. It had been some time since she had last visited the sleepy fishing village, and she arrived with mixed emotions. On the one hand, Namba Heads was the source of great delight; its craggy coastline and superb surf spots had delivered her with such rich memories. On the other, it was the scene of the tragic deaths of a young surfer, Jake Thompson, and a local trawlerman, Dave Fletcher. She had still not made good on her commitment to bring the perpetrators to justice. Hopefully, this trip would yield the results she craved.

Jim Grady and his wife had checked into the caravan park and secured keys to two cabins, tucked away and side by side. Ange was pleased that she could park her car and access her cabin without being seen. She had stayed in the caravan park many times and knew that the manager missed nothing—he would surely see through her disguise.

Once she was settled in, Jim Grady popped over and the pair worked through the arrangements of their surprise visit to the local police station and Sergeant Darren Billings. Grady would keep a lookout and confirm when Billings was present at the station. Ange would then ring Grady before entering the station, leaving the call active so that Grady could record the conversation. Ange wore her exercise leggings, the ones with the stretchy pocket on her thigh for a mobile phone, something that she stress-tested with Grady first. The speech was a touch muffled but clear enough for their purposes.

Just after 3 p.m., Ange received the thumbs-up text from Grady and she drove her hire car around to the police station. Grady had parked on the river foreshore, just around the corner, looking for all the world like a tourist enjoying the view.

Parking on the verge, she pulled her cap down over her sunglasses and walked into the station, awash with adrenaline. She jangled her way through the screen door and into the drab and vacant reception. Nobody came out to greet her. She pounded on a small round bell mounted on the counter, identified with a crudely fashioned sign that suggested help would shortly be on the way. None was forthcoming. After another impatient minute, just as Ange was preparing to give the hapless bell an even more resounding clap, a young constable loped through the doorway. 'Can I help you?' he asked.

'Hi. Can you tell the sergeant that Lily is here to see him, please?'

The young man looked at her strangely. Perhaps he was wondering if the beer fuel boasts of his boss were true and he was a ladies' man with a bit on the side. 'Can I ask what you need to see him about?'

'Just tell him my name. Lily. It's important.' As she uttered those words, Ange rubbed her lower abdomen gently, suggestive of protecting Darren's love child. She felt certain that Billings would have bragged about his supposed proficiency with the fairer sex. She could be cruel at times, particularly to the likes of Darren Billings.

The constable's eyes widened at this news. He raced back through the doorway and into the bowels of the little station, so small that she could hear her message being passed on. She swore that Billings practically ran out of his office in response before screeching to a halt and composing his best officialdom face at the doorway.

This was the part that Ange had been playing over and over in her mind all morning. She almost felt guilty at the pleasure her reveal was going to bring forth. She casually removed her cap and sunglasses.

'I hear that you've been looking for me, Sergeant?' Ange's slow, deliberate voice was a taunting mixture of irony and import.

Billings' face went through a series of phases. First surprise, then concern, ultimately setting on his favourite—indignation.

'You! You're not Lily. What's all this about?' spat Billings, his belligerent tone further raising Ange's ire.

Ange took a moment to calm down and slowly reassembled her cap and sunglasses. 'Let's go outside for a chat, shall we?' she suggested. After such a salacious entrance, she had no desire for eager ears to bring things undone. Billings followed Ange out through the jangling screen door, disturbing a determined squadron of flies who were itching to get at the staleness inside. The pair spilled onto the wide grassy verge, brown and crackly from a lack of rain, before Ange silently led Billings behind the faded metal garage that sat against the rear boundary of the station property.

Judging them to be clear of earshot, Ange continued. 'I gather someone has asked you to look for a certain Lily. I'm here to find out who that someone was. As you can see, Lily and I are close.'

Indignation instantly disappeared as fear infiltrated his being, surfacing first in his eyes before it infected his whole demeanour. The normally tall and arrogant Sergeant Darren Billings morphed into a lesser person, a puppy cowering from an impending flogging, perhaps. He pulled himself together and gave himself one last shot.

'What do you mean? I've done nothing wrong. I was responding to an anonymous tip-off that I received from a concerned citizen.'

Ange was now even more disgusted. He might have regained a modicum of her respect if he had the balls to admit to his wrongdoing. 'We've been monitoring your activities for months now. We know about your gambling debt and we know that you've been running errands for criminal elements. Major Crimes caught you on video at the Bangalow markets speaking to Lomax and Smith, the murderers who killed Dave Fletcher. We also know that you helped pass off Fletcher's death as a suicide.'

She let that sink in and his fear grow. Billings said nothing. He just stood there like the proverbial deer in the headlights. Ange let this awkward situation hang in the air for a full ten seconds before providing him a way out.

'The crazy thing is that I'm probably your best bet to survive this. Darren, you've gotten yourself mixed up with some seriously dangerous people. If you help us now, then you'll be helping yourself. Not only can we protect you, but it should help with sentencing. I guess I don't need to tell you how the other inmates treat ex-coppers in jail.'

Billings seemed dumbstruck, now more resembling a stunned mullet than the puppy or deer of moments before. Ange pressed on. 'So, tell me, Darren. How do you make contact?'

Billings made no reply, staring dejectedly at the ground in front of his feet, as if standing on a precipice and looking down, gauging how far he might fall and what perils lay below. Once he took that next step, there would be no way back.

He teetered. Ange piled on the pressure. 'I'd like you to set up a meet-and-greet.'

This brought him back from the edge. Billings snapped his head up to look at her. 'You're crazy. They'll kill you for sure. Probably kill me as well.'

'Darren,' said Ange, trying a little I'm-on-your-side ploy, 'now that we're in this deep, they won't leave you alone. I have no option but to bring this to a head. The best thing you can do is to stand by my side so we can protect you.'

'So how do you propose that? You'll hit them with your handbag? Believe me, those guys are thugs.'

Ange's expression instantly turned to steel. 'Don't patronise me, Sergeant. I'm well aware of how dangerous your two friends are. Luckily, the guys I have on my side are even tougher. With your help, we'll also be better prepared.'

It was time to deliver her ultimatum. 'Either you agree to help me, or I'll leak information. Something that we know will get to Lomax and Smith and tease them out, with you as the bait. Perhaps we'll let slip that you came to Major Crimes with a proposal to cooperate. We can pick them up when they come and pay you a visit,' she said, gilding the lily perhaps—the flower, that is, not the person.

'What's it going to be, Darren?' Ange paused on that good-cop ending and waited. Billings was no hardened criminal; he was just a small man with an oversized ego. There was only one viable option—step off the precipice and hope that Ange and her colleagues would catch him and keep him safe. Ange held her breath and waited, sensing not to push Billings any further.

'We communicate via a tipping forum,' he said, his voice barely a whisper, a beaten man. 'It's like a chat room where gamblers exchange tips.'

'Good. I want you to send them a message that you've found Lily and that you want to pick her up and bring her to the site where they buried Jake Thompson, the young surfer. Tell them she wants one hundred thousand dollars in exchange for Ted Kramer's wallet address and recovery phrase.'

'What the hell is a recovery phrase?' Billings asked belligerently.

Ange fixed him with a death stare before deciding to let his attitude slide. He had a lot to process, after all. 'I don't have time to explain, and you don't need to know. Remember, Lily wants a hundred K in return for Kramer's wallet address and recovery phrase. Suggest 3 p.m. tomorrow. Offer no more information than that. Do I need to write that down for you?'

'No, I've got it,' came the sullen reply.

'Good. You'll get a text this evening from Sergeant Grady from Byron Bay. I believe you called on him last week, so his contact won't be entirely out of order. The text will ask you whether you found the missing woman. Don't reply straight away. If you've successfully organised the meeting, text back *Yes—all good, thanks*. If not, text back *No—still looking*. If we can't make tomorrow work, try Thursday and then even Friday if necessary.'

'Why the cloak and dagger? Couldn't I just call you?'

'We can't risk any leaks. They could very well be monitoring your phone. After all, we have been.' She let that piece of news sink in for a moment. Billings looked back towards the office with a worried look. Ange was one step ahead. 'Don't worry about your constable. He thinks you're a ladykiller and that I'm pregnant with your love child. Sorry, terrible choice of words,' she said, smiling at her own faux pas and indelicately relieving the tension.

'What happens when the meeting is confirmed?'

'Jim Grady will pay you a social call at some stage during the morning of the meeting and brief you then. Are we good, Sergeant?'

Billings mumbled a barely audible 'Yes' before turning and shuffling back into the station, defeat oozing out of every pore.

'Talk about pathetic,' Ange thought to herself.

Once Billings was out of sight, Ange walked briskly to her hire car and drove back to the cabin, where Jim Grady was already waiting for her.

'Brilliant work, Ange. How you played Billings was masterful. I recorded the whole thing, but I'll bet it was more fun in person,' said her old boss with a big smile.

'I reckon the constable assumes Billings got me pregnant. As if that could ever happen. What a tool,' commented Ange, the corner of her mouth turning upwards in disgust as she spat out those last few words. Catching out Billings like that had been exhilarating.

Now that she'd successfully executed step one of their game plan, a sombre dose of the reality that lay ahead replaced her adrenaline rush. 'Careful what you wish for, heh, boss?'

## Chapter 43

# Preparations

Sally Anders rang late Tuesday afternoon to confirm that the feds had offered three officers for support and they were on their way. All three were trained marksmen, and one was also good at surveillance tech. He would bring along his box of magic tricks. They would stay alongside Brett Tompkins at a drive-up motel, inland from the coast and just off the highway. Ange then rang Brett and asked that he text her the address as soon as the backup arrived. She offered to pick up some takeaway Chinese and they could work through their plan of attack over dinner.

She filled in Grady and waited for the text. What was bugging her was how the syndicate seemed to know their every move. It couldn't be Billings—it had to be someone close to them in Major Crimes. She called Billy to check how he was going.

'Hi, Billy. How are you enjoying your current assignment?' she said sweetly, suggesting an ulterior motive in her loaded question.

'Bree and I are fine, boss,' replied Billy, his trailing tone showing what he thought about her puerile question. 'Anders has got me looking through phone records of several of our colleagues. She seems convinced that we have a snitch on our team. And, no, you're not on the list.'

'Have you found anything?'

'Nothing yet. It's painstaking work. Why do I get all the good jobs?' he enquired to no one in particular. 'Anyhow, I've been thinking through suspicious events, times when we lost ground and someone may have given the other side a heads-up. I'll then build an algorithm to look for any patterns around those events. So far, working backwards, I have the visit to Tedesco to retrieve his painting, and the time you were going to detain Eddie Falconi on the Gold Coast. Anything else significant that you thought suspicious, boss?'

'Frankly, it would seem unlikely that a criminal in our midst would use their own phone. It's more likely that they would use a burner like Ted Kramer did. I suppose they could have slipped up somewhere. It happens,' commented Ange before thinking back in time to answer Billy's question. 'How about when we logged that tracking device on the Mitsubishi that Lomax and Smith were driving? They seemed to know all about that tracker. I can't remember the exact date, but it should all be on file. I'll let you know if I think of anything else. Oh, while I think of it, can you text me Kramer's RedBrd wallet address? It wouldn't be ideal to suffer a bout of amnesia in the heat of the moment. I'll act as if I have his recovery phrase written down in an envelope. Hopefully, that won't be needed, but I may well need to trade something. I guess I should make the phrase credible. Is there a list of phrase words that I should use?'

'Sure is. I'll text you the wallet address and email you a link to a list of recovery words. By the way, I agree about the burner phones. Let's hope someone was stupid or lazy.'

'Thanks, Billy. Wish us luck. It might get ugly. You have fun with your babysitting duties.'

'You just couldn't resist one last dig, could you?' replied Billy in response. 'Stay safe, boss.'

Her phone buzzed a few minutes later with the requested text from Billy. Checking her emails, she clicked on the link that he'd forwarded, which revealed a long list of recovery words, arranged in alphabetic order. Tearing a leaf out of her notebook, she chose her make-believe recovery phrase. It was harder than she thought, trying to make her selection seem random. It made her think about the concept of randomness. If she chose two words beside each other in the alphabet, was that random or not? What even was random, anyway? It was not unlike her investigations. The trick, or one of the tricks, was being able to sense when seemingly random events were just that, and when they weren't random at all.

Bogus recovery phase selected, safely sealed in a crumpled envelope she dug from her laptop satchel, Ange then spent the rest of the afternoon looking over the satellite picture of her proposed meeting site. She remembered the spot well and closed her eyes to recall the imagery that was etched in her memory. That had been a terrible day, uncovering Jake Thompson's body from his shallow grave.

One never forgot experiences like that.

Ange pictured the low coastal scrub, beaten by the prevailing south-easterly winds, mostly around shoulder-height and perfect for what she had in mind. With the warm, almost summery weather they had been enjoying, early season cicadas would sing their mating song, layering a white-noise blanket that wavered over the landscape. In her mind's eye, she looked up and to the right, picturing the long white scar on a prominent sandy hillock to the south, a straight line of cleared scrub meant to contain the inevitable bushfires that would be sparked by the violent electrical storms of summer.

She visualised the car park to Bushies Beach, a portal to the spectacular coastline and a wide expanse of ocean. She imagined wandering down the beach towards the glorious headland that formed Sliders, her favourite surf break on the planet. This was a stark contrast with her chosen meeting place, already a place of death and sadness. It was possible that more would follow, and she hoped that nobody would mourn her in the coming days.

A text from Brett jumped her from this reverie. Apparently, the guys had arrived, and his message contained the address of the motel where they were staying. She didn't know the place, but it would be easy to find. She then rang her old friend Jimmy from the local Chinese takeaway. He was as brusque and impatient as usual, and Ange whisked off a series of dishes from memory, having frequently enjoyed his delicious food.

'Big order. Thirty minutes,' was Jimmy's way of saying thanks for the business. He had been of immeasurable help during her time in Namba Heads, and his quick thinking and security video had been pivotal in breaking the case open.

She rang Jim Grady. 'Hi, boss. The guys have arrived, so I've ordered takeaway Chinese from Jimmy's around the corner. It will be ready in thirty minutes. The order is in the name of Grady. How about you pick up the food and then swing back and collect me? Will Barb be OK?'

'It's Parma Tuesday at the Services Club. Barb will be fine. I'll swing back to pick you up once I have the food. It'll be after dark, so nobody should see you.'

Ange took a shower and put on some respectable clothes, applying whatever scant makeup she had in her travelling cosmetics kit. It was this very caravan park where her whirlwind romance with Brett had first ignited, their coupling seemingly inevitable after the best day's surfing of her life. She hadn't seen him for ages and wanted to look her best at this certain moment of weirdness.

As she heard Grady's car pull up outside, she closed her laptop and stuffed it into her backpack on the way out. 'You look nice,' was the blank-faced greeting from her old boss. He was no fool.

It took less than twenty minutes to find the motel. Brett had secured a large family unit in the corner, and they arrived to find the crew waiting for them. The food smelled amazing and won everyone's attention in a second. Brett introduced Ange and Grady to the guys from the federal police. Matt, Andy, and Will greeted them in a slow and measured manner. They oozed competence and inspired confidence. Sally Anders had secured talent from the very top shelf. She must have really put on a show.

They devoured the food over small talk before Ange opened her laptop and started the briefing. Brett's initial reserved demeanour gradually broke down as the combination of good food and lively comradery displaced any discomfort that sat between them.

She pointed at the image on her screen. 'This is the spot where I've arranged the meeting. The low scrub is about head-high and should be perfect for you guys. Brett, this white track here is a firebreak that runs up a ridge to a high point. You've probably noticed it before on the drive over to Bushies Beach. It's less than a kilometre from the site. You should be able to see any movement through binoculars.'

'How do you access the site?' asked Matt, a man of few words, having been silent throughout dinner.

Ange pointed to the track that led from the bitumen road. 'Billings and I will drive down this track and park here, to the northern side of the clearing. I doubt that whoever is coming will choose this method. Let's assume it will be Lomax and Smith for the moment, and that they aren't coming to give us kisses and cuddles. It's a rough track in, so we would easily hear any vehicle coming in that way. There's nowhere else to park between the turn-off and our clearing, and I can't see them wanting to leave a car parked out on the main road.'

'Who is Billings, and why isn't he here?' Matt asked abruptly.

'Because I don't trust him. He's the local sergeant and a complete moron. I've been able to convince him it's in his best interest to help us out. He's setting up the meeting.'

Matt again. 'Given that you don't trust him, do you plan to tell him about us?'

'He knows that I have some form of protection, but he's such a tool that he'd give us away if I provided any specifics. I don't plan to tell him much at all,' replied Ange.

'Will you be able to control him?'

"I guess you guys will step in if Billings goes rogue on me?' asked Ange.

Matt nodded his answer. 'Definitely. So, which way do you expect Lomax and Smith to approach the site?'

Ange was forming an opinion that Matt was the chief tactician. 'There are only two other ways in, but I'm almost certain that they will park their vehicle near this car park.' She pointed to the large public car park for Bushies Beach. 'There are plenty of places to park around here where they can remain unnoticed.' She traced her finger along the faint sandy walking trail that wound its way from the car park, where it joined a network of trails that ran through the scrub, passing through the clearing of their plans.

'The other way is from the rear,' said Ange, pointing to the more substantial fire trail protecting the houses built on the south-eastern fringe of the township. 'I don't think they'll choose this way in. It's far too open and quite a long walk. However, I suggest that you guys should approach the site this way.' She pointed to the trailhead nearest the township. 'I've walked this track many times, and you can park your vehicle here. It'll be out of sight and not obvious.'

Matt stared at the screen for at least a minute before verbalising his succinct opinion. 'Makes sense.'

'I'm trying to set up the meeting for 3 p.m. tomorrow, but I suggest you guys head out early to avoid any risk of being spotted. It'll get hot out there, so take some sun protection and pack plenty of water, but I guess I don't need to tell you guys how to suck eggs. I'll let you know if the meeting gets postponed.'

Ange looked around the team, checking for questions before continuing. 'That brings me to the crunch. I feel sure that Lomax and Smith will be the guys paying us a visit. I'm also guessing that they were recently in the Hunter Valley helping tie up loose ends. We know of at least four people who have probably died at their hands, so they won't come empty-handed. Do you have any protection we can use?'

'Definitely. We'll run through all of that, but we have these new super high-tech vests. They stop a bullet, but it'll pack a punch if you're hit. They're impressively slim. However, I suggest you wear loose-fitting clothes. We have other options, but I think they're too obvious,' said Andy. He stood up, retrieved two black vests from a large duffle bag and handed them to Ange. 'Here, take these with you and experiment with your clothing. I presume you want the snake to wear one as well? '

Ange grimaced. 'Yes. As much as it pains me. Billings isn't evil like our other two guys, just stupid. They reeled him in over a gambling debt.'

'It happens,' observed Andy drily.

She bounced the flimsy vests up and down in her hand. 'Are you sure these things will stop a bullet? They seem ridiculously thin.'

Will spoke up for the first time. 'I know, they're amazing. Made of carbon nanotubes. Trust me, they work.' He lifted his shirt and pointed to a faint bruise on his upper abdomen. 'You still don't want to be hit. We'll make sure that doesn't happen.'

'What about comms?' asked Brett.

Andy pulled out some earbuds. The first two sets that he handed to Ange were minuscule. 'Ange, you wear one of these. It's up to you whether you give the other one to Billings. Personally, I wouldn't, at least based on what you've said about him. He's likely to get distracted or react to what's being said. Being so small, the battery life is only two hours, so don't turn them on until the last minute. What's the mobile reception like at the site?'

'Good. I've used my phone from there before. Brett will be fine. The ridge is the highest point and probably even closer to town. I presume he'll act as lookout. Won't he be too far away for these tiny earpieces?'

'Correct,' replied Andy. 'However, once Brett is in position, I'll set up a high-powered repeater station in the tallest tree that I can find and check that we're all online.' He looked at Grady and handed him a larger style of earpiece, looking for all the world like everyday earbuds people used to talk on their mobile phones. 'Since you won't be in the thick of things, I've given you a more powerful headset that also has a longer battery life. You should base yourself nearby so that you can hear what's going on. Hopefully, we won't need you. I synced all the units together with our comms.'

He stopped and showed Ange and Grady how to turn their earbuds on and off before performing a short bench test. Ange couldn't believe the clarity; they were obviously extremely high-quality units.

Andy watched and waited for the testing to finish before continuing his tech briefing. 'I'll also set up a WhatsApp group that we can use to communicate. Brett will let us know when he sees the bad guys, and we can post a message for you to turn on your earbuds. Brett, as soon as you're in position, send a test message to our WhatsApp group. We've got time to work something out if you don't have adequate phone service. Unlock your phones, guys, and I'll set up our WhatsApp group.'

Ange, Brett, and Grady handed over their phones and Andy fiddled around before handing them back. 'I called our group Sandstorm.'

'WhatsApp is perfect for this stuff,' said Grady.

Ange was surprised to hear that Grady was comfortable communicating in this manner. She secretly thanked Billy for forcing WhatsApp onto her phone. Grady's phone buzzed with a text message. Ange looked over at him expectantly. The room went silent, sensing that the message had importance for their project. He read the text and looked up before speaking. 'We're on for tomorrow.'

Their plan now had teeth, and Grady finally asked the question that was most concerning him. He gestured towards the three federal officers. 'Where will you three guys be? This is not worth risking Ange's life over.'

Ange looked at her old boss with affection. He was a good man. Grady did not express similar concern over the safety of Darren Billings. Nobody corrected this omission and Ange surmised that her less-than-glowing depiction of the man had not helped his cause.

Matt answered his question. 'It's best that Ange doesn't know where we'll be. Otherwise, she might be tempted to look and give our position away. I plan to deploy a tiny wide-angle video camera in the bushes to record proceedings, but we can also use the live feed should something get in the way and compromise our line of sight. It's a terrific location that you chose. Plenty of cover.' He paused and fixed Ange with a direct stare. 'We won't hesitate to take these guys out if things turn ugly. We've done this before. However, gear failure is always a possibility.' He paused and looked at Ange. 'In case we lose comms, we need to agree on a signal you can use if you want us to move in. You should decide what that signal should be, Ange. Something obvious that you'll remember and we wouldn't miss.'

Ange thought for a while before speaking. 'I'll be carrying a crumpled white envelope. It supposedly carries a recovery phrase to a digital wallet. The signal could be me waving this around above my head, sort of like a white flag.'

'That sound perfect,' replied Matt.

'Don't confuse this with me pulling it out of my pocket to show them, but

I'll be careful to keep it below my head. Also, you need to move in at the point that I hand over the envelope. By that stage, I'll make sure I have every skerrick of information I can get out of them.'

'Understood,' said Matt. He looked at the other guys, who all nodded to show that they also understood these arrangements. 'Ange. If it all goes south, don't hesitate to use that signal, even if we seem to have comms. It's better to be safe than sorry,' concluded Matt.

The group went suddenly silent on the back of that sombre note, before Ange stood up and grabbed her new kit. 'OK, then. I guess I *won't* see you tomorrow,' she said with a smile that showed far more bravado than she felt.

## Chapter 44

# Restless Moments

To say that Ange had a terrible night's sleep would be an understatement of monumental proportions. Her fitful dreams provided no comfort for the day that lay ahead, yet she was feeling alert and ready for action. Adrenaline could be a powerful ally.

She had put her phone on silent in a last-ditch effort to get some sleep. This must have worked, as she had arisen to see a WhatsApp message from Brett, alerting the group that they were on the road. He had sent the message at 4:30 a.m. Theirs would be a long day. She fluffed around in her little cabin, willing Jim Grady to wake. She needed coffee but had no desire to jeopardise their plans, potentially being seen in the main street by the wrong person. At 6:30 a.m., her phone buzzed with another WhatsApp message.

> *Hi, I'm in place. If anyone can see me, let me know. Let's check everyone is online. Please respond, Brett*

Within seconds, the three federal officers had responded in the affirmative. Nobody could see Brett. Ange posted the last message. This was no dream.

> *Thanks, guys. Will keep you posted if anything else develops, Ange*

An hour later, Grady knocked at the door to take her breakfast order. She added some raisin toast to a large triple-shot flat white.

She felt even more energised after the caffeine and some sustenance—if that were possible. The plan for the day was to have a large and early lunch, enough to ensure that there was no energy drop come 3 p.m. Ange had settled on her outfit for the day, finally finding a use for the denim overalls that she had carted up from Sydney. Ange considered she looked absurd and vowed to dump the tragic outfit in a charity bin as soon as the day was over. They did, however, hide her high-tech bulletproof vest to perfection. Plus, they had a large pocket inside the bib that concealed her revolver nicely. She traded texts with Sally Anders.

**Ange:** *Hi, boss. Everyone is in place and we're on for 3 p.m.*
**Sally Anders:** *Don't do anything stupid. Stay safe!*

Ange simply texted back a fingers-crossed emoji. Nothing else seemed appropriate in the circumstances.

Grady rang Billings mid-morning, speaking in riddles and suggesting that he was in town and would like to pop over and pay his respects. He, like Ange, had absolutely no respect for the corrupt sergeant. Grady returned at lunchtime, laden with bread rolls from the bakery, some fruit, some more coffee, of course, and a delicious-looking vanilla slice. Such a richly flamboyant dessert was not something that Ange would normally partake in, but she figured her nervous energy would make quick work of the extra calories. It proved the perfect end to their substantial meal, helping to settle the butterflies that were going crazy.

At 2 p.m., Billings drove up in his police-issue twin cab 4WD. He knocked on the door and came into Ange's cabin. She was pleased to see that he was in uniform. Ange handed him the second bulletproof vest and gestured towards the bathroom. 'Here. Put this on. You'll need to put it under your clothes and fiddle with it until you're certain it's not visible.'

Billing weighed the vest in his hands. 'What, this flimsy thing? Are you sure this will stop a bullet?'

'I certainly hope so, as I'm wearing the same thing,' replied Ange. 'While you're at it, give me your gun.'

'What? You're sending me there unarmed? What about you?' asked Billings indignantly.

Jim Grady came to her aid. 'Don't be an idiot, Billings. Nobody trusts you. I'm sure you would do the same thing in our position.'

'You can still jump ship, Darren, and deal with these guys on your own terms. Speak now or forever hold your peace,' said Ange.

'We're not getting married, Detective. More like my funeral, if you ask me. I'll feel better with my service revolver. Plus, it will be safer for both of us,' grumbled Billings as he snatched up the vest and handed over his service revolver.

'Point taken. Jim and I will discuss this while you're getting changed, Darren,' said Ange, using his first name as a team-building exercise. No matter how low her opinion of Billings was, it would serve them better to have his full cooperation.

Ange and Grady got into a heated discussion over whether it would be helpful for Billings to be armed. Grady was dead against it, but Ange was vacillating one way and then the other. 'It's your funeral. Sorry, awful choice of words,' was Grady's last opinion on the matter as he turned away and fiddled with his phone, annoyed that she wasn't in absolute agreement with him.

That they had used twice the word 'funeral' in the last five minutes was a telling insight. She made a snap decision to take a halfway position and quickly removed the ammunition from his revolver. She placed the weapon back on the table and dropped the bullets into the side pocket of her overalls. Speaking loudly enough that Billings could hear, Ange feigned support for his trustworthiness.

Grady was calling her a deluded fool when Billings emerged from the bathroom. Both Ange and Grady agreed that his new vest was indiscernible. Ange exaggerated her reluctance to hand the revolver back to Billings. 'Don't make me regret this, Sergeant.'

Billings smiled smugly in response, as if he had won a major victory, his ever-present ego a distraction from properly checking his weapon. Grady dispatched a scornful stare at Ange as Billings holstered his weapon. Ange knew Billings was an absolute snake, and Grady's obvious disgust forced her to take one further step. 'Darren, I want you to confirm that you're doing this of your own free will.'

'I would hardly call your ultimatum a case of free will,' said Billings dismissively.

'Don't mess with me, Darren. Say the words and then we can get on our way.'

'OK. I'm doing this of my own free will,' Billings replied, petulantly enunciating each word in an exaggerated manner.

Grady looked up from whatever he was doing on his phone and exchanged a nod with Ange, prompting Ange to glance at her own phone. It was showing a time of almost 2:30 p.m.

'OK, then. Let's do this,' she declared, putting on her garish cap and oversized sunglasses and making for the door. As she walked past Grady, she slipped him the third earpiece. After that last discussion, Ange had established that she couldn't risk Billings with comms. He was an unreliable ticking time bomb, and not one she wanted exploding in her face.

Ange allowed Billings to play the boss for a moment and lead her to his car, inserting her in the back seat for the sake of optics, just in case Lomax and Smith were watching.

After Ange's text, Sally Anders sat at her desk, nervously and aimlessly pushing papers. Naturally, she worried about placing her officers in danger, but they were operating essentially against orders, adding significant professional risk to all concerned.

Billy rang just before lunch.

'Hi, Billy. I hope that you're behaving?'

'What do you mean?' replied Billy in reflex before realisation dawned that she was joking with him. 'Oh, that. Ha ha. Actually, I've been hard at it and I've discovered something odd in the phone logs. You won't like it.'

Sally Anders' tone quickly sharpened. 'Get on with it, Billy. It is what it is,' she replied impatiently.

'I built an algorithm to look at patterns between leaked events and calls made, stuff that seemed out of character. The only person whose calls showed any correlation was Peter Fredericks.'

Anders fought to keep her composure before asking the next obvious question. 'Who was he contacting? Please don't tell me it was Lomax or Smith, or any other of the bastards we've been chasing.'

'No, I rang the number, and that's the weird thing. Fredericks was ringing your boss. Chief Superintendent Bold.'

Clarity came to Anders like a lightning strike, clear, bright, and shocking. It explained everything. Her heart was racing with this news. It needed some deep thought.

'OK, Billy. That actually makes perfect sense. Thanks for your work. No need to keep looking further, and you can leave this to me. Can you just email me the relevant records from Peter's phone? By the way, you haven't spoken to Peter about what Ange is up to, have you?'

'No. I've become a bit paranoid myself. Peter did know that I was looking into some crypto trades, but I'm certain that I never disclosed any specific details.'

'Ok. Good. Just sit tight and wait to see if Ange needs any help. It's going down at 3 p.m. today.'

After hanging up, she sat and pondered what to do. Before she accused one of her trusted lieutenants, or worse still, her boss, she needed to be sure. If she wanted to stress-test whether Peter was leaking crucial information to Bold, then she needed something big as bait. The idea came easily, a thorn in her side that had been stinging for ages. She called Peter Fredericks. 'Hi, Peter, can you pop over to m y office when you get a chance? There's something that I need your help with.'

Peter Fredericks knocked and opened the door to her office in under ten minutes. 'What's up, boss? By the way, where's Ange and Billy? I haven't seen Ange for days.'

'Ange took some stress leave. We sent her down to Tasmania to get away. This business of being watched was getting to her. Billy's feeling sick. I've sent him off to work from home. I can't afford to lose any more staff. Are you feeling OK, by the way? Get tested if you feel crook.' Sally Anders was a consummate fibber when the situation was called for. 'Anyway, you probably heard about Ethan Tedesco's death?'

'Yes, that was tragic. What a waste.'

'Yes, quite. Anyhow, his father was a director of some companies that we have suspicions about. I'm preparing a warrant to bring him in for questioning, and I'll need you to get a magistrate to sign it. Can you check and see who might be available?'

'OK. How soon will you need it done?' asked Fredericks.

'I've just about finished. Hopefully, later this afternoon. Keep your calendar clear. It's important. I'll let you know when it's ready.'

The call she was expecting came within the hour, such was the smug confidence of Anders' boss. They hadn't been on good terms for months. 'Senior Detective. I hear a rumour that you're going after Eric Tedesco. This is totally out of line. Especially after the tragic death of his son. I told you to back off this imaginary crusade of yours. Given your history with Tedesco, this sounds more like a personal vendetta than anything of substance. If you take this any further without my authority, I'll suspend you for insubordination.'

Sally Anders sat there impassively, grim-faced even, taking both barrels that Bold unloaded her way. She did not object or argue, simply waited for his onslaught to finish. At least it confirmed what the outcome for her career might be if she got things wrong. She suspected Bold had been itching to throw the threat of suspension her way for some time.

'Of course, boss. I'll back off Tedesco, and I promise to come to you first before I do anything,' she replied, seemingly as meek as a church mouse.

'That's good, then. I don't want to have this conversation again, Sally.'

'You won't, sir,' she said, hanging up from the call and immediately starting another.

'Hi, Inspector Paulson. It's Sally Anders here from Major Crimes. I wondered if you could trace two names for me. I suspect we might connect them with the Ndrangheta. A gentleman named Peter Fredericks, who works with me, and a Chief Superintendent Gary Bold. He's my boss.'

Cam Paulson whistled in response. 'Boy, that's a big name, Detective.'

'Yep, almost as big as it gets. I would prefer that you handled this personally, Detective. It's not a hot potato that I want handed around the office.'

'I hear you. I hope it turns into nothing, for your sake at least.'

'So do I, but I seriously doubt it. Make sure that you look carefully. Anyone who could attain either position in the service will be an expert in covering their tracks.'

After the call was complete, Anders sat back in her chair and thought through the implications. She was almost certain that Paulson would confirm her suspicions. The pieces fitted perfectly. It would cause a massive ruction in the police service. In her experience, whistle-blowers rarely got any pats on the back for exposing police corruption. There was usually collateral damage.

Anders spent the rest of the day working through strategies that might prevent her and her trusted team from being collared.

## Chapter 45

# Poor Timing

Ange and Billings had barely made it out of the caravan park when her phone rang with a WhatsApp call.

'Ange. It's Brett. Lomax and Smith have beaten you to the site. I'm almost certain it's them. You'd best get set with your comms now—otherwise you won't have time. When you get to the clearing, park immediately to the right, the north-easternmost spot you can find. Lomax and Smith are to the west and we don't want your vehicle getting in the way. You guys try to stay as far east as you can. Don't worry, we've got eyes on them. They won't be able to sneeze without a world of pain raining down on them.'

'OK, Brett. Thanks for the heads-up,' replied Ange. She slid across the seat so that Billings couldn't see her in his rear-view mirror, inserted her earbud, and turned it on. She could instantly hear the chatter from her support team. It was crystal clear.

As they drove over the bridge and past the fish co-op, Ange casually asked Billings if Sharon Fletcher was still in town. 'No, she's sold up and moved to Coffs Harbour,' said Billings in answer to her seemingly innocuous question.

'We got that, Ange. You're good to go,' came Brett's voice in her ear.

Their turn-off was less than two minutes away, and Billings slowed to make the turn. The track was even bumpier than she had remembered. The sand was dry and loose and not showing any distinctly new tyre tracks. They bumped and jumped their way along the track until they reached the clearing. Following Brett's earlier instructions, Ange directed Billings where to park. Once the car had slowed to a stop, she slid across the rear seat and opened the door on the driver's side, keeping the vehicle between where she knew Lomax and Smith were hiding.

Billings sat fixed in the driver's seat. Not a good start.

'Get out of the car, Sergeant, or I'll shoot you myself,' she muttered angrily to him through gritted teeth. This seemed to work, and Billings warily opened his car door and stood nervously beside the car. Ange did the same. Her watch showed that they were ten minutes early. Lomax and Smith stayed hidden, no doubt ensuring that the pair had come alone.

Ange walked slowly clear of the car and took in her surroundings, enveloped by that curious version of silence that the coastal scrub could deliver, one of constant noise as millions of animals went about their chores. The cicadas played their background song, while birds sang amongst the dense foliage, picking up any insects that broke cover. In the distance, she heard the screech of some yellow-cheeked black cockatoos, one of her favourite birds in the area, comically perched atop some tea trees in a distant hollow. Setting the team in place early was a sound strategy, as these cockatoos were always on the lookout for trespassers. Once disturbed, the flock would take their large frames to the air amid a cacophony of piercing screeches. Not great if stealth was your aim.

From her vantage point, she glimpsed where Jake Thompson had once been crudely buried amongst the bushes. The relentless coastal scrub was quickly reclaiming its territory. By the end of summer, evidence of that dreadful event would be erased from the record. A sudden wave of futility washed over Ange as she realised that her life and all her efforts were the tiniest blip on the continuum. Insignificant; potentially meaningless, in fact.

She leapt from this unhelpful thought when Lomax and Smith emerged from the bushes and silently entered the western side of the clearing. Billings was looking eastward, cluelessly assuming that they would also arrive down the track. Lomax and Smith were both blatantly armed, their revolvers lengthened by noise suppressors. Smith carried a cheap blue duffle bag, presumably containing the $100,000 which Lily was expecting. The two groups stood some twenty-five metres apart.

'We've got company,' said Ange, more to her colleagues than for any benefit of Billings, who snapped his head around 180 degrees in response. A measured voice spoke through her earpiece. 'You need to draw them further into the clearing. We don't have a clear line of sight.'

She then addressed Lomax and Smith. 'How are we going to do this? How about you put the bag in the middle of the clearing and then I'll give you Kramer's wallet address and recovery phrase.'

'Not so fast. How do we know you have this information?' said Lomax.

'And how do I know that the duffle bag contains the money I requested?' responded Ange.

Smith opened the bag and pulled out a stack of bills. He waved them around in the air. 'There. Your turn.'

'You guys place the bag in the centre of the clearing and I'll text you Kramer's wallet address. Once you're happy with that, I'll collect the money and leave the recovery phrase in its place.' Ange paused and pulled the creased envelope containing the recovery phrase out of her overalls, taking care to keep it no higher than her waist. 'Once you're in, we can go our separate ways.'

Lomax and Smith looked at each other before Lomax nodded. 'OK. You seem to know your way around. I gather this isn't your first shakedown.' The pair walked cautiously into the middle of the clearing. Lomax lifted his gun and trained it on Billings.

'Why me?' pleaded Billings. 'I've been helping you all along. I'm on your side.'

'Your job is to keep an eye on her until we've emptied Kramer's wallet. Pull out your gun and do your job,' said Lomax menacingly.

Lomax had just given a ringing endorsement for Ange's decision to empty Billings' gun and keep him out of the loop during preparations. Billings had no clue that his impotence was being recorded on video.

Billings cautiously complied with this request, hesitatingly training his weapon on Ange. Despite his assurances concerning whose side he was on, covering a fellow police officer with a revolver was starkly symbolic of his betrayal.

Reaching what approximated the centre of the clearing, Smith dropped the bag onto the ground. 'OK, now text me the address.'

'Good work. We've got them,' whispered a voice in Ange's ear. She quickly weighed up her options, deciding that it would be best that Lomax and Smith felt relaxed about how the exchange was going down, thinking that they held the upper hand. She reached into the pocket in the front of her overalls and pulled out her phone, finding the text containing Kramer's wallet address which Billy had sent the day before. She selected the 'forward text' option, poised ready to enter the recipient's details.

'What's your number?'

Lomax called out each of the ten digits of his mobile number and Ange punched them into her phone. Once that was complete, she read back the number to check she had entered it correctly. After Lomax nodded his approval, she pressed send. She heard his phone buzz, even from the ten-odd metres that they stood apart.

Lomax looked down at his phone, then instantly looked up and raised his gun. 'Detective Watson, you've been busy.'

'Crap,' said Ange out loud, more to alert her colleagues that things were trending south than anything else. It simply hadn't occurred to her that Lomax would have stored her number on his phone. It was a trick that she had employed herself to help dodge reporters during the SACC investigation. She should have planned for that eventuality. Basic mistakes could ruin even the best of plans.

'Don't shoot. Let's talk,' said Ange. She needed information and hoped that her colleagues would take the hint. 'I thought you might like another mole in the police service. I'm sick of putting my life at risk and living on the poverty line.' She had rehearsed this ploy as she tossed and turned during the night. It was an eminently plausible proposition, as the pathetic pay was the root cause of most cops who turned dirty.

'You simply have no idea about who you're dealing with, do you, Detective?' said Lomax.

'I've been wondering whether you guys are just hired muscle or card-carrying members of the Ndrangheta family network. Lomax and Smith sure don't sound Calabrian to me. I thought I would help with your dirty work. Plus, we can share in Kramer's crypto nest egg. You know that once I take this money, I'm yours—just like Billings. Given my position, a hundred K is cheap.'

'I'm surprised that you, of all people, would think that only the male side of the bloodline would define family ties. Anyhow, we don't work like that. We come to you, not the other way around.'

While Smith trained his gun their way, Lomax fiddled with his phone, evidently trying to enter Kramer's wallet address. Once he seemed satisfied that the address was valid, using his revolver as a pointer, Lomax gestured towards Billings. 'Billings, bring her over. You'd better hope for both your sakes that the recovery phrase works.'

Brett's voice whispered in Ange's ear. 'Enough, Ange. We need to close this thing down.'

'One last question for you before I give you all my bargaining chips,' said

Ange, hoping that Brett understood what was going on. 'Who's been making me look like an idiot, always one step behind you guys? You know my boss suspects something. We'll have to give someone up if my proposal is to be of any value. That would place me in an even more trusted position.'

Lomax's face had suddenly taken on a dark hue, as if an ominous thought had just crossed his mind. He turned to Billings, who was yet to move a muscle. 'Did you know anything about this?'

Despite his role in setting up the meet-and-greet, Billings seemed legitimately bamboozled by Ange's latest ploy. 'No, absolutely nothing. I had no idea,' replied Billings, pleading his ignorance, slithering this way and that, in perfect accord with his character.

With that, Smith shot Billings in the leg without warning. The shot was barely a whisper, one that blended almost seamlessly with the cicadas' mournful melody. Ange wasn't sure her colleagues would even have heard this turn of events. Billings fell heavily to the ground and started screaming in agony. The twittering wildlife turned instantly silent, his cries briefly fracturing their rhythm, rebooting a moment later upon realising this turn of events did not concern them.

'Why did you shoot him?' yelled Ange.

Smith looked down at Billings, his chilling sneer one of abject disgust. Billings was writhing on the ground and looking up at his assailant, a cocktail of fear and pain coursing through his eyes.

'Shut the fuck up, Billings,' said Smith, spitting the words out, not dissimilar to the way his silenced revolver had just spoken. 'Either you brought her here and didn't know what she was up to, or you're in on the shakedown. Which one is it?'

Suddenly, a red dot appeared on each of Lomax and Smith's torsos. Ange understood that this conversation had reached its end point.

'Stop there,' Ange said quietly yet forcefully. 'Look down at your chest.'

The two assassins each glanced at the red dot on the chest of the other. The realisation that they were marked men dawned in an instant.

'Put down your weapons. We'll protect you if you come in peacefully,' said Ange loudly, needing to make sure every player in this deadly dance heard her offer.

The pair shared a glance, a look of resignation perhaps. 'You can't protect us. We're dead anyway,' said Lomax in a decidedly matter-of-fact manner.

With that ominous admission, the pair fired their weapons, dispatching a series of shots before the hidden federal officers opened fire, bringing Lomax and Smith down and killing them instantly.

The first bullet slammed into Ange's chest, knocking the wind out and jolting her backwards. The second bullet never registered as such, nothing more than a sting from an angry wasp. Such was the blow to her torso. She stumbled and fell, suffering a blow to the head as she landed on something hard, rendering her instantly unconscious.

## Chapter 46

# Mopping Up

When Ange came to, she was lying on the ground and had absolutely no idea how much time had elapsed since the shootings had occurred. One of the federal officers was crouched over her and peering intently into her eyes, with Jim Grady looking over his shoulder.

'It's Will, Ange,' said her colleague. 'Stay where you are. An ambulance is on its way.'

Ignoring this request and almost in reflex, Ange tried to get up. Pain shot through her rib cage and she instantly collapsed back down. Her head ached.

'The vest stopped the bullet, but you've probably got a fractured rib. You need to stay still. A broken rib can be serious. I'm also worried about concussion.'

Ange carefully raised her throbbing head and peered down at her right leg. Someone had sliced her overalls open and she could see that her thigh was heavily bandaged.

'You also took a shot through the thigh. You were bleeding badly, so I've wrapped a pressure bandage around the entry site. It'll need surgery. I've stabilised your leg just in case. The Lismore hospital is waiting for you. I hope these overalls aren't your favourite. I made a bit of a mess, but I needed to gain access to the wound,' said Will, trying to calm her down to take her mind off things.

'I was planning to donate them to charity after this. What about the others?' said Ange, suddenly alert as adrenaline kicked in.

'Lomax and Smith are toast. Billings is in worse shape than you. He took another bullet that missed the vest and smashed his left shoulder into a million pieces.'

'I didn't even get my gun out,' said Ange, as if admitting a grave failure.

'That would have been dumb. Those guys were pros. They would have gotten even more shots away. What you did was incredible, Detective. I can't believe how cool you were through that entire episode. Now stop talking and take it easy.'

'There's some ammunition in my left front pocket. Can you take it out? I don't want anyone accidentally getting hurt at the hospital.'

Will and Grady exchanged looks. 'What ammunition? There was nothing in your pocket. You must have been mistaken.'

In her dazed state, Ange took that answer at face value before lying back down. One of the other guys came and propped her head with his rucksack. She looked across at Billings. They had afforded him no such creature comforts.

As Ange lay there, waiting for the whine of the ambulance to shatter the peace, she looked up at the clouds and listened to the coastal scrub talking to her, having instantly returned to its normal self after the battle. No doubt hallucinating, her subconscious alerted to her location, lying in the lonely clearing where she had found Jake Thompson's dead body. Ange imagined she could hear his voice, carried in the pulsing drone of the cicadas' song, thanking her for bringing Lomax and Smith to task. Of course, this was nonsense, wasn't it?

When she saw that Brett Tompkins was calling her, Sally Anders' heart skipped a beat. 'What's up, Brett?'

'The meet-and-greet turned sour. Don't worry, Ange is OK.'

'What do you mean by that?' Anders demanded.

'Lomax and Smith opened fire and shot her. Twice, in fact. The high-tech vest the feds gave her stopped the first bullet. The second hit her in the thigh. She's in surgery now. She'll be OK. She might have trouble surfing for a while, but nothing that she shouldn't recover from.'

'What about Billings?'

'He'll live, but he's in worse shape. Smashed kneecap *and* shoulder. Couldn't happen to a nicer guy,' replied Brett sarcastically.

'Lomax and Smith?' asked Anders.

'We had to take out both of them once they started shooting. It came out of the blue. Matt, one of the feds, said he heard one of them say that they were dead anyway,' replied Brett. 'The guys got it all on video. I'll get them to send it to you. Don't worry, nobody screwed up. Lomax and Smith just snapped. There was no other option but to take them out.'

'Thanks, Brett. Let me know when Ange is out of surgery. I wouldn't count on there being no blowback. Did Ange tell you we have a mole in our midst?'

'No, but Ange tried to get a name out of Lomax and Smith. No luck, I'm afraid, but they sure didn't deny it. Do you have any ideas?' asked Brett.

'Yes, and it's going to be a shitstorm,' was all Sally Anders would reveal.

'Ange was amazing, by the way. As cool as a cucumber. She rolled with the twists and turns right through the engagement. The feds called a halt to it—otherwise I reckon Ange would have still been trying to pry information out of them. Billings would have given up the farm in a heartbeat. I'll ring you back when I know how the surgery went,' said Brett, before hanging up.

Sally Anders had rarely ever been so furious. The depth of anger that surged from her core brought a metallic taste to her mouth. Emotions rarely got the better of her, but she marched around to Peter Fredericks' desk and all but dragged him back to her office, slamming the door and demanding that he sit on the chair opposite. She remained standing.

Anders channelled this rage towards her subordinate. 'Ange has been shot and you are partly to blame.'

Peter Fredericks was giving nothing away. 'What do you mean? I though that she was on leave. Anyway, what have I done?'

'How about leaking critical details and undermining our investigation into the syndicate? Without your snitching, we could have reeled in Lomax and Smith months ago and prevented this mess from ever happening.'

'I wasn't leaking information. I was keeping your boss in the loop. Evidently you weren't,' Fredericks shot back.

'You're a smart guy, Peter. Didn't you join the dots? Every time you passed information to Bold, we lost the upper hand. I can think of at least three crucial times you thwarted our investigation. I'm sure there are more,' yelled Anders. She paused, reflecting on what this meant. 'What did he offer you? My job, perhaps?'

The look on Fredericks' face said it all. His expression then hardened. 'We all know that you only got this job because you're female—just like the commissioner.'

Sally Anders had heard that self-serving hypothesis many times before, so it slipped by like water off a duck's back. 'Is that right? I presume by we, you mean you and Bold.'

'I've done nothing wrong and there's nothing you can do about it. What are you going to accuse me of, responding to a demand from your boss because he doesn't trust you?' replied Fredericks, puffing himself up and trying to secure some moral high ground.

Sally Anders realised Fredericks was correct. He had already thought through this defence. Such premeditation made her even angrier. 'Perhaps, but nobody will work with you once they realise what a snake you are. Get out of my sight.'

With that, Sally Anders opened the door to let him out. 'Oh, and by the way—give me your phone. If you contact Bold in any shape or form, I'll have you for insubordination and endangerment of life.'

Some of Peter Fredericks' chutzpah slipped away, and he made his way back to his desk. That was certainly not the last word that Sally Anders planned to have with him on the matter, but there were more important fish to fry.

Once some semblance of calm had been restored to her demeanour, Anders called Cam Paulson. 'Any luck with Chief Superintendent Bold? I know for sure that he was receiving information from within my office. I probably acted precipitously and fronted my snitch of an employee, but one of my officers just got shot and I lost my cool. You met her, Detective Angela Watson.'

'I'm sorry to hear that. I hope she's OK.'

'She's in surgery now, but her colleagues assure me she should be fine.'

'I was planning to call you tomorrow, but we've found a link. Bold is an English name, so we got sidetracked looking at his mother's bloodline. It was my colleague, Caroline Russo, who worked it out. Bold's father changed his name from Boldo, which is a fully blown Calabrian name. It's not uncommon with post–WWII immigrant families to change their names like that. Once Caroline had us back on track, we could confirm links between his family and other likely members of the local Ndrangheta.'

'OK, I want you guys to take a serious look at Bold and promise not to back down. Internal Affairs will be like a snail on sleeping tablets. Who knows what damage Bold will do in the meantime.'

'I think we have enough reason to look. We're also running Eric Tedesco to the ground. I suspect he'll rue his flamboyant son by the time we're finished.'

'Thanks. That last piece of news makes me feel a little better. I know you can't keep me fully informed, but I would appreciate a heads-up if anything's going to blow back my way.'

'Will do. By the way, thanks for these leads.'

Brett called Anders around 9 p.m. 'The surgery went well. The bullet that entered the outside of her thigh fractured her femur. They've removed the bullet and stabilised the fracture, but they needed to insert some screws to help piece it all back together. The surgeon said that she's resting comfortably and they expect a full recovery. She was lucky. The surgeon pointed out what would have happened had the bullet struck the inside of her thigh. The carnage would most likely have severed her femoral artery and she would have bled out in minutes. Billings suffered a significant amount of damage and he's still under the knife. It's lucky for him I'm not the surgeon.'

With a sense of relief, Sally Anders called it a day. One like no other. She needed a stiff drink.

## Chapter 47

# What Next?

Ange spent the next day dosed up on morphine, in and out of sleep, her body purging the anaesthetic used during surgery the day before.

Billy and Bree were the first to visit Ange the following morning. 'You didn't need to take a bullet for me, Ange. How are you feeling?' asked Bree, her expression filled with compassion for her injured mentor.

'Like a truck ran over me. Lucky for the drugs that they have me on. I gather surfing might be a challenge for a while,' Ange joked, her wry humour relieving some of the concern on the face of her visitors.

'What was it like, being shot?' asked Billy. His expression showed his concern. Being shot was an unpleasant risk of their chosen career.

'It was like being slammed in the chest with a baseball bat. I never felt the second bullet, as I was probably already out of it,' replied Ange.

'We're just so relieved that you're OK. It was a shock to hear what happened when your boss called Billy with the news,' said Bree, heartfelt concern showing in her eyes.

'The boss is flying up on the weekend,' said Billy, effectively sidestepping any emotional outpouring. 'I gather that she's made some progress on our mole.'

'Who is it?' asked Ange.

'She's not saying. You know how tight-lipped she can be,' replied Billy.

Ange looked at each of them, standing shoulder to shoulder beside her bed. 'So, how are you guys getting along?'

The red tinge that flushed Billy's face said it all. Bree was much cooler and responded on the couple's behalf. 'Quite well. We're both due some holiday leave, so we're having a week off.'

'Sounds fun. That's a good idea. There will be a mountain of admin to deal with once the dust settles, particularly with me being out of action. Where are you planning to go on your holiday?'

'We're planning to stay put. No point in wasting money going anywhere else when everyone wants to come to Byron,' replied Bree, evidently the spokesperson for the duo.

From the look of the smiles on their faces, Ange had a sense of what they might get up to during their staycation. 'Have fun. Don't go hacking any more crypto companies on your holiday, you two. Hopefully, I'll be out of hospital soon and we can have dinner together.'

Her parents called. Seeing as Ange had no significant other, Sally Anders had rung them as her next-of-kin to inform them about what had happened.

Ange was miffed that her parents seemed to take her being shot so easily in their stride. She shouldn't have. The combination of farm machinery, quad bikes, motorbikes, horses, and other large farm animals, not to mention a constant cycle of floods and bushfires, meant that accidents and the occasional tragedy were an all-too-common part of rural life—where the word 'risk' was personal, not the remote concept discussed in management meetings.

Her dad had summed this up succinctly and in the typically laconic style of country folk. 'Well, that's good, then. Your mother's pleased you're OK. Remember, what doesn't kill you can only make you stronger.'

Ange was not yet fully on board with that concept.

Later that day, Brett Tompkins paid Ange a visit. 'Has the surgeon seen you?' he asked once the pair had exchanged a peck on the cheek.

'Yes. I gather no surfing for a while.'

'You were lucky, Ange. I've seen the video footage. Who would have thought that Lomax and Smith were basically going to commit suicide and try to take you with them?'

'Those guys are Calabrian mafia. I guess they knew what failure would mean for them, potentially also to their families,' Ange explained. A sudden look of concern clouded her face. 'Was everything OK with the video, Brett? Did I make any stupid mistakes?'

'Everything's fine, Ange. The guys from the federal police were super impressed with how you handled the situation. Actually, I think that they're all secretly infatuated,' replied Brett with a broad smile.

'Thanks, Brett. That's a relief. Everything happened so fast in the end. I've been wondering if I should have been quicker or done something differently.'

'Not a chance. Lomax and Smith just went crazy, without warning. There was nothing you could have done.'

Ange looked at her former lover, needing to get something else cleared up. 'What about us, Brett? I can't just drift away like nothing ever happened between us. I was super pissed off when you dumped me on the phone like that. That wasn't fair,' she declared. Despite her stoic facade, the hurt showing in her eyes was impossible to conceal.

A pained expression came across Brett's broad suntanned face. 'I'm so sorry, Ange. That was gutless of me. I was grappling with so many contradictions in my life—but that's no excuse. I loved our time together, but I need to focus on my family. It's not perfect, but we're making it work. After what I did, I owe it to them. I hope you'll forgive me one day. I'd like us to remain friends.'

'You should have met me in person, Brett. I might still be pissed with you, but I'll get over that in time. If I'm honest, I'm sure that I'd make the same decision in your shoes,' said Ange, her expression turning to one of understanding and genuine affection, more telling than words.

Her last visitor for the day was Jim Grady. 'Hi, Ange. How are you holding up?'

'Pretty good, boss, considering,' replied Ange. Old habits died hard. She couldn't shake that moniker, even after all they had endured over the past few days.

'I'm pleased. Barb is giving me hell for letting this happen to you. I tried to tell her you probably outrank me now, but she's having none of that argument.' He held up a duffle bag. 'Barb packed you some things. I threw in your tablet so you can watch some shows and help keep your mind off the pain. We can bring you more clothes when you know about being discharged.' He glanced down at her heavily bandaged thigh with its uncomfortable splint. 'I guess what to wear below might need some thought.'

Ange smiled, not having thought about such practicalities. 'Terrific. Thank Barb for me. I'll get Kerrie on the case about what to wear. I think long skirts might be in order for a while. What about Billings? How is he faring?'

'He's a mess. Smashed knee and shoulder.'

'When Lomax and Smith realised Billings was complicit in our sting operation, Lomax simply shot him in the knee without warning. It was an excellent shot. They were probably eight to ten metres away, so I guess they'd done this before. Anyway, Billings was curled up, clutching his knee and writhing around, when they snapped and tried to finish us. He wouldn't have been an easy target to hit. What will happen to him?'

'Not sure. You'll need to speak to your actual boss about that. Sally rang to tell me she's booked to come up and visit on the weekend. She mentioned some loose ends that need to be dealt with before she could get away.'

'Boss, one thing that's bothering me is Billings' gun. When I came to, one of the guys had cut my overalls open. I asked him about the bullets that I'd taken from Billings' service revolver. He said that there wasn't anything in my pockets. I felt sure that's where I'd put them.'

'When it all went pear-shaped, I was sitting in my car at the Bushies Beach car park. I was on site within a couple of minutes at most. The old Camry might need some underbody work, given how fast I drove along that goat track. Anyhow, when I arrived, the feds were securing the site and checking who was alive. You were still out cold. Will, I think his name was, had removed your revolver from your overalls. Billings had also passed out, and his revolver was on the ground. I checked each weapon to make sure their safety catch was on. Both had full magazines, and neither had been fired.'

'That's so weird. I was certain that I took the ammunition out of his weapon. Remember, we had that discussion about whether we could trust Billings?'

'Yes, I remember the discussion, Ange. You seemed to be on his side at the time. You were so amped up. Maybe you're confusing that with when you handed me the spare earpiece. Anyhow, I saw the footage. Billings' gun was lying on the ground when Lomax and Smith opened fire, and you never had time to lay a finger on yours. Don't waste any time worrying about Billings. Get yourself better.'

Ange remained confused, but the facts were the facts, weren't they?

The cocktail of painkillers allowed Ange a respectable night's sleep, although moving around in bed caused some sharp pain that even drugs failed to quell. Kerrie and Mike were her first visitors on Friday morning.

'My darling friend, what the heck have you been up to? Your old boss rang me last night,' said Kerrie, as she went to give Ange a big hug.

'Careful,' said Ange defensively. 'Broken rib. Thank goodness for my bullet-proof vest. Otherwise, we wouldn't be having this conversation.'

Tears streaked down Kerrie's cheeks as the reality dawned on her about what might have happened to her dear friend. She refrained from hugging Ange but held her face close, her salty tears dripping onto Ange's own cheek. Pulling herself together, Kerrie handed her phone to Mike, demanding that he take a picture with her hero—Kerrie's words.

Once the photo shoot was complete, Mike handed over a white cardboard box. 'Lisa dropped these over for you. Some of her famous chocolate brownies, I understand. She's super busy today but promised to swing by tomorrow after the Bangalow markets.' Ange had often given Lisa a helping hand with her cake stall, so she knew this box contained dangerous stuff, particularly in her bedridden state. Lisa's creations were impossible to resist.

Kerrie stood back and appraised her wounded friend, making a pained gesture towards Ange's new hairstyle. 'This is a new look for you. It will take a while to grow it out,' she commented, irony dripping off her tone of voice.

'Well, perhaps you can consult on my new image, Kerrie? I'm thinking something edgier than my pre-gunshot version. I'm not going anywhere flash for a while, but the sooner we get me sorted the better, at least going by the look you just gave.' Ange grimaced, holding back a laugh on account of the pain in her ribs. She looked down at her leg. 'I'd really appreciate you picking up some things for me to wear. The doc says six weeks in a cast, so I won't be able to wear pants for some time.'

'We'll come and see you again soon. Perhaps we can work out what to do with you then,' said Kerrie. 'By the way, I let Gus Bell know what happened. He's also going to visit you today sometime,' she added, glowing with a most mischievous smile.

As Kerrie had intimated, Gus Bell came by mid-afternoon. 'What the hell, Ange? We could have lost you,' was his opening charge.

'I'm a tougher nut to crack than you give me credit for, Gus. I'll be OK.'

'I've spoken to Kerrie, and we both think that you'd be best staying at my place in the hinterland. It's completely flat and I have an entire guest house you could use. Kerri and Mike's place is no good with all those stairs,' Gus blurted out, giving Ange the distinct impression that this proposition came well-rehearsed.

'I feel like I've been set up,' said Ange, unable to suppress a belly laugh that brought forth a stabbing pain. Her face softened at the concern showing on Gus's face. 'That's very kind of you, Gus. Let's talk about it once I know what I'm in for. The surgeon said that I'll be on crutches for at least six weeks, so stairs will be a problem,' she conceded. The prospect of staying in Gus Bell's guest house was far more appealing than Ange was letting on.

By late Friday afternoon, Ange had fielded calls from both Jake Thompson's mother and Sharon Fletcher. Gus had rung Joy Thompson, as there remained a strong connection through the JayTee Foundation. 'I know that Jake's death was an accident, but I still blame those mongrel drug traffickers. I gather that those two men who were killed are the same people who buried Jake so callously in the scrub. To think. They would have left me wondering what happened to Jake for the rest of my life. That was until you came along.'

Sharon Fletcher, the wife of the trawlerman murdered at the hands of Lomax and Smith, best summed up her family's gratitude. 'Terry Scott rang me, Detective Watson. I'm so pleased that you will be OK. I know it doesn't bring Dave back to us, but it gives us some closure. It would have been terrible to go through life knowing that his murderers had gotten away with it. I'm not a vindictive person, Detective, but good riddance to them.'

Neither Sharon Fletcher nor Joy Thompson would ever know the half of it.

## Chapter 48

# A Clarity of Sorts

Ange was spending her Sunday morning reading when Councillor Terry Scott and his lovely wife, Jenny, swung by just after 10 a.m. She had great affection for the couple, country folk who she had gotten to know during the Namba Heads investigation. Ange was genuinely pleased to see them.

Jenny explained the origin of their visit. 'That lovely Brett Tompkins rang to tell us what happened. I didn't realise that you two had been an item?'

Ange wondered what details Brett had divulged. Hopefully, he was just keeping his cover as a property developer intact. Terry looked decidedly uncomfortable as his wife fussed and bothered over Ange.

'He doesn't like hospitals,' explained Jenny conspiratorially, as if this was a peculiar affliction that only affected her husband.

'Who does?' said Ange with a dry smile.

It was only the mention of Darren Billings that forced Terry to brighten marginally. 'If someone else hadn't shot him, I pretty sure I eventually would have,' he observed dryly. Terry Scott had never been a fan of his lazy local sergeant.

Even Joe Kramer called by just before lunch, which yielded a moment of genuine awkwardness as he muttered and stumbled over his thanks and well wishes.

'I saw on your friend's social media post that you'd been badly injured,' explained Kramer, looking as uncomfortable as could be. Ange should have known that Kramer would follow Kerrie's lifestyle blog, such was Kerrie's influence around town with the social and moneyed sets.

She steadied their painful clumsiness by asking about a mutual friend. 'How's Bluey going? You know he played an important part in tracking down the guys who killed Ted?'

'How so? Although it doesn't surprise me. Bluey has become the official mascot of the society. He's also the chair of my volunteer selection committee. I don't know how he does it, but he's proving a way better judge of character than I've ever been. He's helped purge a few bad eggs from our ranks.'

Ange evaded responding to the first part of his question. 'Give him a tousle for me,' she answered instead.

While Ange appreciated Kramer's visit and despite their mutual affection for Bluey, she was pleased to see him go after the series of long and uncomfortable pauses, when even inane small talk eluded them.

Lisa swung by after lunch to lighten the mood and bearing another box of goodies, fresh from her stall at the Bangalow markets, a real treat after the bland hospital sandwiches that Ange had just forced down. She had to send Lisa away in the end, such was the pain of laughter as Lisa gave a rundown on the day's difficult customers. There was always at least one self-important shopper who tried to give them grief. Ange and Lisa had developed a sure-fire strategy to prevent self-important and clueless individuals from upsetting them, and they would hilariously replay these encounters over lunch at the pub. Lisa was quite the mimic.

Sally Anders finally arrived just before 4 p.m. 'Hello, Detective. I thought I told you to stay safe?'

'Yes, it didn't quite go down as expected. Who would have thought that Lomax and Smith would basically commit suicide?'

'We should have thought. Well, at least I should have expected that.'

'How so?'

'Lomax and Smith were hardened Ndrangheta. If we'd done our research properly, we might have predicted their behaviour somewhat. The Ndrangheta have been keeping a closed shop for generations. Typical Aussie way of doing things. Here we are, isolated on our island at the far end of the earth, yet we believe everyone thinks and behaves like us. Those guys operate under a very different set of rules and values.'

'Perhaps, but I'm not sure we would ever have predicted the way they snapped,' observed Ange.

'Had we taken the time to understand the Ndrangheta, you would have played it differently and not tried to pry too much information out of them. I've seen the footage, Ange, right until the end.'

'When was that? Remember, I was out cold.'

'The video feed stopped soon after Jim arrived. He filled me in on what happened after that.'

It seemed like an odd place for the video to stop, but that was something to revisit at another time. It was the perfect segue to something she was worrying about. 'Given that you've seen the video footage, do you think we'll have any hassles with Internal Affairs?'

'I would normally be up to my armpits in crocodiles until next year, at least. However, I'm not expecting any blowback on this occasion.'

'Why on earth not? Two people killed, and two police officers shot and badly wounded. I would have thought IA would have a field day over this,' suggested Ange.

'There's been an interesting development. Have you been in contact with your colleagues?'

'Yes, but they haven't mentioned work. I guess they want me to take it easy.'

'OK. Well, you wouldn't know that Chief Superintendent Gary Bold went missing two days ago, ocean swimming in rough conditions. We'd all heard the legend of him being an active member of the Balmoral Ocean Swimming Club, but it turns out that he was also an active member of the Ndrangheta.'

'You're kidding! He was the mole who was causing us all that grief?'

'Well, one of them. Peter Fredericks was the other. Bold had pledged my job if Peter fed him updates on our progress. Peter wasn't doing anything illegal, and that's why he didn't cover his tracks. Billy identified the link easily. Nobody in the service will trust Fredericks once his betrayal of trust leaks out,' explained Sally Anders with a most determined look on her face, a clear signal on the likely source of those leaks.

'I can't believe it. Peter. I never had a bead on Peter. It seemed like he had some sort of chip on his shoulder,' replied Ange, visibly shocked as she processed this news.

'Yes. It seems as if I was the chip he carried around.' Anders grimaced.

'Talk about being stuck in the middle of a snake pit. No wonder we kept being bitten. Do you think Bold's death is an accident or suicide?'

'I doubt it was an accident. You know about my lack of faith about coincidences like this. It could have been suicide, or the Ndrangheta killed him and then staged his disappearance. His body hasn't been located and the coast guard feels a shark attack is plausible. He wouldn't be the first ocean swimmer to be taken this year. It's all too convenient for my liking.'

'Yes, I see what you mean. And messy. So how does this help you with Internal Affairs?'

'IA have been on my case ever since Eddie Falconi's death. They've had a field day, accusing me of overreaching my authority, police bullying, you name it. They recently ramped up this campaign against me once we started looking into Ethan Tedesco. It was all an enormous distraction and IA weren't the slightest bit interested in my concerns over leaks and breaches of confidentiality. Of course, all of this pressure was at the behest of Bold.'

'It's like a BBC crime series. The chief superintendent, of all people,' observed Ange.

'Yep, it doesn't bear to think about all the damage Bold has caused us over the years. Ironically, he probably also played a part in the disposal of Falconi and Tedesco once we started closing in.'

'That explains a lot,' said Ange thoughtfully, thinking back to their investigations and the timing of when those two met their demise.

'Anyhow, I may have pointed out to our colleagues at Internal Affairs how badly this looks for them, and that I was thinking of making an official corruption complaint. I suggested they imagine the headlines: *Internal Affairs and High-Ranking Mole Join Forces and Subvert Efforts to Investigate the Ndrangheta Mafia.* They weren't at all comfortable with my suggestion. IA prefers to throw the mud, not the other way around.'

'Now you're just being vindictive, boss.'

Sally Anders offered her the most wicked smile at that observation. 'They'll still need to follow protocol and interview you, Ange, but I hope it will be nothing more than a box-ticking exercise. If they turn officious on you, you might also mention these failures and how they put officers' lives at risk because of their inappropriate bullying tactics. I'm finding that threatening the B-word seems to work a treat these days. It also helps if you mention the word corruption along the way.'

'Will do. I'm sure that my indignation will be very real in the circumstances. Let's hope it goes better than my SACC performance,' replied Ange with a wry smile. Her upcoming conversation with Internal Affairs would have been very different had Sally Anders not flushed out Bold.

'The feds and the tax office are already scrapping over any assets, including all the crypto and NFTs that we put them on the trail of. At least all that mopping up is off our hands.'

'It will be interesting to see what happens when Eddie Falconi's overseas art collection hits the market. I wonder how many others he duped with his forgery scam,' observed Ange.

'I hadn't thought of that. I suppose there isn't much they can do in the circumstances,' replied Anders. 'Drug enforcement will take over the leads for the dealers identified by the BuzzyBat NFT and cryptocurrency transactions, but we're all so under-gunned in this area. After this sorry episode, I hope my request for additional resources will bear more weight.'

'That will make Billy happy. The way crime is heading online, he might very well be after your job soon enough,' Ange joked.

Despite her own smile, Sally Anders knew that there was undoubted truth in Ange's satire. 'I'll be long gone by then. Anyhow, it's the feds who need to be worried at present. The task force may well have a Ndrangheta mole in their midst, which would be ironic. Bold went missing within days of being implicated. This is all a monumental mess of epic proportions. I can't see that it will be in anyone's interest to make it any bigger. Better that we praise our brave police officers for saving lives and bringing criminals to justice.' said Anders, making air quotes over her last sentence. 'At least Bold was a bachelor and we won't have to sit through any widow telling us what a wonderful and generous man he was on the evening news.'

'Speaking of police officers, what about Billings?'

'What a mongrel. He's already tried to play the victim card. Billings complained we coerced him into the altercation with Lomax and Smith against his will, basically blaming you and Jim for putting him in danger. Jim put Billings in his place by playing back a recording of him accepting the assignment of his own free will and in complete contradiction to his claim. That was smart of you and your old boss. Everyone now knows that Billings is an abject liar and nobody wants to have a bar of him,' explained Anders.

'I didn't realise Jim recorded that discussion. He must have done that behind my back while I was negotiating with Billings. I guess I owe him. Frankly, I never would have thought Billings would try that on when Jim was there as a witness. I suppose he didn't know that we'd also recorded him when Lily White paid him a visit at the Namba Heads station. What will happen to Billings? Will we prosecute him?'

'I doubt it. Given that he was technically assisting, plus the extent of his injuries, I doubt it will make sense to waste taxpayers' money going through a lengthy and complicated court case. Not to mention how distracting it would be for all of us. Anyhow, Billings is even less than a minnow in the grand scheme of things. I figure he'll pay for his transgressions every day, limping through life looking over his busted shoulder and waiting for the Ndrangheta to pay him a visit. Frankly, I doubt they'll feel the need to waste ammunition on that lowlife.'

'When I started this whole saga back in Namba Heads, looking for a missing young surfer, I never would have thought that I would come face to face with the Ndrangheta mafia,' reflected Ange.

'Or get shot,' added Sally Anders.

The pair stared blankly ahead as they contemplated some of the ugly realities of life as a detective. Sally Anders ultimately broke the gloomy mood, gesturing towards Ange's damaged leg. 'By the way, did I mention my policy on this?'

'What policy?'

'The one where any of my officers who get shot must take three months' leave.'

'You have a policy for that? How often do you need the policy?' interrupted Ange.

'Not often. Actually, you're the first to benefit. The policy only came into effect last week,' replied Anders. Ange laughed instantly at her boss's frank explanation, then grimaced in pain, an occupational hazard in her current state.

Anders continued while Ange regained her composure. 'Your surgeon told me you should be up walking again in six weeks, but I figure you'll need another six weeks of rehab. I reckon you should stay in Byron Bay rather than boxing yourself in that little flat in Sydney. I can get any of your stuff sent up. Do you have anywhere to stay?'

'Funny you should mention that. I'm working on it,' said Ange with a knowing smile.

# Epilogue

Ange was slowly crawling out of her haze, where either pain or painkillers dulled her daily existence. She had been treading a fine line, needing the relief offered by heavy medication, yet fearful of becoming another sad entry in the ledger of opioid addicts. It had been more than a week since she'd moved from the hospital into Gus Bell's guesthouse, perched on the hinterland behind Byron Bay. Until the past few days, she hadn't been able to fully appreciate the view, which was genuinely impressive. Gus had been a sweetheart in his efforts to help Ange through this period, administering to her needs, even acting as gatekeeper to manage her many visitor requests.

She hadn't been sleeping well. The combination of a cumbersome cast and shooting pain had killed off any chance of a solid night's sleep. Most days had drifted aimlessly from one to another, medication bringing intermittent slumber to help dull the passage of time. Yesterday had finally seen the return of an old adversary, a suggestion that she might get back on her feet, so to speak. Ange rarely did boredom at all well, so the onset of this nemesis was bittersweet.

She was pleased to be receiving visitors today, but it wasn't without some concern. Sure, it made sense that Billy might visit before heading back to Sydney, but not with Sally Anders. Flying up again from Sydney, so soon after her last visit, seemed out of character for her boss, someone not prone to time-wasting or virtue-signalling. Ange felt a twinge of anxiety on hearing the car arrive and sat pensively as her two colleagues scrunched their way across the gravel courtyard toward the guesthouse.

'Nice view,' said Sally Anders with a big smile as she stuck her head in the door, prone to under-exaggeration as she was. 'It looks like you've landed on your feet. Excuse the pun.'

'Thanks, boss. I can't say that I've really been in a state to take full advantage, but yes, I could do a lot worse. So, what's this visit about? I'm certain you're not here to admire the view,' replied Ange, her apprehension as to the reason for this visit cutting short any chance of witty small talk.

Sally Anders appraised her invalided colleague with an uncertain gaze. 'There's been some developments in our last case.'

Ange was onto her in an instant, adrenaline dismissing any pain or discomfort she might have been feeling. 'Seeing as you flew all the way up from Sydney to see me in person, I'm guessing that these developments aren't good ones.'

Sally Anders didn't dispel Ange's summation. 'The charred body that we'd recovered from Ethan Tedesco's Mercedes wasn't who we expected.'

'Who was it?' asked Ange, all edgy and impatient.

'It took us some time to work it out, but the body was that of John Williamson, the former CEO from Jack's Constructions. It was lucky for us that his current employer had raised the alarm that he was missing. We still had Williamson logged as a person of interest, so the alert came through to us and we put two and two together. Dental records have confirmed that the body was that of Williamson.'

This was not as surprising to Ange as it could have been. Compromised over a massive gambling debt to eZee Bet and Eddie Falconi, Williamson had gotten himself embroiled in helping the syndicate import narcotics concealed in building products. His handlers had been none other than Lomax and Smith. It seemed that Williamson had paid the ultimate price for his gambling addiction.

'So, what happened to Tedesco?' asked Ange, her anger building that he might have duped her yet again.

Sally Anders looked at Billy. 'Seeing it was you who worked it all out, why don't you fill Ange in, Billy?'

'Within days of ET going missing, all his tech companies fell victim to a massive cyber breach, one that has sent them all to the wall. An administrator has been appointed but has remained tight-lipped about the details. The tax office is owed a packet, as well as lots of mum-and-dad investors who will have lost the lot. The media are blaming Russian hackers, but that seems way too convenient a whipping boy for my liking. I must be learning something from you guys, as I no longer believe in coincidences either. My theory is that the Russian hackers were a convenient ruse for Tedesco himself,' explained Billy.

Sally Anders seemed most impressed with his work and opted to blow Billy's trumpet for him. 'Billy cleverly cross-checked the movements of Tedesco's private jet. It had made a trip to Switzerland two days after the car crash. What's more interesting is that the flight made a detour through Portugal, ostensibly to pick someone up. My theory is that they discreetly dropped off a couple of passengers at the same time.'

'You say passengers, plural. Who would the other passenger be?' asked Ange.

'I'm suspicious that Bold has also gotten away. His body still hadn't been located,' elaborated Anders.

'Let me guess. Tedesco owned a large boat to go with his Lamborghini and private jet,' observed Ange.

'Correct. Billy was on the same wavelength and checked that out. Tedesco's boat wasn't in its berth on the day Bold went missing. Unfortunately, all this is very circumstantial. The only thing we know for sure is that the body recovered from the burnt-out Mercedes is not Tedesco. Everything else is mere supposition.'

'How much did they get away with?' asked Ange.

'All they stole was cryptocurrency, according to Nelson, but they pocketed over seven hundred million dollars' worth. We reckon they must have been setting this up for months,' replied Billy, his friend in the tax office again proving invaluable.

Ange's face was full of surprise at the full extent of this heist. 'Holy moly! That's an eye-watering sum of money. Tedesco won't be going hungry, that's for sure. I know Portugal has rather lax crypto exchange regulations, but can't you trace the currency using your amazing piece of software, Billy?'

In answering this challenge, Billy's downcast eyes said more than his words. 'Yes, normally, but Tedesco is one step ahead. It looks like he's running it through a mixer. We can't trace a thing anymore.'

'What the heck is a mixer, Billy?'

'Mixers, or tumblers, as they're called, de-identify transactions by mixing them with other coins from other users, making them virtually impossible to track. Of course, it's difficult to mix that large a sum in one batch, but they can accomplish that progressively over time,' explained Billy.

'Why doesn't it surprise me that such an application exists in the crypto space?' observed Ange sarcastically. 'Surely mixers aren't legal.'

'They're mostly frowned upon, but they aren't inherently illegal. There could be legitimate privacy reasons for mixing cryptocurrency. However, mixing platforms are slowly making their way onto sanction lists in places like Australia and the USA.'

Ange thought about this for a moment before voicing her conclusions. 'So basically, other than eight dead bodies and some financial carnage, we have absolutely nothing to show for our efforts, assuming one excludes some painful gunshot wounds.'

'That's a bit harsh. Let's remember that we've stopped three major drug and money laundering operations and prevented untold pain and suffering. We'll need to brief Interpol and get them on the job of tracking down Tedesco and Bold, but I can't see we have any more threads to pull on this case,' summarised Sally Anders, attempting to mollify her colleague. The reality of the financial carnage that Tedesco's cyber raid had foisted on his unquestioning investors was clear to everyone.

Despite these sentiments, Ange was no longer feeling that she had achieved anything at all. 'I think it's safe to assume that the Ndrangheta will have their contacts in Interpol as well, probably more so than we experienced. We might have chopped off one arm of this octopus, but it will grow back soon enough. If you exclude us, everyone connected with this operation is dead or has escaped. Hang on, what about your old friend Eric Tedesco?'

Billy rescued his boss from responding to this troublesome question. 'When the hackers came in, they sanitised any links between Eric Tedesco and his son. That sure was lucky, wasn't it?' explained Billy, his mocking tone making it clear what he thought of this coincidence.

'I've already had a call from the minister, who told me in no uncertain terms, and I quote, *Eric Tedesco is a prominent and respected business leader. He's the victim here and you need to stop this personal crusade against him*,' said Sally Anders sarcastically, thereby giving Ange another education on the political realities of life in the public service.

This was now the second time that Eric Tedesco had used his political capital to thwart Sally Anders. Ange knew how galling this would be to her boss and tactfully changed direction. 'Are you saying that we need to sit and wait until the Ndrangheta comes out from the shadows, maybe get lucky and basically stumble across their next project?'

'The feds have a dedicated task force in play, so we need to leave the Ndrangheta to them, at least for the time being.'

'Do you think we're in any danger?' asked Ange, the cold, hard reality of this news restoring a pained expression to her face, one easily misinterpreted in the circumstances.

Going by her ready response, Anders had already given this prospect some thought. 'It makes no sense that they would take the risk of going after Major Crimes. If my suspicions are correct, the Ndrangheta already have tentacles into the feds and will remain well informed on any developments that might affect them. It's almost laughable. I don't think you need to worry, at least until we poke the bear again. Sorry to intrude on your recuperation, Ange, but I didn't want you to hear about all this second-hand.'

'I guess time will tell on that,' observed Ange, her grim and grey expression offering a telling insight into how safe she really felt. 'Thanks, boss. I appreciate you making the effort to come and visit.'

'Get well, Ange. Let's speak in three months once you're recovered,' said Anders before she and Billy said their goodbyes and drove off.

Despite his best attempts that evening over dinner, even Gus couldn't ease her frustration and anger. She hobbled to bed that night feeling deeply depressed.

Suddenly finding Gus in her life was a pleasant surprise, although without Kerrie, Ange probably would have left him to drift around aimlessly in her sea of failures. She almost felt guilty at how generous and lovely Gus had been, taking her in and providing companionship and comfort. Heaven knew the state she might be in without Gus and Kerrie.

Waves of self-doubt washed over her as she lay in bed, turning the events of the past twelve months over and over, following the moonlit shadows as they inched across the ceiling. She felt a crack appearing, a chasm that widened with every fresh doubt, fracturing her continuum and threatening her mission to keep moving forward in life.

Despite her successes, there were too many errors to bear thinking about. She had severely underestimated her quarry for one, and, in the process of making these innumerable miscalculations, she had threatened the lives of herself and her colleagues. Was she so callous as to privilege her ambition over her friends and family, the things that really mattered in life?

A sense of despondency appeared and ripened, stalking her, prowling around the edges of reason. The breathtaking self-interest of some of her so-called colleagues, those supposedly on the same team, made her question everything. 'What the fuck am I doing working in this snake pit for?' seemed a reasonable question and an inevitable conclusion. Only thoughts of Billy, Bree, Jim Grady and Sally Anders helped quell a creeping resentment.

Chief amongst her doubts were those of adequacy. Was she cut out for a career as a detective in Major Crimes? Was she actually the diversity hire that some of her more puerile colleagues claimed? How would she cope when thrust back into the heat of battle? Would she be like one of those police dogs who, once shot, recoiled forever at the sight of a gun? These were just some of the question marks which swirled across the mottled ceiling until the early hours of the next morning, when she finally drifted off into a fitful sleep.

That was when the nightmares started.

## Trashed – Book One of The Songbird Tragedies trilogy

Join Ange on a new case and a fresh crusade.

Scan or click here to purchase Trashed though Amazon:
**https://www.pg-robertson.com/trashed**

Scan or click here to join the author's mailing list to stay alert to new releases and hear the latest news:
**www.pg-robertson.com**

 facebook.com/profile.php?id=100090607141784

 instagram.com/petergrobertson/

 amazon.com/stores/P-G-Robertson/author/B0BY4B55VP?ref=ap_rdr&store_ref=ap_rdr&isDramIntegrated=true&shoppingPortalEnabled=true

## Now read the beginning of Trashed.....

The woman painstakingly moved aside the cardboard boxes, straining to make as little sound as possible. She knew them to be pizza boxes, yet she had never eaten pizza until a few nights ago. In her opinion, pizza was overrated and not the delicacy suggested by the countless bootlegged movies she had watched back home.

Once clear of those smelly boxes, she carefully pushed open the lid of the large plastic bin and took in a deep breath, savouring the fresh air, a stark contrast to the putrid odours that she had endured for the past few hours. She had experienced worse back home. Ironically, she had been running for her life then as well. It had taken weeks to rid herself of the smell of those pigs.

Despite it being the dead of night, the surrounding countryside was awash with the sounds of unfamiliar birds and animals, going about their nocturnal business. She heard the bleating cry of a calf somewhere off in the distance, no doubt urging its mother to provide food or comfort, perhaps both. The woman slowly raised herself up and carefully folded over the lid of the bin, taking a moment to stretch muscles that had started cramping. The next move was tricky and she could not risk a sudden muscle spasm.

A mere slip of a girl, with shoulders that barely broached the rim of her smelly hiding place, she stood silently and surveyed her surroundings for a moment. She slowed her breathing as best as she could, forcing herself to remain calm. A rushed or panicked move at this point could spoil everything. She looked skyward and saw that some heavy cloud was moving across the sky. Timing would be crucial.

Satisfied that nobody was watching, she then carefully pulled herself up and straddled the two sides of the bin. Luckily, the woman was still young and flexible, able to balance herself precariously and avert tipping the bin over, a disaster that would destroy the solitude that was both an ally and an enemy of her escape. A crow cawed, fracturing the dead of night, as if warning that death and evil were afoot. Fear and superstition overcame the woman, causing her to slip ever so slightly. She steadied herself and waited for a handful of seconds until she was certain that only the crow was watching. Those ominous birds missed nothing, especially when food was involved.

As soon as her extraction was complete, she stood perfectly still, waiting for the cloud cover to extinguish the slivered moonlight. Once under cover of darkness, the woman moved away from the buildings as quickly as she dared, suppressing any temptation to run and potentially trip over. The night was now as black as that crow, yet she knew that there was a road straight ahead somewhere, having heard cars rumble past during the day. The young woman eventually came up against a barbed wire fence, and she stopped for a moment to look back, straining to see the outline of the farmhouse where those men were staying.

She turned to her right and followed the fence line until she came to an opening. She was pleased to have taken things slowly; otherwise she might have broken her leg on the strange contraption that lay on the ground. Made from a series of metal bars, spaced perfectly to catch the unwary, it was an obvious trap of some sort. She had seen nothing like it. Whether it kept things in or out, she couldn't be sure.

Having painstakingly negotiated that torture device, she walked onto the road that would be the conduit for her escape. The woman looked left and then right, weighing up her only two options. In the distance, to her right, she could see the faint glow of a yellow light, so she started walking in that direction. She already knew that cars were not a concern at this time of night, so she stuck to the middle of the road and moved as quickly as she could. Without shoes, the gravel and sharp stones cut at her feet, and she knew she would struggle to go much further than that yellow beacon.

After what seemed an eternity of pain, the woman stopped and surveyed the situation. Fear gnawed at the pit of her stomach as she decided whether to seek refuge or keep walking. No torture device guarded this entrance, confirming her suspicions about the place she had just escaped from. Hopefully she could find safety here.

The tiny woman climbed over the gate and silently made her way toward the house. She waited for a dog to bark. She had heard them off in the distance before. Surely it would smell the remnants of her past few hours. Thankfully, she remained undetected.

She spied a parked utility vehicle in the shadowing light cast by the lone light bulb and decided in an instant that this would be her best option. She climbed into the rear of the vehicle and slid under its canvas tonneau cover. Fortunately, except for a spare tyre that she bumped into, her new hiding place was empty.

The woman pushed herself into a corner, where she curled up as tight as a ball and promptly fell asleep.

Woken after what seemed only seconds, although it was probably hours, she listened as a door over at the house opened and then closed. She held her breath as thumping footsteps came her way, assuming the worst. A man muttered to himself and secured the corner of the canvas cover that she had used to enter her hiding place. Phew.

She breathed another enormous sigh of relief when the car barked into action and drove toward the road. The driver left the car running while he got out to open the gate. She heard him mutter a curse to himself. Although she didn't speak his language, she knew from all her movie-watching that it was a curse, repeated as he completed this little dance for a second time to close the gate.

Finally, they were off, heading away from that dreadful place. So far, so good.

If you would like to continue reading Trashed, scan the QR Code, or visit:

**https://www.pg-robertson.com/trashed**

**Also By....**

**Read the previous two volumes of The Saltwater Crimes trilogy**

Scan the QR code or visit
**www.pg-robertson.com/books**

 facebook.com/profile.php?id=100090607141784

 instagram.com/petergrobertson/

 amazon.com/stores/P-G-Robertson/author/B0BY4B55VP?ref=ap_rdr&store_ref=ap_rdr&isDramIntegrated=true&shoppingPortalEnabled=true

# Authors Note

The characters in this book are entirely fictional. I have created them from good friends, work colleagues, acquaintances, strangers I've encountered, some people that I've met in the surf, and others that are purely imaginary. Even though the storyline is purely fictional, personal experiences and events have influenced many of the situations and ideas that support the plot. Likewise, except for any household names, the companies and enterprises that underpin the plot are figments of my imagination and similarly fictional.

My heroine, Detective Ange Watson, is a mixture of friends, some who surf and some who do not. I trust you have grown to like Ange as much as I like my friends.

Sydney, the Gold Coast, Surfers Paradise, Byron Bay and Brisbane are real places. Namba Heads is a purely fictional town but is based on the small coastal villages of the Northern Rivers region in New South Wales, Australia. I hope my writing has done justice to these spectacular places.

Much of the story is set on the traditional lands of the Bundjalung Nation, which extend from Yamba in northern New South Wales up into southern Queensland, a region much loved by most Australians. I acknowledge the Bundjalung people, who are the traditional custodians of this magnificent place, and pay respects to the Elders, past, present and emerging of the Bundjalung Nation.

# So Many To Thank

Thank you for reading Snaked and The Saltwater Crimes trilogy. I hope you enjoyed in the journey. The fact that you have persevered to read my books is incredibly gratifying. I hope you are looking forward to reading The Songbird Tragedies.

Of utmost importance, is the need to thank all those who gave me the encouragement to push on and write the series. I probably should list you all individually, but the list is long and I risk missing someone important! Hopefully, I have already told you in person how much your input has meant to me. I cannot thank you all enough.

The Island Book Club deserves a special mention. I will forever remember the scene of our inaugural book club meeting, sitting on the beach in our camp chairs one glorious afternoon, champagne in hand and laughter in our hearts.

I am also grateful for my 'media team', Annabel Robertson, Sophie Robertson, and Ben Hall, whose skills and comfort with new media amaze me. I must also thank my editor, Eliza Dee, and my cover designer, Karri Klawiter, for their dedication and forbearance in enduring my many rookie errors.

Finally, if you have a spare minute, I would appreciate you posting a review of Snaked on Amazon via your purchase history.

## Surfing Terminology

A brief description of some of the surfing terminology that I have used throughout The Saltwater Crimes series follows:

**'Tombstoning'** occurs when a surfer is held under the water by a wave following a heavy wipeout. Whilst the surfer is being dragged deep beneath the water, their surfboard is straining on the surface, connected as they are by a fully stretched leg rope. An obvious metaphor for a perilous situation, tombstoning is never a good sign and rarely fun for the surfer, although bystanders or fellow surfers will invariably find it all most amusing after the fact.

A **'left-hander'** is a wave that breaks to the surfer's left. That is, as the surfer catches the wave, he or she will turn to the left. Obviously, a **'right-hander'** breaks to the surfer's right.

A '**goofy-footer**' is someone who surfs with the right foot forward, and a ' **natural**' is someone who leads with their left foot. The decision to choose one side or another is instinctual and set for life.

Surfing '**forehand'** indicates that a surfer is facing the wave face, **'backhand'** is the reverse. Most surfers find surfing forehand easier, particularly in steep demanding waves. Hence, a 'right-hander' favours a 'natural', and a 'left-hander' best suits their 'goofy-footed' cousins.

The **'line-up'** is the term used for the queuing area where the waves start breaking.

The **'peak'** of a wave is a term commonly used for beach breaks. It defines the apex of the wave face. Once perfectly positioned at the 'peak' of a wave, a surfer can choose to go left or right. The other descriptor for perfect beach breaks is 'A-frames', but these dreamy situations are disappointingly rare.

A **'rip'** is where seawater, carried in by the crashing waves, combines into a channel and rushes back out to sea. Dangerous for swimmers, they can be a godsend for surfers to help ease a long and tiring paddle.

Being **'inside'** means the surfer is the one closest to the breaking point of the wave, which is the surfer who is farthest inside on the line-up. On a headland or reef break, this would be closest to the rocks or reef, and inevitably the most ambitious take-off point. The surfer sitting farthest 'inside' technically has a right of way, a case of fortune favouring the brave. It does not always work that way, wi th **'drop-ins'** being the scourge of surfers around the world, usually spoiling the wave and often dangerous to all concerned.

Jostling for the premier position at the take-off zone is part strategy, part bravado, and part aggression. Called **'hassling'**, this can easily spiral out of control, and fights in and out of the surf are not uncommon in crowded surf breaks, and where localism is rife. **'Dropping in'** on an aggressive local will usually end badly. The old way to surf was to take turns. As the 'inside' surfer departed on their wave, the next would slide across and assume the vacated spot in the line-up, gaining rights to the next wave, and so on. This type of surf etiquette is now relegated to isolated or sparsely populated breaks.

A **'grommet'** is surfer slang for a young school-aged surfer, a term usually reserved for those with talent, their lightness, speed, and flexibility sometimes grating on the older surfers around them.

The **'rail'** on a surfboard is the outside edge, the shape and taper of which are critical in how a board performs.

The '**rocker**' of a surfboard describes how the nose turns up. Boards made with a pronounced rocker are more forgiving when tackling powerful, steep waves. Boards fashioned with minimal rocker make catching smaller and fuller waves easier, but are prone to nosedives during steep or late take-offs—but this might be my age talking.

**'Longboards'** and **'shortboards'** create quite different surfing styles and favour different wave formations. Longboards typically range from eight to eleven feet, or 2.5 to 3.3 metres. Shortboards are under seven feet, or 2.1 metres. The weight of a surfer will often dictate the type of board they choose, and the division between a longboard and a shortboard has blurred over time.

The number of fins on a board varies depending on the style of board. **'Single fins'** are mostly reserved for longboards or surfers wanting a traditional style. The original surfboards were all single fins. **'Twin fins'** are highly manoeuvrable, usually earmarked for small wave boards. A **'thruster'** sports three fins and is the most popular and versatile configuration for shortboards. **'Quads'** have four fins and sit somewhere between a twin fin and a thruster in terms of functionality.

A **'quiver'** is simply a collection of surfboards used by a surfer, as in a 'quiver of arrows' used by an archer.

Finally, a **'tube ride'** is when the surfer positions themselves within the curl of the wave, precariously covered over by the breaking lip, but remaining relatively untouched within the eye of the storm—so to speak. It's the most exhilarating of all surf manoeuvres, and waves that are 'tubing' are highly prized, yet relatively rare. Surf spots that regularly produce tube rides are usually very popular, difficult to travel to, or jealously guarded secrets.

## Australian-isms

For the benefit of non-Australian readers, below is a short explanation of some idioms that I have used on occasion.

**'Back of Woop Woop'.** Far away from everywhere and anywhere. Beyond the black stump is another synonym.

**'Bad egg'.** Someone who is rotten to the core.

**'Berko'.** Going crazy mad, angry and out of control. The Tasmanian devil goes berko if cornered while eating their dinner.

**'Buggered, stuffed, screwed, rooted'**—you get the drift.

**'Bushie'.** Someone who lives in the country, most commonly on a rural farm/property/station, and well away from any major towns or cities. In general terms, one's degree of 'bushie-ness' is also directly proportional to the distance one lives from the coast.

**'Curly request or question'.** Refers to a difficult request or loaded question.

'**Deckie**'. A shortened name given to the deckhand working on a fishing trawler.

**'Feeling crook'.** Feeling sick or unwell.

**'Firey'.** Slang for firefighter.

**'Larrikin'.** Part rogue, part joker. The sort of person to enjoy a beer at the pub with, but not someone to risk with the family jewels. Larrikin is often used to describe the affable kookaburra, one of the coolest and most personable birds in Australia, also a ruthless killer of small birds and animals.

**'Nong'.** An idiot or fool, a term used endearingly and in jest toward a friend or loved one.

**'A park'**. A park can refer to either a park with grass and trees, or a single parking place for a car. Go figure!

**'Roached'.** Has its roots from the word cockroach. Being roached normally refers to the situation where someone has scuttled behind your back to do no good.

**'Rort'.** Another word for scam or con.

**'Seachange & Greenchange'.** Seachangers leave their lives in the city and move to the coast. Greenchangers move to the country.

**'Spit the dummy'.** A dummy, in Australian vernacular, is also known as a pacifier. When a baby is about to throw a tantrum, their face with turn sour, before they spit out their dummy and go berko. It's a wonderfully descriptive phrase—part facial expression, part change of mood, part warning for the carnage about to be unleashed.

**'Stunned mullet'**. Refers to someone who is in a form of temporary shock. An actual stunned mullet will be floating helplessly on the surface and unable to swim away.

www.ingramcontent.com/pod-product-compliance
Lightning Source LLC
Chambersburg PA
CBHW072350110726
47909CB00003B/663

* 9 7 8 0 6 4 5 7 0 0 0 5 3 *